someone
you
know

OLIVIA ISAAC-HENRY

Published by AVON
A division of HarperCollins*Publishers* Ltd
1 London Bridge Street
London SE1 9GF

www.harpercollins.co.uk

A Paperback Original 2019
1

A catalogue copy of this book is available from the British Library.

ISBN: 978-0-00-831778-2

Typeset in Birka by Palimpsest Book Production Limited,
Falkirk, Stirlingshire
Printed and bound in UK by CPI Group (UK) Ltd, Croydon CR0 4YY

MIX
Paper from
responsible sources
FSC
www.fsc.org
FSC® C007454

About the Author

In addition to writing novels, Olivia Isaac-Henry is a crime drama lover, occasional keyboard player, and backing vocalist in the band The Protaganist. She grew up in Worcestershire but now lives in London, where she loves the theatres, food markets and festivals.

For Sylvia and Kester

Chapter 1

Tess: June 2018

Walking home, it's nearly light. The constant drum of water on my skull melts into the bass beats still looping through my head and the slap of my feet on the pavement. The weather's broken, thunderstorms have driven people from the streets and I have London to myself. Almost. I can hear Edie behind me, the faint splash of her footsteps.

I come in and drink a glass of water. Until it touches my lips, I don't realise how thirsty I am. I down two more. Only when I finish do I notice the trail of mud and rain through the flat. I can't be bothered to mop it up.

In the bathroom, I rough-dry my hair and put it into a topknot, then tiptoe to the bedroom, pull on an old T-shirt and creep in next to Max. It's my turn to take the lounge, but I can't face a night alone on the lumpy sofa. Asleep, Max forgets we're no longer together. He rolls over to put an arm across me and I curl up against his chest, absorbing the warmth of his body. Feeling his bulk and soft breath against my skin lets me pretend nothing has changed, until I catch the faint whiff of perfume, Chanel, not mine. Has he found someone else already? I don't care. I can't be alone tonight.

I close my eyes, but sleep is far away. At some level I'm aware my body is tired and my limbs ache. But my mind is running fast. Images of bars, dancers, grubby hands grabbing at me in grubby cubicles... Then Edie. Always Edie.

Twenty years have passed quickly, but the individual days are long and the nights even longer. Wherever I've been, whomever I'm with, whatever I've taken, it's never enough, I always see her.

*

'Tess.'

Edie's voice. I sit up. My mobile's ringing. It feels like seconds since I shut my eyes. Max's imprint in the sheets is cold. He must have gone to the gym hours ago. Was he angry with me for sneaking in next to him when I should be on the sofa, or did he wake, his arms around me, and wish for a moment that we were still together? I look to the bedside table in hope. There's no mug. He used to make me a cup of tea before leaving in the morning.

The mobile's still ringing. I pick up.

'Tess, it's Cassie. You're late.'

'Shit.'

I look at the clock, it's nearly ten.

'Nadine's asking for you. You better get in quick; there's a meeting at half eleven.'

'I'm on my way.'

I roll off the bed. Pain runs up my ribs and back and I land on my knees. I slip my fingers under my T-shirt. Some of the material is stuck to me. I peel it back. The sharp sting makes me shudder. A thin scratch runs from the bottom of my shoulder blade to under my left breast and my front ribs are bruised, not too bad but a little raised. I think back but can't remember hurting myself.

The blood leaves a faint iron smell. And I smell. Not of me, but of other people's clammy bodies.

The shower is as hot as I can take it. Water and steam scald my skin, the pain doesn't matter. I have to cleanse myself of last night.

Afterwards, I dab at the scratch with TCP. I don't have to worry about Max noticing now he's broken up with me. Judging by the lingering scent of Coco Mademoiselle last night, he's not changing his mind.

Cassie once asked why I was with someone as dull as Max. Maybe because he is dull. He reminded me of Dad, quiet and caring. 'Be careful of the road,' became 'You shouldn't drink so much, you shouldn't take that stuff, you don't sleep enough or eat properly.' I never did. He was familiar, safe and knew me from back home; he knew Edie, too. So there's none of the awkward pauses I get when I tell people about her, a shuffle of the feet, oh I'm so sorry, then change the subject. We're two mixed-race kids from a nowhere Midlands town who've lost their mothers. Mine was killed by a drunk lorry driver. Max's ran off with his school physics teacher, Mr Kent. Max always changes the vowel. There's nothing to hide or explain. Being with Max was easy. He's kept me anchored. Without him, I'm worried I'll float away, adrift in disarray. Last night was just a glimpse of the chaos waiting to swallow me up once he goes and I'm alone again. If there wasn't three months still to run on the tenancy agreement, which neither of us can afford on our own, he'd have left already. I don't even know where I'll go. Back to a room in a shared house, my milk missing from the fridge, other people's hair stuck to the side of the bath. And what else? Meeting men in bars, lost weekends, lost jobs, Dad having to come and take me home because I've stopped getting out of bed. I'm nearly thirty-five. Other women my age have houses, husbands and children. I'm on the verge of being homeless and alone.

But what Max wants, moving back home and having children, terrifies me more than the chaos. How could I ever have a child and stay sane? She'd not be allowed to walk to school alone or go to sleepovers or have boyfriends. I'd never leave her side knowing one day she could disappear like Edie and I'd be left forever wondering. A child raised in a glass cage. And what sort of life is that for a child or for me? Max always thought I'd change my mind about having children. I won't.

My phone beeps with an incoming text. Cassie: **GET A MOVE ON**.

Half an hour of dawdling between the bedroom and bathroom to clean my teeth, spray on deodorant, put on a loose-fitting blouse, jeans and strappy sandals, comb my hair, drag mascara across my lashes and I'm ready to leave the flat. Last night's rain has raised the humidity and the tube's heat and claustrophobia will be too much today, so I catch the bus. It's slower but I'm already late and at least I'll be able to breathe.

A red light halts our two yards of progress along the Caledonian Road. From the top deck I watch a girl pass by on the street below. She's in school uniform with curly hair that hangs to her waist. It's not her. I know it's not her. I'm not going to look. The bus lurches forwards. I turn around. Sensing my stare, the girl glances up. Other than the hair, she's nothing like Edie and she's a schoolgirl. I forget Edie's grown up now. I have to believe she's grown up.

*

At work, the office intern is hovering by the door. I smile at him.

'Be a love and get me a coffee will you, Oliver?'

'Sure,' he says. 'And it's Oscar.'

'Of course, sorry. Oscar. Americano.'

'No milk, no sugar. I remember.'

'You're a star.'

I head for my desk. It's not unusual for people in our office to turn up late and dishevelled. In advertising sales most of our pay is commission, so it's your own loss. And on my good days I bring in a lot of sales. Only there haven't been so many good days recently and I can't remember the last time I was at my desk by nine. The laptop flickers to life and I lean back in my chair. I used to be able to switch myself on and off like that computer. Not any more. Now the previous evening lingers until early afternoon.

My coffee arrives. Oscar tries to make small talk. I tell him I've too much work to do to sit around chatting. I sip the coffee and stare at my screen for ten minutes then open a spreadsheet. My mobile rings. It's Dad. He works for his brother, my uncle Ray, so gets away with doing very little. He often rings up during the day to pass the time and chats on about the weather, how it's affected the garden or the mid-week West Brom match. He asks after me and after Max. We never mention Edie. From our conversations, you'd never know I had a twin.

I'm not in the mood today and send his call to voicemail.

5

Whatever was keeping me buzzing last night has long since left my system and my mind has gone the same way as my body. Caffeine isn't doing the trick. I need rest, so head for the toilets. As I walk past, Nadine taps her watch.

'Ten minutes,' she says.

Not enough time for a nap.

Instead, I splash water on my face.

'Your mascara's gonna run.'

A figure emerges from the cubicle behind me. Flawless skin, neat hair, ironed clothes. Cassie. The last time I'd seen her was about 3 a.m., when she was dancing with some vaguely famous DJ. Now, she turns up looking like someone who's had eight hours' sleep whilst being drip-fed wheatgrass.

'How do you manage it, Cass?' I say. 'Weren't you out as late as me?'

'Out, but not out of it. You need to slow down, Tess Piper.'

'Yeah, yeah,' I say.

I pat my face dry with a paper towel. Its rough texture scrapes against my skin.

'Seriously, you look terrible,' she says.

'Thanks,' I say.

'Anytime.'

We laugh, which hurts my ribs.

There's something about Cass that reminds me of Edie. Despite being cousins, they don't look alike. It's more the elegance she gives her clothes. If I wore a tight-fitting top with short feather sleeves, I'd look like a drag queen. Cassie looks like a model, long-necked and glossy. You'd imagine her to be highly strung, but she's easy-going and fun. Nadine passes on our not so infrequent fuck-ups to her and soon the clients are cooing.

She pulls a can of Red Bull from her bag.

'Even with a good night's sleep you'd need one of these to get through Nadine's strategy meetings.'

'Thanks.'

I take it and tug on the ring pull. It smells of bubble gum and makes me wrinkle my nose.

'Drink it,' she says. 'You shouldn't even be here in your state.'

'I've come in worse.'

'But y'know... with what you told me.'

The drink's sickly sweetness bubbles on my stomach. What the hell did I tell her?

'You've been with Max for nine years. You're not going to get over it in one night.'

I don't remember telling her this. I've made a point of not telling anyone, hoping Max will change his mind and we can limp on as we are.

'Cass, I'm fine.'

My stomach contracts. I think I'm going to throw up.

Cassie finishes washing her hands.

'Maybe you two can still work things out.'

I give a non-committal, 'Hmm.'

Cassie gives me a quick smile and squeezes my shoulder.

'Three minutes,' she says.

I wait till the click of her heels disappears down the corridor, then dive into the nearest cubicle. All the sugary red fizz shoots straight up my nose as I retch into the bowl. Cass is right, I need to slow down. I shouldn't have told her about Max.

I return to the sink and rinse my mouth out. It's less than

one minute till the meeting and Nadine always starts on time. In the mirror I look old and the strip light gives my skin a muddy-green tinge, my face looks drawn and puffy at the same time. Maybe in natural light I only look tired.

I sit down at the central desk just as Nadine is organising her papers. The meeting starts with Nadine banging on about professionalism and commitment. I look round the table, as if this applies to everyone but me. My phone rings. Dad again. Nadine glares at me.

'We turn our phones to silent before meetings,' she says in the manner of a teacher reprimanding a troublesome pupil.

'Sorry,' I mutter and send Dad to voicemail again.

Nadine moves on to monthly targets. I stare out of the window. Last night's rain is just a memory and a relentless heat, unnatural to the English summer, reclaims the city. Hot air shimmers off the buildings and people huddle in bus shelters, desperately seeking out the tiniest sliver of shade.

Why can't I remember what I said to Cass? I need to remember. I need to slow down. Something has to change.

I look round the table. Soraya's my age. She'll have dropped her kids off for nursery before work and has a nutritionally balanced packed lunch to put in the fridge. Her linen dress looks freshly pressed and her shoes are dust-free. Adrianne's a couple of years younger than me. She and her boyfriend have bought and renovated a house in Tufnell Park. They regularly eat at Le Gavroche and attend cultural events at The Barbican. Her city shorts and cotton blouse strike just the right balance between fashionable and professional. These are the women I should be emulating, not the chaotic twenty-somethings like Cassie, who can go out all night and wake up in the morning daisy fresh. For them it's a phase, in two or three years they'll morph into Soraya and Adrianne. By then I'll be nearly forty.

I don't notice the meeting has finished until people stand up and start drifting away. Nadine is still tapping on her laptop.

'A word before you go, Tess,' she says, still typing.

'Sorry about being so late, there was— '

'Yes, I know,' she says. 'The traffic, the trains. I didn't realise you were the only person in the office who uses public transport.' She looks up. 'I don't want to have to take this to HR, so it's an informal chat this time.' She lets her words sink in. My mouth's still open mid excuse when she continues, 'But you're not adding much value to the team right now. The lateness, missing targets, complaints from clients.'

'I'm sorry.'

'I'm looking for a bit of passion or, better still, some new ideas. It's why we hired you.'

'I know. I'm sorry. Things have been a bit difficult lately. I'll sort myself out.' I can't lose my job on top of everything else. 'And I've got some ideas, good ideas, new social media strategies. I've been working through them this week. I'm just not ready to present.'

'Really? Tess, that's great. We'd love to see you back on form.'

Christ, she's genuinely excited about this. I'm not even that enthusiastic about my vices any more. I strain my jaw into a smile, which sets off a throbbing in my temples, and I go back to slump behind my desk and pretend to look at spreadsheets until Nadine goes to a meeting in another building. Then I go to the Café Nero over the road for another Americano. I smoke a cigarette outside with the coffee before returning to my desk to browse the Net-a-Porter website for clothes I can't afford, ones that will turn me into Soraya and Adrianne. My phone rings. It's Dad again. This time I pick up.

'Tess.'

His voice sounds different, strained and breathless.

'Tess,' Dad repeats.

The phone feels suddenly heavy in my hand.

'Dad,' I say.

'Something's happened, Tess.'

'Where are you?'

'I'm at home. The police are here.'

The edges of the room begin to blur.

'What's happened?'

Cassie puts down the folder she's holding and looks over to my desk.

'Tess, I don't know how to tell you.'

'Stop it, Dad. You're frightening me.'

Cassie's by my side. My throat tightens, I can't breathe. I know now why he's been ringing. I know what he's going to say.

'Sweetheart,' he says. 'It's her. They've found Edie.'

Chapter 2

Edie: August 1993

Edie gulped in the smoke drifting towards the kitchen door. Tess was helping Dad pile up the coals on the barbecue. Soon, the blackened lumps would stop smoking and Uncle Ray would cook her burger. It had to be Uncle Ray. His were the best, not burnt on the outside and raw in the middle like Dad's. Then they'd cut the cake, open the presents and it would really feel like their birthday.

She ran out onto the lawn calling to Tess, who turned around just as Mr Vickers came out of his back door. The smoke was billowing across the garden and over the fence. He waved his arms around as if about to suffocate. Dad was too busy fussing with the coals to look up. In the end, Mr Vickers stomped back into his house and slammed the door.

Edie grinned at Tess, who rolled her eyes, old sucking lemons. They laughed and Edie grabbed Tess's hands and span her round. Sucking lemons, sucking lemons. She leant back and they span faster, round and round. Edie tipped her head to the sky and was momentarily blinded by the high sun. She closed her eyes and absorbed the heat, leaning further back, spinning faster and faster.

'Too fast, Edie,' Tess said.

She sounded far away. Blood rushed round Edie's head. She felt as if her feet could lift off the ground and she would fly.

'Too fast, Edie.'

She relaxed her grip. Tess's hands slipped from hers and she shot towards the lawn and landed flat on her back. She opened her eyes to the empty blue sky and started laughing before pulling herself onto her elbows. Tess was splayed in the flower bed. Edie laughed harder. Dad ran over from the barbecue.

'Tess, love, are you hurt?'

Tess's face was scrunched up ready to cry.

'I'm OK,' she said quietly and rubbed her arm.

Dad pulled her to her feet.

'Are you sure you're alright?'

'Yes, Dad.'

He glanced down at the flattened flowers, the pretty blue ones he'd planted for Mum. They were difficult to grow in the heavy clay soil, but he had found a way. He didn't say anything about them and brushed Tess down instead.

Edie jumped to her feet. Tess still looked as if she were about to cry. She mustn't cry, not on their birthday.

'I'll get you some lemonade,' Edie said.

She ran into the kitchen via the side door. The dim light and cold contrasted with the day outside. Edie looked through their lounge to see Auntie Becca bustling her way through the front door, two bowls of salad, a lasagne and a trifle balanced in her arms.

'I thought I'd bring these, Gina.'

A blur of black and tan tore past. Auntie Becca's knees jerked forwards and her body fell backwards into the wall, as her Welsh terrier rushed to jump up at Edie. She flapped him away. He sniffed the bottom of the stairs, gave one bark, before running through the kitchen and out into the garden.

Mum dashed towards Auntie Becca.

'Are you alright?'

Somehow, Auntie Becca had held onto all the dishes. Mum took them from her and put them down on the kitchen counter. Edie examined them. The trifle looked alright, but there was no point in a lasagne when they were having a barbecue and Mum's salads looked better than the pile of limp leaves in Auntie Becca's patterned glass bowls.

'Thank you, Gina,' Auntie Becca said.

She straightened up and smoothed down her trousers with her palms.

'These look good.' Mum indicated towards the food. 'Lucky they didn't end up on the floor. That dog's quite a handful.'

'Oh, Pepe. He just gets so excited in new houses. Likes to make himself at home everywhere. I took him to my aunt Jeanie's the other day, he jumped straight on her lap. I'm surprised she let him leave, she was so besotted,' Auntie Becca said. 'And happy birthday to you, Edie.'

She pressed Edie into her squishy belly. Hugs from Mum meant having sharp hip bones poking into her ribs. Even so, hugs from Mum were better.

Auntie Becca let her go.

'And let's find Tess,' she said and walked towards the back door.

'Bring the salads will you, Edie?'

'Where's Uncle Ray?' she asked.

'Finding a parking space.'

Edie ran from the kitchen, through the lounge and out of the front door.

'Edie, help Becca first,' Mum called after her.

The street's narrow two-up two-downs left little room for cars, but Ray was parked right outside and talking to Valentina Vickers. Edie was running so fast she only just managed to skid to a stop and avoid crashing into them.

Valentina took a step back.

'Happy birthday,' Uncle Ray said.

He picked her up and hugged her. She wrapped her arms around his neck. Uncle Ray's hugs were even better than Mum's.

'Happy birthday,' Valentina said. 'I made a cake for you and Tess.'

A round yellow tin decorated with white flowers was perched on the roof of Uncle Ray's car.

'Wow, thanks, Valentina.'

'You're welcome.'

She smiled at Uncle Ray and walked off into her house.

'Why did Valentina want to speak to you?' Edie asked.

'Oh, nothing much,' he said. 'Her old man made her come out and say I have to leave him plenty of space when I park.'

It sounded like the sort of things Mr Vickers would say. Edie looked at Uncle Ray.

'Old sucking lemons,' they said together and laughed.

He set her back down on the pavement.

'You're getting too big for that, you know.'

'Aww, Uncle Ray,' Edie said.

'Well, maybe for a little longer.'

Edie smiled, grabbed his hand and began pulling him towards the house.

'Come and see the cakes, we've got two now. What present did you buy me?'

'Presents?' Uncle Ray struck his forehead with his free hand. 'I knew I'd forgotten something.'

Edie turned and smiled. Uncle Ray would never forget.

'What is it?' she asked.

'Wait and see.'

*

'Looking good, Gina.'

Uncle Ray kissed Mum on both cheeks when he came into the house.

'What's that?' Mum asked, looking at the tin.

'Valentina made us a cake,' Edie said.

'That was nice of her,' Mum said. 'Take it outside with the salads, will you? Becca's been calling you for ages.'

Edie took the bowls and cake out to the garden. The smoke had disappeared and the barbecue glowed silver and red. The table stood in the sliver of shade by the back wall of the house. Auntie Becca sat beside it and Pepe lay underneath.

'It's better away from the heat,' she said.

Edie put the food down. Auntie Becca was right, it was getting hot. Dad had been fussing about the plants for weeks. Had they enough water, had he overwatered? Their garden wasn't like the others on the street. She could see them over the low fences. They were either paved or looked like junk-yards. No one else had an array of flowers and shrubs and a winding pebble path. Raquel, their neighbour on the other side, had laughed and asked what the point was, but her mum said it was a nice change to have something pretty out there.

Edie looked back to the kitchen door. Where was Uncle Ray? She was starving; he should have started by now. And afterwards she could show him the new dance moves she'd practised.

'Uncle Ray, where are you?'

He didn't reply at first.

'Uncle Ray.'

'Coming,' he said eventually.

He came out of the kitchen door, ruffling Edie's hair as he came past.

'You're so impatient,' he said. 'There's no rush.'

But Edie was in a rush. It wasn't really her birthday until they'd eaten burgers and cut the cake, then she'd be a year older. She'd be allowed to do new things and go new places. She wouldn't be a child any more, or at least, she'd be less of one. Not so grown up Uncle Ray wouldn't give her proper hugs.

Auntie Becca had left her seat in the shade.

'Get the meat on, Ray. You always boast how good you are.'

'What is it with everyone today? We've got all the time in the world,' he said.

'Where's my lemonade?' Tess asked.

'I forgot,' Edie said.

Tess's face turned sullen.

'Look, I've something to show you,' Edie said. She pulled Tess over to the table. 'Valentina made it for us.'

She opened the cake tin. Tess peered into it. Inside was a chocolate sponge with chocolate icing, a ring of violet sugar flowers and in matching lettering, the words 'HAPPY 10th BIRTHDAY EDIE AND TESS' had been piped across the top.

'Wow,' Tess said. Her face lit up, the fall forgotten.

Edie picked off one of the flowers.

'Edie, don't,' Tess said. 'It's for afters and it doesn't look right now. Look, there's a gap.'

'Open up.'

'Edie, you shouldn't.'

Edie winked at her. Tess opened her mouth. Edie placed the flower on her tongue. She took another and put it in her own mouth, closed her eyes and tilted her head to the sun, so that all she could see was red. The sugar flower's sweetness spread across her tongue. She opened her mouth and laughed. This was going to be the best birthday ever.

Chapter 3

Tess: June 2018

The last time I saw Edie she was slipping through a gap in the hedge at the back of our school. One moment she was there, the next she was gone, like Alice Through the Looking Glass. And like Alice, I thought one day she'd return.

My train is sitting at a red signal, a fire on the line outside Coventry is causing delays and we're already forty minutes late. People tut and glare at their phones. I'm the only one hoping the signal stays red.

We've received calls before to say a body's been found. Only to be told later that it's too old, too young, the wrong height. This will be another mistake. So why is my heart thudding against my chest, why is Dad so certain it's her this time, when he's been through so many scares before, why do I dread the train ever reaching its destination?

The gap in the hedge led to a route home via the canal. The police searched its towpath repeatedly in the week after Edie's disappearance. Only her leather school bag was found, flung in the water, its strap caught on the bars of a discarded shopping trolley. In it were her schoolbooks, comb, Discman and a purse holding four pounds twenty-two pence in change.

She even left one of her records, a Northern soul track Ray had given her.

The police brought the bag to me.

'Do you recognise everything, is anything missing?' a policewoman asked.

'The photograph,' I said.

'What photograph?'

'Edie keeps a photograph of us. She always carries it with her.'

It was the sole copy of a family portrait, the negatives lost long ago. In it we're about three or four years old. Edie is sitting on Mum's lap, looking up into her face. Mum gazes back, smiling. Dad's turned towards them, proud and protective. I'm on Dad's knee, swivelled away from the rest of the family, pointing to something out of shot.

There aren't many snaps of Mum; we didn't own a camera. Uncle Ray took them. I have the one of Mum at nineteen, just before she married Dad. She looks so like Edie, tall, slender, graceful. Her expression is difficult to read, a half-smile flickers round her lips, her eyes slightly turned from the camera, as if a full gaze would be giving too much of herself away. And there are pictures of birthdays and Christmases. But Edie loved that one of us all together, when we were very young.

'Are you certain she had it? When was the last time you saw it?' the policewoman asked.

'I'm not sure, but she'd never leave it. She must have taken it with her.'

'She may have removed it from her purse or lost it months ago.'

'She wouldn't remove it or lose it,' I said. 'She took it with her.'

The policewoman smiled, made a note and started asking me if Edie had been in any trouble recently.

Over the years I repeated to Dad, Uncle Ray and Auntie Becca about the photograph, that Edie would never leave it behind, she took it from her bag, which means she must be alive. None of them listen. Perhaps Edie knew that too, that only I would realise its significance. A message to me alone.

So I never believed she was dead, never gave up hope, but my heart still thuds as the train lurches forwards for the final stretch of the journey. Is it Edie?

Chapter 4

Edie: August 1993

'This one's called "The Snake".'

Even though Edie had heard it a hundred times before, Uncle Ray always announced the songs. It was part of the ritual. And this time it was her record player, the one Uncle Ray and Auntie Becca had got her for her birthday. Tess had got a portable CD player. But Edie knew she had the best present. All Uncle Ray's Northern soul tracks were on vinyl and that first crackle before the song came on, then the drum roll, gave Edie goosebumps.

As the trumpets came in, Uncle Ray swung his leg sideways before stepping left then right. He didn't sing along like Edie, his arms and legs slid into patterns and his eyes focused on the middle distance.

'Spin,' Edie shouted.

He kicked one leg high then brought it down with a snap, sending him swirling so fast the stripes on his T-shirt blurred. Then he was back into his diamond pattern steps.

'Your turn,' he called to Edie.

She'd been practising. Uncle Ray had made her a cassette

of some of the top tunes, as he called them, though a few of her favourites were missing. She couldn't play it on the stereo in the lounge if Dad was watching TV, which was most of the time. So she practised upstairs, which she preferred anyway, because Tess wouldn't try and join in. With her clumsy hopping about, she looked like a puppet with half of its strings cut. At Christmas, Uncle Ray had bought them their own cassette player for their bedroom, which Edie loved. But Tess said she felt bad because Dad had wanted to buy it for them and couldn't afford it. Edie thought if he wanted to buy them stuff that much, he'd get a job.

Auntie Becca came in and leaned on the kitchen door frame.

'You should be outside on a day like this, Edie. It's your birthday; everyone else is in the garden. It won't be summer forever.'

Edie ignored her and kept swinging her hips from side to side before copying Uncle Ray by kicking her leg up by her head, then pulling it down to put her into a spin.

Auntie Becca shook her head.

'I'm not sure you should be teaching her that, Ray,' she said. 'She should at least be wearing trousers.'

Edie didn't listen. She was watching Uncle Ray's next move. He lunged to the side with his right leg and dragged his left foot along the floor behind him. Edie followed. They stepped left together. Edie squealed and hissed the 's' of snake in the chorus.

'Ray,' Auntie Becca said.

'Give it a rest, Becs,' he said. 'We're just having a bit of fun.'

Auntie Becca shook her head again and left.

Why didn't Auntie Becca ever want anyone to have fun? Edie thought. It didn't matter, she was gone now and Edie was going to dance how she liked.

'What are you doing?'

Tess was at the kitchen door. Edie and Uncle Ray were too intent on their dancing to reply.

'What's this one?'

Edie did another spin. Tess jumped into the room and started skipping from side to side, trying to copy Edie.

Mum came in from the kitchen just as Uncle Ray was changing tracks. He put down the single he was holding and swapped it for another.

'This is "You Didn't Say a Word" by Yvonne Baker,' he announced.

'My favourite,' Mum said.

She pushed the sofa as far as it would go against the wall and moved the coffee table into the alcove by the fireplace.

She began to dance, singing along to the track. Edie hadn't seen Mum dance in this way. She was good, better than Edie, despite all her practice. Not as good as Uncle Ray, but nearly. Tess was now bouncing up and down, oblivious to the beat.

Auntie Becca came back and stood at the door, looking as if the entire family had gone mad. Dad stood behind her and stared at Mum.

'Come and dance, Dad,' Tess said.

'Not just now, Tess,' he said.

'But Dad,' Tess pleaded.

She grabbed his arm and pulled him away from the door. 'Come on, Dad.'

He danced a few steps, just moving from side to side before

looking over at Mum and Uncle Ray with their coordinated jumps and spins. He moved back to the door.

'I'll leave it to the experts,' Dad said and left to go for a smoke out the back.

*

They danced until it was dark and Mr Vickers banged on the wall and told them to shut up. Then they ate cold sausages from the barbecue and more cake. Uncle Ray let Edie sit on his lap and sip his beer, which she pretended to like but it made her screw her face up and she vowed never to touch it again. By the time Uncle Ray and Auntie Becca left it was gone midnight and Tess was half asleep on the sofa.

'Come on, you two, time for bed,' Mum said.

'Not tired,' Tess said as her head flopped on Mum's shoulder.

'I know you're not,' Mum said and propped Tess against her arm.

Edie followed them up the stairs. She wasn't tired either, but she wanted the day to end now, when it was perfect. She was ten years old. Double digits. Nearly grown up.

Chapter 5

Tess: June 2018

It's nearly midnight by the time I reach Aspen Close, the street lamps' pooled light hinting at the neat lawns and clipped hedges in the shadows. From the end of the road I can see Dad leaning against the door frame, his cigarette a tiny glow against his silhouette. Once he sees me he throws it to the ground and runs to meet me. He puts both arms around me and squeezes hard. When his grip relaxes I look at his face. It's gaunt, the artificial light exaggerating the shadows under his eyes.

'It's not her, Dad,' I say. 'I'm sure it's not her.'

He looks around, as if someone's watching, picks up my case and walks back to the house without answering. Once inside, he turns and slumps onto the stairs and leans his head against the banister.

'Dad?'

He closes his eyes.

'The police seem pretty certain,' he says.

'But there's still a chance...'

Dad sighs.

'No, Tess. There's no chance.'

'They've made mistakes before. It could be anyone.'

His certainty frightens me.

'I've just got a feeling. A bad feeling.'

He opens his eyes; they're red with tiredness.

'I'm sorry, Tess,' he says.

He takes my suitcase and drags it upstairs.

It's never been like this before. He's always been the one to reassure me, when I've been frantic, terrified that all my instincts telling me Edie is still alive are wrong. The fight has gone out of him this time, maybe it's just been going on for too long. Maybe he wants it to be her, so he has a definitive answer to what happened to his daughter. The only answer I want is that she's been found alive. I won't believe this girl is Edie.

I go into the lounge and slump on the sofa. The new chocolate brown leather looks out of place against the faded abstract-patterned wallpaper and scuffed laminate floor. When we first came to Aspen Drive the rooms seemed enormous and the newness was intimidating compared to our tiny terrace on the Limewoods Estate, which was, and still is, a byword for unemployment and minor criminality. Now, the house's décor is more than a decade out of date. In a Victorian house, it would be charming shabby chic. On a nineteen-nineties executive housing estate it's just shabby.

Edie would like this sofa, it's minimalist with clean lines. A spasm grips my stomach. What if she's not around to like anything any more? Whenever I shop, I consult Edie's aesthetic. Whether she would choose the music, clothes or homewares I've selected. When would she play it, how would she wear it, in what way should it be arranged? I try to do that with the sofa but can't push away images of the cold dark water and the sailing dinghies circling above her, engrossed in their sport on the reservoir's surface, just a few feet away. But it can't be her. She ran off with her boyfriend to London or Tuscany or Marrakech.

I take a cigarette to calm myself. Dad thuds down the stairs.

'I'll make you some tea,' he says.

'Nothing stronger?'

'I keep some whisky in the sideboard for Ray. Don't know how much is left. Or there's cooking sherry in the kitchen.'

I go to the sideboard. Dad's not much of a drinker. It interrupts his smoking. But tonight he lets me pour him a glass of Laphroaig and sits down in his armchair.

The whisky burns my throat. It's bitter and smoky, but better than nothing.

'What did they tell you about...' I'm not going to say Edie. 'The girl in the reservoir?'

Dad manages to grip the whisky glass with both hands and hold his cigarette at the same time.

'She's a teenager, been down there for years.'

My fingers feel hot. I look down to see the cigarette's burnt to its butt. I stub it out and reach for another.

'How can they be sure?'

'Dunno. Tests.'

We fall silent. Dad switches on the TV, it's showing a football match. He sits back and stares at the screen, chain-smoking. I'm sure he has no more idea of what's going on in the game than I do. It's just his fear of silence and what I might choose to fill it with.

A girl, a teenager, dumped in a reservoir thirty miles away. She's been down there for years. How many explanations are there?

*

27

After the match, I pour another large glass of whisky and make an excuse of an early night.

'Alright, love, sleep well.'

Dad sounds relieved and opens a new packet of cigarettes.

I take a look at Edie's room before I go to bed. It was never a shrine, though when she first disappeared, I used to go and curl up on the bed, willing her to come back. I'd smell the clothes that held onto her scent and try them on; they were too large and looked dull and sexless on me.

Later, the room became a home to unwanted objects, a broken Hoover, old cardigans, a garden fork, but enough remains for it still to be Edie's room, the same furniture in the same place, the walls the unpleasant shade of peach we thought fashionable at the time. In the corner sits the record player she was so proud of, along with a stack of LPs. I should clean them; they're thick with dust. Edie would hate that. Her books are in a similar condition: Angela Carter, Woolf and Solzhenitsyn. She was always so much more sophisticated than me. The only book out of place is our old scrapbook. In large marker pen the title 'The Case of The Missing Cakemaker'. My childish attempt at creating a mystery, involving a neighbour who left her husband.

I take it down. It's covered in the same rosebud wallpaper we used for our schoolbooks. Where it came from, I don't know, we never had that pattern on a wall. The pages fall open, lots of notes and diagrams and a sketch I'd done of the missing woman, Valentina Vickers. It's a good likeness for a ten-year-old. Of course, Valentina was never really missing. I saw her shopping in House of Fraser a few years later. By the time I'd crossed the store to speak to her, she'd disappeared into a lift. It left me disappointed. I had wanted so much for there to be a mystery and she'd simply moved away. That's why I've never believed Edie was dead. One day she'd just turn up, like Valentina.

Wouldn't I know if she was dead, feel it, sense it? We're twins, we shared a womb, we're part of one another and I can almost see her in front of me, laughing, dancing, arguing. I can't think of her as dead when every cell in me screams that she's still alive.

A few pages have been ripped out of the scrapbook, betrayed by fraying scraps of paper along the stitched spine, probably used for a list of records Edie wanted to buy.

My room has survived better, the same single bed against the wall and only a few stray objects having made their way on top of the wardrobe.

I flop onto the bed and close my eyes. The whisky mingles with the dark and Edie's standing before me. She smiles and turns to walk into the night, wearing a silver top and thick mascara, and I'm left on my own in the bedroom of our old house on the Limewoods Estate. I'm fully-grown but lying in my childhood bed and my feet stick off the end. I can see the red of my eyelids as the light breaks through the curtains. The smells of Mum cooking breakfast float up my nostrils. If I turn my head, Edie will be in her bed next to mine. The rain patters at the window and I'm sinking back into the soft mattress.

'Tess,' a voice says.

Two hands grip my wrist and tug. I nearly tip out of the bed.

'Edie,' I say out loud.

'Tess,' Dad calls.

I can smell bacon cooking downstairs.

I daren't lie back in case I fall asleep again. Instead, I swing my feet to the floor.

'Are you up, love?'

Maybe he heard me shout out.

'Yes. I'll be down in a bit.'

My hand's shaking. I distract myself by checking my phone: three missed calls, two from Max, one from Cassie. I text back, promising to call them later.

In the kitchen, Dad's lost in the thick smoke from the frying pan. We lived on ready meals after Mum died. Only after Edie disappeared did Dad discover the cookery channel and we started having huge stews, curries and roasts. I got fairly porky before my art foundation year, when I replaced them with boys, cigarettes and speed. I think he did it so he could pretend that we were a family, just the two of us, and to show that he loved me, which he's never been good at saying. And here he is again, with a plateful of eggs, bacon and mushrooms, as if cholesterol can counteract heartache.

'I thought you could do with a proper breakfast,' he says.

I eat as much as I can but hand my plate back nearly as full as when Dad gave it to me before switching to coffee and cigarettes.

The house phone rings and Dad dives into the lounge. I can't hear the conversation. He comes back into the kitchen and sits next to me; he won't look me in the eye.

'Tess, that was the police. They're coming to pick us up.' He takes my free hand and squeezes it. 'We have to go to the station.'

Chapter 6

Edie: September 1993

'A record player.' Raquel said the words with a mixture of disbelief and pity. 'My mum's got one of those. Plays her old LPs on it. I wish the bloody thing would break.'

'I wanted a record player,' Edie said.

'Next time my dad visits, he's going to buy me a whole stereo with a CD player, not just one with a cassette. Then I won't have to listen to Mum's Matt Monro albums.'

'Uncle Ray doesn't play Matt Monro,' Edie said.

Not like Granny McCann, she could have added. Raquel's mum was twice the age of the other kids at school, something she was sensitive about. Almost as sensitive as she was about her dad never actually visiting or her reading problems.

'Tsk,' Raquel said. 'You should've got a CD player, like Tess.'

Edie decided not to challenge Raquel. If that was her reaction, what would girls like Deanne or Caitlin say? She looked round for them as they entered the schoolyard. They were standing together, a little way from the gate, in a group of about ten. Edie caught their eye; both sides ignored the other. Caitlin was as tall as Edie but twice as broad. Her older sister, Moira, had also been the school bully and Caitlin was trying to live up to the family reputation. She'd started on Tess a few times, but being Edie's twin and Raquel's friend, had held her back. Caitlin was especially wary of Raquel, since she'd given her a black eye after one to many Granny McCann jibes. Still, being the start of a new school year, Edie was cautious around Caitlin; though Tess seemed unconcerned as she walked past, swinging her canvas bag.

The bell rang and they filed into school and found their new classrooms. Raquel's 'Mc' for McCann was not close enough to 'P' for Piper to be in the same class and she went down a different corridor. Edie knew her new class teacher, Miss Armitage, because she also took them for music. The room was familiar: a piano sat in the corner, the walls lay bare, waiting to be filled by their creations throughout the coming year.

'Stand at the back and I'll call you to your places,' Mrs Armitage said. 'You'll notice each table has the name of one of the great composers on it. You will each be assigned a composer and sit at that table. I will be referring to these groups by the name of the composer throughout the year. Please pay attention.' She rapped the desk with her knuckles to bring the class to order. 'Beethoven,' she said. 'Miele, Jaspinder, Deanne, Tyrel, Ian and Edie. Go to your table, please.'

Edie looked at Tess. She hadn't noticed the error. They always sat together.

'Hadyn.'

Tess looked up. Suddenly realising something was wrong, she was trying to catch Miss Armitage's attention.

'Tchaikovsky,' Mrs Armitage said. 'Tess, Ricky, Noah, Imran, Harrison, Joelle.'

The class chattered as they took their seats, no one quite satisfied with where they'd been placed.

'Quiet now,' Mrs Armitage said.

Edie stuck her hand up.

'It's Edie, isn't it?'

'Yes, miss. I think there's been a mistake, miss. I always sit next to Tess.'

'Tess?'

'My twin.'

'No mistake,' Miss Armitage said.

'But we always sit together.'

Miss Armitage pursed her lips.

'You know, Edie, in many schools, twins are put in separate classes altogether. I've put you on tables according to your ability. At your next school, I doubt you'll be in any of the same classes.'

Deanne sniggered.

'So I suggest you need to acclimatise to being a whole ten feet apart,' Miss Armitage concluded.

Deanne's shoulders were shaking hard. Edie glanced at Tess, who was staring determinedly at the table.

'Now,' Miss Armitage said, 'I'm handing out your new textbooks for English and maths. Your first homework will be to cover them in wallpaper to prevent their getting damaged. It will be your own responsibility to keep the books in good condition until the end of term.'

She stood up and opened a cupboard, her back to the classroom.

Deanne turned to Edie and rubbed her eyes as if crying.

'Boohoo. I can't be next to my sister all the time.'

Edie kicked her under the table. Deanne yelped.

'What's that?' Miss Armitage spun around.

'Nothing, miss.'

Deanne glowered at Edie.

Miss Armitage returned to retrieving armfuls of books from the cupboard.

'I'll get you for that,' Deanne said.

*

Until the morning break, Miss Armitage passed the time by explaining that the whole year was just a preparation for 'big school'. Edie couldn't help wondering if calling Bridges Academy, where most of them were heading, 'big school' was helpful in making them feel more grown up.

She flicked through her new maths textbook. Whenever she looked over to Tess, she was staring out of the window. It wasn't surprising she'd fallen behind. She never listened in any class except art.

At last the bell rang. Tess was waiting for her at the door and they ran outside to catch up with Raquel, eager to hear about her new class. Deanne and Caitlin were waiting at the entrance to the playground with a handful of hangers-on. Deanne whispered something in Caitlin's ear, a smirk on her face.

Caitlin swaggered towards them. Edie caught a whiff of the slightly sweet-stale odour from her clothes. She wrinkled her nose and stepped backwards.

'If it isn't the famous twins,' Caitlin said. 'I heard you cried when you weren't put on the same table.'

'Shut up, Caitlin.'

34

'Bet you're gonna marry the same bloke, all share the bed together.'

Titters rose from the hangers-on. Edie pushed past Caitlin. It was a mistake. Caitlin turned around and moved across, separating her from Tess.

'I don't believe you're twins anyway. Look how small she is.' Caitlin jerked her head backwards to mean Tess. 'Reckon she's adopted.'

'Yeah,' Deanne said. 'From the special unit.'

Edie tried to push back to Tess but Caitlin stood firm. Edie glanced around.

'Looking for Raquel? Not coming out till lunchtime. Miss Clitheroe's keeping her back. In trouble already.'

Tess looked frightened. She was shorter than the other girls, who had begun nudging her with their shoulders.

'She's not special and she's not adopted,' Edie said.

'Just thick then?' Caitlin said.

'Smarter than you.'

'I could do it if I wanted. Can't be bothered. Her, she's just stupid. Staring into space like some retard.'

Edie felt her face getting hot. Tess was no longer visible among the surrounding girls.

'Actually, I do believe you,' Caitlin said. 'She's not adopted. If there's more than one it's bound to happen. Like puppies. There's always a runt.'

Caitlin threw her head back and opened her mouth to laugh. She was cut short by a small fist, darting out from the group of girls and smashing into her nose. Caitlin looked more surprised than hurt, until another fist drove into her mouth. Blood spurted across her face and down her blouse. She fell to the ground. Tess jumped on her. It was like a terrier attacking a bear. Caitlin's thick arms flailing around, unable to stop the blows being rained upon her by Tess's skinny ones. Deanne tried to drag her off and received an elbow to her nose. She fell backwards and started whimpering.

Edie stood, stunned and motionless. Tess had always relied on others to fight her battles. Edie was about to try and stop Tess, when Mr Everett dragged her off. Tess spun round, her bloodied fists balled, her arms straight and tense. For one moment, Edie thought she was going to hit Mr Everett. Her eyes bore into him, then she brought her fists to her face and started crying. Deanne was also crying, while Caitlin lay gasping on the floor.

'She just attacked me. For no reason,' Caitlin said.

Tess pointed to Caitlin.

'She said, she said...'

But Tess couldn't finish her sentence.

Chapter 7

Tess: June 2018

I lean my head against the cold of the car window and watch people, shops and traffic stream past my eyes. Post-rush hour, the roads are clear, and we pass swiftly through the town centre and out towards the police station. It sits on the edge of town, where industrial estates mix with the suburbs. Most families of the missing long for resolution, an answer, any answer. But I don't know what I'll do if this body is Edie. Only hope has allowed me to survive this long.

I don't have to know the truth. I could get out at the next set of lights and walk away, start a new life and never come back, as I imagine Edie did. At this moment she could be harvesting grapes in the Loire or surfing in California. It can't be her lying on a table, her bones being picked over, photographed and catalogued.

Detective Inspector Vilas sits in the front passenger seat, his hands smoothing the light creases in his grey trouser suit, with his hair swept back from the temples, his appearance speaks more of business executive than serving police officer. He's polite but distant. The driver, Detective Sergeant Craven, is a little friendlier.

'I've daughters of my own. I can't imagine how difficult this is for you,' he said when he picked us up.

We turn off the main road, then down a small lane running between two neat rows of semis, the inhabitants probably unaware of the horrors adjoining their pristine lawns.

Craven pulls up next to a police car and two other unmarked vehicles parked in front of a low concrete building with ramps either side of its main entrance.

DI Vilas leads us inside and talks to the receptionist, who passes him two lanyards, one each for Dad and me. We're then buzzed through a set of double doors and led down a long, narrow corridor to a windowless room with a desk and chairs and a large mirror on one wall.

'I'll just be a moment,' Vilas says and leaves us.

He returns, carrying a sealed black bag, and takes the chair on the opposite side of the table.

'Are we going to see...' I don't know what to say, Edie, the corpse? I settle for 'her'.

Vilas looks confused.

'No. I thought you knew. The body's been in the water for twenty years. We found a skeleton, no soft tissue.'

Is his coldness an attempt to stop a torrent of emotion from us?

'Then I don't understand what we're doing here,' I say.

'Certain items were found, which the lab are hoping you'll be able to identify.'

Lab. Images of cold examination tables with metal tools designed to scrape, break and probe. This girl is no one to them, whoever she is. With no soft tissue, no face, no eyes, she's just a bundle of bones and 'items'. They could be items in a shopping trolley. Under the table, Dad takes hold of my hand.

Vilas removes a clear plastic bag from the larger black one and places it in front of us. Dad looks away. I lean over. Inside is a short-sleeved polyester dress, dirty and degraded. I can see that it used to be bottle green with a thin white stripe and a white Peter Pan collar, now badly stained with brown blotches.

'I've been informed this was the standard summer dress at Joseph Amberley Girls School from 1994 to 2001,' he says.

'I had the same dress,' I say.

Dad's grip on my hand tightens.

'Can you see anything that indicates this belonged specifically to Edie?'

Dad still won't look.

'I can't see the size,' I say.

'It's a medium,' Vilas says.

'Lots of girls would have been a medium. Lots of girls would have worn that uniform.'

Vilas's face softens. Perhaps he's human, after all.

'This uniform was found wrapped round the remains of the girl found in the reservoir. Her height and age match Edie's and forensics estimate they've been down there for around two decades.'

I push the bag away. Vilas waits a moment before placing another, smaller bag on the table.

'Could you look at something else for me?' he asks.

The contents are too small to see clearly. I lean down so that my nose nearly touches the plastic. A silver chain lies flat against the table surface. Attached to it is a pendant, its once silver wings eroded but still identifiable. I raise my left wrist. A tiny matching pendant swings round on the chain of my bracelet.

'It was a set?' Vilas says. 'So this belonged to Edie.'

The room goes very cold and I start to shake. Vilas leans over to examine my bracelet.

'It's some sort of bird. What is it, a dove?'

'A swift,' I say. 'It's a swift.'

Dad makes a strange gasping sound. Mum's maiden name was Swift. Grandpa Len bought the necklace for her, with a matching bracelet, for her eighteenth birthday. After she died, Edie wore the necklace and I took the bracelet.

'Is there any chance...' I trail off.

Vilas takes a deep breath.

'We're running dental records and checking DNA, but even before you identified the necklace and dress, we believed this to be Edie.'

I won't accept what he's saying. There must be another explanation. I look to Dad. He's turned away from me, so that I can't see his face.

He says softly, 'I knew it was her this time.' His back rises and falls in silent sobs. I can't stop shaking.

'I'm sorry, this must be a terrible shock,' Vilas says.

The empathy doesn't reach his eyes. He stands up, places the dress back into the black bag and reaches for the necklace. I put my hand on it.

'No,' I say.

Vilas glances at Craven, who leans forwards.

'Tess,' Craven says. 'This is evidence. It will help us find out what happened to Edie. DI Vilas will need to take it with him.'

I let go and fall back on the chair. Vilas picks up the bags. I watch the bulge of Edie's dress press against the plastic.

'Was it...' I hardly dare speak the words. 'Was it an accident?'

Craven sits back down.

'All the evidence points away from an accident,' he says.

I think of the stain on the dress collar, it wasn't brown originally, it was red, bright red.

'Edie was wrapped in plastic sheeting and weighted down. There's little room for ambiguity,' Vilas says. 'DS Craven will be assigned as your family liaison officer. Edie's case is being changed from a missing person to a murder inquiry.'

Chapter 8

Edie: September 1993

Caitlin needed two stitches in her top lip. If she hadn't had a reputation as a bully, Tess would have been suspended. Instead, she was dragged before the headmistress. Edie came as a witness. Mrs Stanton declared it to be 'six of one and half a dozen of the other'. Tess, Caitlin and Deanne would be given lunchtime detention for the next week and a letter sent to their parents.

'Make sure you give it to Dad, not Mum,' Edie whispered as they came out of the head's office.

*

'Nice one, Tess,' Raquel said as they were leaving school. 'Wish I'd been there.'

Raquel wasn't the only one who admired Tess. The whole school was happy to hear about Caitlin being taken down, and tiny Tess doing it made it even funnier.

'Are you coming to Roswell?' Raquel asked.

Mum had told them to keep away from Roswell Park. Older

kids went there to smoke, drink and worse. Besides, they'd got in enough trouble for one day.

'Valentina said to go round and tell her what our first day was like,' Edie said.

'She's always having you over. Mum says it's cos she's no kids of her own. But she never asks me. What do you do there, anyway? You'll have more fun at Roswell.'

'She makes cakes for us,' Tess said as if this explained everything.

Raquel looked at her sideways.

'Suit yourself.'

*

Valentina must have been looking out for them, because she opened the door before they knocked. Her hair was in its usual chignon and she wore a suede skirt and long boots.

'Edie, Tess,' she said and motioned for them to come in. 'You have to help me eat this gingerbread. I always make too much. Mr Vickers never eats it.'

Edie knew Valentina really made it for them. It was their favourite. She skipped into the house without stopping. Tess hovered at the front door.

'Don't you want any, Tess?' Valentina asked.

'Maybe we should go and see Dad first,' Tess said.

'He won't miss us,' Edie answered.

Every day Dad sat in the same chair, smoking the same brand of cigarettes, watching the same programmes. It didn't matter whether she and Tess were there or not. Tess trudged inside.

The Vickers' home always seemed so much brighter and larger than their own. It had a small extension at the back, so that the kitchen could fit a large chest freezer, for Valentina's casseroles and stewed fruit. It was so clean and tidy you wouldn't think anyone lived there. Only Valentina brought it to life, as she filled the air with baking and Chanel No. 5.

One day, Edie would have a home like this, clean and calm, until she arrived, and she would be Valentina, brightening the rooms with her presence, filling the air with warm spice and perfume. People would call her Edith, not Edie. She wouldn't have a husband who sat in his armchair smoking all day or one like Mr Vickers who came home, only to start barking complaints the moment he stepped through the door. If she ever married it would be to a man like Uncle Ray, handsome and fun. She could never remember Uncle Ray raising his voice or not wanting to take her to the park or saying no when she wanted something. Why did men like Uncle Ray marry Auntie Becca and women like Valentina marry Mr Vickers?

'And how was your day, girls?' Valentina asked as she put the tray down.

There was a pause. Edie glanced at Tess, best not to mention Caitlin.

'Edie's on the top-stream table, I'm not,' Tess said sulkily.

'That's a shame,' Valentina said.

'Tess will catch up,' Edie said.

Valentina smiled and passed Tess a plate.

'And you're so good at drawing, Tess,' Edie said. 'You can't be good at everything.'

Tess seemed to cheer up and took some cake.

'I was always hopeless at maths and things like that, Tess,' Valentina said. 'Much better at cookery and art.'

Neither spoke while Valentina fussed, pouring the tea and cutting the cake. Edie ate her gingerbread and Tess broke hers into small pieces without bringing any to her mouth. Valentina tried to hand her a teacup twice before she noticed.

'Your mum says you're going away this weekend,' Valentina said.

'We're going to London with Auntie Becca,' said Tess. 'To see Aunt Lola in Kentish Town.'

'That'll be fun. Are you going to see all the sights?'

'No,' said Tess. 'We've been before. We'll probably go down Oxford Street.'

Edie was less thrilled than Tess. Aunt Lola gave their cousins money to shop, whereas Tess and Edie could only watch. Still, she liked her cousins, Cassie was too young to be of much interest, but Corrine and Ashley were older and a lot more fun than Tess. She dreamt of being their age or older and living in London by herself. That was until she married and had Valentina's house.

'Dad can't come though, Uncle Ray's busy with work and someone has to look after Pepe,' Tess said.

'Who?'

'Auntie Becca's dog. Do you and Mr Vickers ever go away for weekends?'

'No,' Valentina said. 'Not our thing.'

'Why not?'

'Mr Vickers doesn't really like travel. I persuaded him to go to Portugal once, he hated it.'

It was odd how Valentina referred to her husband as Mr Vickers, as if he were a teacher. Edie couldn't imagine Mum calling Dad 'Mr Piper'.

Valentina glanced at her watch.

'You know what,' she said. 'I'll put the rest of the cake in Tupperware and you can take it with you for your journey. You'll be a few hours on that coach.'

'We're taking Uncle Ray's car. Auntie Becca wants to buy lots of clothes,' Tess said.

Edie giggled.

'She'll only get black tops and trousers like all her others.'

'I don't care why. It'll be nicer in the car.'

Edie thought about it. Uncle Ray's car had leather seats and a stereo. The coach had dirty toilets and old ladies trying to talk to you.

'I suppose so,' she said.

'Well take the cake anyway,' Valentina said.

She took the gingerbread back into the kitchen and returned with a plastic box.

'Bring the Tupperware back when you've finished, will you?'

'We will,' Edie said.

Tess stood up. Edie had hoped to stay for another slice. She saw Valentina's eyes flick to her watch again.

'Mr Vickers had a meeting in Stoke this afternoon and he's not going back to the office before coming home.'

Edie understood. She got to her feet and thanked Valentina for the cake.

*

The smell of stale tobacco drifted from under their front door. Edie felt the gloom before they even stepped inside. Tess ran over to Dad and kissed him. He patted her on the head, cigarette still in hand; a little ash fell into her hair.

'Hi, Dad,' she said.

'Hi, girls.'

He spoke softly, as always.

'We've got some cake, do you want some?'

'Not now, Tess,' he said.

'I'll put it in the kitchen.'

Edie followed her. She had just got the plates out for a second slice when the shouting began next door.

'I can smell it. Baking all day for those bloody urchins and what do I get when I get in? Sardines on effin' toast.'

They couldn't hear Valentina's reply.

'What's the time got to do with it? I don't work every hour God sends to feed the neighbourhood waifs and strays.'

A door slammed.

Tess and Edie looked at each other. Tess looked like she was about to cry. Edie started to giggle.

Chapter 9

Tess: June 2018

I lie in bed. Dad brings me cups of tea I don't drink. Cassie and Max make calls I don't answer. Dad will have told them what's happened by now and anyway, it's all over the news. DS Craven comes in and asks if he can have a word. I say no and Dad tells him to leave me alone.

'You should really eat something,' Dad says.

I'm sure he's had nothing himself. He leaves a plate of Welsh rarebit on the side table.

I turn over and stare out of the window; the rain trickling down my reflection in its pane provides the tears I'm unable to cry.

The only reason I moved to London was because I thought I'd find Edie. She'd dreamed of living in the city and it didn't matter how many millions of people lived there, I knew one day I'd bump into her on Oxford Street or at Waterloo Station.

But she was never there. The whole time she was lying at the bottom of a reservoir, wrapped in plastic and weighted down. She would still be there now if the police hadn't dragged it after a tip-off about a drugs stash, but there were no drugs, just the body of a young girl, another one. We've had many messages from the police over the years. An unidentified young female, you may need to prepare. And then you hate yourself for being relieved at another girl's death. Anyone's as long as it isn't Edie's. And now it is.

Anger rushes through me. How could this happen? How can Edie be dead? I find the energy to get up and go to her room. There have to be answers somewhere, she must have left me something. Where's the photograph, where are the missing pages from the scrapbook? I start with the tallboy. I find a couple of old Record Collector magazines and an NME from 1998 with Blur on the cover. I turn every page, to see if anything's cut out or ringed. Nothing. Her make-up bag's still here. A Rimmel eyeliner pencil and mascara in black, cherry-red Boots Seventeen lipstick, dried and cracked. I leap on a scrap of paper crunched up in the corner. It's covered in silver powder from a long since disintegrated eyeshadow. I press it flat against the wall and hold it to the light. I can just about make out a till receipt from Topshop dated April 1998. I screw it up and throw it back then pull the drawer out completely, turn it over and shake its contents on the floor to make sure I've not missed anything.

I start pulling out the other drawers, rifling through them, spreading old birthday cards, mismatching earrings and desiccated cough sweets across the carpet. Nothing.

I go to the wardrobe. Her faux suede jacket is still hanging there and her dress with the fitted body and full skirt, that was unfashionable back then but everyone wanted when they saw it on Edie. I go through the coat pockets and a couple of bags: more receipts and a few bus tickets. Flinging the clothes on the floor, I then run my hands in the corners to make sure I haven't missed anything. It's empty.

I start pulling books from the shelves. She could have hidden the missing pages from the 'Cakemaker' scrapbook in their leaves. I flip through the pages then hold their spines and shake each one out. A couple have magazine clippings slipped inside, mostly about bands, but no loose pages from the scrapbook. I try her school exercise books. A little hope. A phone number and address I don't recognise. No names, though. I take a photo with my phone anyway.

The last things left are her records. I don't touch them. Edie wouldn't have written anything on those or stuffed something inside the sleeves. They were too important to her.

I sit down in the pile of clothes, books and junk in the centre of the room. Is this all that's left of Edie? This and the necklace I'm not allowed to have because it's evidence. I pull my knees to my chest, lay my head on them and start to cry. I can't believe she's gone. Every last thread of hope has been pulled from me. DS Craven told us the DNA and dental records are a match. This is all there is, a pile of clothes and some junk.

'Here you are.'

The door opens and Auntie Becca comes in.

'I was worried when you weren't in your own room.'

She kneels down next to me and I raise my head; her eyes, too, are puffy from crying. She takes my head in her hands.

'At least you know now. You won't have to keep wondering forever.'

'I don't want to know. I always thought we'd find her. I always believed that.'

'Sweetheart, I'm so sorry. When's Max coming?'

'He's not.'

'I didn't think he'd leave your side at a time like this.'

I could not tell her, but she'll just keep asking questions until she knows the truth. Dad hasn't asked me about Max, which is why I know he's already spoken to him.

I curl up tighter.

'Has something happened?' she asks.

'He's met someone else.'

I can't be bothered with the details. Somebody else is easier to blame than my failure to meet his ultimatum, and what other conclusion can I draw from another woman's perfume clinging to him?

'Oh, Tess, and at a time like this.'

'I don't care any more,' I say, and it's true. What is Max to me? He's been a support system. Well, now there's nothing left to support. Whoever slung Edie into that reservoir may as well have thrown me in, too. Becca seems to read my thoughts.

'Tess, your dad needs you. He's not strong and you're all he's got.' My own misery has made me oblivious to his. 'Vince is looking sick. I don't think he'll get through this without you. Especially when the press turn up.'

'Are they here?' I ask.

'Not yet, but they're coming. Maybe you could come and stay at ours for a bit.'

'They'd only follow.'

'Parasites,' she says. 'Look, Tess, why don't you have a shower and come downstairs, try and eat something, talk to Ray. He's taking this hard; you know how close he and Edie were. And most of all, you have to pull through this for your father.'

'I'll try,' I say.

'And there's a police officer downstairs, Tess.' She looks at me nervously. 'I came straight up and didn't speak to him. What's he doing in the house?'

'He's the family liaison officer.'

'I think you should get rid of him.'

'He's alright, Becca, he's trying to help.'

She shakes her head.

'You weren't here, Tess, you've no idea how bad it got. The way the police treated Vince, the way they questioned him, as if he'd ever hurt Edie. You need to go downstairs and support him. Don't let that liaison officer trick you into saying anything about Vince or Ray. The police are not our friends, Tess.'

*

I go through the mechanical routine of undressing and showering, and arrive downstairs bare-footed and with wet hair. DS Craven's in the lounge sitting on the sofa next to Dad, his arms in a triangle on his thighs. Ray's perched on the side, his chin resting on his hands. When he looks up his eyes are red. He comes over and hugs me and I rest my head on his shoulder.

'Christ, I'm glad Gina didn't have to go through this,' he says.

Mum. Throughout all of this we've not mentioned her once. And my short-lived resolve at being strong for Dad crumbles. My legs go limp and I fall into Ray. He supports me and pulls me into the armchair. I want Mum, I want her to take me in her arms and tell me everything's going to be OK, like she did when I was a little girl.

Ray kneels next to me.

'You're so much like her, Tess,' he says.

Have I become like Mum? I try to picture her face compared

to mine. Then I get it mixed up with Edie's and become confused.

She and Edie were so alike, not just in looks, but they were also both animated and excitable. With no effort, people were drawn to them and wanted to be friends. Often, I'd arrive somewhere with Edie and people would say to her, 'I didn't know you had a sister,' when they'd met both of us before; only Edie was remembered. And she's never coming back.

Craven's hovering in the background. Ray sees him looking at Becca.

'This is my wife, Rebecca,' he says. There's barely disguised animosity in his voice. 'This is Detective Sergeant Craven.'

'Tony,' Craven says. 'I'm the family liaison officer.'

He offers Becca his hand. She gives it a cursory shake and purses her lips in substitution for a smile.

'When can we have Edie back? We want the funeral to be as soon as possible,' she says.

Craven's on edge. Dad's made it clear he doesn't want him here and his manner is exaggeratedly calm, as if permanently fending off an overwhelming panic; he's new to the job, I think.

'The coroner will release the body once a second post-mortem has been carried out. It's just a formality, so in about a week.'

'Do they have an exact cause of death?' Becca asks.

I ball my fists tight to brace against the answer.

'The pathologist noted she'd received a blow to the head,' Craven says. 'Significant enough to render her unconscious, though she doubted it would have been fatal.'

'So she drowned.'

'We can't be certain.'

53

'You're telling me they don't know?' Becca says.

'The pathologist couldn't give a definitive cause of death. I'm afraid it's not uncommon in cases where the victim isn't found for many years. I know you want answers and we're going to do everything in our power to get them. We'll be re-interviewing everyone and put out a fresh appeal for witnesses.'

'After twenty years?'

'You'd be amazed what people do remember. We can combine the appeal with a press conference and of course there'll probably be a reconstruction.'

'No chance,' Dad says.

'We've asked journalists to stay away from the house,' Craven says. 'But they're only agreeing to a twenty-four hour period to let the family grieve. After that...' He gives a slight shrug. 'It would be easier if you just arranged to speak to them. We can discuss the appeal another time perhaps.'

Dad glares at Craven.

'We'll also be looking at any similar cases,' Craven says.

'Similar cases? Are you talking about a serial killer?' Ray says.

My mind scurries away down dark tunnels. I look at Dad.

'Please no,' I say.

'It's just a possibility,' Craven says quickly. 'There's no evidence of a sexual assault. She was fully clothed. Though, again, we can't be certain.'

Ray brings his hands to his face.

'Do you think someone held her, before they...' I can't say the words.

'We believe Edie was killed soon after she went missing. The original investigation surmised this when they found her bag in the canal. And there's an additional indication of this being the case from the post-mortem.'

Ray takes a sharp breath.

'What indication?' he asks.

'The indentation to the skull contained tiny fragments of rust. It's consistent with the composition of metal on the bridge crossing the canal. Unfortunately, the ironwork along the bridge wasn't checked for blood at the time. Edie's injury indicates she was attacked from behind and her head hit the metal struts.'

Becca flinches. Dad doesn't move and remains staring at his hand. Ray looks from one to the other then to me.

'Tess,' he says. 'Oh God, Tess. How could this happen?'

I can see it as a film running through my head, Edie bouncing along the path unconcerned, enjoying the June day, the shade by the canal, the dragonflies drifting through shards of light shooting between tree branches. Then it's all gone. Just cold and endless darkness.

'What happened to the photograph? Was it with her?' I ask.

'Which photograph?' Craven asks.

Ray glances at Dad. They never believed my theory and it turns out they were right.

'Edie always carried a photograph with her, of us as a family. It was missing when they found her bag.'

'I remember now. It was in the notes but...' Craven looks embarrassed. 'Detectives at the time weren't sure of its existence.'

'They thought I'd made it up?' I say.

'No, it's just you couldn't say when you'd last seen her with it.'

'She always took it with her,' I say.

'It wasn't with her, Tess,' he says. 'And who else would have wanted it, or have known it was there? The new evidence only confirms the conclusions of the original investigation. That she was killed along the canal. We haven't advanced much beyond that right now. Hopefully, a fresh appeal will bring new witnesses forward.'

*

When Becca and Ray leave, I return to the bathroom and stare into the mirror. Do I look like Mum? I lean in close. My hair's started to dry, half is stuck to my face and half is sticking out. My eyes are red, but there is a resemblance. Not the pretty heart-shaped face and high cheekbones of the Swift girls, which she shared with Edie, just a light sketch of her features on my long, oval Piper face. Is that what Ray meant? Or was he just seeing what he wanted to see? Because it should have been the tall, beautiful twin standing here, not me, the small, plain one.

Passing Edie's room on the way back to mine, I realise I've left the clothes, books and general junk in piles on the floor. Dad mustn't find it like this. I start replacing the clothes on their hangers in the wardrobe and returning the books to the shelves. I pick up 'The Case of the Missing Cakemaker' scrap-book again. The cover's torn where I threw other books on top of it; I try to tuck the hanging strip back inside the pages. As I do so, I see a piece of paper's come loose. It must have been stuck under the cover. I pull it out. It's a cutting from a newspaper dated from March 1994:

56

Sentencing in Gina Piper Death

Judge Lavinia Darlington sentenced Nathan Bexley to a two-year jail sentence, suspended for twelve months following his conviction for death by dangerous driving earlier in the week. Bexley was found to have blood alcohol levels two and a half times above the legal limit and was travelling at excessive speed when his HGV hit the thirty-year-old mother of two, whilst she was crossing the eastbound carriageway of the Hagley Road on 15 December last year.

Judge Darlington added that Mr Bexley's lack of remorse and attempts to shift the blame on to Mrs Piper had caused her family additional distress. However, in mitigation, she did note that Mrs Piper's actions could be considered reckless and this was taken into account when handing down a suspended sentence.

The article doesn't tell me anything I don't know. And I'm not sure why Edie took the trouble to hide it, until I see her bold, swirling handwriting in faded blue biro on the white border, a single word: Suicide.

Chapter 10

Edie: September 1993

Caitlin and Deanne kept their distance after the first day. And when the letter was sent, Edie and Tess managed to keep it away from Mum.

'It wasn't Tess's fault,' Edie told Dad. 'Caitlin Powell's a big, fat bully.'

He wasn't quite the pushover they'd expected.

'But fighting, it's not like you, Tess, is it?'

'I won't do it again, Dad. Promise. You won't tell Mum, will you?'

'I think she needs to know, Tess. Have a chat with you.'

'Please, Dad.' Tess's eyes brimmed with tears. 'She'll go nuts.'

He sighed.

'Alright then. But if it happens again...'

Edie wrote out the return letter for Dad to copy.

*

She'd been so anxious about the letter and making sure she and Tess didn't run into Caitlin and Deanne outside school that she didn't notice straight away that Valentina was gone.

It wasn't like they went round every day, just most days, and sometimes Valentina would go shopping or visit her sister. But she was always home in time to make Mr Vickers' dinner. Now, Edie saw him park his car, slam the door with more force than usual and stride up the path. Valentina was nowhere to be seen. After a week, Edie and Tess started to miss her. Without Valentina, the only things to look forward to at home time were a smoke-filled house, Dad's boring sports and gardening programmes, and nothing but toast to eat until Mum got back. Sometimes Edie would go and listen to her records. 'The Snake' was still her favourite. But it was ruined by Tess complaining and wanting to listen to pop music on her CD player. Coming home was rubbish if they didn't go and see Valentina first. They couldn't ask Mum where she was. For some reason she didn't like them spending so much time at the Vickers'.

'You could ask Mr Vickers,' Tess said.

'Why me?' Edie said. 'Why don't you ask him?'

'You're much better.'

'All you have to say is, "Where's Valentina?" It's not a big deal, Tess.'

'You do it then.'

Edie huffed.

'OK, I will.'

'Tonight?'

'Tonight,' Edie said.

*

A knot formed in her stomach. She had always made fun of Martin Vickers and did impressions of his rants about 'those bloody kids', 'eating me out of house and home', 'should be taken into care if their parents can't look after them'. Tess would laugh then check over her shoulder, as if Mr Vickers were hovering there. Edie would never admit she was actually scared of him. She'd never seen a man so angry. Raquel told them that when her dad lived with them, he sometimes hit her. Edie wasn't sure whether to believe it or not. Their dad never so much as raised his voice. Even when one of their ball games destroyed his beloved plants, he'd just sigh and say, 'Please be careful, girls.' They never were. Uncle Ray laughed all the time and let them have anything they wanted. When Auntie Becca said, 'You spoil them,' he'd say, 'Of course I spoil them, who wouldn't spoil them. Look at them.' Mr Vickers was different. He didn't think she and Tess were 'just so cute' and he was angry all the time, even when he had a posh car and beautiful wife who made cakes. She didn't understand him and that made her scared. What if he was like Raquel's dad?

Mum came home at half past five. She asked them how their day had been, unpacked some shopping and started to chop vegetables. Just before six, Edie and Tess slipped out of the house. On cue, Mr Vickers' car drew up. He got out and walked towards them, his face set in a scowl. Edie's stomach tightened. She opened her mouth as he walked past but no words came out. Tess nudged her. The words still wouldn't come. As he was about to enter the gate, Mr Vickers spun round. Edie took a step back.

'What the hell are you two gawping at?'

'We...' Edie began.

'Get lost. There's nothing for you to scrounge today.'

He marched up the path and entered the house, slamming the door behind him.

Edie and Tess looked at each other and went back inside without speaking. Dad didn't look up from the TV.

'In here, you two,' Mum called from the kitchen.

She was standing by the sink, her arms crossed.

'Sit down.'

Edie and Tess shuffled onto the chairs under the kitchen table.

'Was that Mr Vickers you were speaking to?'

'No,' Edie said. 'Well, sort of.'

'I've something to tell you,' Mum said. 'This is going to be difficult for you to understand, but Valentina's gone away.'

'We know,' Tess said.

'Is she at her sister's?' Edie asked.

'I don't know. The thing is, she's not coming back.'

'Why not?'

'It's hard to explain.' Mum looked down at the table. 'Sometimes couples stop being friends.'

'Like Raquel's dad running off with that slag from the travel agent's?'

'Don't use words like that, Edie.'

'It's what Raquel calls her.'

'And Mrs McCann,' Tess added.

'Raquel and her mum can say what they like. I don't want you two speaking like that and using words when you don't understand the meaning.'

'I do know what it means, Raquel told me.'

'That's enough, Edie. Don't use those words and don't go bothering Mr Vickers. He's got enough to worry about without being pestered by a couple of silly ten-year-old girls, poor man.'

'Poor, he's not... he's ...he's ...' Tess spread her arms.

Edie took up the sentence. 'He's a horrible, cross, mean and bad-tempered—'

'I said enough.'

'No wonder she ran away.'

'Edie, I'm telling you once and for all to leave that man alone. You don't understand. You're just a little girl. One day you'll realise...'

But Mum never told her what she'd realise. She'd turned away. When she turned back her eyes were wet. Edie hadn't seen her mum cry since Grandpa Len died. She didn't know what to do. Tess ran over and wrapped her arms round Mum's waist.

'I'm sorry,' Tess said. 'I'm so sorry.'

Mum buried her face in Tess's hair. She remained there a moment stroking it before standing straight again. 'Now, go and sit down with your dad. I'll call you when dinner's ready.'

Dad's eyes pointed unfocused towards the TV screen as he drew on his cigarette. He didn't notice when they slumped on the sofa, nor when Tess nudged Edie, pointed to the ceiling and they sneaked upstairs.

'Why's Mum so upset?' Tess said when they reached their bedroom.

'I don't know.'

'Valentina's not come to see her. What does that mean?'

'I don't know,' Edie said.

'I think Valentina's dead.'

Edie considered this.

'They'd tell us and if they didn't, Mrs McCann would.'

'What if they don't know for sure?'

'How could they not know?'

'I think...' Tess lowered her voice to barely a whisper. 'I

think he killed her. Mr Vickers murdered Valentina and said she's gone to her sister's.'

Edie pulled a face.

'I don't think...'

'He's always shouting at her.'

It was a big step from shouting at someone to killing them. But maybe Tess knew more than she did. Edie remembered her attack on Caitlin. If Tess had been bigger, if Mr Everett hadn't stopped her... On the other hand, Tess obsessively watched detective shows on TV. Miss Marple, Inspector Morse, Sherlock Holmes. Not to mention all the true crime programmes. Her imagination was running away with her.

'I'm not sure,' Edie said.

'If everyone thinks she's at her sister's and no one's looking for her she could be dead. On the news I saw about a man who said his wife had run off with another man and twenty years later they found her body in a lake.'

'But what if Valentina is at her sister's?'

'Then why hasn't she come back to see us?'

'She doesn't want to bump into him.'

'He's not back until six. She could come every day.'

It was true, Valentina was supposed to be fond of them and when Edie thought about it, she was a little hurt that Valentina had not come back. She still couldn't see Mr Vickers as a murderer. Not that she was entirely sure what one looked like. On the news they had cold, hollow-eyed expressions and didn't smile. A bit like a passport photo. If you don't smile, if you just stare, you look like a murderer. It was true Mr Vickers never smiled.

'That's why Mum's so upset. Valentina hasn't come to see her. I don't think she's even rung her,' Tess said.

'Even if he has killed her, how could we do anything?'

'Follow him.'

'If he's thrown her in a lake he won't be going back and anyway, there aren't any lakes round here.'

'There's the reservoir at Lickey and it might not be a lake, it might be a canal or something,' Tess said.

'The canal's too full of shopping trolleys.'

'Or she could be in the freezer. I saw another programme where—'

'Tess, she's just gone away. You watch too much TV.'

Tess looked hurt.

Edie dismissed Tess's ramblings. She loved her TV shows too much and was so desperate for a mystery in real life she invented strange motives and secrets to the most ordinary people. When their former teacher, Mrs Edge, had left midterm, Tess linked it to a large jewellery theft she'd seen on the news. Raquel's dad's infrequent visits were due to his work in espionage, despite Raquel telling them he was a boiler engineer at British Gas. But unease trickled into Edie's mind when she thought about Mum's reaction to Valentina leaving. Something was wrong, still, she dismissed what Tess had said until the following evening. Mum was out and Dad was in the garden when Tess ran up to Edie.

'Quick or you'll miss them,' she said.

'Miss who?' Edie said as Tess dragged her to the front window.

Tess pressed her face to the pane so that her breath left a mark on the glass.

'I told you,' she said.

A police car was outside, double-parked next to Mr Vickers' Rover. Edie was just in time to see two uniformed police officers go into next door. She caught the words 'Mrs Vickers'.

'See,' Tess said.

She ran to the wall and put her ear against it.

'I can't hear what they're saying,' she said.

There was no need to have her ear to the wall for what happened next.

'I bloody will not,' Mr Vickers shouted.

Tess jumped back.

The crash from next door was so loud it made the room shake.

Another voice.

'You need to calm down right now, mate.'

Some more scraping, another crash. Then the front door was open.

'They're coming back out,' Edie said and Tess was back at the window.

They weren't the only ones, the two houses opposite had the whole family gaping from indoors and Mrs McCann had come outside to watch. Raquel must have gone to Roswell Park, because there was no way she'd miss out on this.

A policeman led a handcuffed Mr Vickers from the door, his eyes fixed to the ground. The second policeman came out rubbing his jaw.

'He must have hit him,' Tess said.

Edie hadn't seen Tess so excited since their school trip to Tutbury Castle, the most haunted castle in England. Ghosts were a close second to criminals in Tess's list of interests.

'He must be scared to hit a policeman, knows they're on to him. Why do you think he didn't run away before now? He must have known they'd come.'

The second policeman opened the car whilst the first shoved Mr Vickers into the back.

'Do you think they've found the body?'

More neighbours were spilling into the street, unashamed of their gawping. The police car drove off.

'You didn't believe me, Edie, but this proves it. He's a murderer. He killed Valentina.'

*

When Mum came home, Mrs McCann rushed out of her house and accosted her before she could even get to the door, no doubt filling her in on what happened at the Vickers'.

'Did you hear what happened?' Tess asked as Mum came into the lounge.

'It would be difficult not to. Eileen's a lovely woman but...'

'But what?' Tess asked.

'Never mind. Just make sure you two don't go around constantly gossiping and making up any bits you don't know.'

Tess pulled an innocent face as if such things had never occurred to her. Mum walked through to the kitchen and left the door open. Tess wriggled on the sofa, desperate to talk to Edie about Mr Vickers. She pointed to the ceiling and Edie followed her upstairs.

'What do you think happened?' Tess asked.

Tess seemed more elated than horrified at the thought of Valentina's death and Edie wondered how much she really believed it; though Mr Vickers' arrest did support Tess's theory.

'Let's watch the news,' Edie said.

'Yes, he's bound to be on it,' Tess said.

They watched the early evening and late news, national and local, without any mention of Mr Vickers and were sent to bed, disappointed. And they were further disappointed

66

when a car pulled up outside and Mr Vickers arrived home.

'How could they let him go?' Tess asked, her face pressed to the window. 'Do you think they can't find the body?'

'Maybe it's nothing to do with Valentina.'

'What else could it be? If we could find the body we'd help the police solve it.'

'You've never solved a crime, Tess. Guessing the end of Poirot doesn't count.'

Tess scowled.

'You can stay here listening to your records if you like. I'll solve it on my own.'

Despite Edie's sneer about Poirot, she'd always wanted to be a detective, though she fancied herself more like an American private investigator with a gun and a fast car. She knew it was silly and childish, but they had little else to do. Since turning eleven, Raquel considered herself a grown up and was spending most of her time at Roswell Park, hanging out with older kids. She even had a boyfriend, who was thirteen. 'I know what he wants but he's not getting it.' Mum was working the whole time. Uncle Ray was 'snowed under' with the business and hadn't been to see them for ages. And Dad was just Dad, as likely to leave the sofa as he was to fly. Being an investigator might be fun.

'OK, but we'll have to keep it from Mum,' Edie said.

'We'll go undercover,' Tess said. 'Starting tomorrow.'

Chapter 11

Tess: June 2018

Phone calls, knocks at the door and calls through the letterbox. Flash bulbs firing, a TV camera crew outside. The day's grace we've been granted by the press is up. Now, we're under siege. Would we like to get our story out there, let the public know the real Edie, quash rumours that the family were involved, she ran off with an older man, was mixed up in drugs. The first time round I was spared this by being packed off to stay with Aunt Lola in London, while Dad had to cope with the intrusions and insinuations.

DS Craven, I can't think of him as Tony, tries to deal with them. Dad looks grey, ill and so thin he could disappear into his armchair, where he sits smoking, tapping, missing the ashtray and finally crushing the butt before reaching for another cigarette. We can't open the windows to lift the fug for fear of being filmed. Not by the journalists but the thrill seekers, real crime enthusiasts, men obsessed with teenage girls and their deaths. Craven says it's normal.

'How the hell is that normal?' Dad says.

The whisky's finished and I've started on the cooking sherry. I don't know what normal is any more, either. It's still light but I've no idea what time it is. Edie's scrawled note on the newspaper clipping, 'suicide', plays on my mind. I can't see how it's linked to her murder and yet I can't shake the feeling that it is. I don't want to cause Dad any more pain right now by asking him. If Edie didn't speak to me about it, did she tell her friends, did she tell Michaela? Would she really speak to them before me?

I must have fallen asleep, because I wake up with the sherry still in my hand, calling for Edie.

Voices are coming from the kitchen. I go in to find Max standing next to Dad, who looks apologetic, a cigarette smouldering in his hand. Max is blinking rapidly. He hates smoke.

'You wouldn't answer your phone,' Max says before I can speak.

Dad looks at us.

'I'll go to the lounge,' he says.

'No need, Vince,' Max says. 'We can go into the garden.'

He leaves by the side door. I turn to Dad.

'You shouldn't have let him in. You know he finished with me.'

'I couldn't just leave him sitting on the step, could I?' Dad says.

'Why not?' I say.

'There's a photographer still out there.'

I sigh, take a cigarette and follow Max. When I reach him, he stares at the cigarette and looks as if he's going to object, then decides against it.

'Why haven't you been answering my calls? I had to find out from Vince that it was Edie, that's she's dead.' He stops. Pain flashes across his face. 'That she was murdered. One phone call, one, that's all it would have taken.'

'Do you know what it's been like here? Police, press, I don't even know what day of the week it is. You've absolutely no idea.'

'Because you've not been speaking to me,' he yells. 'I've had to keep ringing Cassie.'

I check the kitchen door and hope Dad can't hear.

'I can't deal with this right now, Max.'

He takes a deep breath.

'Look, I didn't come to argue,' he says. 'I came here because I'm worried about you. You shouldn't go through this on your own.'

'I've got Dad.'

'How is he?'

I shrug. In truth, I am on my own.

'He looks ill. Have the police interviewed him again?'

'Not yet.'

'What about you?' Max asks

'Not properly. I have to go in sometime, go over my original statement.'

Max shifts his weight to his other foot.

'I've got to speak to them tomorrow.'

'You?'

'They're talking to everyone from Joseph Amberley who knew Edie, the boys' and the girls' schools. I'm only going to tell them what I told them before, that I knew her from the odd party. It's just, you know...' He shifts his weight again. 'Going out with you, they might make a big deal about it.'

'Why would they?'

'I don't know. But make sure they don't twist it, to make our relationship seem odd. And tell them I had no reason to

70

harm Edie. And me seeing you, it was just a chance meeting. I mean, it's the truth.'

It's the truth, the sort of expression people use when they're lying, along with honestly and swear on my mother's life, which wouldn't count for much with Max, given that he hates his mother. I've never thought of our relationship as odd, imbalanced and dysfunctional, but not odd. I like that Max remembers Edie and understands when I say, 'Edie would like this', 'Edie would hate that'. It's always been something positive and held us together. Why would it be odd and why did Max just tell a lie, which I'm sure he did?

I think of another woman's scent, lingering in his hair the night before I left.

'Who's the girl you're seeing?' I ask.

'What are you talking about?'

'I smelt her on you, that last night I spent in London.'

'She's no one. And you'd just dumped me...'

'You dumped me,' I say. 'You told me it was over.'

'That's not true. I still want to be with you.'

'If I move back here and have seventeen babies.'

'Two would be fine.'

His face sets into its habitual sulk.

'Now isn't the time, Max,' I say.

'It's never the time with you, is it, Tess?'

'Not when I've just found out my sister's been murdered, no.'

'Why do you push everyone away? I came here to be with you. I'm upset about Edie because of the pain it's causing you and you turn it into something else. I don't know what I can do right for you, Tess, I never have. You think you don't need anyone, then you end up in a mess and expect me or your dad to sort you out. Well, neither of us are going to be here forever,' he says and stamps back into the house.

*

'Do you mind me asking who that was?' Craven asks when I come back inside. Max has disappeared and Dad must have gone upstairs. 'We're supposed to keep tabs on who comes to the house. Just procedure, you understand.'

'That was Max,' I say.

'Max Arnold?' Craven looks confused. 'Do you mind me asking what he was doing here?'

'He came to see me.'

'Any particular reason?'

The police contacted me through Dad and can't have noticed that I have the same London address as Max. I think about explaining that we're not in a relationship, only we sort of are but we're not together, even though we still live in the same flat, then decide that's all too complicated. And I'm saved from answering by Dad crashing back into the room, waving a notebook in front of him. Craven takes a moment to recognise it as his.

'I have to ask for that back,' he says sternly.

'Are you interrogating Tess now?'

'Just asking a few questions. And I do have to insist you hand over my notebook. That's part of an ongoing investigation.'

'I've told you to leave her alone.'

'I'm not a child, Dad.'

'Don't say anything to him, Tess,' Dad says.

Craven looks bemused.

'Don't you want to know, Mr Piper? If it were one of my daughters who had been murdered—'

'It's not one of your daughters though, is it? Tess is my daughter too and I'm not having you lot harassing her. We've already had journalists poking around. Don't you think we've been through enough? You say you're here to help but look what I found...' Dad holds the notebook at arm's length and starts to read. 'V. Piper – detached – two question marks. T. Piper reliable witness – three question marks. Aunt and uncle hostile – exclamation mark.' He glares at Craven as he throws the book to the floor. 'Here to help? You're here to set us up.'

'I can assure you that's not the case, Mr Piper. However painful, there has to be an investigation,' Craven says. 'And we need to ask questions of everyone involved from that time, including the family, if we're to get to the truth.'

'You lot aren't interested in the truth. I remember from before. How had I coped since my wife died? Wasn't it awful to be a man on my own? Didn't I miss having a woman around the place? Did I love my daughter? Did it make me jealous, knowing she'd started getting interested in boys? I knew what they were asking. Making me ashamed to admit I loved my own daughter, twisting it into something dirty and disgusting.'

I had no idea what Dad went through back then. I was shielded and kept safe. I had been a victim, but Dad had been a suspect.

Craven picks the notebook up and starts to speak in a slow, even-toned voice, no doubt some training manual calming technique.

'As a father myself, I can't imagine how awful it must have been for you,' he says.

'No, you can't,' Dad says. 'No one can ever know.'

73

'And we won't be repeating those mistakes, Mr Piper.'

Dad steps towards Craven.

'Get out,' he says. 'I've had enough.'

'Mr Piper, please.'

'Out.'

Craven looks to me.

'Perhaps you could come back another time,' I whisper.

Dad hears.

'No, you can't come another time. You're just a snoop.'

Craven has already moved to the hall. I follow him and shut the lounge door.

'I can see your father's upset, it's understandable. But we're not looking to implicate the family. DI Vilas hasn't ruled out a stranger killing. I think the support we can provide...'

There's a roar and a crash from the lounge.

'Yes, but not right now.'

I virtually push Craven through the door and slam it shut, thankful the press have left for the night.

I run through the hall and back to the lounge. The coffee table lies four feet from Dad, the remains of my sherry dripping down the wall opposite, the glass smashed to pieces on the floor.

'I can't do this again, Tess. I can't.'

Dad falls back onto the sofa and puts his head in his hands. I kneel down beside him.

'We'll get through this, Dad,' I say.

'No Tess, you don't understand,' he says. 'This is never going to end. It'll never be over.'

Chapter 12

Edie: September 1993

'I followed him for twenty minutes and he didn't see me,' Tess said.

It was late morning. Tess was in disguise, wearing a woolly hat and an old green anorak that Dad used for gardening. The sleeves swallowed up her arms and the hem hung well below her knees.

'Where did he go?' Edie asked.

'Only to the newsagents and the chippie. He turned around a couple of times but he never spotted me.'

Tess was taking her detective duties seriously. The investigation log was an A4-sized notebook, which she'd covered in the same cream with rosebuds wallpaper they'd used for their school textbooks. It was filled with diagrams and notes. She'd drawn a floor plan of the Vickers' house, a mirror image of their own, with the addition of the small utility room at the back and a sketch of Mrs Vickers with her hair in a chignon.

Edie had to admit the likeness was impressive. Less impressive were Tess's conclusions. Valentina was definitely dead. It was just a case of finding her body. Possible hiding places: under the floorboards, in the freezer, buried on waste ground, submerged in the canal. On the front of the book, in thick black marker pen, was written: THE CASE OF THE MISSING CAKEMAKER.

'That's a really stupid title,' Edie said.

'Dr Watson always used titles like that for Holmes' cases.'

'That's made up, Tess. Police cases are called things like operation something or other.'

'Well, you can call it Operation Cakemaker, if you like, but it's my book. This afternoon I'm going to go through his bin.'

'What for?'

'Clues. He might've put Valentina's clothes in there.'

'She left three weeks ago.'

'I know,' Tess said. 'I wish I'd thought of it sooner.'

Edie wasn't sure about spending the afternoon riffling through rotting vegetables. Mum rescued her.

'Becca's just rung. She's invited us over.'

'But we've got plans,' Tess protested.

'What plans?' Mum asked.

'Nothing,' Edie said.

'Good, get your coats. Your dad and Ray'll come along later.'

*

Auntie Becca called it an Indian summer and insisted they sat outside.

'It may be the last good weather we get this year.'

Edie thought India was supposed to be hot, she was freezing, the low, bright sun was blinding her and the egg mayonnaise sandwich she was eating had fallen apart, its filling leaking down her arm. Mum was in the deckchair opposite, a cup of tea balanced on her lap. She wore black jeans, a camel-coloured jumper and large sunglasses. She'd been quiet since they arrived and sat rubbing her temples. Auntie Becca, oblivious to the cold, was wearing her usual black trousers and black top. Tess had nabbed Auntie Becca's discarded sunglasses to copy Mum. Edie wished she had some. She moved one hand over her eyes as a shield. Pepe took his chance to jump up and take a bite out of the remains of her sandwich.

'No, Pepe, bad dog,' Auntie Becca said.

She didn't sound like she meant it.

Pepe ignored her and leapt at Edie again. She moved her arm away, then decided she didn't want the dog-licked sandwich and threw it to him.

'Don't give him that. He's a delicate digestion. It'll make him sick,' Auntie Becca said.

'Too late,' Edie said.

The dog swallowed it in one gulp and set off running around the garden. Usually Edie liked animals, but she wasn't sure about this one, all it did was run in circles, bark and eat. It never seemed to lie down or want stroking. A funny looking thing too, a Welsh terrier, with a tan body and black back. She was surprised Uncle Ray had let Auntie Becca have Pepe, she knew he didn't like dogs. And it was odd that Auntie Becca, who was so fussy and house-proud, wanted one, a dog meant mess. Then there were all those vases and figurines to knock over.

Pepe hurtled towards the flower bed, growled at a rose bush then ran to the garden gate, put both front paws on top of it and started barking.

'I don't think we'll be staying here long, Gina,' Auntie Becca said.

'No?'

Auntie Becca and Uncle Ray were always moving and Mum sounded bored. She was no fun today. Edie hoped Uncle Ray would turn up soon. He'd promised her a tape with new tracks and maybe a single on vinyl from the record fair he'd been to the weekend before.

'The garden's too small for Pepe and as for that lot...'

Edie knew what was coming: the neighbours, feckless parents and feral kids.

'They let those children run wild. And the parents are no better. We thought this was a nice area.'

'They looked nice enough when I saw them,' Mum said.

Edie had also been surprised on seeing that the neighbours wore clean clothes and combed their hair. The word feral made her think of cats, she'd expected them to have mange.

'They may look nice,' Auntie Becca said.

'Isn't he a bank manager?' Mum said.

'That means nothing. That boy, I can't remember his name, kicked a ball right over the fence into my washing. It splattered everything with mud. I had to do it all again. Not one word of apology from his mother, let alone him.'

'Kids are always making a mess, Becca, and maybe his mother doesn't know.'

'How could she not know?'

'You can't keep an eye on them all the time.'

'She should do. That's how these children turn out so rough, even if their father is a bank manager.'

The way Auntie Becca went on you'd think it had happened for the twentieth time that morning, not once, two weeks ago. And Pepe was worse than any kid, he was still at the gate barking loudly. Uncle Ray had told Edie that Pepe had got out and torn up next door's roses. When they complained, Auntie Becca said he was just a dog and didn't mean any harm. Uncle Ray had had to go around and pay for the damage later. It was their secret to laugh about, Edie wasn't to tell anyone.

'Yes,' Auntie Becca said with a nod. 'Time to start looking elsewhere. Are you alright, Gina? You don't look well.'

Mum's head was slumped over her cup.

'I'm just a little hot.'

'But it's freezing,' Edie said.

'I'll go and splash some water on my face.'

She stood up, which drew Pepe back from the gate so he could jump up at her instead. Edie batted him away. He growled back at her.

'Stay where you are, Edie,' Mum said. 'I'll be fine.'

Pepe continued to circle Mum until Auntie Becca called to him.

'Gina's not quite herself, is she?' Auntie Becca said when Mum was inside.

'It's since Mrs Vickers left,' Tess said.

Edie tried to catch Tess's eye, to shut her up, but Tess wasn't looking at her, deliberately, Edie thought.

'Val Vickers,' said Auntie Becca. 'She can't be much of a loss, if she's anything like her sister.'

'She's always nice to us,' Edie said.

'You know Valentina's sister?' Tess said at the same time. Her eyes lit up.

'I knew her. At school, Lillian Harlith. My God that girl gave herself some airs and graces. You'd think her father was a lord not a trader on the Rag Market. I'm sure some dodgy dealings were going on there. They always had fancy cars, cruises, fur coats. You don't make that much money selling a few yards of cloth, do you?'

'And Valentina was at school with you, too?' Edie asked.

'No. She's a few years younger. I couldn't believe it when she moved in next door to you. I'm sure that's not what her father had in mind. I've no idea what happened there. Rumour had it that her husband was a gambler; it would explain where all the money went. Because I know when their father sold up he gave them a pretty penny. Lillian bought that huge place over by the rose gardens. I don't know what Valentina did with her money. Whatever it was it didn't last. A Harlith girl on the Limewoods Estate. I'd never have believed it.'

'We live on Limewoods,' Edie said.

'I know,' said Auntie Becca. 'But it's not forever, is it?'

'I don't want to move.'

Auntie Becca screwed up her face.

'At least our neighbours aren't feral,' Edie said.

Auntie Becca turned to her. She looked angry and was about to say something, when Tess asked, 'Does Lillian still live by the rose gardens?'

Auntie Becca was still looking at Edie when she replied, 'I don't think so. I was driving past there not so long back and another family came out of the house.'

'So you don't know where she is?'

'Where who is?'

Mum had returned without them noticing.

'Nothing,' Tess said.

'Oh, they were asking me about your neighbour, that awful Harlith woman or Vickers or whatever she is these days.'

Mum's forehead contracted.

'I told you not to interfere, girls.'

Neither Edie nor Tess looked up.

'So she's upped sticks, has she, Val Vickers?' Auntie Becca said.

Mum didn't reply.

'I heard she wanted children,' Auntie Becca said. 'Maybe he doesn't. Maybe he can't afford it.'

'I really don't know, Becca. It's all I can do to keep these two from sticking their noses in.'

She picked up her coat.

'It's time we were off.'

'Not before Ray and Vince get back,' Auntie Becca said. 'Ray wants to see you and he's giving you a lift.'

'I've got a headache,' Mum said. 'We'll get the bus.'

'But the girls can stay.'

'No, they can't.'

Tess was already on her feet and Edie took one look at Mum before getting up. Usually she would have argued, but she remembered Mum's tears from the week before.

'Ray will be disappointed,' Auntie Becca said.

'I'm sure he'll get over it,' Mum said.

Auntie Becca frowned. Mum grabbed the girls' arms and pulled them towards the door. Pepe, who had barked loudly when they arrived, now didn't want them to leave. He crouched in front of them, arched his back and growled.

Mum looked at Auntie Becca.

'He's harmless, Gina. Just ignore him.'

Edie hung slightly behind Mum. Pepe wasn't a large dog but his teeth looked big and sharp. Mum walked forwards. Pepe shuffled in front of her, blocking her path and still growling. Eventually, Auntie Becca got up.

'Pepe, Peps,' she called.

The dog ignored her. She walked over, grabbed its collar and pulled him back. Edie inched past him with Mum and Tess.

'Bye, Becca,' Mum said.

The dog was still pulling on the collar and growling as they left.

*

Edie didn't dare complain about the cold wind and standing at the bus stop for twenty minutes. It took an hour and two changes to get home. Mum didn't say a word during the whole trip.

'Go to your room,' Mum said when they got through the front door.

'We only wanted to know if Valentina is at her sister's,' Tess said.

'I'm disappointed in both of you.'

Edie shot Tess a warning look.

'We didn't stick our noses in,' Tess said. 'Auntie Becca started talking about her. Did you know she used to have loads of money and Mr Vickers gambled it away?'

'That's pure gossip.'

Mum's face was getting angrier. Why wouldn't Tess shut up?

'But what if she's not at her sister's? He could have done something to her.'

'Enough, Tess.'

'He might have killed her. Her body could be in the freezer or under the floorboards. John Christie used to—'

'That's enough!' Mum rarely shouted and Tess looked up as if from a trance.

'If I find you've been snooping around...' Mum said.

'We haven't,' Edie said.

'I'm ashamed of you. After I told you to leave that man alone. He's going through enough.'

'Mum. He's... he's...'

Mum was glaring at Tess, daring her to say the words. Tess closed her mouth.

'Mr Vickers is a very unhappy man,' Mum said. 'And he can do without two silly little girls tormenting him. And if I find out there's been any more snooping you'll be grounded till Christmas.'

This time Tess stayed silent.

'Now go to your room. I don't want to see either of you right now.'

Edie and Tess slunk off.

'You shouldn't have said all that,' Edie said when they were upstairs.

'She has to know,' Tess said.

'I think Mum does know.'

'Knows what?'

'What happened to Valentina.'

'Then why won't she tell us?'

'I'm not sure.'

'You're not making any sense, Edie. If she knew where she was she'd tell us and she wouldn't be so upset.'

It made no sense to Edie, either. But she was sure she was right, that Mum did know something. And despite her promise, she was desperate to find out why.

Edie read her book, the sixth in a series. She'd got bored after the third but wanted to find out the ending. Tess was lying on her bed fidgeting and looking across at her. Edie carried on with her book.

'Edie?' Tess said after a long bout of rustling.

'I'm reading.'

'But, Edie.'

'Shut up, Tess.'

'I'll find her on my own.'

Edie put her book down.

'How?'

'I'll go to the library. Harlith's not a common name. There can't be that many.'

'She might not even live nearby any more. Auntie Becca said she'd sold her house and if she's married she won't be Harlith, anyway.'

'I didn't think of that,' Tess said.

'I know.'

'I can still try. If I find which house she used to live in we can get her name from an old phone book.'

'You won't be able to do that without asking Auntie Becca, and Mum will find out.'

Usually, Edie was the one to break the rules and she would have gone along with Tess. But Mum's reaction had upset Edie. It wasn't like her to be sad or serious.

'Tess, I think you should forget about Valentina. She hasn't come back to see us because she's not that bothered.'

'She can't come and see us if she's dead.'

'She's not dead, Tess. Mr Vickers did not kill his wife. She left him. I know you love detective books, but they're just stories. If she'd actually disappeared, the police would know. You're being a baby.'

'Don't call me a baby.'

'Don't act like one.'

Tess didn't reply. She switched off her bedside light and

pulled the duvet over her head. Her breathing was uneven and Edie wondered if she was crying. She carried on reading for a few minutes before turning off her light, then lay back on her pillow and stared up at the ceiling.

They were too old to be sharing a bedroom but there was no choice in this tiny house. It seemed unfair that Uncle Ray and Auntie Becca had five bedrooms to themselves, whilst they were squashed into a two-up two-down terrace. Edie turned on her side and sighed. It won't be forever, Auntie Becca had said, but what was going to change?

Her eyes were drooping towards sleep when she heard Tess say, 'I am going to find her.'

Edie was too tired to argue but if anyone was going to find Valentina, it would be her.

Chapter 13

Tess: June 2018

I tell Dad to go to bed and get some rest. He refuses, switches the TV on and stays in the lounge. As the press have gone for the day, I sneak out to buy some vodka from the corner shop, ignoring the curious stare of the woman behind the counter. I'm back in my bedroom and pouring myself a glass, when Vilas rings.

'DI Vilas here, is your father with you?'

'He's resting.'

'Good. I understand your father became upset with DS Craven. It's to be expected as he's under so much strain.' The irritation in his voice contradicts his sympathetic words. 'Of course, you're not obliged to have a family liaison officer. But it is advisable. If Mr Piper is finding DS Craven too intrusive, we could find someone more experienced.'

So I was right about Craven, he is new to family liaison.

'Dad doesn't want anyone around,' I say. 'Is it true you made accusations against him when Edie went missing?'

Vilas clears his throat.

'That was a long time ago, before I even joined the force, and he was never accused. We do have to ask difficult questions of individuals closest to the victim, if only to eliminate them as suspects. We'd be negligent if we didn't follow every line of inquiry.'

'Dad's not a line of inquiry. He's Edie's father and he's really not coping with this. DS Craven hanging around is making things worse. You know he's had problems in the past. Before Edie disappeared, even before Mum died.'

'We've got that on our records. A breakdown. That was a long time ago. He's on antidepressants, isn't he? Aren't they working?'

'What, after he's just found out his daughter's been murdered? Strangely enough, they're not doing much.'

This man's skills are better suited to working in an abattoir than dealing with bereaved families. Vilas is either ignoring or oblivious to my sarcasm.

'If you're determined not to have a new FLO...' he says.

'We are.'

'...I'll assign a point of contact for you within the investigation team. Do you think you could cope with Craven doing that? It saves bringing anyone else up to speed.'

'As long as he doesn't come to the house,' I say. 'Dad's made that clear.'

Better Craven than having to run through everything again with a new officer.

'I'll sort that out. And I'll be seeing you tomorrow at eleven thirty.'

'Tomorrow?'

'We're going over your witness statement from 1998. I'm sure DS Craven's mentioned it to you.'

He probably did.

'Eleven thirty then,' I say.

*

The low sun pours through the window. I sit cross-legged on the bed, a glass of vodka in one hand, a cigarette in the other. I'm playing a game. I press my eyelids shut then flick them open. For a moment the sun blinds me, then when I close my eyes again they're filled with purple blobs that float across the darkness. If I try and focus on the blobs, they vanish. The trick is to look without looking.

My mobile rings. I ignore it, happy in my land of purple and warmth. I try the purple blob trick again. The sun's disappeared behind the rooftops and it doesn't work. The phone rings once more. It's Max. I let it go to voicemail and I'm about to switch it off, when I think about the newspaper clipping. Why did Edie think Mum's death was suicide? I haven't dared to ask about it. Dad's a hair's breadth from a breakdown. He disappeared once when we were children. Mum said he'd gone to visit a distant cousin. Raquel laughed when I told her. Didn't I know? He was at the funny farm. Edie hadn't believed her and neither had I, but we never met Dad's distant cousin. I'll have to ask Ray and Becca about Edie's note, though Ray's looking nearly as fragile as Dad.

If Edie spoke to anyone about Mum it would have been Michaela and she might know about the boyfriend, too. Much as I loathe her, I need to get in touch. I try the phone number I found in the exercise book and am told it doesn't exist. I look up the address online: the bungalow was bulldozed ten years ago to build a block of flats.

I decide to download the Facebook app instead. A long time ago I had a profile. It was fun finding out what my friends were doing and to catch up with them. Then too much started catching up. Photos you're tagged in from nights you don't remember. Too many questions from Max. I deleted myself from social media. I may as well not exist. My new profile name is Laura Andrews. Not too obviously made up but dull enough to skim over if you don't recognise it. I upload a photo of two Labrador puppies as my profile and write that I live in the area and am married with no children.

Raquel pops up when I enter my primary school. She's still living on Limewoods and runs a gardening business with her husband, Gavin. They have one child. I want to contact her, but it seems wrong under a fake profile. Instead, I send her a private message, saying my real name and does she want to get in touch.

Then I search the Joseph Amberley Girls' School group. There's a general, anyone-can-join group with nearly eight hundred members and a smaller closed group, The JAGuars, which I apply to join. I didn't have any friends until the morbid glamour associated with Edie's disappearance made me a school celebrity and girls who'd ignored me suddenly wanted to be my friend. Not Michaela. She was a year older and left school the summer Edie disappeared.

JAGS alumni start popping up. Natalie Clarke, divorced, has one boy, works as a structural engineer, likes dance music and watching romantic comedies. Charlotte Wansford (née Lanark), a home manager, married with two daughters, Mimi and Lucy. She likes salsa, golf and healthy eating. Aveline Clements is an architect, separated, no children and no interests, but lots of pictures of her with her sister, Vonnie, and her friend, Gemma, (relationship statuses single) at clubs, parties and on holiday. All these girls attended JAGS at the same time as me. So did Hannah, Esme, Ade, Leanne, Anji and Rhiannon. But no Michaela. No link to Michaela, no mention of Michaela. She was the one Edie gravitated towards, shared secrets with and left me behind for. I need to speak to her. I check all the girls I can see from my year, the year above and all of their friends. I copy my Laura profile to Twitter, Snapchat and Instagram. Still no Michaela.

If social media had existed when we were at school, she would have ruled the world. Her vlog on music, boys and fashion would have turned her into a celebrity. It's made for her. Where is she?

The vodka's blurred my thoughts. I put the phone down and light another cigarette. The sky's the smoky colour it turns just before going black. I want the sun back, so I can play the purple blob game.

I play it with Michaela instead. Her skirt is the regulation school length but she's so tall it's halfway up her thighs. Her tousled hair hangs loose and her eyeliner is smudged. She smokes Russian cigarettes. Her boyfriend drives a red car. I see her leaving school and walking along the canal, heading towards the iron bridge, and I know what's going to happen. She's treading in Edie's footsteps at the back of school, stalked by an unknown attacker. She will bang her head, be wrapped in plastic sheeting and found in a reservoir twenty years later. I have to warn Michaela. I turn my gaze to her and she vanishes. You have to look without looking.

I've had far too much to drink and my imagination is running away with me. If something had happened to Michaela, I would have heard, even if I don't keep up with my school friends. But where is she? Who doesn't have a social media profile?

When I open my eyes it's fully dark. I turn the side light on and slosh more vodka into my glass.

On Facebook, I've just been accepted into the closed JAGuars group. Whoever the administrator is obviously isn't checking if a Laura Andrews actually attended the school. I click on Aveline and her sister, Vonnie. Michaela could be friends with them, perhaps she's also using a pseudonym. I don't find her; instead, the first thing I see is a post showing the front page of a national newspaper: **Missing Girl Dredged from Reservoir**.

I've deliberately avoided the papers. The word 'dredged' reminds me why. As if she's silt or rubbish to be removed. The picture shows Edie in her summer school dress, leaning against Ray's old sports car. It's the last photo we have of her. Ray must have taken it kneeling down, the lens points up at her and she's showing acres of bare leg. Edie didn't even like short skirts. The dress had been bought the summer before and was far too small for her by then.

Sad face emojis

Under the picture Aveline posts:

Devastated. Poor Edie. I always thought it would turn out this way. My thoughts are with her family.

Typical Aveline. Know-it-all, trite and insincere.

Charlotte: Yes, so sad. I've been crying all evening. Thoughts with the family.
Natalie: *raised eyebrow emoji*
Aveline: What Nat?
Natalie: You know.
Hannah: You think she had a boyfriend?
Charlotte: The police asked me back then if she had one. I know for a FACT she didn't. I was her BEST FRIEND.

91

You wish, Charlotte Lanark.

Aveline: I thought Michaela was her best friend.

Nice dig, Aveline.

Charlotte: Michaela just used Edie. And look at where
she is now.

For once be useful, Charlotte, and give me an answer. Where
is Michaela now?

Charlotte: It wouldn't surprise me if she had something
to do with all of this.
Aveline: No way. She could be a cow, but she wasn't
dangerous.
Charlotte: Michaela got in with some weird people
when she went out with that Bob.

God, they all want to get in on the act. With everything
that's happened, I'd forgotten what vacuous bitches Edie's
friends were. To them she's just a headline in a short skirt,
one that brings a little reflected fame because they knew her,
something a bit spicier than the usual pictures of their kids,
pets and holidays.

Aveline: Do you think the press will want to talk to us?
We could give an interview together.

Knew it. She'll have already booked in for a blow-dry.

Charlotte: Might do, but we can hardly go around accusing Michaela or some non-existent boyfriend.

Aveline: There'll be an appeal by the family, there usually is, anyone with information. Maybe the press will want to speak to us after that.

Natalie: The police do appeals to watch the family's reaction. No one's going to remember anything worth-while after twenty years. If the police ask them to do an appeal, they're listening to what I told them at the time.

Charlotte: What do you mean?

Natalie: Boyfriend, Michaela? You two are both way off target. You know who my money's on and I told the police. It's Edie's sister. That creepy twin.

Chapter 14

Edie: October 1993

'The Case of the Missing Cakemaker' lay under the bed. Tess's carefully drawn maps unused, her theories untested. But as Tess told Edie, from her extensive knowledge of criminal investigations, every case needs an element of luck.

It was the last day of the autumn half-term. At five thirty the street lights were already lit and outside a light drizzle was falling. Edie's searches for Valentina's sister were going nowhere. The only L. Harlith in the local directory turned out to be a Lionel, who didn't know any Lillians. Edie had rung numbers all over the country, using the payphone on the high street; she'd spent a fortune in ten pence pieces and got nowhere.

Tess still insisted Valentina was dead. It was just a matter of finding the body. Her latest hunch was under the Vickers' patio. The paving slabs were slightly out of alignment, indicating Mr Vickers had replaced them quickly for fear of being caught. She was considering ways to lift the stones, when Edie pointed out that the slabs were set in concrete and Mr Vickers would need a drill to get them out. They hadn't been moved for years.

'We have to rule out Valentina's sister first,' Edie said.

So when she saw Mr Vickers walk up to their door and drop an envelope through the letterbox, Edie raced downstairs. Tess had beaten her to it and was holding the envelope. Mr Vickers must have been in a hurry to leave the note without ringing the bell. Mum was at work and Dad was watching cricket being played somewhere on the other side of the world, where the sun was shining. On Gladstone Road it had been raining all day.

The envelope was unsealed. Tess lifted the flap and pulled out a sheet of paper. Edie peered over her shoulder:

I've waited in all day for the plumber, he hasn't come and I need to pop out. If he bothers to turn up, can you let him in please?
Martin

Tess turned the envelope upside down and shook it. Two Yale keys fell out. Tess held them up and turned them over in her hand.

A shout from Dad, a run, a dropped catch. He wouldn't be disturbing them. Edie looked at Tess.

'We can't,' Tess said.

'I'll go without you then,' Edie said.

Tess looked over at Dad, his eyes were still fixed on the cricket.

'I suppose one of us needs to keep a look out,' she said.

Edie smiled. She knew Tess couldn't resist. This had been her investigation, after all.

'We should do it now in case the plumber arrives or Mum comes back.'

Tess didn't move.

'You're not chicken, are you?' Edie said.

Tess glanced towards the TV, thunderous applause from the cricket ground.

'What if someone catches us? What if Mr Vickers comes home? Or you find Valentina's body?'

'I don't think you're going to make it as Sherlock Holmes, Tess,' Edie said. 'Just keep a lookout, OK?'

Tess went to the window.

'You'll need a torch,' she said. 'You can't turn the lights on once you're inside, people will know someone's there. Dad keeps one in the shed.'

'You get that. I'll go and change my clothes.'

Sometimes Edie wished Raquel was her sister, not Tess. She would be perfect for this, if she hadn't got such a big mouth. She'd have fought Edie to be the one raiding the house and then blabbed to the whole estate about it the next day.

'Mum'll be home at six,' Edie said. 'That gives us twenty minutes. We'll have plenty of time if we do it now.'

Edie spoke with confidence but she knew the timings were tight. The knot in her stomach she got, when she thought about Mr Vickers, returned. She could see his face, unsmiling, like a passport photograph, like a murderer.

By the time they left the house, the drizzle had turned to driving rain. At Tess's insistence, they walked to the end of the street and Edie changed clothes. She pulled her coat hood tight over her head, hiding her face, so if anyone did notice someone going into the Vickers' house, they wouldn't recognise her.

She left Tess on lookout at the end of the road and walked back to the Vickers' house. In her pocket the key felt very cold and her hand very hot. She had never noticed that the Vickers' gate squeaked, but now it groaned loudly when she opened it. Her hand shook so badly it took three attempts to get the key into the lock. She pushed the door open, switched on the torch and flicked the beam around the front room. The place looked like it had been burgled. Newspapers were scattered across the floor, drawers lay open and foam takeaway boxes piled up on the side. Valentina would never have let this happen.

Edie wasn't sure where to start. At home, the address book was kept next to the phone. She couldn't remember seeing Valentina's phone. She moved through the piles of papers on the floor, trying to put them back where she found them, though she was sure Mr Vickers wouldn't notice.

On the shelves either side of the chimney breast were more stacks of paper, where Valentina had kept glasses and photos. Either she had taken them with her or Mr Vickers had got rid of them. On the lower shelves, folders, binders and boxes were piled on top of one another but no telephone.

It was impossible by torchlight. A stack of bills sat on top of the fireplace. She was getting nowhere when the phone rang. She jumped and had to breathe to calm herself. It was coming from behind one of the armchairs. She pulled it back. The phone was still ringing.

It was then she heard the car pull up right outside. It had to be Mr Vickers.

She should leave, kill the torchlight and go. But she kept searching. She had to find that address. The car's engine died and its door clunked. Get out, get out. Her torch scanned evermore frantically.

'Hi, Mr Vickers, how are you today?'

Tess was shouting so that Edie could hear her.

'Huh? What are you after?'

'Nothing. I just wanted to know how you are.'

'Push off,' he said.

The torch beam landed on a red book, half stuck under the chair. Edie pulled it free, it was marked 'Addresses'. She grabbed it, ran to the kitchen and tried to get out by the side door. It was locked and without a key. The front door lock was turning. She couldn't get out in time. The chest freezer stood at the back of the kitchen in the small utility room. She turned off the torch. Fear crept over her. If she opened the freezer she'd find Valentina's body, scream and alert Mr Vickers to her presence and he would find the opportunity to add a second body too good to miss.

He was inside the lounge now. Edie darted into the utility room, pulled the door shut behind her and squeezed into the gap next to the freezer and the wall.

Footsteps. The kitchen light came on. Would he notice the utility room door was open a fraction, would he want food from the freezer?

Pouring water, a kettle hissing and the smell of warm spices. He'd brought a takeaway home, Indian. He wouldn't need the freezer tonight. Edie heard the slosh of liquid in a cup, the light was flicked off and his steps moved away towards the front room. He'd left the kitchen door open. She wouldn't be able to leave without him noticing and so knelt down in the narrow gap between the wall and the freezer. It kept humming, singing to her to have a peek inside. She should ignore it.

Mr Vickers switched on the TV news. Edie stood up and tiptoed to the front of the freezer. Its lid came open with a soft smack and the inner light came on. Too scared to look,

Edie leaned over it with her eyes shut. What if Valentina's frosted face lay there, staring up at her? She opened her eyes.

Nothing, only her breath puffing into clouds. Nothing at all. She shuddered. The emptiness disturbed her. Valentina kept it full. Everything was gone as if her whole existence had been erased. The freezer's chill crept into her skin.

Valentina could have been placed here and moved. It felt like a coffin, small, confined and dark. Was death like this, no feeling, just endless black and cold? She shut the lid, returned to her hiding place and continued to shiver.

By the time Mr Vickers came back into the kitchen, Edie's teeth were chattering so loudly she was sure he would hear. He didn't even turn the light on, just threw something in the sink and walked out. At last he shut the door to the front room and turned the volume up on the TV. Her legs were stiff from kneeling and the cold and she had to use her arms to pull herself up.

The side door was on a wheel lock, she'd not noticed in her panic. Uncle Ray and Auntie Becca had a similar one in their last house and she knew how to use it, turning it one way then the other and relock from outside by pushing the handle up.

It was still pouring with rain when she escaped Mr Vickers by the side door. She looked across to her kitchen, their back door and safety. The fence that separated the houses was too high to jump. A dustbin stood next to it, Edie used it to clamber over. The lid was slippery from the rain and her stiff, frozen legs made her clumsy. Her foot slipped, the dustbin tipped backwards, she tipped forwards, her stomach slammed onto the top of the fence, winding her, the momentum carried her over. She put her hands out to break the fall. Her wrist

crunched onto the concrete the other side and straight afterwards her head. Pain shot through her. She stifled a cry.

The Vickers' light came on and the door flew open. Edie
flattened herself horizontally across the bottom of the fence.
Her wrist was throbbing and blood trickled down her forehead.

She heard Mr Vickers step outside. He waited for what
seemed like an age, then swore under his breath, picked up
the bin and returned to the house.

Edie still didn't dare move. She lay shaking, pressed against
the fence. The Vickers' kitchen light stayed on.

Then another light came on. Their own kitchen light and
Tess was at the back door.

'Get inside,' she hissed.

Edie tumbled into the house. Tess's eyes were wide with
fright, her cheeks streaked with tears.

'You're bleeding. What did he do to you?'

'Nothing. I fell. My wrist is killing me.'

'We have to go to hospital.'

'No. Mum will find out. Get some cotton wool and a
bandage. She can't see me like this.'

Tess ran to the bathroom and Edie was alone again. With
her good hand she pulled the address book from her pocket.
A crack ran across the plastic cover, behind which were the
indented pages, A, B, C. She stuffed it back in her pocket.

Tess returned and began dabbing at Edie's forehead with
TCP. Edie winced.

'What happened? Did you find anything?' Tess asked.

'No. Nothing,' Edie said. 'Nothing at all.'

Chapter 15

Tess: June 2018

For a moment after I wake, the pain shooting behind my eyes and gnawing at my temples makes me forget where I am and why I'm here. Then I peel my lids apart to find myself in a single bed in my old room at Dad's and the misery floods back, the police station, the investigation, Edie's remains found lying in a reservoir.

The Facebook conversations loop through my head, that creepy twin, was just the beginning. More joined in: Anji, Rhiannon, and other girls I don't even remember. I was 'weird', 'obsessed with Edie', 'possessive' and 'jealous'. Edie and I had just lost our mother when we went to Joseph Amberley Girls' School. Clinging to her seemed natural, I never considered my behaviour obsessed or possessive. I recall one of the few parties I attended at Joseph Amberley, where I was standing at one end of a large hall, looking at a painting. Edie was at the other chatting with a group of her friends. I turned from the picture, moved towards her and caught a flash of panic on her face. That's what these girls saw, not me, but Edie's reaction to me. I was going to embarrass her. She'd have to acknowledge me. She wished I wasn't there.

Instead of deleting the Facebook account and pushing it from my mind, I go back and reread every line before moving on to Twitter and scrolling through the #EdiePiper tweets. 'It's always one of the family.' 'Why was one twin taken and one left? Suspicious.' @EverydayDarling, who I don't recognise says, 'I knew Tess at art college. Wild. Not a murderer.' And one more voice of reason: 'How does a fourteen-year-old girl kill another girl and dispose of her body thirty miles away? Needs upper body strength and car.' Followed by @AlphaTruth: 'How short was that dress? #slut #askingforit.'

I'd love to give @AlphaTruth what he's asking for. Thank God Dad's a stranger to social media. He's too fragile for this. All these years she's been missing I've been the one falling apart, making bad choices, taking wrong turns, with Dad arriving in time to pick up the pieces. And now, when we've found her, it's him who needs me.

My phone rings, displaying DI Vilas's number.

'We were expecting you half an hour ago,' he says.

I check the time, it's a quarter to twelve.

'I'm on my way,' I say.

My voice is croaky with exhaustion and too many cigarettes.

'The sooner the better,' Vilas says, his words clipped in irritation.

Too much alcohol is swilling round my system to drive, so I call a cab. With no time to shower, I just wash my face, spray on deodorant and pull some clean clothes on. As I get into the taxi, I catch my reflection in the car window and realise I've forgotten to comb my hair. It's still twisted into the low bun I wore to bed last night, half of which has fallen out and now just straggles at random angles from my scalp. It's too late to fix now.

I make the taxi driver stop on the way so I can buy more cigarettes and a large bottle of water. My mouth is dry and my tongue furry. I gulp the water down on the back seat of the taxi, the driver watching me in the mirror.

Does he know who I am? Will he be on Twitter the second I leave the car? Saw sister of murdered twin. She doesn't look too upset, if you know what I mean.

We take the same route to the station as my first trip to see Edie's clothes and necklace, and I relive the sick realisation that it's her, scrabbling around for a reason to doubt it and all the time knowing that there's no alternative. It is Edie. She's dead. I'll never see her again.

By the time we reach the station I'm ready to ask the driver to turn around and it's only his look of curiosity that makes me leave the car. The fear of what comments he'd post if I refuse to attend my interview.

Not willing to face the music. Make what you want of that.

I pay him and consider having a cigarette until I see Vilas has come out of the building to collect me. He looks me up and down, unimpressed by my dishevelled appearance.

'Miss Piper, shall we?' he says and motions to the station door with his arm.

The over-formal address puts me on my guard. And I remember what Dad said, how they tried to lay the guilt at his feet, and Becca's words, the police are not our friends.

Vilas leads me to the same interview room we were taken to identify Edie's belongings. This time I'm aware of the two-way mirror on the wall and that I'm being assessed by unknown observers.

'This is DC Patterson,' Vilas says as a woman joins us.

She's young, in her twenties, and seems wary of Vilas,

waiting for him to sit down before she does and watching him for cues.

'I see you've brought your water,' Vilas says. 'Need anything else?'

A cigarette would be good.

'I'm fine,' I say.

'We'll make a start then. As you're a significant witness, we will be making an audiovisual recording of this.'

Patterson fiddles with a camera, presses a button and a red light comes on. Vilas states the date, time and my name then clears his throat.

'I've read the original interview you did in ninety-eight. But I'd like you to tell me in your own words about the last time you saw Edie, if that's OK.'

The truth is I can't tell him. It's gone around in my head so many times, I'm not sure what I did see, what I thought I saw and what I've been told. I picture Edie pushing through the hedge, she puts her headphones on, straightens her back and crosses the road towards the canal. But I couldn't have seen any of that, because the school's perimeter hedge was too high to see the road beyond. Her Discman and headphones were found in her school bag, so she wasn't wearing them. That memory is false, taken from the description the police gave of the route she must have taken, with other memories of Edie and imagination filling the vast gaps in my recall.

'We were at school,' I say.

'Just for clarity, this is Joseph Amberley Girls' School,' Vilas says.

'Yes. I was standing by my locker, which was near the main entrance. Edie went ahead of me out of the front doors, then came in again and left by the back. I saw her walk across the

104

playing field. There was a gap in the hedge you could get through. We weren't supposed to use it.'

I stop.

'And that's it?' Vilas says.

'Yes.'

So little to remember her by.

'Why didn't you leave together?' Vilas asks.

'We often went home separately.'

'Do you know why she left by the front then came back?'

I hesitate.

'No. But she always left by the back, that last term. I don't know why.'

Vilas raises his eyes to meet mine.

'Are you sure?' he says. 'You didn't ask her? You were sisters, twins, didn't you automatically share everything?'

'That's a myth about twins,' I say.

Patterson leans forwards and gives a faint smile.

'You know, Tess, I've got two girls,' she says. 'They're really close, would do anything for one another, but my God, they fight like cat and dog, at any moment over anything. And there's slamming doors and of course they're never going to speak to each other again. It all blows over in five minutes. It doesn't mean anything...' She pauses. 'Had you argued with Edie that day?'

Had I? The day's images twist and blur.

'I don't remember,' I say.

It sounds so weak.

'I find that odd,' Vilas says. 'Usually people have a pretty clear recollection of significant events, however long ago.'

He's right. I remember the day Mum died and her funeral like it were yesterday. But Edie's disappearance is a haze. How must I look on the video footage? At best stupid, at worst a bad liar. I scrape around for something concrete.

'I think we had argued.'

'Can you remember why?' he asks.

'Edie kept secrets. I didn't like it.'

'What sort of secrets?'

I think of the notebook, 'suicide', but Vilas would dismiss this as the police had done with the photograph. Me seeing what I wanted to see, believing what I wanted to believe.

'I think she had a boyfriend,' I say.

'You're not sure? Your dad said she definitely didn't have a boyfriend.'

'Dad wouldn't have known. After Mum died, well, he struggled.'

Dad barely registered the day of the week. Becca had to remind him of our birthdays and school holidays. She bought our uniforms and attended parents' evenings. Other girls were jealous of our freedom, we could go to parties, stay out overnight, hang out in clubs. Of course, only Edie did these things.

'Why do you think Edie never told you about him?' Vilas asks.

'I'm not sure. I think that's why we argued.'

'And you've no clue who this boy was, or if he even existed?'

'Auntie Becca saw them together once. Edie said he was just a friend.'

'You think she could have been meeting this boyfriend that afternoon?'

'I suppose.'

'Was it quicker going home that way, by the canal?' Vilas asks.

'No, it was slightly longer. I walked that way sometimes, when I wanted to be alone. It was pretty along by the canal.'

'The Herrick Canal where her bag was found during the original investigation?'

'We just called it the canal,' I say.

'Which way did you go home that day?'

I'm running through the trees along the rutted towpath. Brambles tear at my dress and my knees are bloodied. 'Edie. Edie. Are you there?' I fall over and drop my art folder. 'Edie.' Another false memory.

'I left via the front of the school and walked to my auntie Becca's.'

Vilas nods.

'Your aunt, Rebecca Piper? Is there a reason you went to her house that night?'

'Dad and Uncle Ray were at the cricket.'

'And you couldn't be left on your own, at fourteen?'

There's a hint of scorn in his voice, I wonder if it will be apparent on the recording.

'It was just a habit we'd got into. From after Mum died. Auntie Becca made proper food. Dad could only just use the microwave back then,' I say.

'And when did you first learn Edie was missing?'

Again it's hazy. I can't tell Vilas that or the watchers behind the two-way mirror, or a future audience watching the recording, they won't believe me.

'She didn't arrive at Auntie Becca's and she rang Dad to see if Edie had gone home. I don't know what time it was, but Dad and Uncle Ray went out looking for her.'

'So this would be early evening?' Vilas says.

'I suppose.'

'I understand Edie was a typical teenager, a bit rebellious, she'd go out late, clubbing and drinking.'

'A little.'

You stink of smoke, Edie, and alcohol.

Go back to your own room, if you don't like it.

'So it wasn't unusual for her to be out late. Do you know why your father and uncle were so worried so early?'

Edie was always staying out late and Dad rarely had any idea if she was at home or not. For the first time this strikes me as odd, that they made a fuss so early in the evening. The camera's flashing light reminds me of all the seconds passing when I'm not answering Vilas's question. I see the pain on Dad's face as he tells me, 'They thought I'd hurt Edie, my own daughter.'

'She stayed out late, but she was always on time if you arranged it. She'd never just not turn up.'

Vilas nods and gives a false smile. I hope Becca and Ray give the same explanation.

'Did you ever go out with her to these clubs?' he asks.

'We had different friends.'

'And who were Edie's closest friends?'

I think back.

'Aveline and Charlotte, she hung out with them a fair bit.'

Vilas must know of them because he doesn't ask for surnames.

'Anyone else?'

I don't want to say her name.

'Anyone older?'

Vilas is fishing for what he already knows.

'Michaela. Michaela Gossington.'

Oh my God, that Tess girl can't really be your twin, can she, Edie?

'Michaela,' he says. He smiles slightly and I wonder what's been said about her. 'And who were your friends?'

Edie was my only friend. I can hear a chorus of JAGS: 'jealous', 'possessive', 'obsessed'.

'Ermm...' I search for names. 'Natalie and er... Hannah.'

'That's all?'

'They were my main ones.'

'Surnames?'

'I can't remember. We went to different sixth forms and lost touch.'

Vilas flicks through some pages. I glance at the two-way mirror, unsure if the shadow moving across is real, a trick of the light or my imagination.

'OK,' Vilas says at last. 'Can I bring you onto another matter that's been brought to my attention. Max Arnold.'

Aware of being filmed, I try not to scowl.

'What about him?'

'We interviewed him in ninety-eight. Did you know that?'

'Yes.'

'And it doesn't bother you?'

'Should it? Didn't you interview everyone she knew?'

'Yes,' Vilas says and pauses. 'It was suggested to us that Max had a bit of a crush on Edie.'

'Maybe, most boys did.'

I say it as casually as possible, to disguise my unease. Max never mentioned a crush, only that he'd met her a couple of times.

'You knew Max at the time?' Vilas asks.

'We may have met once or twice. I can't really remember.'

A small boy at a party, the other boys laughing at him, taunting him about his mother's affair with a teacher. Mr

Kent's whore. I'm not telling them that. It's none of their business.

'And it was sometime after school that you met up with Max again.'

'About nine years ago. We met in a pub in Islington. Max was up in London for an interview.'

'By chance?'

'Yes.'

'Did you post on Facebook that you were going?' Vilas asks.

'I don't know, it's nine years ago. What's this got to do with Edie?'

Vilas flick through his notes.

'The thing is, Miss Piper, I don't believe in coincidence.' He flicks through more papers. He's just doing it for effect and it's beginning to annoy me. 'We're looking for someone who may have had a reason to harm Edie. Romantic rejection is pretty high on the list. I would have dismissed Max's interest as a teenage crush, but his pursuit of you strikes me as a little odd. Do you really think it was a coincidence you met in that pub?'

It's not something I've ever questioned before. Just as I never questioned how well Max knew Edie. Vilas is looking at me, waiting for my reply.

'What else could it be?' I say.

'Tess,' he says. It's the first time he's used my Christian name. 'I just get the feeling someone's not telling me the whole truth about the afternoon Edie disappeared. I don't buy these blanks in the memory. If for some reason you're covering for Max...'

'Why would I?'

Vilas raises his eyebrows and continues. 'If you are shielding him, for whatever reason, I'd like you to reconsider.' He indicates to Patterson to turn the video off and doesn't look at me when he says, 'If I were you I'd be careful.'

'What do you mean?'

He turns around.

'I mean, I think you need to protect yourself.'

From what, from Max? It never occurred to me it was anything other than chance we met in that club years ago. And even if it wasn't chance, does that make it sinister? I watch Vilas gather his notes. Patterson also watches him, her eyes slightly narrowed, her wariness of earlier resurfacing. Is she being dragged along by her superior, grasping at straws, throwing suspicion on Max in an attempt to divert attention from the fact that they've yet to find Edie's boyfriend, or any meaningful leads? On top of which, they're implying I'm withholding information.

'Have you tried to find her boyfriend?' I ask. 'I'm sure I told the police, back when Edie first disappeared, that he followed her to the house once and Dad had to chase him off.'

Vilas stops gathering his notes.

'Your father has no recollection of that, and I think he'd remember, don't you?'

Another thing, like the photograph, that no one will believe.

He takes the jacket from the back of the chair and puts it over his arm before adding, 'Your aunt saw Edie with a lad, she said he was only a friend. You'd never met him, her own sister. None of the friends who are cooperating know anything about him.'

'Who's not cooperating?' I ask.

'I can't tell you that. The truth is, we don't have many leads and the family is usually the main source of knowledge.' And the main suspects. 'Mr Piper refusing to have an FLO isn't helping. We need fresh evidence. An appeal by the family is our best option.'

The police do appeals to watch the family's reaction.

'No,' I say.

'It's the next logical step.'

'No one's going to remember anything after all this time,' I say.

'You'd be surprised. You need to have a long, hard think about this. Our options are limited. If we don't find fresh information and we're not making progress, I'll be under pres-sure to start reassigning resources.'

'I'll talk to Dad,' I say.

'And I'll get the appeal organised,' Vilas says.

'I said I'll think about it.'

This is all the confirmation he needs.

'DS Craven will contact you.'

If the police ask them to do an appeal, they're listening to what I told them.

Chapter 16

Edie: October 1993

Mum was singing in the kitchen, the strains of Julie London's 'Cry me a River' carried into the lounge.

'Mum,' Edie called from the door.

She continued singing, her voice rising for the chorus.

'Muuuum.'

She paused from stirring a stew.

'We're going out with Raquel,' Edie said.

'OK. Stay away from Roswell Park.'

Edie turned back through the lounge where Tess was waiting at the front door.

Raquel was already outside her house, sitting on the low wall in front, kicking her heels. She jumped up as Edie and Tess came outside.

'I said I'd meet Clark later at Roswell.'

'I thought your boyfriend was called Daryl,' Edie said.

'Him. Nah. Got bored with him.'

'We're not allowed to go to Roswell,' Tess said.

'You don't always have to do as you're told, Tess.'

Raquel looked over to Edie. She was curious about Roswell Park and wanted to meet Raquel's boyfriend. But she had a vague fear Caitlin might be there. She'd left them alone at school, but if her older sister was with her, she wouldn't miss the chance to get her own back.

Edie wondered if Raquel was thinking the same, because she didn't argue when Edie said, 'It's too cold to go to the park.'

'How about the garages then?' Raquel said. 'I can't smoke here.'

The garages belonged to the tower block at the edge of the Limewoods Estate. Cans, condoms and the occasional needle littered the tarmac, but in the early evening they were deserted except for a ragged fox, which slipped under the wire fence at the far end as they arrived.

Raquel leant against a garage with 'Carlos suck my dick' sprayed across it. She placed one foot on the metal door, one on the ground, then lit a cigarette she'd stolen from her mum.

'Did you find out what happened to Val Vickers yet?' she asked.

Tess shook her head and glanced at Edie. She must have told Raquel about it when Edie was out of earshot.

'I did,' Raquel said.

She let out a long stream of smoke and smiled. Tess glanced at Edie again.

'Where is she?' Tess asked.

'She doesn't know anything,' Edie said. 'How could she?'

'Well if you don't want to know...' Raquel said.

'Tell us,' Tess said.

Raquel tossed a look at Edie to see if she had any more to say. Edie kept quiet. She wanted to know as much as Tess and it wasn't like they'd gone snooping again.

'You were right, Tess. All that stuff about her staying at her sister's was a load of bull.'

'I knew it,' Tess said.

'She's gone off with her fancy man.'

'Oh.'

Tess looked disappointed.

'How do you know?' Edie asked.

'Mum's hairdresser told her.'

Raquel's mum's hair was set in a solid block, high on top of her head. Robert's salon on the high street created the exact same style for all the old ladies.

'How does he know?' Tess asked.

'Hairdressers get to know everyone's secrets.' Raquel spoke in a slightly posher voice as if quoting a grown-up. 'And Ursula Mowbray told Robert she'd seen Valentina Vickers with a new fella.'

Edie snorted.

'That's Marcia's gran and even Marcia can't stand her. She made it all up because she's got nothing better to do when her hair's stuck under those driers.'

Raquel stood up straight and flicked her cigarette butt across the tarmac.

'Why else would she go off then?'

Edie didn't reply.

'Who was he?' Tess asked.

'Ursula didn't know,' Raquel said.

'It could be Mr Vickers who put the rumour about,' Tess said. 'That's what he wants you to think. He could still have killed her. I saw the exact same thing on—'

'TV, yeah, we know,' Edie said and rolled her eyes.

Tess scowled.

'You're soft in the head, you are,' Raquel said. 'Why would he kill her?'

'Jealousy, he—'

'Shut up, Tess,' Edie said.

She'd been dragged along by Tess into this murder mystery plot. When it was just the two of them, Edie half believed it. Tess was so enthusiastic, so convincing. But said out loud, in front of Raquel, it sounded silly and childish.

'The police came and took him away,' Tess said.

'That was because of money. You know he's a gambler?' Raquel said. 'That's why they're posh with no money. Y'know the way he speaks, all la-di-da. You, girl, stay away from my car.'

She pronounced it in the harsh voice of Mr Vickers. Edie giggled and Tess looked anxious.

'It's not funny,' she said. 'The police wouldn't put him in handcuffs because of gambling; it's something more serious. Men always say their wives have run off when they've killed them. John Christie's wife was under the floorboards.'

'Who's John Christie? Edie's right, you watch too much TV. She's got herself a fancy man more like. The place is on the same road as her sister, that's all, she's with a fella, I'm telling you.'

'I don't believe it. I'm going to find where her sister lives. If Valentina's not on the same road we'll know he's lying. Or we could find out who the man is,' Tess said.

'Mum knows something but she won't tell me,' Raquel said.

'Why did she bother telling you anything at all then?' Tess asked.

'She didn't. I was listening to her talking to Sharina's mum in the kitchen; they didn't know I was at the back door until I sneezed.'

'They could have been talking about anyone,' Edie said. 'You're really dumb sometimes.'

116

She regretted the words as soon as they left her mouth. Raquel would think Edie was talking about her reading problems.

'I'm not dumb. I heard them say her name. You think you know everything, don't you, Edie Piper?'

'I didn't mean...'

'If you're so smart, tell me why your mum married your dad?'

'What's that supposed to mean?'

Edie took a step towards Raquel, who stared hard at her then slumped back onto the garage. The metal door banged against its frame.

'Nothing,' she said.

None of them spoke for a while. They rarely argued. Edie was wrong to call her dumb. Then again, Raquel shouldn't have talked about Mum and Dad. Tess looked scared. Raquel stared at the ground.

In the end, Tess said, 'Shall we go up the high street? I want a magazine.'

Tess read comics but called them magazines to make her sound more grown up.

'Alright,' Raquel said. 'I'll get some more cigarettes.'

'They won't serve you,' Tess said.

'I wasn't going to the shops,' Raquel scoffed.

They wandered up to the high street in silence. Edie thought about what Raquel had said about Mum and Dad. It was probably something else she'd overheard and half understood. Still, Mrs McCann must have said something. Why did your mum marry your dad? Because they were in love. Isn't that why people got married?

Only the off-licence and newsagents were open on the high

street. Raquel walked straight past them to a group of lads sitting on a bench, smoking and drinking cans of Skol. They were older, about fifteen or sixteen. Edie and Tess hung back as Raquel walked up to them.

One of the boys glanced up then looked away again. No one acknowledged her until she was right in front of the bench.

'Hi,' she said. 'I'm after some fags.'

'Piss off,' said the boy in the middle who'd looked up.

'Come on, you sold me some before.'

'What?' he said.

One of the boys standing behind him whispered something in his ear.

'Alright then,' the first boy said.

Raquel gave the boy at the back a brief smile and placed a couple of coins in his palm. The first boy gave her four cigarettes.

'They're bad for you, y'know,' he said.

'Yeah?' Raquel said.

She waved the cigarettes in front of her as she walked back towards Edie and Tess.

'Told you.'

They were about to leave when some other girls arrived. From their height, Edie guessed they were a similar age to the boys, but they behaved more like adults. They didn't slouch and their hair, worn loose, had a satisfying swish as it swung from side to side. Edie became aware of her own unruly curls pulled into a haphazard ponytail or worse still, Tess's close crop that made her look like a boy.

All the boys stared at these new girls. The one who'd told Raquel to piss off sat up and smiled. Edie couldn't hear the exchange, but she saw one of the girls hand him some notes and he passed her a small packet.

Later, she couldn't remember which girls she had seen, or if she met them again. All she remembered was the word.

'They're JAGS,' Raquel hissed.

JAGS. Just the word, the long vowel, hung in Edie's memory long after the girls had left.

'They're what?' Tess asked.

'JAGS,' Raquel repeated. 'Joseph Amberley's Girls' School. JAGS.'

'What does that mean?' Tess asked.

'It means they're stuck up and they're sluts. They only come over this way to buy weed; wouldn't bother speaking to Bridges Academy boys otherwise.'

'We're going to Bridges Academy,' Tess said.

'I'm not going back to school, so it doesn't matter,' Raquel said.

'You can't not go to school,' Tess said.

Raquel laughed.

'Sharina and Mel all hang out in Roswell Park. You can join us if you get bored.'

'Mum says they do drugs there.'

'Don't be daft,' said Raquel. 'Honestly, Tess, you're such a kid sometimes.'

The conversation went on, Raquel insisting she wouldn't be going to secondary school and Tess insisting she didn't have a choice.

Edie was still thinking about the JAGS. Raquel had spat the word out but there had been envy in her voice. Edie, too, was envious. Somehow, she knew these girls with the swishy hair and leather bags would grow up to be like Valentina and smell of cake and Chanel No. 5, not Domestos and B & H like Mrs McCann. Edie understood Raquel's venom. She didn't care. She didn't want to go to Bridges Academy, she wanted to be one of them, she wanted to be a JAG.

Chapter 17

Tess: June 2018

'You need to go into fifth, Becs,' Ray says.

Becca obediently changes gear. The 4 x 4 engine roars then drops and we glide past a slow, chugging Fiat.

'Stay in the middle lane,' he says.

I don't know why he doesn't drive himself if he thinks Becca's incapable. But she doesn't seem to mind his instructions and it saves us from having to talk. Dad's not spoken since I told him I was thinking about doing the police appeal.

DS Craven sounded alarmed when he rang up to arrange it and I wouldn't give him an answer. Vilas called, too. If I don't want justice for my sister. The thing is, I agree with Natalie, it's a trap, after the speculation last time, and I don't want to put Dad through that again. Then again, it could lead somewhere.

We pull onto the slip road. 'Keep left, stay in third,' and drive up a winding residential street before reaching the cemetery, where Edie's to be buried, next to Mum. I want to see it before the funeral.

Once, it must have been a beauty spot, lying on a hill overlooking fields. Now, the West Midlands conurbation sprawls below and the air is polluted from the nearby motorway. It's like a little town with a flower stall at the entrance and roads running in a neat grid.

I can't remember the last time we came here together. I can't remember the last time I came on my own, and if Dad visits, he never tells me.

We slide out of the car and though we've not discussed it, we're all wearing black. I've forgotten the location of Mum's grave. Ray leads the way, in a well-cut wool suit, which is far too thick in the fierce summer heat. Light perspiration speckles his brow. Becca's swapped her usual slacks for a long skirt and Dad's wearing trousers and a shirt with frayed collars and cuffs.

'Edie hated this place,' I say.

Ray slows his pace and turns to me.

'I can't say I blame her.'

Faint whisky fumes carry on his breath. That's why he didn't drive.

'She said it wasn't a proper graveyard,' I say. 'No cracked lopsided headstones or yew trees. Just rows of graves mapped onto a grid, like a diagram you draw in maths.'

'It's a cemetery,' Becca says. 'Churches have graveyards.'

'Ordered and heartless. That's why she wouldn't come.'

'She could be stubborn,' Ray says and smiles.

We've come to view the family plot, to decide what's appropriate and what will fit on the headstone, and to make sure it's the right place.

'It is,' Dad insists.

He was horrified when I suggested a cremation.

'She should be with her mother,' he said.

Mum's plot is row G31. The large curved headstone is of

122

black granite flecked with gold, and the lettering is gold: Gina Piper, beloved wife and mother, 12 April 1963–17 December 1993. It's hideous. Mum would never have chosen it. I don't know who did. A desiccated bunch of lilies is lying on the flat stone. I bend down and pick them up.

'Who left these?' I ask.

Dad stops a couple of yards behind us and doesn't answer. Becca looks at Ray. He takes them from me. One of the greying blooms drops off.

'It was probably your dad.'

Dad always used to bring blue delphiniums, Mum's favourite. I pick up the fallen lily and stick it in my pocket.

Becca and Ray have a bunch of roses each, one red, one pink. They place them on the grave. Dad catches up and places his bunch there, too.

I scan the cemetery: a few families, but it's mostly individuals. Some are just standing, others are sweeping away dead wreaths and placing fresh flowers in pots. Perhaps Dad did leave the lilies. He's showing no interest in the grave now he's placed his flowers; instead, he stares up at the sky and passing clouds.

I realise Ray and Becca are looking at me.

'Shall we go?' I say.

'Eh?' Dad says.

'Go,' I say and gesture back up the hill with my head.

He nods and we trudge back to the 4 x 4. Ray places the dead lilies in a bin. I want to rush over and retrieve them; instead, I place my hand in my pocket. The flower has disintegrated into individual petals. I rub one between my thumb and index finger and extract the tiny drop of remaining moisture.

'I don't know about you, but I could do with a drink,' Ray says.

'Me too,' I say.

'Becs?' Ray says.

She gives a thin smile and opens the car.

'The Gypsy's Tent?'

'Sounds good to me,' he says.

Ray gets the drinks in: two whiskies and two pints for him and Dad. Becca has an orange juice. I go for wine, house red.

The pub is bustling with Sunday trade. We take a table by the window, the remains of the previous occupants' lunch still strewn across it. Dad and I sit opposite Ray and Becca. The glass panes magnify the sun's heat. Becca is flushed, but even the heat can't erase Dad's tired grey look. Only Ray appears healthy.

A woman in her forties with glossy black hair comes over and starts clearing the table.

'Sorry about the mess. Two staff called in sick and we're so busy today.'

'No worries,' Ray says.

'Can I fetch the food menu for you?'

'Just drinks today, thanks.'

'Well let me know if you need anything.'

She smiles at Ray.

'We'll let you know, thank you,' Becca says.

I suppose Ray's attractive for his age. He looks younger and taller than Dad, even though they're the same height and Ray's two years older. Dad's shoulders slump and though thin, his middle sags and his face is being pulled into bags and jowls. I'm sure he never gets smiles from waitresses. It's a shame, in old photos he's just as good-looking as Ray.

You'd imagine Ray with one of those women who retain their allure long into middle age, slim, with expensively maintained hair and tailored clothes, not Becca. She's always been plain and plump, living in black slacks and shapeless tops. Though the last time I saw her, the slacks hung more loosely around her thighs. Either she's lost weight or she's buying a size up.

'To Gina,' Ray says.

He sounds falsely cheerful. I wonder how many drinks he had before the cemetery.

'And Edie,' I say.

'And Edie,' Ray agrees and downs his whisky.

I drink the wine. It's slightly sour and I wish I'd chosen a short. I touch the petals in my pocket again.

Ray starts on his pint.

'Drink up, Vince,' he says to Dad, whose whisky lies untouched.

Becca sips her orange juice.

'We were thinking, after the funeral, we could invite people back to ours.'

Becca's super house-proud, lots of strangers wandering around, bringing in dirt and spilling drinks, would be her worst nightmare.

I look at Dad. He's staring out of the window.

'That's kind, Becca, but I thought we could use the church hall, where Mum's was held.'

She pulls a face.

'It's not a nice part of town, Tess. I bet you've not been back. We can have it at ours.'

'You know we can't ask people to take their shoes off,' I say.

'We can get carpet cleaners in afterwards,' she says.

'What do you think, Ray?' I ask.

'Becca's right and there's less chance of press intrusion. I can ask one of the lads from the site to check the guests.'

I look at Dad for his approval.

'I need a cigarette,' he says and stands up.

He'll be gone for at least three. He leaves his drink on the table.

Becca watches Dad go before she leans over and says, 'I know you didn't want Edie buried, but it was important to Vince to have her next to Gina.'

'I know.'

I sip my wine and look to the garden, where I can see Dad smoking and staring into space. When I turn back, Becca is nodding at Ray.

'Look, Tess, I wanted to talk to you,' he says. 'Vince told me the police have convinced you to make an appeal.'

'The main detective said they'd run out of leads.'

He looks to Becca. She's nodding again.

'Don't, Tess. They're using you. They're not looking for new leads, they're looking to trip you up somehow.'

'Trip me up?'

'You weren't here before. It got out of hand. They accused your Dad and accused me.'

'That's insane.'

'To you, not to them. Nothing's insane to them. They said that we were disposing of the body when we went out looking for her. Said we shouldn't have been so concerned so quickly. Can you believe it, we were too concerned for her?'

'Why did you go out so early?'

'Because she didn't turn up. There'd been a couple of

unsolved murders in the year before Edie went missing, so of course we were worried.'

'But shouldn't I do it, if Edie's killer is still out there?'

'It was twenty years ago; nothing like that has ever happened since. Whoever did it is probably dead.'

I place my elbows on the table and rest my chin on my hands.

'Mum would know what to do,' I say. 'I miss her. Though I'm glad she hasn't had to go through this.'

Neither Becca nor Ray say anything.

'Do you think they're linked? Mum's death and Edie's?' I ask.

'How could they be?' Becca says.

Ray frowns.

'I don't know,' I say. 'But I found a newspaper clipping.'

He looks at Becca.

'It's about Nathan Bexley.'

'Bastard,' Ray spits.

'Edie's written on it.'

Becca glances at Ray for a second, then back to me.

'What did Edie write?' Becca asks.

'Suicide.'

Ray bangs his glass down.

'That piece of shit. It was a lie,' he says. 'A total lie. Should have done what I said at the time. Tracked him down and ripped his head off. No remorse. He blamed Gina. Gina, when he was drunk, twice over the limit, speeding around in two ton of metal. How guilty do you have to be?'

Ray's voice is rising and people are looking round. Becca puts a hand on his arm and speaks softly.

'The court found him guilty, Tess,' she says.

'So Mum wasn't?'

'Wasn't what?'

'Unhappy.'

'How could she be? Don't you remember? She was always so cheerful. Always singing, the life and soul of every party.'

Dad's coming back through the door. Becca spots him. She reaches over and rubs my hand.

'Leave it for now, Tess,' she says.

Dad sits down.

Becca leans over to me.

'Do you feel better for going, Tess?' she asks.

What can I tell them? That I see Edie all the time. That I'm out every night drinking and taking God knows what to make myself feel better, only it just makes things worse. That I hate Dad because all he's ever done is sit and smoke, and he did nothing to protect his wife and daughter. That I hate Becca because she knows what it's like to lose a mother young, but bangs on about an overlooked garden and inadequate shops as if it actually matters. And I hate Ray because he's always happy and can't see what's happened to his wife and brother.

'I just miss them,' I say. 'Both of them.'

My voice is cracking and I realise I'm on the edge of tears.

We finish our drinks in silence. Dad takes a few sips of his pint but doesn't have the heart for it. Ray sits, morose and silent. He takes the whisky he bought for Dad and drinks that as well.

'I think we should go,' Becca says.

Ray gets up without answering. Dad follows.

As we leave, Ray takes my arm and pulls me to one side.

'It was all lies,' he slurs. 'Gina had everything to live for:

you two, Vince. Bexley should have got life. She loved you girls more than anything. She would never have killed herself, never.'

'Ray,' Becca calls. She's standing upright and tense. 'We need to get going.'

Ray lets go of my arm and walks towards the car. He's more upset about the newspaper article than Edie. I'd say it was the booze, if it hadn't been for Becca's reaction.

Chapter 18

Edie: December 1993

'Sorry, Edie. You can come next time,' Auntie Becca said.

They both knew there wouldn't be a next time. Tess was going on a Christmas shopping trip to London with Auntie Becca. If she'd taken Uncle Ray's four-seater Mercedes, Edie could have gone, too. Instead, she was driving her own two-seater MG, not a sensible car to drive down in the snow. It was revenge for Edie's comments about feral neighbours.

'Tess always talks so much about London,' Auntie Becca added.

Tess pulled a face.

'I really wish you were coming too, Edie.'

Edie shrugged.

'Got better things to do here anyway,' she said. 'And you'll be freezing in that tiny car.'

'I'm sure we'll be fine with the heaters turned up,' Auntie Becca said.

Edie pulled on her thick coat, scarf and furry trapper's hat and headed for the front door.

'I'm going out.'

'Where you off to?' Mum asked.

'I'm meeting Mel.'

'You need your boots as well,' Mum called.

'I'll bring you something back,' Tess said.

Edie banged the door behind her.

She would have loved to go to London. It made her think of her glamorous cousins. Tess would see the Christmas lights on Oxford Street. They might even go to a show, Auntie Becca said. There was nothing to do at home. Mum was still in a really weird mood, Uncle Ray was away on a business trip to Scotland and Raquel had a rare day out with her father. Edie was too old to play in the snow that had been falling for the past few days. The weekend would be really boring.

Halfway down the street, she realised Mum was right, she should have worn her boots, snow had started to melt through her thin-soled trainers. The icy, damp socks pleased her, it gave her more right to be angry. Angry with Auntie Becca and Tess and especially with Mum. She should have told Auntie Becca she had to take them both. But Mum wasn't herself recently. She'd stopped singing and took no interest in their school life.

Edie wasn't sure why she hadn't told Tess about Lillian Harlith's, now Congleton's, address. But she was glad she hadn't. It had been under 'L' for Lillian, rather than her married name. Too easy really. She'd copied the address into 'The Missing Cakemaker' scrapbook then ripped it out, jealous of her discovery. She was glad she'd done that now, Tess should have refused to go to London without her. Finding Lillian, without telling Tess first, would teach her a lesson. Edie would go and watch the house and find out, once and for all, the truth about Valentina. She couldn't wait to see Tess's face when she told her the whole 'Cakemaker' business was a lot of childish nonsense. Fenton Road was the other side of Stevenson Park. It was less than fifteen minutes to the park and another ten to cross it.

Muddy slush covered the main road; it sprayed up with every passing car. As she crossed over she noticed some girls in front of her. She was sure they were JAGS. They didn't look overstuffed with layers like the other pedestrians. They wore fitted coats with quilting and fur trim. They had long boots also trimmed with fur. Since Raquel had pointed them out, Edie saw them every time she left the estate. They fascinated her. How did they do it? It wasn't just money. Auntie Becca had money and she wasn't like that. Edie watched them, aware of her enormous trapper hat that made her look cute. She didn't want to look cute, she wanted to look like a JAG.

She stopped at the entrance to the park. The JAGS carried on down the road. Edie watched them until they disappeared around the corner.

The snow still lay thick and white in much of the park. Some young boys were having a snowball fight. To avoid becoming their target, Edie skirted around the edge, in the untrodden snow near the bushes. It came up to her knees and by the time she'd reached the other side of the park, she'd forgotten how angry she was. All she could think of was the cold and how long she might have to sit outside Valentina's sister's house. Fenton Road was directly opposite her nearest exit, about a hundred yards away. An enormous snowman, with its head knocked off, seemed to point the way with its long twig hands.

She had started walking away from the bushes and towards the main path when she saw a couple enter the park. The man was wrapped up tight against the cold, in a dark blue peacoat, a scarf wound up to his nose, a woolly hat pulled down to just above the eyes. The woman wore a cream ski jacket that pulled at the buttons across her belly where it was far too tight. If she hadn't pulled back her hood and shaken her hair, Edie wouldn't have recognised Valentina. Even with the cold eating into her face, she was beautiful. Flakes of snow landed in her hair. She laughed and shook her head some more. The man brushed the flakes away with his hand.

She should look down, in case Valentina saw her, but Edie couldn't tear her eyes away. Here was Valentina, whom they'd missed and worried about, alive and happy with a new man. Raquel had been right all along. Edie carried on staring.

They stopped. The man stood behind Valentina and clasped his arms around her belly. He pointed to the headless snowman. Valentina said something. He held his head back and laughed. The scarf fell from his face.

A prickling heat replaced the icy cold that crept up Edie's neck. She should have guessed from his height and build. She should have remembered that blue peacoat from when he'd taken her and Tess out to the hills to go sledging last year.

Uncle Ray bent his neck and kissed Valentina's face. She twisted round and kissed him back, on the mouth this time. Then he took her arms and they turned and left using the entrance they had come from.

Chapter 19

Tess: June 2018

Shouts of 'Is it true Edie was a drugs mule?', 'Was she held captive before she was killed?' blend with the click of camera lenses as Becca drops us back to Aspen Drive. I feel sorry for the neighbours, to me the journalists are only wall-paper, and I'm sure Dad doesn't hear them at all. In truth, it's a bit half-hearted. There's only a fraction of the number as when the news first broke and the TV crew has now gone. A transatlantic political spat, a footballer videoed in a hotel room with a couple of prostitutes and a mound of cocaine, and suddenly a murder case from twenty years ago is not so exciting.

'What was Ray saying to you in the car park?' Dad asks once we're inside.

If Ray can't handle questions about Mum, Dad definitely can't.

'Something about the catering for the funeral.'

'I thought Becca would be on top of that.'

I shrug.

'Dad, about the appeal...'

'No,' he says.

'But if it helps find Edie's killer.'

Dad doesn't speak for a moment.

'They're not interested in catching her killer. They're interested in getting a conviction. Last time...' He stops and takes a long, deep breath before continuing. 'Last time they said it was me, they just couldn't find the proof.'

'But if there's new evidence it will clear you, won't it?'

'After twenty years, it's not going to happen.'

'It will look weird if I do it on my own. People will want to know why you're not there, like you're hiding something.'

'I don't know, Tess.'

'At least think about it,' I say.

Dad answers by going into the lounge and falling into his armchair, cigarette, TV routine. I follow him.

'I'm going to do it, Dad. Even if I have to do it on my own,' I say.

He doesn't reply.

'I'd rather have you with me,' I say.

Dad takes his time before he replies.

'I'll do it for you, Tess,' he says.

I guess that's as much as I'm going to get.

I open the Absolut Citron vodka I bought on the way home, pour a glass and check my phone. Like a loose tooth, I can't stop playing with the pain. I log onto my Laura Andrews Facebook account.

Natalie: Police came to see me today. Apparently, Tess had told them I was one of her close friends. AS IF!!!
Hannah: I got exactly the same too *Angry red face emoji*
Charlotte: She didn't have any friends, just hung

around with Edie in the hope that someone would talk
to her.

Aveline: She probably said Michaela was her friend
LOL.

Natalie: I asked if they're doing 'an appeal for information'. They wouldn't tell me. I'm watching this one.

Aveline: I never liked her but a killer? Anyway, how
would she get the body to Worcestershire?

For once Natalie, Hannah and Charlotte don't have an
answer and the thread ends.

On Twitter, @AlphaTruth is back. Why are the police
wasting time finding the killer of this silly tart. Haven't they
got CRIMINALS to catch, like whoever clipped my car last
week? *Crying with laughter emoji* #ediepiper #slut

'What are you looking at?' Dad asks.

'Nothing.'

I switch the screen off.

'I don't understand people staring at their phones for hours
on end.'

Dad's got a smartphone but only uses it for making calls.
Even email is a mystery to him.

'It's no different from staring at the TV, Dad.'

'There's stuff on TV.'

I let it lie; the last thing I want him to do is discover
Twitter.

'I was looking at some posts from Joseph Amberley Girls'
School.'

'What do you want to do that for?'

'I was trying to find someone. Do you remember a girl
called Michaela Gossington? She was one of Edie's friends.'

136

'Was she the girl from that big house out towards Bromsgrove?'

'Was it Bromsgrove?'

'Not far from the golf course. I had to drive Edie out there a couple of times.'

'Right.'

'Why are you asking?'

'I wanted to find her and ask her about Edie, see if she really had a boyfriend.'

Dad's eyes move from the TV screen.

'She didn't. Don't get involved. Leave it to the police.'

'You keep saying the police are a waste of space.'

'That doesn't mean you should get involved. It could be dangerous.'

'How?'

'If someone had a reason to hurt Edie, they knew her, which means they knew you and probably still know you. And if it's a stranger, there's no link, so you're wasting your time. What do you think the killer would do if he knows you're after him? DI Vilas might be useless, but he's paid to take risks. You have to stay safe, Tess, promise me that.'

His breathing becomes uneven. I think about what Becca says, I'm all Dad has left. I go over and sit on the arm of his chair and place my hand on his shoulder.

'I'm going to be fine, you mustn't worry about me, OK?'

'So you'll not go looking for this girl?'

'No. I promise.'

I don't have to look for her, Dad's already told me where she is, Bromsgrove. So much for the Internet. You just have to ask.

Chapter 20

Edie: December 1993

Edie went straight to her room when she got home, took off her wet socks and trainers and lay on the bed. She put one of Uncle Ray's CDs in her Discman, closed her eyes and listened to the thrum of the bass.

She was still lying on her bed when she heard Auntie Becca's car pull up, the door open and rapid voices downstairs. Edie rolled onto her stomach and turned the volume up on the Discman. Thirty seconds later, Tess bounded into their room. She jumped and landed on the bed next to Edie. The mattress bounced up and flipped Edie onto her side.

'Look, I got you something. It's a video; we can watch it later.'

Tess pushed a bag into Edie's hand. She threw it to the floor without opening it.

'You're not still in a mood, are you?'

Edie didn't reply. Tess tried a different tack.

'What did you do today, did you see Mel?'

'None of your business,' Edie said.

'Don't be like that. It's only one day. We can't always be together. When we grow up—'

'God, Tess, does it only take one day with Auntie Becca for you to start talking like her?'

'It's true though.'

'Go and watch your film,' Edie said.

'Auntie Becca will take you next time.'

'I wouldn't go with Becca if you paid me. I've better things to do.'

'Like what?'

'You wouldn't understand.'

Edie knew any suggestion that Tess was slow or less mature made her furious.

'Auntie Becca's right about you,' Tess said.

Edie wasn't going to give Tess the satisfaction of asking what Auntie Becca was right about.

'Yeah, remember that next time you want to tag along with me.' She copied Tess's whine. 'Please, Edie, I want to come too.'

Tess leapt from the bed as if she'd been slapped. She grabbed the video and ran downstairs.

Edie pressed play on her Discman. Right now, the space between her headphones seemed the only safe place.

Chapter 21

Tess: June 2018

'Did I wake you up?' Cassie asks after I roll over and pick up the phone.

'I should be up anyway.'

'I waited till eleven. Were you up late?'

Another night of alcohol-induced oblivion and falling asleep with my clothes on. I stink of yesterday's cigarettes and lemon vodka.

'Couldn't sleep.'

I make a gap in the curtains and peek out, the light hurts my eyes and I let them fall back.

'Are you at work?'

'Yeah. By the way, Nadine says to take as much time off as you need.' I feel a little guilty about my general contempt for Nadine when she's being so kind. 'I'm sorry I can't be there. Mum's in hospital again; I'm sure it's the shock that made her Crohn's disease flare up. She wanted to come up but the doctors are keeping her in. I can't leave her right now. But I've got a meeting with a client in Birmingham tomorrow, that's not far, is it? We could have lunch. I'd like to see you and Uncle Vince.'

'Dad hardly leaves the lounge. We went to the cemetery yesterday but he's not going to come to lunch,' I say. 'I need to see you though, Cass. I'm losing my mind here. I know I've got Dad and Ray and Becca, but I feel completely alone.'

'God, Tess, I can't even imagine. You need to keep busy.'

'I'm trying to catch up with some of Edie's old friends.'

'That's a good idea, talk about Edie with people who knew her. It'll help the grieving process.'

Cassie's degree was in psychology.

'You don't get it,' I say. 'They're total bitches, the last people I'd go to for help. You should see what they've been posting online. They were hateful at school and they're hateful now.'

'Stay off the Internet, Tess. That way lies madness.'

'I'm halfway there.'

'So why do you want to speak to these girls, if that's what they're like?'

'I think Edie had a boyfriend I didn't know about and I wanted to ask if they knew who he was. And I found this newspaper article that might be linked to Edie's disappearance; she could have discussed it with one of those girls. Her best friend Michaela's not online anywhere, but I found out where her parents live. I'm going there later.'

'Shouldn't the police be dealing with that?'

'They're not getting anywhere. They're doing a reconstruction and an appeal, which looks like a last resort to me.'

I think how gleeful Natalie will be at the information, confirming her belief in the family's guilt.

'Actually, Cass, could I ask you about it?'

'Me, sure, but what could I know? I was eight when Edie went missing.' There's talking in the background. 'Look, gotta

141

go. Nadine's on the warpath about the Fairbrother account. We'll talk tomorrow. Text me the venue.'

*

Michaela's parents are easy to find online. I crawl out of bed in the early afternoon and make my way to their enormous nineteen-thirties house, with electric gates at the front and a gravel drive with two Range Rovers and a sports car on it. I knew her parents were wealthy, both doctors in private practice, and I have some recollection of inherited money as well. How overawed we were, when we moved from Limewoods to our modern, square detached house, and yet it was probably smaller than their garage. I now realise why Michaela never bragged about money, she didn't need to.

I pause before I press the intercom button. What if Michaela's there? A lingering fear of her scorn hovers over me twenty years since she last saw me as a scrawny fourteen-year-old with bad clothes and wayward hair. I imagine her leaning against the door in a cashmere lounge suit. 'Well you haven't changed,' she'll drawl.

I had a couple of pre-mixed gin and tonics on the way to calm my nerves. I decide she can't still be living at home and press the buzzer.

'Mrs Gossington, I'm a friend of Michaela's,' I say when a woman answers.

As I walk up the drive, Michaela's mother comes to the door. She's short, plain and rotund. Hovering in the background is her father. He's similarly round and has a bald head. I wonder what quirk of genetics produced a slender beauty like Michaela. Whilst they may have welcomed her beauty,

I'm sure leaving school at sixteen with no qualifications had not been part of their plan.

'Michaela's friend?' Mrs Gossington asks. The door only opens a few inches. Her husband hangs back, looking over her shoulder. 'She doesn't live here, you know.'

'I thought she probably wouldn't. I just wanted to get in touch.'

'Why?'

Perhaps my denim cut-off shorts, grey T-shirt and Converse aren't smart enough.

'We were at school together.'

She lets the door open a fraction more and folds her arms. 'Which one?'

'Joseph Amberley,' I say.

'I don't remember you.'

'I'm Tess. Tess Piper.'

She uncrosses her arms and covers her mouth with her hand.

'You're that girl... I mean your twin sister, Edie... I saw it on the news. And I'll never forget when she went missing.'

Mr Gossington clearly has no idea what she's talking about. He ambles over to the door.

'Sorry, who's your sister?'

'You remember, Simon. The girl found in the reservoir.' She glances at me. 'I'm sorry, I don't know how else to put it.'

Mr Gossington looks uncomfortable.

'Of course. Terribly sad,' he says.

'I can see the resemblance now,' Mrs Gossington says. 'Come in.'

She leads me to the lounge. It's spotless and boringly tasteful.

143

'I suppose you must have been good friends with Michaela if Edie was.'

I nod.

'But you never came here much.'

I never went there at all.

'No. We lost touch after I left school. And I couldn't find her on the Internet.'

'No.'

She says it slowly, extending the vowel.

'Is she OK?'

Mrs Gossington looks embarrassed.

'Michaela's living out near the airport, the Glades.'

She says it so brightly you could forget the Glades makes Limewoods look like Kensington. It's mostly tower blocks with vandalised lifts, burnt-out cars and nervous police. That's what Charlotte meant by 'look at where she is now'.

'She's had a bad few years,' Mrs Gossington says.

'I'm sorry. What happened?'

The Gossingtons look at each other. It's my turn to feel uncomfortable. I'm saved by the sound of the front door opening and heavy footsteps running in our direction.

'Hi, Gran. I'm back.'

Mrs Gossington moves towards the door. Mr Gossington decides to straighten the cushions. A girl of about seventeen stomps into the room. Despite the heat, she's wearing a hoodie and Doctor Martin boots. Earbuds hang from her neck.

'Shoes, Arabella,' Mr Gossington calls.

She ignores him and dusty footprints cross the carpet.

'Can you give me forty quid for Saturday, Grandad?'

'What for?' he asks.

'Does it have to be for something?' she asks.

144

'Yes it does.' Mr Gossington sees me watching them. 'We'll discuss it later.'

'But, Grandad—'

'Later,' he says.

Arabella turns from her grandfather and eyes me up for the first time.

'Who are you?' she says.

I want to ask her the same question.

'Don't be rude, Arabella,' Mr Gossington says.

'I'm only asking.'

'This is Tess,' Mrs Gossington says quickly. 'She's a friend of Auntie Ros.'

'Oh,' Arabella says.

The information is obviously boring and she dives into her bag, pulls out an iPad mini and stomps out of the room.

Mr and Mrs Gossington look at me. What's Michaela done that she can't even be mentioned?

'I can see you're busy. Perhaps I can leave you my number. Or if she's on Facebook, I'm on as Laura Andrews. Sorry, silly name, but the press are trying all sorts to contact us.'

'Of course.' Mr Gossington fetches a pen and pad.

I write down my details, though I suspect they'll never reach Michaela.

'Bye then. Thanks for your time.'

I try not to sound sarcastic.

The Gossingtons are looking at each other, not sure what to do. I move towards the hall. Before I get to the door a man steps into the lounge. He's late thirties, tall, scruffy, not bad-looking.

'Alright, Simon, Lucinda. I'll drop her back the same time tomorrow.'

Unlike the Gossingtons, he has a warm local accent.

'That's great, Jem.' Mr Gossington says.

Jem is standing in my way. He doesn't seem to register my presence at first, even though I'm right in front of him. Then he does a double take and looks puzzled.

'It's Tess, Tess Piper, isn't it?'

'Yes.'

I don't recognise him.

'You know each other?' Mr Gossington asks.

'Sort of,' Jem says.

'Of course, Tess was one of Michaela's friends,' Mrs Gossington says.

'Yeah.'

He sounds amused.

'I have to go,' I say.

Jem doesn't move out of my way and I have to slide past him. He follows me with his eyes. I close the front door and I'm halfway to the gate, when I hear footsteps behind me.

'So, Tess, what brings you here?' Jem asks when he catches up.

'How do you know who I am?'

'I asked first.'

'I'm looking for Michaela.'

'Your friend?'

'Yes.'

'Come on, you and Michaela were never friends.'

I keep walking.

'You haven't answered my question,' I say.

'I knew your sister. I heard what happened. I'm really sorry.'

'How did you know Edie?'

'Through Michaela, I guess.'

'And what are you doing here?'

He stops walking and without thinking, I stop, too.

'It's complicated and it's been a long day. I could do with a drink. The White Horse is just down the road. We can talk there if you like.'

I hesitate. I don't know this man, but he might have some information about Edie and I could do with a drink.

'Which way?' I ask.

Chapter 22

Edie: December 1993

Two days had passed since she saw Uncle Ray and Valentina in the park and roadside slush was all that remained of the snow. Edie hadn't told Tess about Valentina. She hadn't told anyone. She wished she didn't know herself. The secret infected her, left her unclean. Since Tess's London trip, Edie had spent most of her time listening to the music Uncle Ray had brought her back from his supposed trip to Scotland. Tess was always hopping from foot to foot trying to start a conversation. Edie refused to look up. Tess, thinking Edie was still in a mood about not going to London, had given up and was out in the garden with Dad, tidying up after the snow.

Uncle Ray had not just betrayed Auntie Becca, he had betrayed all of them, Edie especially. She was his favourite, after all. He tried with Tess, but everyone knew. Uncle Ray, who went out of his way to find songs she'd like, who'd brought her a Discman when no one else at school had one. Uncle Ray, who she secretly wished was her dad not her uncle. He was a liar. Was that true? He'd never lied to her, but keeping secrets was the same thing.

And Valentina, Edie had wanted to be her, that snake. Valentina's kindness to them had only been to impress Uncle Ray. Now she'd got him, she and Tess were forgotten.

Edie was desperate to ask someone what she should do. Usually, she spoke to Uncle Ray if she had a problem. Who could she turn to now? Tess wouldn't understand. They were the same age but Tess was still such a baby. Raquel would understand, then go and blab it to anyone who'd listen. And Mum had told her not to interfere. She could say she came across Valentina by accident, which was almost true.

*

The smell of fruit, cinnamon and rum drifted up the stairs to her bedroom. Mum was making Christmas cake. She followed the scents down to the kitchen. Mum was standing over the worktop and waving a spoon over a ceramic bowl.

'Come and give it a stir, Edie, and make a wish.'

Mum's voice was calm but her eyes were rimmed with red. Edie took the spoon from her and began to turn it through the gloopy golden mixture.

'Are you alright, Mum?' she asked.

'Yes, why wouldn't I be?'

'No reason,' Edie said.

'My eyes are only red from cutting onions earlier.'

Edie stirred the cake some more.

'I saw someone the other day,' she said.

'Who's that?'

'Don't be angry. I wasn't looking for her. I was just in the park, Stevenson Park, you know, when Tess was in London.'

'Who did you see, Edie?'

Mum's voice was quiet.

'Valentina.'

Mum didn't speak.

'She was with someone.'

Edie looked across. Still Mum said nothing.

'A man,' Edie said.

'I see.'

Mum was still turned away from her. Should she say it was Uncle Ray?

'How did she seem?' Mum asked.

'Happy, I suppose. Laughing. But she's got fat.'

'Fat? How fat?'

'Her belly's huge.'

Edie demonstrated by making a circle in front of her with her arms. Mum walked towards the window at the back of the kitchen.

'I'm not in trouble, am I?' Edie asked.

'No, Edie, you're not.'

'I thought you'd want to know that Valentina's alright.'

'Thank you.' Mum remained facing the window. 'Have you told anyone else, Tess? Your dad?'

'No.'

'It's best if you don't say anything.'

'Why?'

Mum didn't answer at once. Tess and Dad were clattering about just outside the back door.

'I think Valentina wants to be left alone,' Mum said. 'It's better that way sometimes, Edie. Do you understand?'

'Yes,' Edie said, even though she didn't. 'I think the cake's done now.'

She let go of the spoon.

'Leave it there, I still haven't lined the tin.'

She was about to return to her room, when Mum called her back.

'Edie.'

'Yes.'

'I don't know what you and Tess argued about, but make it up. It's silly not talking. You're sisters. You're lucky to have each other.'

'OK.'

'And Edie, did you see the man, get a look at his face?'

Something in Mum's voice disturbed her.

'No,' Edie said. 'He had his hat pulled down.'

'I see.'

'He was wearing a blue peacoat.'

She looked at Mum for signs that she knew, but she'd turned away.

'Do you know who he could be?'

Mum didn't turn around.

'No,' Edie said. 'I've no idea who he is.'

Chapter 23

Tess: June 2018

I watch Jem move across the beer garden, weaving through the other drinkers, a glass in each hand. He's relaxed and smiles at people in his way, who nod or say something and make space for him. Max is always wound up tight, worried about what people think, imagining unspoken slights. It's hard to picture Jem ever being stressed about anything.

He puts a large glass of white wine on the table we're standing at.

'I've not been here before,' I say. 'It's alright, isn't it?'

'Yeah, I normally go to The Crown. I should come here but it's a bit far from where I live,' he says. 'It's good in the summer.'

The pub's garden is larger than you'd expect from the front. Wooden tables and chairs stand under large gas heaters, not yet switched on. A sign saying: **Barbecues at the Weekends – Families Welcome**. Today it's full of the after-work crowd, white shirts and blouses, drinking too fast and talking too loudly, glad the day is over and it's a hot summer's evening. Jem swigs his lager.

'Why were you at the Gossingtons'?' I ask.

'You don't know?'

'I wouldn't be asking if I did.'

He shrugs.

'Arabella's my daughter with Michaela.'

'You're too young,' I say.

'I was twenty-two back then. I thought you'd know.'

I shake my head.

'Most people round here do,' he says.

'I live in London.'

'Right.'

'And Arabella lives with her grandparents?'

'It's your turn to answer a question.'

'OK.'

'Why do you want to see Michaela?'

I take a sip of the wine. It's cold, acidic and tastes good.

'It's complicated. Are you two still together?'

Jem splutters.

'No. We are not.'

'Well, do you know where she is? Her mum said she's living on the Glades. What's she doing out there? I thought her parents would rather she died than end up somewhere like that.'

'They'd be less embarrassed if she had died,' he says. For the first time the smile fades from his face. 'Don't go and see her, Tess. Cala's not in a good way.'

'What do you mean?'

He swirls his pint.

'It's funny. Her parents did everything they could to break us up. Cala should be with one of those nice university chaps, who ends up being a doctor or something, not a failed electrician like me.' He laughs and shakes his head. 'I bet they'd give anything for her to be with someone like me now.'

'What's happened to her?'

'Drugs.'

'Michaela? You're kidding.'

'Seriously. I don't even know what she's on. She lives with some guy out there. I don't know what they do for money. I don't want to know. I do know that Arabella's never going near the place.'

He swirls his pint again before taking another gulp.

'So Michaela never sees her?'

'She used to try. Came over to her parents shouting, causing a scene. They got a court order in the end.'

'Against a mother seeing her daughter?'

'You don't know the state she was in. They don't even mention her in front of Arabella, it upsets her too much.'

'Why doesn't she live with you?'

'My place isn't big enough. But I pick her up from school every day; she's at Joseph Amberley,' he laughs. 'You'd think they'd have learnt their lesson.'

'Michaela's parents pay?'

'Yeah.' He frowns. 'Sometimes I think I must embarrass Arabella. I'm not like the other dads.'

'Is it still like that? I remember dying every time Dad came to school.'

'Really? I thought you were posh.'

'Not really. Not at all. After Mum died my uncle Ray gave Dad a job at his company. Charity really. He doesn't do anything useful. But it gave us the money to move and Ray paid the school fees. Before that we lived on Limewoods.'

Jem nearly spits his drink out.

'You're joking.'

'No.'

'Edie never said.'

'She wouldn't.'

I think of Raquel, still living on the Limewoods Estate, and how we promised to go and see her and never did.

'You still haven't said why you want to see Michaela,' Jem says.

I hesitate.

'Tell you what. I'll fetch another drink and you can think about it,' he says.

I down the last of my wine. Evasive answers aren't going to get me anywhere with Jem.

He returns with another large glass of white. I notice his phone's in his other pocket and wonder if he's made a call. He puts the drinks down and wipes his hands on the back of his jeans.

'So, what is it with you and Michaela?' he asks.

'It's about Edie. They were friends. There's stuff I need to know.'

Jem frowns.

'Aren't the police dealing with that?'

'They're not getting anywhere. The post-mortem didn't provide any more clues, except she was definitely attacked by the canal.'

'The canal, just by the school, so close?'

He looks more upset than before and I remember Joseph Amberley is also Arabella's school.

'But that hasn't got them any nearer to finding the killer. They've asked us to take part in an appeal, but Dad doesn't want to. I don't either, really, but if it's the only way of finding new leads I don't know what else to do. The detective's talking of "directing resources elsewhere" if there's no progress soon. A twenty-year-old murder is not a priority.'

'So what are you going to find out that the police can't?'

'I think if anyone knows who this guy she was seeing was it will be Michaela. The police don't seem to think he exists.' I could tell Jem about the newspaper clipping I found and about Mum but decide against it, he's a stranger. He could go straight to the press. 'I need to talk to Michaela.'

'Seriously, I'd stay away if I were you. Ask the police to go,' Jem says.

'I think they've gone. The detective mentioned old friends being uncooperative.'

'Sounds like Cala,' he says.

'You couldn't ask her, could you?'

'You're kidding. She'd probably get her fella to knife me.'

'You've no idea who he was, do you?'

'Who?'

'This guy she was supposed to be seeing.'

He shakes his head.

'I don't remember her having a boyfriend. It was a long time ago. There was that kid who used to follow her about.'

'Max?'

'Was that his name? I doubt it was him. A bit of a wimp.'

To avoid his eyes, I look down into my glass. It's nearly empty.

'I have to find out, it's killing Dad and it's my fault. I'd argued with Edie, we weren't speaking. If we'd walked home together maybe...'

'Maybe you'd both be missing,' he says.

He raises his glass and tips it to and fro to demonstrate its emptiness. 'Another one? You look like you need it.'

He's right.

'My round,' I say.

'Nah, let me.'

He wanders off before I can reply.

I should leave now, while I'm half sober, but the claustrophobia of home, another night of silence in front of the TV with Dad, keeps me where I am and there's something soothing about Jem. His sympathy is not expressed by cooing and fussing, he's calm and a good listener.

The beer garden is full now and Jem has to snake his way through the drinkers to reach me. Another couple have come and stood at our table. Jem manoeuvres himself so that they have to stand back. He takes up the gap they leave and we've a little more space. He's carrying a bottle of wine this time.

'Saves keep going to the bar,' he says.

He's smiling. I wonder if I'm amusing him or if something's happened in the pub. He's a little drunk, too, I think.

He leans in and says in my ear, 'You're not really from Limewoods, are you?'

'Yes. We went to St Luke's Primary School.'

'I can't believe Edie never told us.'

He shakes his head and curls his hands round his beer glass. He has thick fingers with callouses on each tip.

'Did you know her well?' I ask.

'Not that well. She used to come out with me and Cala sometimes. I think she liked to hang about with someone older. When I was out of the room she giggled a lot. She was just a kid really.'

'So was Michaela.'

He frowns.

'Not that young,' he says.

I calculate how old Michaela was when she had Arabella. She was in the year above us and Arabella is about seventeen,

157

so Michaela can't have been more than eighteen or nineteen at the time. She'd left school but I was surprised I'd not heard she'd had a child. Maybe her parents packed her off to some old aunt by the seaside in true nineteen-sixties style.

Jem relaxes as quickly as he ruffled.

'Sorry. I guess I'm touchy. Her parents act like I snatched her from the nursery. Her dad would have been after me with a shotgun if he'd had one. As if Cala had nothing to do with it, like she was some innocent. I wasn't that old myself. My mum was nineteen when she had me and she's still with Dad.'

'Did you never try to be a couple, you and Michaela?'

'We tried but we never stood a chance with her parents breathing down our necks, criticising me all the time. They'd wanted Cala to have an abortion, then they wanted Arabella adopted. Something they choose to forget now they're playing the perfect grandparents. We moved into mine for a couple of months, the same place I'm in now, but it's too small. And Cala wouldn't stop whining, she was worse than the baby. I told her to go back home and I went abroad for a bit.'

'Where?'

'Spain. Worked as a holiday rep. You're out every night, it makes it easy to forget.'

I can relate to that.

'I hope Arabella never finds out. First her grandparents want to get rid of her. Then I left and then Michaela. When I got back, Arabella was with Simon and Lucinda, and Cala was with some other guy.'

'A drug dealer?'

'I wish he was, at least he'd have some money. No, he was just a user.'

'Michaela, too?'

He nods.

'She's had a few different men since then. All the same. Simon and Lucinda were a bit nicer to me after the first, realised I wasn't the worst boyfriend she could end up with. And a child needs at least one parent. I started seeing Arabella again. Now, I can't believe I didn't want her to be part of my life.'

The sun is fading now. He's leaning on the table, his head right next to mine. I should ask him if he's found anyone since Michaela. But never ask a question you don't want to answer yourself.

'And there's no contact with Michaela?'

'Not from me. I think Simon and Lucinda help her out. Well, Simon mostly. He tried to get her to leave and sort herself out but she won't.'

It's hard to think of Michaela leading a squalid, drug-dependent life. She had such poise, the girl everyone wanted to be. But that wasn't the cause of my jealousy. It was her hold over Edie. Michaela replaced me as her best friend and confidante. At the time I was angry with Edie for her betrayal, now I'm angry at her judgement. I imagine Michaela now, stick thin, sores round her mouth and bruises up her arm, limp on the shoulder of some snarling, tattooed thug. Is this who you wanted to emulate, Edie?

My head's getting fuzzy.

'I should go,' I say.

'It's early,' Jem says.

'No, really.'

'I'll come and get a cab for you.'

He places his hand on my lower back and I shiver. I won't look at him. It's nearly dark. The gas heaters are on and

159

people's faces are illuminated in an orange glow. Just before we enter the back of the pub, Jem steps in front of me, his hand still resting on my back. His face is nearly touching mine.

'Are you sure you want to go?'

I shiver again and bend my head to his shoulder. It would be so easy to go back with him. I don't owe Max anything, he's already moved on, got someone else. No doubt the move-home-buy-a-house-have-babies plan has transferred to her. Still, guilt nudges at my conscience.

'I can't,' I say.

I look up. He's smiling. He's not expecting anything.

'Thanks for the drink.'

'Come on, I'll call you a cab,' he says.

While we wait outside, Jem takes my phone from me and punches in his number.

'In case you're in the area,' he says.

A cab stops. I'm about to climb in. He's half turned to go back into the pub.

'Do you live far?' I say.

He smiles and gets in the cab next to me.

'Park Road please, mate,' he says.

Chapter 24

Edie: December 1993

Only one of Rudolph's antlers was lit up on the local high street Christmas lights. It fought a losing battle against the gloom of the dark December evening. Edie thought of the lights Tess must have seen in London, brilliant and beautiful, illuminating the sky, not this sorry display.

She knew Tess wasn't to blame for Valentina and Uncle Ray, but that shopping trip and Stevenson Park seemed like a single event. One that would never have happened if Tess had refused to go to London.

Today was the third day they'd not spoken, when normally their fights only lasted minutes. It was lonely, very lonely, but every time she saw Tess, she saw Uncle Ray and Valentina, too. Edie had been avoiding her and had spent the day with her friend Mel, staying out as late as she could without Mum worrying.

Edie turned off onto a side road. The lights on people's houses were more impressive than those on the high street, and Santas, stars and angels lit her way back to the house. Their decorations weren't up yet. She would remind Mum. It was only a week until Christmas.

Uncle Ray's car was outside the house. Edie didn't want to see him. She'd been glad when Dad told her that they were cancelling lunch at Auntie Becca's the previous Sunday, because Mum was feeling unwell. Edie wasn't sure how to act around him.

She pushed the front door open.

Dad was sitting in his armchair smoking. The only thing in the room she recognised. Everything else seemed to have changed. Tess was curled up in his lap, her arms round his neck, sobbing. In the corner, Auntie Becca stood with Uncle Ray, his head on her shoulder. He sobbed harder than Tess. Edie tried to make sense of what she was seeing, when a policewoman rose from the sofa. She was large, her black uniform frightening. Edie looked up at her.

'Where's Mum?' she asked.

'It's Edie, isn't it?'

She looked to Dad. His face was blank. Ash dropped from his cigarette to the floor. Uncle Ray and Auntie Becca were still huddled in the corner.

'Where's Mum?' she repeated.

'Sit down, Edie,' the woman said. 'I'm afraid I've some bad news for you.'

Chapter 25

Tess: June 2018

I agree to meet Cassie in a café just off the canal at the back of the National Indoor Arena. One of those chains that pretend to be Italian but their food's mostly American. Not the sort of vegan place Cassie prefers, nor a pub, which would be my choice, but at least they serve alcohol. I get there first and order a glass of white. Cassie's a few minutes late. She's dressed in Zara, making it look like Chanel. Several guys look up as she saunters past them and sits down.

'How have you been? You look terrible,' she says.

'Enough of the compliments.'

'Seriously, Tess, you look ill. You need to take care of your-self. I know that look, too much drink, not enough food.'

'So pretty normal then.'

'Stop it, Tess. You've just found out Edie's dead. You can't go around pretending it's not happening. Drinking, cracking jokes.'

'If I throw myself on the floor and wail will it make things better?'

'Tess, please.'

'Look, Cassie, I'm as OK as I can be at the moment.'

She raises her hands in surrender before calling the waiter over. I order another wine and a bowl of spaghetti alla puttanesca. Cass goes for the superfood salad and a green juice.

'How's Uncle Vince?' she asks.

'Not good. I don't know how to help him.'

'I wish I could stay. What about you? Did you meet up with Edie's friend?'

'Not exactly.'

'What do you mean?' She tilts her head. 'Tess?'

I tell her about Jem. I expect her to be shocked but she just looks sad.

'Tess, there are better coping strategies than getting drunk and having one-night stands with a complete stranger.'

'He's not a stranger, at least he didn't feel like one, he remembered Edie. It felt like I knew him.'

'But you don't know him, he could be anyone. You need to be around people who are going to take care of you. Short-lived pleasure is just that, short-lived. And you'll end up feeling worse.'

Cassie's never suffered real loss. If she had, she'd understand the need for oblivion, in losing yourself in a moment, forgetting where or who you are and leaving the pain behind, even if it's for a single second.

'Max wants to see you,' she says.

'You coincidentally bring up Max after telling me off about Jem?'

'He's in a bad way, too.'

'He can't be that broken-hearted. The night before I got the call about Edie, he reeked of another woman's perfume.'

'That's not proof and even if he is seeing someone else,

I'm sure he'd drop her in a heartbeat if he thought he had a chance of getting back with you. This whole thing has made him rethink. He's freaking out, says you won't answer his calls. He phones me instead, talks about Edie, talks about you. I don't know what to say to him.'

'Block his number if he's bothering you,' I say.

'I can't. He needs to talk to someone; it should be you. He still cares, you know. And from what I can tell, he's as devastated about Edie as any of us. I didn't know he knew her so well.'

'He didn't.'

The waiter brings our order and I pour the last few drops of my first glass into the second. I don't fancy the spaghetti any more and just pick out the olives.

Cassie looks puzzled.

'They weren't friends?'

I think about telling her what Vilas told me, that Max had a crush on Edie. But it's not something I want to think about myself.

'They hardly knew each other,' I say.

'It's just because of you then, that he's so upset. He can't watch you in so much pain. Oh, Tess, can't you get back together. I'm sure you could work it out.'

I think of a child on a swing, she looks like a young Edie, her head's flying backwards, laughing with delight as it takes her higher and higher. Then the swing is empty, its motion jolting as its chains loosen on the vacant seat. My child would not be allowed to go to the park and sit on a swing. Max and I will not be working it out.

'It's not going to happen, Cass,' I say.

Cassie's parents, my aunt Lola and uncle Jake, have been

married for thirty years. When I go over, they're curled up on the sofa together like a couple of newlyweds. It's easy for Cassie to think men and marriage are a simple option. I drink more wine. I'm not in the mood for arguing about relationships with an idealist and change the subject.

'Can I ask you something without you saying anything to anyone? Especially not Aunt Lola.'

'Sure.'

'I found a clipping from a newspaper article about Mum's death. At the trial, the lorry driver claimed that Mum threw herself in front of him deliberately. The jury didn't believe him, but I think Edie did. I'm not sure why.'

'Right,' Cassie says.

She picks up her fork and concentrates on pushing green shoots around her plate.

'You knew?'

I put my glass down and wine sloshes onto the table.

'Is everything alright, miss?'

The waiter comes over and starts mopping it up.

'Everything's fine,' Cassie says.

She smiles at him. He returns the smile and glances at me.

'Really, we're fine.'

He nods and moves away.

'You knew and you didn't tell me?'

'Tess,' she says.

'How long have you known?'

'I don't know anything for sure. You know Mum, she never drinks except at Christmas, so after two glasses of wine she's babbling away about everything and nothing, then she got really maudlin, started talking about Auntie Gina, what a great sister she was, how much she missed her and she'd always wonder if it was deliberate. I asked her what she meant and she said about the accident, if what that man—'

'Nathan Bexley.'

'...had said was true, that Gina stepped in front of the lorry deliberately. She said Gina was unhappy but wouldn't tell me why. Then Dad told Mum she should go and lie down. And when I asked him about it he said she always got upset about Auntie Gina at Christmas and it didn't mean anything. Can't you ask Uncle Vince?'

'Dad never talks about Mum. I asked Uncle Ray, he lost it a bit and went on a rant about Bexley, said Mum had no reason to kill herself.'

'I think Ray's right. I don't remember your Mum too well, but she was always smiling. Not depressive like...'

She starts pushing her salad around again.

'Like Dad?'

'I'm sorry.'

'It's OK.'

'Even if your mum was unhappy, the jury had all the facts and found this Bexley bloke guilty. You've got enough on your plate with Edie. Raking up all this stuff about Auntie Gina isn't helping you or Uncle Vince.'

'But what if they're linked? Mum's death and Edie's.'

'They're years apart in completely different circumstances.'

'I know. I just feel there's something right in front of my face that I'm missing. Could you ask your mum again?'

'I can't risk upsetting her. She's just starting to get better. She's determined to make it to the funeral, even if Dad has to carry her.'

I imagine my elegant aunt Lola getting a piggy back from Uncle Jake, a black Jimmy Choo pointing each side of his waist. The image makes me laugh. Cassie looks at me as if I'm going mad.

'What's so funny?'

'I don't know.'

I'm feeling a little light-headed. Cassie looks concerned.

'I don't think you're well, Tess,' she says. 'Why don't you and Uncle Vince come and stay with us for a few days?'

I escaped to Cassie's last time. Auntie Lola barely left my side. My cousins Ashley and Corinne would try to interest me in their music and magazines and Cassie, who was only about eight at the time, would bring me books and toys to cheer me up. I would love to go to Cassie's, but Auntie Lola's in hospital. Cassie's at work and Ashley and Corrine have long since left home.

'We can't, Cassie. We've got to do the appeal and then there's the funeral.'

'When is it?'

'End of next week sometime. Becca's dealing with everything. I can't face it.'

'Oh, Tess, we'll be there on the day. And I know it's not the same, but I'm always at the other end of the phone.'

'I'll be OK, Cass. I'm just so exhausted, it feels like this has been going on forever.'

'Are you sure you can't come and stay at ours?'

I shake my head.

'I'm needed here.'

Cassie leans over and gives me a hug.

'Well, get some rest. And try to eat something.'

She glances at her watch.

'I've got to get back.'

She calls the waiter over and hands him her credit card.

'This can go on expenses. Call me if you need anything,' she says.

She waves as she leaves the restaurant then jogs across the canal bridge.

I stay and finish my wine then decide to walk into the city centre. I should go home and be there for Dad, but there's only so much cricket and cookery I can cope with. And I need to think. Aunt Lola thought Mum was unhappy. Ray was sure she had everything to live for and Becca didn't want him to talk about it. I need to know why. But what if Cassie's right? It's got nothing to do with Edie's murder and I'm just causing myself more pain? I need to find Michaela. If anyone knows, she does. I check Facebook on my phone to see if she's been in touch. She hasn't, but there's another message with a phone number next to it:

Hi, Tess, it's Raquel. Terrible about Edie. What's with the Laura stuff? You should come and see me. I'm still on Gladstone Road. Call me.

Chapter 26

Edie: December 1993

A unt Lola sat on the sofa, Tess across her lap, her head flopped on her aunt's shoulder, her hands in tight fists pulled to her face. She looked like she was sucking her thumb. Even little Tess was too old for it to be comfortable, her legs hung down so that her heels knocked into her aunt's calves.

Edie watched from a chair the other side of the room. Since Aunt Lola arrived that morning, Tess hadn't left her side. She looked like Mum, the pretty heart-shaped face, her voice the mellow tones that sang when excited. Her accent had changed, from years of living in London and working in the civil service, so that she sounded more BBC than Coseley. She was a little shorter and fuller-figured, but still Tess stared when she'd arrived at the door, as if their mother had returned, and she had followed Aunt Lola around, worried she'd disappear again.

But she wasn't their mother and Edie couldn't look at her. It was a cruel joke. She loved her aunt and her cousins. She knew it was wrong to wish Mum were here instead of Aunt Lola, to wish her cousins were suffering instead of her. And still every inch of her wanted it, all the time knowing she must be wicked for such a thought to enter her head. Perhaps that's why God had chosen to punish her.

God hadn't featured much in their lives until now. The local vicar, Reverend Corby, came to their primary school once a week to speak about sheep and angels or donkeys and crosses, depending on the time of year. But they didn't go to church. No one was even sure what church the funeral should be held at. Mum and Dad had married in a registry office. Grandpa Len had been a Baptist, Grandma Dot an Anglican. Aunt Lola was sure they'd been baptised but couldn't remember in which church. Auntie Becca said it was all the same God anyway and St David's Church of England was Victorian and had a beautiful vaulted ceiling, whereas the Baptists had that hall, which looked like a school gymnasium. Everyone else was too drained to take the matter further.

So the only time Edie met a priest other than the Reverend Corby was the vicar of St David's, who came to the house to ask about their mother. He offered his condolences and told them of God's mercy and love and had left believing he offered comfort, when Edie recalled some of Reverend Corby's other words that didn't include sheep and donkeys. God's wrath, cities destroyed, plagues and pestilence sent to punish the wicked. And she was wicked, for wishing her beautiful aunt Lola dead and being angry with Tess for transferring her love to a faulty copy of their mother to find comfort.

Edie had no comfort. Her dad was lost, barely spoke. When she went to him he lifted his arms to her, a reflex action to hold his child, whilst his face never changed. The doctor had come to see him and given him some tablets 'to make him feel better'.

'Can I have some?' Edie asked.

The doctor's eyes filled with tears when she looked at Edie. 'No,' she said. 'They only work on grown-ups.'

Edie's face fell. When would she ever feel better, how would she ever feel better?

The front door rattled, the key wriggling back and forth by someone unused to its quirks. Uncle Ray came in. He was always too large for the front room and today seemed to fill the whole space. He came straight to Edie and scooped her up in his arms, hugged her so hard she thought her ribs would break. His eyes were red and his voice hoarse.

'What are we going to do without her, Edie?' he said. 'What are we going to do?'

Edie clasped her hands round his neck, not wanting to let go.

'That man Bexley,' he hissed in her ear. 'Don't worry. If the police don't nail him, I'll find him myself.'

The policewoman had explained that Mum had been hit by a lorry. The driver had been travelling too fast and had drunk too much alcohol. No, they didn't know what Gina was doing walking along the dual carriageway, but Bexley was still culpable.

'We'll be charging him with death by dangerous driving.'

'It should be murder,' Uncle Ray had shouted.

Now he was whispering, 'Don't worry, we'll find him, we'll get him.'

Again and again, Edie pictured the crash in her head, the screech of brakes, the front of the lorry, its cold, hard metal crunching into Mum and her lying there in the sleet, blood seeping from beneath her, turning the grey and white slush bright red.

'Uncle Ray,' is all Edie could say. 'Uncle Ray.'

Because there was no answer to the question: What are we going to do without her?

*

Aunt Lola nudged Tess from her knee and stood up.

'Can I get anyone anything?' she asked for the hundredth time. 'You really need to eat something, girls.'

They shook their heads.

'I could do with a drink if you've got one, Lola.'

'Tea's all there is.'

It was the fourth time Uncle Ray had come round since Aunt Lola's arrival. Each time she'd excused herself and left the room until he'd gone. Tess looked around, unsure whether to follow her, before deciding to join Edie. Uncle Ray sat on the armchair facing the window and pulled them both onto his lap.

'My little Swifts, I'm going to have to keep you safe.'

Edie nestled into his lap and stared out of the window. It was frosted with cold, the day outside grey and bleak. Then a flash of pink streaked past. It was Raquel riding a bright new bike.

'Be careful,' Mrs McCann called.

Raquel came haring back at an equal pace, the bike flying into the air as she left the pavement for the road. Raquel's bike was blue and too small for her. Edie wondered where she'd got this new one. Then she looked across the street to the angels and stars twinkling in the houses opposite, and she realised it was Christmas Day.

Chapter 27

Tess: June 2018

I've rented five flats in London and lived nine years at the new house on Aspen Drive before that, but to me, our terrace on the Limewoods Estate will always be home.

Twenty-five years has shrunk Gladstone Road and I'm surprised to see a family of four spill out from one door. It seems impossible we ever fitted into one of these tiny two-up two-downs.

Raquel lives next door to our old house. Her neat lawn contrasts with ours, which has been paved over. Crisp packets are tangled in the nettles and green shoots have forced their way through some of the cracks in the slabs of concrete, the remnants of Dad's planting or just weeds? The door's red paint is scuffed, so the original green is visible round the keyhole and letter box.

I want to go inside and see what's left. I want to touch the walls and walk in the back garden, where some trick of time will let me see Mum and Edie again.

If Mum were alive, this might still be our family home. She would have stayed as a vet's assistant, Dad would be unemployed. We would never have gone to JAGS and Edie would still be around. We wouldn't know we were poor, just as we wouldn't know we were happy.

A woman comes to the window and glares at me. I don't know how long I've been standing there. It feels like twenty-five years.

I can't go into Raquel's house and walk through a replica of our own. I won't be able to pretend that it's a happy reunion. I'll be searching for Mum and Edie in every corner.

I turn and walk down the street without looking back.

*

'Tess.'

I turn around. Her hair's pulled into a loose bun and she looks relaxed in indigo jeans, black ballerina pumps and a marl-grey jumper, with just the slightest pull across her belly. Not like someone off Limewoods. I can't shake my JAGS education, viewing people as I was viewed. Raquel agreed to rearrange and we're meeting in this coffee shop on the edge of respectable suburbia.

She rushes over and hugs me.

'I still can't believe it, Tess. I was sure Edie'd turn up some-where, someday.'

Her eyes fill with tears, the same deep-set eyes she always had with that tight button mouth. Faint lines have started creasing the corners of her eyes. We are not children any more. I feel a rush of affection for my childhood friend and wish I'd known someone else had never given up hope of Edie returning, until all hope was wiped out.

A grubby hand is poking over the top of the sofa. It's followed by a round face smeared with blackcurrant juice.

175

'This is my daughter,' Raquel says.

I'd forgotten she had one. It explains why she insisted on a coffee shop not a pub. She's about two years old. Raquel picks her up and rests her on her hip. The girl reaches for Raquel's wet cheeks.

'Mummy's sad,' she says.

'Yes, Mummy's sad,' Raquel says.

I smile at the girl.

'Hi, I'm Tess,' I say.

'Say hello to Tess, Fleur.'

The girl turns and buries her head in Raquel's neck.

'I'll get the drinks, what are you having?' I ask.

'A hot chocolate with cream please; Fleur's already had her juice.'

I order the hot chocolate and a black Americano for myself.

'How did you find out?' Raquel asks.

I tell her about the call. The trip to the police station, the dress and necklace. I realise I've not spoken to anyone about it before. Raquel sits and listens, she's easy to talk to, as if we still lived next door and saw each other every day. By the end we're both in floods of tears and Fleur is, too.

'Stop, Mummy,' she says.

'I'm sorry,' Raquel says. 'She's not used to seeing me upset. Have you got kids?'

'No.'

'Maybe one day, eh? You with anyone?'

'No.'

The last thing I want to do is talk about Max, especially after Vilas's reaction to our relationship.

'That's a shame.'

Raquel pulls a tissue from her handbag and blows her nose.

'I can't believe it, Tess. That Edie could just disappear. That no one knew anything. Have the police got anywhere? Do they have a suspect?'

'No, but the Internet does.'

She sticks her tissue in her pocket.

'Yeah, I've seen it. They accepted me into the JAGuars, as well. I joined when I was looking for you. They're not very careful who they let in, are they? You could sue them for saying those things.'

'Do only pervs and bitches go online? It feels like it. And they all reckon they're expert psychological profilers.'

'They must have dull lives, if they've nothing better to do,' Raquel says.

'You're right, screw 'em. I wanted to ask around about Edie but I can't with all that going on. I found something out. I'm not sure it's connected with what happened to Edie, but it seems weird. You remember when Mum was killed?'

'Of course.'

'It was before any of us had the Internet, but were there any rumours?'

'What sort of rumours?'

I don't want to plant ideas, so leave it open.

'Anything odd?'

Raquel pulls a puzzled look.

'I thought you'd know, Tess.'

'Know what?'

'It's probably nothing...'

'Come on, Raquel.'

She pulls at a strand of hair and tucks it behind her ear.

'It was only a rumour.'

I wait.

'Are you sure you want to know?'

'Yes.'

Raquel looks embarrassed.

'People said that something was going on between your mum and Mr Vickers.'

'What the fuck? That's a joke, right?'

Raquel's made a mistake, my mother and ill-tempered Mr Vickers with his slicked-back hair, oversized glasses and tufty moustache, it's unthinkable. Old sucking lemons, Ray used to call him. He treated me and Edie like a couple of delinquents. Whatever I was expecting, it wasn't this.

The coffee shop's customers start looking round. Raquel's daughter stares up at me with large, scared eyes. Raquel reaches down and scoops her onto her lap.

'It wasn't true,' Raquel says.

'Of course it wasn't true.' Customers are still looking. I lower my voice. 'Who goes spreading shit like that about?'

Raquel looks as scared as her child and I wonder if her mother was involved in the gossip. I take a breath.

'I'm sorry. It's just, she was my mum.'

'I know,' Raquel says. 'I can understand.'

She leans over and squeezes my shoulder.

'Why would they say that?'

'I think your mum spent a lot of time with Mr Vickers after his wife left. She was just being kind to him.'

Mum was always a magnet for waifs and strays. People she barely knew would come crying to her about broken hearts and bereavements. And this was her payment. Rumours about Mr Vickers.

I can see Dad may not have been enough for Mum. He was unemployed, uncommunicative and mostly inert on the sofa. If she did look elsewhere, would it have been this horrible man, whose own wife couldn't stand him? And if he felt anything for her, wouldn't he at least have pretended to like us?

'Does he still live on Gladstone Road?' I ask.

'No. He left years ago. Not long after you. No idea where he is now. The street's not like it used to be. I hardly know anyone.'

Did Dad hear the rumours? Did it deepen his depression? The same type of minds constructing lies on JAGuars were at work on Gladstone Road. I can hear them talking in the newsagents, at the hairdressers. I'm not one for gossip but... I couldn't help noticing that... it wouldn't surprise me if...

Raquel's watching me with concern. I try to lift the mood.

'What's it like living there now? Your husband's Gavin, right?'

'Yes.'

'How did you meet?'

'Horticultural college. He was my first proper boyfriend.'

'Come on, Raq. I remember you having boyfriends at eleven!'

'You didn't believe all that, did you?'

'Of course I did.'

She laughs.

'Oh my God, that was a joke. None of those lads would give me the time of day. I just used to hang around with them in Roswell Park and claim they were my boyfriends.'

'And I always thought you were a wild child.'

'So did Edie. She was always asking me about boys. I never

knew what to tell her. No. Gavin was my first; we were seventeen when we met. First day at college.'

I put my coffee down. Edie and I weren't interested in boys at primary school.

'When was it Edie started asking about boys?'

'Can't remember. When we were about thirteen or fourteen.'

'You saw her, after we left the estate?'

'Now and then.'

Edie had transformed into a Joseph Amberley girl so easily with her clothes and accent, her likes and dislikes, no one would ever guess she was from Limewoods. I never fitted in, no matter how hard I tried. And all the time she was sneaking back to the estate and our old life. Raquel finishes her hot chocolate, leaving a faint moustache of cream on her top lip.

'You never came back to see me, Tess.'

'No,' I say.

'Why?'

'I can't remember now.'

Raquel puts her cup down.

'I saw you today, you know, on our street,' she says. 'Why didn't you come in?' There's hurt in her voice.

'I couldn't face it, Raq. Your house is exactly the same as ours. I couldn't go in without Mum and Edie being there. I didn't realise until I was standing outside. I'm sorry I didn't knock and I'm sorry I never came back to see you after we left.'

'Edie managed it,' Raquel says.

'She was always braver than me.'

'That's why I thought you knew about Mr Vickers because Edie did. She came and asked me about him.'

'When was this?'

180

'I'm not sure. The thing is, she was asking something about your mum, too.'

Raquel looks at me, she's anxious, waiting for me to say something. I take my phone out and show Raquel the picture I took of the newspaper article.

'I found this, it's about Mum's death. Can you see the writing on the border?' I point to it. 'It's Edie's handwriting. It says suicide.'

Raquel lifts the phone and holds it close to her face then places it back on the table.

'I didn't know if I should tell you. Edie showed me a cutting once, probably the same one. She asked if I knew why your mum would kill herself.'

I look at the blurred picture of the newspaper article lying on the table between us. A mirror of my family's collective memory, imperfect, only hinting at the truth.

Raquel is still looking away.

'Do you know something else?'

She looks back at me.

'Just that stuff I told you about Mr Vickers.'

'What did Edie do, after she found out?'

'It was so long ago, Tess. I don't remember.'

In the café, people have returned to their coffee and chatter. I look down at my untouched Americano. What else had Edie told Raquel?

'Did she mention a boyfriend?'

Raquel tilts her head to the side, her eyes squinted in concentration.

'Yeah, some older guy, can't remember his name. He upset her. Well, not really upset her, more like bothered her.'

'Do you know who he was?'

'From what she said I think he was married or something. They had to keep it secret.'

'They had to keep it secret because she was underage.'

I feel sick. I remember Becca confronting Edie about having a boyfriend: he's a man, not a boy. I'd thought he might be a couple of years older. Edie said he was eighteen. But what if he was married? That would make him much older, even twenty years ago, no one got married at eighteen. Then again, Raquel could be mistaken. Their caution might only have been to avoid Becca's disapproval. She thought we were too young for boys altogether. Plenty of time for that later, concentrate on your schoolwork.

'I don't know if they were sleeping together,' Raquel says. 'It might have been nothing. You know what it's like at that age. Everything's ten times bigger in your head. You look back and laugh...'

She stops. Perhaps remembering that Edie never did get to look back.

'And she never mentioned she was in trouble or afraid?' I ask.

'Only the problem with that boy, can't remember his name. A little, thin lad, he used to follow her about. You remember him, right? Edie thought he was harmless, but maybe she was wrong.'

'That wasn't the boyfriend?'

'No.'

'Hmm,' I say and don't catch Raquel's eye.

I think of Max. Vilas said he had a crush on Edie. Is he this lad? I push the thought away and realise Raquel's watching my reaction. She was always too sharp.

'I think the police are following that up,' I say.

Fleur starts grizzling and mumbles some baby talk. Raquel turns away and hands her a small tub containing chopped grapes. Fleur grabs a handful and stuffs them in her mouth.

'Why are you asking me all this, Tess? Didn't Edie tell you?'

'We weren't talking at the time,' I say. 'We'd fallen out.'

'She never said.'

At least you were loyal, Edie.

'What did you fall out over?' Raquel asks.

'I can't remember. Probably something stupid. I always think if we'd been speaking, things might have turned out differently.'

'You don't know that and it's normal for siblings to argue. Not that I'd know. I never met mine. I was always so jealous you two had each other. I had no one. I want another, so Fleur can have a brother or sister. A sister, hopefully. I don't want her to be alone.'

'You never hear from your dad?'

'Not much. He never really did the parent thing. Always had something better to do. He's not even in touch with the kids he had with that woman he left us for. He came to see me when Fleur was born and left some money. I don't know how he found out. He lives over the other side of the motorway with a new girlfriend I'm not allowed to meet. She's probably my age. He won't go and see Mum.'

'What do you mean?'

I feel guilty for not asking before. Mrs McCann was so much older than the other parents, she must be in her seventies now, if she's alive. A sad smile spreads across Raquel's face.

'She's got dementia,' she says. 'She's in a home down the road.'

'I'm sorry, Raquel, that's awful.'

Mrs McCann was always a kind woman. I remember when a stray ball from a rough game of football broke the pottery lion in front of her house. It wasn't long after Raquel's father had left, so she must have been feeling short-tempered and probably couldn't afford to replace it. She had come storming out to tell us to be careful, but when Mum told us off, Mrs McCann stopped.

'It can't be helped, Gina. Children have to play.'

She hated the thought of getting us into trouble. Mum made us pay for a new lion out of our pocket money. Mrs McCann sneaked the money back to us.

'How bad is it? Can she recognise you?'

'Usually. Though sometimes she confuses me with Aunt Aggy.'

Raquel's silent for a while.

'Mum was devastated when Gina died, you know. She was so fond of your mum. I think she needed a friend after Dad left. Gina'd come over and chat in the evenings. When all this is over, you should come and see Mum with me. She'll probably know who you are; her memory gets better the further back she goes.'

'I'd love to,' I say.

She looks down at her daughter, who's chewing on a sugar packet. Raquel gently prises it from her mouth, then looks up again.

'I have to go,' she says. 'We're laying a lawn this afternoon. Let me know when the funeral's being held. It was lovely to see you.'

I'm not sure she means it.

We hug and say goodbye. They leave, waving through the

window. I wave back then sit down to my cold coffee, willing it to turn into wine.

I need to contact Mr Vickers. Mum was rumoured to be having an affair with him, he might know something. And I was right about the boyfriend. Edie was seeing someone older, possibly married. I know all of this because she chose to tell Raquel and not me. She's been gone twenty years but the stab of jealousy is still sharp.

Chapter 28

Edie: September 1994

'At Joseph Amberley Girls' we have a policy of putting twins in different classes,' Mrs Cartwright said. 'Let them have a chance to be their own person. Too often they're treated as a single entity.'

Dad nodded. Tess scowled. Edie looked past the woman in the pink tweed to some girls walking by at the end of the corridor. She remembered seeing the girls with the swishy hair and leather handbags when Raquel went to buy cigarettes from those boys on the high street. 'They're JAGS,' she'd said. It had been Edie's first inkling that there was another way she could live her life, away from Limewoods, away from Becca's executive estates and flouncy sofas. And now she was to become one of them. She was a JAG.

'I'll show you to your classes,' Mrs Cartwright said. 'You'll be assigned buddies, to help you settle in. They'll be fine now, Mr Piper.'

The woman stopped and looked to Dad for a response. He was wearing a suit. The last time he'd worn it was at Mum's funeral. He looked towards the exit from the school then back at the girls.

186

'Are you sure you'll be alright?' he said.

'Of course we will,' Edie said.

Tess didn't look so sure. She hadn't wanted to move house or change schools and virtually needed dragging to the car that last day when they left Gladstone Road. Edie was pleased they were leaving. Every day the empty kitchen and the microwave meals reminded her that Mum wasn't there. At school, she'd walk up to a group of friends and they'd stop talking, look sad, and one of them would ask, 'Are you OK?' She couldn't bear it any more. Now Dad worked for Uncle Ray, they could move to a new house and go to a new school. And not just any school: Joseph Amberley Girls'.

'Well then, I'll be off. See you tonight,' Dad said.

'See you,' Edie said.

He walked away without looking back. Tess grabbed Edie's hand. She pulled it away. They weren't at primary school any more.

'This way,' Miss Cartwright said.

They followed her down a long corridor. At their old school the dominant odour was of bleach. Here, Edie could smell hot dust rising through the air vents and the whiff of perfume.

Auntie Becca had suggested the new school when they moved. A new start. She and Uncle Ray would pay the fees, it was the least they could do.

They arrived back at the office where they'd first met Mrs Cartwright. Four girls sat outside. They stopped talking as Edie and Tess approached.

'Edie, this is Charlotte and Aveline. You'll be with them for most of your lessons.'

Edie didn't know what to say. Aveline smiled.

'Come this way,' she said.

'Tess, this is Hannah and Natalie,' Mrs Cartwright was saying as they were walking away.

'You weren't in juniors, why are you starting now?' Aveline asked.

'We just moved,' Edie said. As she spoke, she realised she'd copied Aveline's way of speaking, the newsreader vowels.

'You'll end up talking all la-di-da when you go to Joseph Amberley,' Raquel had said.

Edie had assured Raquel she would not and she'd be back to visit soon. A promise she'd yet to keep.

'Is it for your father's job?' Aveline asked.

'Yes,' Edie said.

'What does he do?'

'He works with his brother. They have a construction company.'

She should have said for not with but it didn't matter. Aveline didn't seem overly concerned.

'Mrs Cartwright said you're taking advanced maths.'

'Yes.'

'Char's doing that, aren't you?'

'Yeah,' said Char. 'My dad made me, but I hate it.'

'Yeah,' said Edie. 'Mine made me take it, too. It's sooo boring.'

Dad had no idea what she did or didn't study and never made her do anything.

'You've seen it all before, but we'll show you round anyway,' Aveline said. 'That way, we'll get to miss the first half of RE.'

*

Edie loved the school library, swimming pool and language labs, and she loved that no one knew she was the tragic motherless girl. She could start again. Char and Aveline chatted away about the school, the girls and what she was to expect. She realised most of them had known each other since they started in the school's junior section. Their parents went on holiday together to places like Tuscany and had job titles Edie didn't understand.

'See you outside,' Char said at first break as Edie went off to use the toilets.

Even the toilets were better than St Luke's. They smelled of lavender and had soft paper and liquid soap. As she washed her hands the door opened and Tess came in.

'I've been looking for you,' she said.

'Aren't you with your buddies?'

'No,' she said. 'I don't like them.'

'You don't know them, Tess.'

'I know I don't like them.'

'Aveline and Char are nice.'

Tess didn't say anything. Edie went to dry her hands.

'Please try, Tess. It can't be like our old school.'

'Why not?'

'We're not children any more,' Edie said.

'I don't like it here. I don't know anyone. They keep using words I don't understand and they can't understand me.'

'Then talk properly, we're not on Limewoods now,' Edie said.

Tess didn't answer.

'Just try to make friends, it's not even been half a day.'

Tess went into the cubicle. Edie slipped out of the door and went to find Aveline and Char.

189

She didn't want to be the tragic twin, she didn't want to be a twin at all. Soon, she hoped no one would ever guess that she was from Limewoods and hadn't always been a JAG.

Chapter 29

Tess: June 2018

Edie walks away from me, the mustard yellow leather bag not quite full enough, her legs too short, her shoulders too broad. She walks with the typical lounging slouch of a teenager rather than bouncing along on her toes, electric with youth, as the real Edie did. How am I to explain to the police that this Edie is wrong, inferior, a faulty copy. Apart from her height, she resembles me at fourteen more than Edie.

I had to return to Joseph Amberley Girls' School, to show the police the spot in the hedge, long since repaired and encircled by a wire fence, where Edie left that day. I've always thought of it as her passing through a curtain to another existence, never believing she was murdered, less than a quarter of a mile from where I last saw her. The original school atrium has been demolished and rebuilt as a much grander glass structure. The change didn't stop my stomach squeezing, the swelling sense of isolation, the remembered hope that today, at school, Edie would spend time with me and not her new friends.

At least it was a Saturday afternoon, so the school was empty and I was spared Charlotte's and Aveline's replacements, perhaps their daughters, staring and making the same judgements passed on me as twenty years ago.

The replica Edie is now far enough from the camera to blur her flaws. Dad watches the screen transfixed as his daughter slides through a hedge. The camera angle changes and she emerges the other side onto the pavement opposite the path down to the canal. She slings her bag over her shoulder and crosses the road, disappearing into the vegetation. The trees are taller and the track has become overgrown since I was last there. They've had to hack the branches and brambles back to recreate Edie's walk. They're chopped to an even length, not the criss-cross and trampled undergrowth of a well-worn path. People must have stopped using it after its association with Edie's disappearance. The camera angle changes again.

The final shot is from the bridge, the last place Edie was believed to be alive, where her bag was found wrapped around an old shopping trolley, where telltale flecks of rust were crushed into her skull. The girl approaches the camera, her likeness to Edie receding with each step. She reaches the bridge and the screen goes blank.

Dad continues to stare at the screen. He's shaking, almost imperceptibly, and clasps his hands together to stop himself.

The thought of not smoking for nearly an hour alarms Dad nearly as much as the rows of journalists. They sit in plastic chairs chatting to one another. They suck on cough sweets and check their phones, an audience awaiting a show.

DI Vilas opens proceedings by thanking the press for their attendance.

'The family will be reading out a short statement but not taking questions. I'll be happy to answer any inquiries afterwards.'

The reconstruction is played and temporarily quietens the journalists. We're then led onto the raised platform. Cameras train on our faces, every muscle and tick exposing us to examination and insinuation. Does anyone feel sorry for the family at these events, or is it just a game, to see who slips up? Who isn't sad enough, just a single tear and therefore cold-hearted? Guilty. Or too sad, sobbing, barely able to speak, laying it on a bit thick, play-acting? Guilty. Or too impassioned, she doth protest too much, methinks. Guilty. Will anyone see past this and think back to a hot summer's day twenty years ago and remember a girl in her school uniform crossing the road?

I am to read the statement, prepared by the police. We're told I'll elicit more sympathy than Dad, being her twin sister. I lay the paper on the tabletop so my shaking hands can't be seen. I look up, take a deep breath and let the words fall from my mouth, meaningless sentences that cannot convey the aching loss, the minute-by-minute torment of losing someone so necessary to me, an integral part of me, a missing limb.

Edie was much loved and is much missed, I say. The family just want answers. Someone, somewhere, must know something or be suspicious, whether it's of a colleague, a family member, spouse or friend. If anyone – look to camera – knows anything, please, please contact the police so our family can have some closure and move on. Dad adds that after the loss of his wife, he tried to be both mother and father to Edie, he failed. All he wants is justice for his little girl. Though whether anyone caught the words, as he mumbled them, his face fixed downwards, is doubtful.

The journalists shuffle in their chairs. Itching to question us when they're only getting Vilas, we're ushered away. Dad's lit his cigarette before we've fully exited the building. The police constable who is accompanying us doesn't pull him up on it. At the back of the building, away from stray photographers, he inhales deeply and lets out a stream of smoke.

'Bastards,' he says. Dad rarely swears. 'Utter bastards. Like they care about Edie. They just want another chance to print that photo of her in a short skirt. I wish Ray had never given that to the police.'

'They could help. What I said in there is true, someone must know something. No one could do that on their own and keep it a secret for twenty years, not telling anybody, leaving no trace.'

'Perhaps you're right. But it felt like a circus in there. They were loving every minute of it. You know, I got a note shoved through the letterbox offering me ten grand to give my side of the story. What side of the story? There's only one side to this story.'

I've had six offers; the lowest was twenty thousand. I don't tell Dad.

'There'll be another big news story soon and they'll leave us alone,' I say.

'No. Every time there's a slow week for news, the press will drag it up, with the same photo.'

'When this is over, maybe you could move away, start somewhere fresh. You'll never move on in that house; it's too big for you anyway.'

'It's never going to be over and, anyway, where would I go?'

He's got a point.

Chapter 30

Edie: October 1997

A large window spanned the three floors from the top to the bottom of Aveline's house. Her father had designed it. He was a well-known architect who'd worked on many prominent buildings in the area. Her mother was a furniture designer, and her sofas and tables filled most of the rooms. To Edie, they looked like posher versions of the old-fashioned furniture they'd had in their terrace on Gladstone Road. The style was retro, Aveline explained.

When she had moved from Limewoods, Edie thought their new house was grand, but it was small and ugly compared to Aveline's. She couldn't believe she'd ever wanted to live like Valentina Vickers. A house like this is what she'd have, one that wasn't rectangular and had paintings on the wall that you had to understand, not just like.

Edie was wearing black jeans with a silver-coloured top and a little mascara on her lashes. It was Aveline's fifteenth birthday party. She'd invited Tess, too. She wore an old top of Edie's; it hung from her shoulders like a cloak and came down to her knees. The cherry-coloured lipstick she'd chosen didn't suit her and her thick curls were twisted into uneven plaits that came to her shoulders. She looked like a child who'd raided the dressing-up box.

Edie had been at Joseph Amberley Girls' School for three years now. Her accent, clothes and hair had changed, but she worried that something of Limewoods still lingered about her. And that something was Tess.

'I can never believe that girl's your sister,' Char said.

Edie was standing with Char and Aveline in the large entrance hall to the house. Tess was at the other end staring at one of the pictures, the cherry lipstick everywhere on her face except her mouth and her plaits making her look more like ten than fourteen. Edie wanted to say no, she's nothing to do with me, but despite being shorter, less clever and having a stupid hairstyle, they were too alike to deny the link. Besides, by then, Tess was dragging herself towards them.

'No one would ever guess you were twins.'

Edie hated the word and hated even more that it meant everyone assumed they had to do everything together. Mums cooed over how sweet they were as a pair. Friends always asked Tess along to any party or sleepover Edie was invited to. That was the only reason Tess was here tonight at Aveline's birthday, as her twin. No one would bother speaking to her otherwise. After three years, Tess still couldn't find her own friends. Wearing Edie's clothes wasn't going to change that.

Tess reached their little group.

'I was saying,' Char said. 'I still can't believe you're Edie's twin.'

'Why?' Tess didn't look up.

'You're so different,' Char said with a fake smile.

'Not that different,' Tess said.

'How's it going in stream three?'

Tess didn't answer. Edie wanted to slap Char. However much Tess embarrassed her, she was still her sister and she knew Tess would be crying over this later.

'I'm sure it's the same in three as one,' Edie said.

'Then why do they split us? My dad says it's a waste of money going to JAGS if you're not academic.'

Edie dug her fingers into her hands.

'Tess is a brilliant painter,' she said. 'She's going to art college.'

Char couldn't make a sarcastic comment about that because Aveline's nineteen-year-old sister, Vonnie, was an art student. Before she could think of an equally snide remark, Michaela Gossington walked past them into the second reception room, the one they'd been forbidden to enter for the duration of Aveline's party.

'What's she doing here?' Char asked.

Michaela was in the year above them. Her parents were rich, she was beautiful, she listened to music no one had heard of, she smoked Russian cigarettes and small amounts of marijuana.

Every home time Edie and the other girls watched as she brushed her hair in the corridor and then swanned out of school, her bag slung over her shoulder. Her boyfriend, Bob, they all knew his name, would be waiting, with his long hair and tight fitting T-shirt. And she'd slide into the car next to him and they'd drive off. She was the girl they all wanted to be.

'She's friends with Vonnie,' Aveline said.

'Michaela's not coming to your party then?'

It was obvious Aveline wanted to pretend she was, but realised she wouldn't get away with it.

197

'No, but she comes around here loads.'

Edie had never seen Michaela say so much as 'hi' to Aveline at school and doubted the Now 37 album playing in the kitchen would be tempting her to stay. Edie longed to play her own music and dance, but when she'd made Aveline and Char listen to it, they'd turned up their noses.

'It's not exactly the Backstreet Boys, is it?' Aveline had said.

Thirty seconds later, Michaela came back into the hall with Vonnie, both in their jackets. Michaela walked straight past them.

Vonnie said, 'Happy birthday, sis,' and handed Aveline a bottle of rosé.

'Thanks,' Aveline said.

Vonnie was already out of the door.

'They're going to The Hub,' Aveline said.

'What's that?' Tess asked.

'Oh my god,' Char said and laughed. 'It's a club.'

She spoke slowly as if Tess were backward.

'How am I supposed to know that?' Tess said.

Char rolled her eyes at Aveline.

'Everyone knows that.'

Edie was too angry with Tess to defend her because Tess did know what The Hub was. She had said it to make Edie's friends dislike her, to get Edie back to herself.

Tess still wanted them to burst out laughing at the same thing at the same time, to read books out loud so they could enjoy them together, to plan trips to far-flung countries they would visit when they were older. She wanted it to be Tess and Edie against the world. Edie wanted to be part of the world, they were fourteen now, fifteen next year.

'I've brought some Smirnoff Ice,' Edie said.

'Let's get some glasses,' Aveline said. 'Drink the rosé before the boys get here.'

'What boys? And where did you get those Smirnoff Ice?' Tess asked.

Aveline and Char either didn't hear her or had decided to ignore her. They went into the kitchen.

Edie hung behind in the hall.

'Will you shut up, Tess,' she hissed.

'Why are we here?' Tess said. 'It's boring and since when do you drink alcohol?'

'You don't have to stay.'

'Will you come with me?'

'No.'

'You're different when you're with them. You become like them. Just stupid and horrible. Drinking and waiting about for boys. It's pathetic.'

'Well go if you don't like it.'

'I want you to come with me.'

'And do what? Go home, watch old movies? Do what we've done every weekend since we were four.'

'Why not?'

'Because we're not four years old any more, Tess. If you want to go home, go home. We don't have to do everything together.'

Tess opened her mouth to speak but Edie had already turned and taken the bottles to the kitchen.

*

The boys could be heard long before they arrived. By the time they reached the drive, their shouts and laughter drowned out the music from the tiny stereo. Aveline left the kitchen; Char and Edie followed her. Behind the front door the boys were chanting.

'Seb, Seb, Seb.'

Edie remembered Aveline and Char both mentioning the name.

'Seb, Seb, Seb.'

Then someone said, 'Nah, it's not his turn.'

Sniggers.

'Go on then.'

Mumbling, more laughter and the doorbell rang.

The lads standing on Aveline's doorstep didn't resemble their voices. They had sounded older. Edie was struck how short most of them were.

'Hi,' said the tallest. 'We brought booze.'

Edie was impressed with Aveline's pretence at indifference.

'Yeah, come in,' she said.

Char should have learnt from her friend.

'Hi, Sebastian,' she said, smiled at him and looked a little shy.

Sebastian smirked at the other lads.

'Hi,' he said.

Edie didn't speak. She wasn't used to boys. She and Tess didn't bother with them in primary school and all their cousins were girls. She glanced at Tess, she was in the corner, behind the door, trying to make herself invisible.

When her friends started hanging about after school to talk to boys, Edie would hang back or slip off home. She'd overheard Aveline tell Char that the boys thought Edie was stuck up. It wasn't that. They made her feel awkward. She had no idea what to say to them or what she was supposed to do with them. Not sex, she understood that. They'd had sex education at school and Auntie Becca had given Tess and her a very long and boring explanation, punctuated with lots of 'when you're old enough', and 'when you find the right man'. All of which was pointless, because several years earlier Raquel had enjoyed shocking Edie and Tess with a far more graphic and useful guide to the whole process. It wasn't the physical side that was a mystery.

Aveline led the boys to the kitchen. From what Edie could see, she benefited from having an older sister. However much she simpered when the boys weren't there, Aveline was cool and dismissive in their presence. Sebastian made far more of an effort with her than Char, who was hanging off his shoulder and laughing at his jokes. In turn, Sebastian's friend, Edie didn't know his name, was trying too hard for Char's attention and she kept batting him away like an unwanted fly.

Edie leant back against the kitchen counter, a little apart from the group. None of them wanted to talk to her. She wondered if it was because she was taller than all of them, or because they'd decided, as Aveline had said, she was stuck up. No one was talking to Tess, either. She felt a sudden urge to do as Tess said, and go home and forget the party.

She was about to sneak away, when Sebastian turned to her. He looked her up and down as if noticing her for the first time. He whispered something to his friend and they both laughed.

'Aren't you going to talk to him?' he asked.

'Who?' Edie said.

They both laughed again. Then she noticed a small boy next to her; he appeared much younger than the rest.

'Hi,' he said.

Sebastian and his friend seemed to find this the funniest thing ever. She wondered if it was the difference in height. He barely reached her shoulder.

'Hi,' she said.

Sebastian nodded at him and turned his attention back to Aveline.

'Do you like this music?' the boy asked.

'No,' said Edie.

She hadn't really been listening to it. But she was sure she didn't like it. All Aveline's stuff was rubbish. Besides, she was annoyed at the way this boy had been placed next to her. She was sure it had been decided beforehand, who was going to talk to whom. Had Char and Aveline been involved? Was this boy picked because they thought it would be funny?

'It's not really my sort of thing either,' the boy said. 'I like—'

'Excuse me.'

Edie pushed herself away from the counter. She looked at Tess, wanting to signal that they were going, but Tess was staring at the small boy and didn't notice her. She'd go to the lounge, Hannah and Natalie were there and they'd let her play what she wanted on the stereo. She was about to push open the lounge door, when she heard loud laughter from the kitchen and Sebastian's voice.

'What's wrong, mate? Don't worry. They're not all like your mum.'

'That one's not gonna run off with Mr Kent.'

Amongst the laughter she heard Char and Aveline. So they'd been in on this. They wanted to make her look stupid. She went into the lounge. She was angry. Angry with the boys, angry with her friends and angry with Tess for being right about how rubbish the party was.

Hannah and Natalie were dancing with some other girls Edie didn't recognise. Her bag lay on the sofa and she reached and fumbled around in it looking for her CDs.

When she looked up, the short boy was next to her.

'Are you following me?' she asked.

'No,' he said. 'It's boring in the kitchen. I wanted to listen to some proper music.'

Edie didn't believe him.

'Just go back to the kitchen.'

'But...'

He stood there for a moment and Edie felt sorry for him. Not sorry enough to be laughed at, though.

'I've seen you outside school. I wanted to talk to you.'

'I'm not interested. Go back to your friends,' Edie said.

She felt guilty being so horrible to him, until she heard more laughter from the kitchen. She wasn't going to be the butt of their jokes. Not Aveline and Char's. Not anyone's.

'OK,' he said and started to walk off. He turned at the door. 'By the way, I'm Max.'

Chapter 31

Tess: June 2018

Ray and Becca have moved three or four times since I left home. Each house is a large, characterless new build, within five miles of where they first started. Sometimes they dislike the neighbours, sometimes the layout proves inconvenient or the local shops inadequate. A 'For Sale' sign stands outside the current one. The garden is overlooked.

I park Dad's car on the drive behind Becca's silver hatchback. Becca comes to the door carrying her bag.

'Are you going out?' I ask.

'Only to the GP's. Routine check-up. I'm a bit early. Come in, I'll make some tea.'

I go into the lounge, which is frilly and flouncy, totally at odds with Becca's no-nonsense character. After a few minutes Becca arrives with a tray, carrying a teapot and cups; she always makes tea properly, never in mugs.

'I saw the appeal,' she says as she pours. 'They wouldn't need to put you through that if they were doing their job properly. I can't believe Vince agreed to it, after the way they treated him last time. How is he?'

'The same,' I say.

'Have they found anything else or was it just a load of crank calls?'

'They haven't got back to us yet. Actually, Auntie Becca, I've a few questions of my own.'

'What about?' Becca asks.

I tracked Mr Vickers down through directory enquiries. 'Absolutely not,' was his response to my request to come and talk to him about Mum. I can't find Valentina. Ray and Dad aren't going to tell me anything. Becca's one of the few people I can talk to. I'm hoping she'll be more open when Ray's not around.

'It's to do with Mum.'

'Your mother? Oh, Tess, you're not going to worry about that nonsense you were telling Ray in the cemetery?'

'You can't expect me to forget it.'

'I think you should do, Tess.'

'Was she unhappy?'

'No, she was always smiling, always singing, lots of fun.'

Fun. If you're fun you can't be unhappy. People at work tell me I'm fun.

Becca puts her teacup down and rubs the bridge of her nose. She's thinner than the last time I saw her, it makes her look older.

'I just want to understand, why did Edie write that? Is it possible Mum was unhappy, even if she did smile and sing?'

'It's going to sound strange, but I didn't know Gina that well. We spent a lot of time together because of Ray and Vincent, but we had our own friends.' I can't recall Becca ever having friends. 'And when we were together, it was always with them or you two. It's not like we had heart-to-hearts.' She picks up the cup. It hovers beneath her chin before she puts it down again. 'She had lots of friends on the Limewoods Estate. I can't remember their names.'

'Eileen. Eileen McCann.'

'Old lady, lived with her granddaughter?'

'Raquel was her daughter, actually. She had her late.'

Becca nods without listening.

'And Valentina Vickers?' I say.

'Hmm. I'm not sure,' she says.

'Lived next door, baked cakes. She was very beautiful, or so I thought.'

'Ah yes. I think I know who you mean. I went to school with her sister, but you used to come to us mostly, so I never got to mix with the people there.'

The Limewoods Estate was not the place for George Lawes' daughter. Not the place for Mum, really, she must have expected better, though you'd never have guessed. My grandfather came over from Jamaica, worked in a factory and studied at evening classes until he qualified to go to teacher training college. There he met my grandmother, eight generations of her family had lived in Coseley and she was the first to stay at school beyond the age of fourteen. Both must have hoped for more for their daughter than for her to drop out of university in her first year to marry Dad and have two children, before becoming a receptionist at a vet's surgery. Their other daughter, Aunt Lola, finished her degree and found a good job in the civil service. But if there was any disappointment, it was never expressed, either by my grandparents or by Mum.

As Becca says, she was always singing or quoting poetry. 'It's Too Darn Hot' would be warbled as ice crept up the inside of single-glazed windows. 'I have measured out my life with coffee spoons' accompanied supermarket brand instant being dumped into chipped mugs. She laughed and chatted with the neighbours who popped in and out. My friends all confided in her and wished she were their mum. Edie and I didn't know we were to be pitied for living where we did.

'You never heard any gossip?' I ask.

'Really, Tess, I'd be the last person to listen to Limewoods' gossip.'

'I suppose it was embarrassing having relatives living there.'

I can't keep the irritation from my voice, not that Becca notices.

'Not embarrassing, depressing. Have you been back? You probably don't remember how awful it was. I was so pleased when Ray gave Vince a job and you could move.' She looks at me and smiles. 'I know what it's like, Tess. I lost my mother young, too. But to tell you the truth, I don't think most people ever get to know their parents. Maybe their parents don't let them. Maybe they don't want them to. I think if Gina had lived you'd have known her longer, not better.'

'Is that how you feel about your mother?'

'Yes.'

'And your father, didn't you travel everywhere with him, after your mum died, the Far East, America, you must have become pretty close to each other?'

She hesitates.

'As I said, Tess, your parents let you see one side of them. The one they want you to see. Perhaps it's for the best. And don't you think you've got enough on your plate, without fretting about Gina?'

'It all seems part of the same thing.'

'It must seem like that sometimes, losing Gina and Edie so close together. But the whole suicide nonsense was cooked up by Nathan Bexley and his lawyer, hoping to get him off the charge. I wish Edie had come to me with that clipping. I hate to think of her agonising over it.' She glances at the clock. 'I do really have to go now or they'll cancel my appointment,' she says.

She puts her teacup down. A thin film is forming across the top.

'Of course,' I say.

I stand up with her. She gives me a little encouraging smile.

'After the funeral maybe then we could all go away for a bit,' Becca says. 'A holiday or something, with Vince and Ray.'

'Yes,' I say without thinking.

At the end of the street I look in the car's rear-view mirror. Becca's still standing at the door. I'm too far away to see the expression on her face. I don't need to see it to know that she was lying. I just don't know why.

*

I pull onto Dad's driveway when my phone beeps. It's a text from Jem:

Fancy meeting up?

The truth is, I do, just as an escape. But I remember Cassie's warning about Jem and I've too much to do. I delete the text and I'm about to put the phone back in my pocket, when Craven calls. There's an unspoken agreement that just as he is our contact in the police, I am their contact in the family. Dad's mood swings between anger and despair. One minute

208

pacing the room, railing against the police and press, the net staring blankly at the television. I worry how long he can go on like this and if he needs the sort of help he'd never ask for or agree to.

'We've had a large response to the reconstruction and appeal,' Craven says.

'Is large the same as good?' I ask.

'Not exactly.'

Twitter has given me a glimpse of the attention-seekers, conspiracy theorists and moral crusaders who will waste police time, claiming close knowledge of the case when they'd never heard of Edie until a few weeks ago.

'We've been through the calls,' Craven says. 'And we have several lines worth pursuing. In particular, a woman remembers the case from the time Edie disappeared. Her former husband was very possessive and she shouldn't have been in the area on that afternoon. She felt sure someone would come forward with the same information as there were other cars around. But no one did, and then she thought it was too late and the police would be suspicious of the delay and she'd still have to explain to her husband why she'd not been at her art class on the other side of town as she'd told him.'

'What did she see?' I ask.

'A schoolgirl, matching Edie's description, arguing with a man.'

I'm revived by the thought that back then Max was only a boy, too small to be mistaken for a man.

'Unfortunately,' Craven continues, 'she only saw him from behind.'

'Do you think it's the boyfriend my auntie Becca saw?'

'We are making additional inquiries. There's also—'

'Speak to Michaela Gossington. If anyone knows who he was, she did. She lives on the Glades.'

'We've spoken to Miss Gossington.' He sounds irritated. 'She or, more importantly, her current partner, are known to the police. Let's just say she wasn't exactly gushing with information.'

As if I could hate her any more. Michaela befriended Edie and the one time her friendship could help, she lets her down.

'The point is, an argument does sound like someone Edie knows,' Craven says. 'The Joseph Amberley boys would have been in uniform, but we'll be asking them. They may have a better idea of who it was, an elder brother perhaps. Boys do like to brag.'

If Edie's boyfriend had bragged, someone would know who he was. Someone who's keeping quiet, because either they don't care or they're afraid.

'I'll keep you informed,' Craven says.

After the call, I phone the Gossingtons and am sent to their answer machine.

'Hi, it's Tess Piper here, who came to see you last week.' I try my work trick of smiling whilst talking on the phone, to keep my voice light and happy, and hide my anger and frustration. 'I haven't heard from Michaela. I'd really like to talk to her. I thought, as one of Edie's friends, she'd want to come to the funeral. It's at one o'clock on Thursday at St David's. It would have meant a lot to Edie to have her there.'

I'm going to find that bitch if it kills me.

Chapter 32

Edie: November 1997

Edie felt a little more grown up and sophisticated today. She wasn't going shopping for clothes or make-up, she was heading to a record shop, a proper one, Irregular Records, not Woolworths or WHSmiths. Aveline's party had been a disaster. Music was her escape.

Uncle Ray had been after 'This is Love' by Joe Curtis and Edie wanted to get it for his birthday. The only copy he had was on a barely audible cassette.

Irregular Records was on the far side of town and she passed Topshop and Boots on the high street. As she moved away from the centre, the shops changed from smart chain stores to second-hand shops, specialist bike outlets and stores selling T-shirts with nationalist logos. She passed Honey Rider, with its rubber-masked mannequins, the sex shop everyone joked about but she had never seen before. When she reached the ring road it started to rain and Edie pulled her hood up. Her enthusiasm for the trip started to fade. Irregular Records was proving more difficult to find than Uncle Ray's single. The rain was driving down so hard that it splashed onto her cheeks despite the hood. She dived into the nearest café.

Ketchup bottles in the shape of giant tomatoes sat on cracked plastic tables and the metal chairs were fixed to the floor. Edie ordered a tea and went to sit down with her polystyrene cup. Three lads were playing on the fruit machine in the corner. They were a few years older, maybe eighteen or nineteen. Another boy sat by the door with his back to her, a guitar at his feet; he was smoking and listening to a Discman. One of the lads by the fruit machine thumped it and laughed as money poured out. Edie looked over. He saw her watching.

'What are you doing here?' he asked.

The others turned round and stared at her. Edie wasn't sure if the boy was being threatening or flirty.

'Nothing,' she said.

The boys huddled together and started whispering.

Edie downed her tea, scalding her throat, then stood up.

The boy at the door looked up. Edie recognised him as Michaela's boyfriend, Bob. He caught her eye. She looked away, hoping he didn't recognise her. Everyone knew him, but why would he notice her out of the hundreds of girls who poured out of the school every evening? She wondered what he was doing in the café. It didn't seem like his sort of place. Maybe he was caught in the rain, too.

As she moved away from the table, the boy who'd hit the fruit machine strutted over and barred her way.

'You're not going, are you?'

'Yes,' she said without looking at him.

'Going shopping in Honey Rider?'

He threw a look to his friends. Edie shook her head.

'Cos if you are—'

'That's enough, Jones.'

The voice came from near the door. Edie knew it was Bob.

'Alright,' the boy said. 'Just having a joke.'

He stepped back.

Edie went to the door. She gave Bob a weak smile before darting outside. Had he recognised her? She hoped not. He'd tell Michaela. Who'd tell the whole school. After her embarrassment with the boys at the party, she didn't need this.

The rain was weakening and looking up, she realised the record shop was only four doors down. She glanced back to make sure no one had followed her out of the café before going in.

The record shop was also full of boys but none of them took any notice of her, with their noses stuck between record covers. Edie headed for the Northern soul section, which she had to herself. The smell of cardboard mixed with vinyl reminded her of Uncle Ray's record cabinet, nothing else smelt quite like it.

'Looking for anything special?'

The man was Uncle Ray's age with a large gut. He wore a T-shirt with the shop's name printed across it.

'I was looking for "This is Love" by Joe Curtis.'

'You'll be lucky to find that,' he said. 'I've not seen a copy for a few years. You could try one of the specialist magazines.'

Edie must have looked blank.

'Is it for you?'

'No, my uncle.'

'Thought you were a bit young. We've some other good stuff. Here.'

He pulled out a couple of singles Edie didn't recognise. Then she saw 'Got to Find Me Somebody' by The Velvets.

Another one Uncle Ray only had on cassette. She tried to act as if she knew what she was doing, inspecting the sleeve and asking the man to pull out the disc.

The vinyl was unscratched but the sleeve was bent at the corner. It was marked at £15.

'It's a bit dog-eared,' she said. 'I'll give you ten for it.'

'Oh, a bit of a dealer. Twelve and it's yours.'

Edie nodded. He took her to the counter and put it in a bag. She was beginning to get her feeling of sophistication back.

'How do you know about this place?' the man asked.

'My uncle comes here.'

'Who's that?'

'Ray Piper.'

'Ray, eh? I know him from way back. We used to go to the Wigan Casino together. Him and that girl, what was her name? Gina. Good dancer.'

Uncle Ray always talked about his Wigan Casino days, but never mentioned Mum. The man must be thinking of a different Gina.

'So you're his niece?' the man said.

'Yes.'

He looked her up and down.

'His actual niece?'

'Yes.'

The man looked amused. He handed her the bag.

'Ray will like this one. Tell him Freddie says hi,' he said.

After she'd paid she wasn't sure if she should carry on looking. She had no money left, but she could impress Uncle Ray with talk about the shop. On the other hand, she was cold from the rain and wanted to get home.

'I didn't know you were into this,' a voice said. 'Took you for another Take That fan.'

Edie looked up from the records. It was Michaela. That's why her boyfriend was in the café, he was waiting for her.

'It's Edie, isn't it? What were you looking for?'

'Northern soul,' Edie said.

She wondered if Michaela would sneer.

'I don't know any of that. You'll have to play it to me sometime.'

'You probably wouldn't like it,' Edie said.

'I might.'

'What are you looking for?'

'Old Stax stuff,' Michaela said.

Uncle Ray didn't rate Stax.

'Anything special?' Edie asked.

'Nah, just browsing. I come here most weeks. I buy loads but that guy always follows me.' She nodded to Freddie. 'Thinks I'm going to nick something, I guess.'

Edie didn't think that was why Freddie was following Michaela, in her minidress and knee-length boots.

'He's alright, he's my uncle's friend,' Edie said.

'You know him?'

'A little,' Edie said.

Not a complete lie. She felt Michaela looking at her with more respect. Then she thought of Bob telling her how pathetic she'd been in the café.

Michaela checked her watch.

'I'd better go,' she said. 'I told Bob I wouldn't be long. See you next week.' Edie watched her stroll out of the record store. She thought of telling Char and especially Aveline, who desperately wanted to be friends with Michaela, how they'd met and chatted about music. How Michaela had asked her if she could listen to some of Edie's records. They'd be so jealous. But what if she told them and Michaela ignored her on Monday? They'd laugh and call her a liar. For now it would be her secret.

Chapter 33

Tess: July 2018

We're back at the cemetery on the hillside for the burial in the hottest summer for over forty years. The cold and grey of January we had for Mum's funeral seemed more fitting. Today, everyone's itching and fidgeting in their formal wear, the black cloth soaking up the searing heat. Like Mum's, the service was held at St David's, and like Mum's, Dad, Ray, Uncle Jake and one of the undertakers carried the coffin. Unlike Mum's, there's a news crew outside the church and a young reporter talking earnestly into the microphone as we leave for the cemetery.

The vicar read out the usual platitudes and like all who die young, Edie is described as a gifted student, well liked and popular, a pleasure to teach. Ray and Aunt Lola gave the eulogies. Neither Dad nor I could manage it. And now the eulogies and hymns are over and the only words left are those of the burial service, spoken by the vicar as he mops sweat from his brow.

'Man that is born of a woman hath but a short time to live, and is full of misery. He cometh up, and is cut down, like a flower.'

Dad's arms are wrapped around my shoulders as if he's

scared I'll fall into the grave and be swallowed up as Edie's coffin is lowered into the earth.

'In the midst of life we are in death.'

Ray is leaning on Becca, his face in the crook of her neck. She stands straight and sad. Cassie and Uncle Jake are comforting Aunt Lola. My other cousin, Corrine, is trying to keep her three young children silent and still. Ashley couldn't make it back from Canada. Some of the Joseph Amberley girls have come. Michaela isn't here and Charlotte hasn't made it but Aveline, Hannah and Natalie are here, along with Mrs Stanley, one of our former teachers.

'We therefore commit her body to the ground; earth to earth, ashes to ashes, dust to dust.'

I can feel the dark and cold around the coffin as earth is thrown into the hole in the ground. As large as the hole inside me I've tried to fill for years, with different men, drinks and pills. But the hole never gets smaller and now I realise I'll always be without her. That's why I had to believe she was alive, so I wouldn't have to face up to being alone. All my shallow friendships and meaningless relationships were just an attempt to feel the same connection with someone else, a connection that never came.

Dad has always been absent in my life. Even before Mum died, his depression ate too deeply into him to be a father. He chose cigarettes and television over his family. Edie's teenage rebellion was against me, my restrictions. Dad never placed any upon us. I'm not sure he knew we were there.

'We give thee hearty thanks, for that it hath pleased thee to deliver this our sister out of the miseries of this sinful world.'

*

Dad and I lean against each other as we leave the grave, neither of us speaking. We should talk to the other mourners, invite them back, but the truth is I wish they were all miles away. I can see the Joseph Amberley girls hovering. They're standing far enough away to ignore them without being rude, but Aveline steps forwards.

'Hi, Tess,' she says.

I look them up and down. Three witches dressed in black. Aveline is a replica of her mother, thin, immaculately dressed, effortlessly negotiating the uneven ground in her Prada stilettoes. I barely recognise the once mildly rebellious Hannah who had a nose stud, red streaks through her hair and wore thick black eyeliner. The nose stud has gone, the only jewellery is a tiny teardrop diamond necklace. The red streaks replaced by long tresses twisted into a low ponytail, a flick of mascara around her eyes. Natalie has changed the least, her face is a little thinner but it's still dominated by large, close-set eyes, framed with heavy brows, giving her an owl-like expression. I let go of Dad's arm. Cassie rushes to take my place and he ambles on.

'You do remember us, don't you?' Aveline says.

'How could I forget?'

My tone disconcerts her, the smile of false sympathy wavers.

'We just wanted to say how sorry we are. It must be so awful finding this out after all these years.'

'We always talked about her,' Hannah says. 'I haven't been able to stop crying. I still can't believe it. Honestly, Tess, I know we haven't kept in touch—'

'For good reason,' I say.

'But if there's anything we can do to help...'

She flounders and looks to the others, who appear similarly

lost for words. I let the silence stew; I want them to feel uncomfortable.

'I think you've done enough for now,' I say at last.

Aveline looks genuinely upset.

'I don't know what you mean, we only wanted to offer our sympathy, to come here and support you.'

'The creepy twin.' I glare at Natalie. 'It's always one of the family. She was obsessed with Edie.'

Natalie has enough decency to look embarrassed.

'It wasn't me who said that,' Aveline says.

'No. You said you never liked me. You're only here for the spectacle. None of you give a damn about her.'

'That's not true,' Aveline says.

She takes a step forwards. Natalie grabs her arm.

'Come on, Aveline,' she says.

Aveline looks around her.

'It's not true, Tess,' she says and lets Natalie lead her away.

Raquel comes over holding Fleur.

'Who were they?'

'Bitches from school.'

Concern creases Raquel's brow but she doesn't say anything.

'It was good of you to come, Raq. It means a lot, having someone from the old days. Someone who actually cared about Edie.'

'I never had friends like you and Edie again, do you know that?'

A tear rolls down her cheek. She shifts Fleur to rest on her hip and wipes her cheek with her free hand. 'It was never the same after you left. So many people came and went. I felt alone, just me and Mum.'

'Where is she?'

'I thought about bringing her, but it would just upset and confuse her. There doesn't seem much point in putting her through that when she won't even remember it tomorrow. But, Tess, I need to speak to you about something now,' she looks over her shoulder. 'In private.'

'Does it have to be today?'

'Yes,' she says.

There's an urgency to her voice. Ray is striding towards me.

'Tell me back at the house.'

Ray arrives.

'We're going now,' he says.

'I'll see you there,' Raquel says.

Ray links his arm through mine and leads me up the path we walked a few weeks ago. He leans against me and again I can smell whisky on his breath.

'You're the last one, Tess,' he says. 'The last one of my little Swifts.'

I press my wrist into my side and feel the hot metal of the bracelet against my skin.

'I remember the first time I saw your mother, she took my breath away. How could I have known it would end like this? Even you're living in London. All the women in my life, gone.'

'You've still got Becca,' I say.

'Ah yes,' he gives a sardonic smile. 'I'll always have the lovely Rebecca, till the day I die.'

He laughs and loses his balance a little so that I have to push him to walk upright.

I never imagined their marriage to be passion-filled, but I assumed a basic affection existed. Ray doesn't criticise or complain about Becca the way other men do about their wives, their nagging, their interfering relatives and constant

221

demands. He lets Becca have her way with the house and the holidays, while he gets on with running the business that once belonged to her father. Maybe it's the mix of whisky and grief that's allowed resentment to bubble up through their Ideal Home lives.

Becca's waiting at the car, her face solemn. I detach myself from Ray. Becca squeezes my arm and I clamber into the back of the car. Ray sits in the middle, Becca follows. Dad's already sitting in the front.

The driver pulls off. I watch the streets streak before me, a rewind of our last trip to Mum's grave.

Becca stares straight ahead, the palms of her hands flat on her lap, her face blank. Ray is sitting bolt upright, the classic pose of a drunk attempting to appear sober. The side of his face is twitching; he's trying not to cry.

Did Ray envy Dad his wife and family? Did he long for children of his own? I can't believe it was his choice to remain childless. He doted on Edie and me. Especially Edie. Perhaps he wanted boys, so he could take them to football and let them take over the firm when they were older. He was old-fashioned like that. He considered a football crowd too rough for us. The same for working in a construction firm. Not a place for a woman. 'It's not my attitude, it's the attitude of other men,' he'd said. So yes, one or two strapping lads would have suited him. Is this why he's resentful of Becca? Because she's given him everything else.

*

Becca's straight out of the car and dealing with the caterers when we arrive. Ray tries and fails not to stumble as he gets out. Dad lights up a cigarette, the second he's on the pavement. His movements are mechanical and he's dead behind the eyes. I join him in a smoke. We don't talk. What's to talk about? The funeral hasn't brought matters to an end. I don't feel better knowing Edie's lying next to Mum. Neither of them should be there.

Mrs McCann's more than twenty years older than Mum would be, drifting around in a fog. Aveline's, Natalie's and Hannah's lives are taken up with gossip and trivia. Edie would have done something with her life, something that mattered. Why are these people still here, when Mum and Edie are gone? I'm alone with Dad, and he is fading. How long until I lose him, too? And where are the answers to their deaths? I'll never know if an unknown dark force pushed Mum to suicide, or if she was just another drink-driving statistic. And I've heard nothing more from Craven about the unknown man seen arguing with a schoolgirl.

I throw the cigarette into the gutter. Other cars start to arrive.

'Come on, Dad,' I say. 'It'll be over soon.'

The buffet looks like a tribute to the century in which Mum and Edie died, a blanket of beige: sausage rolls, vol-au-vents and cheese straws. I opt for a glass of wine instead. There's a general acknowledgement that I'm to be pitied most. More than Dad. It irritates me. I don't deserve it. Dad has suffered more. Seeing Aunt Lola hurts, she looks so much like Mum. A taunt from the dead of what I've lost. All these years Dad has had to look at me, an imperfect copy of Mum and Edie, not a consolation, just an unwanted reminder.

Besides, I don't want their pity. What does it mean? What do they expect from me? Should I lock myself in the bathroom and weep or lie on the carpet wailing in front of them? I've had twenty years of weeping and I did it alone, and I'll do the next twenty alone.

The other unspoken general acknowledgement I can see in their eyes is that I should be the one lying up in that coffin on the hill and my beautiful, brilliant twin should be standing here lost and inconsolable, drinking too much wine and avoiding the cheese flan.

When Mrs Stanley comes over to tell me how talented Edie was and that I must miss her, I lose patience and escape with a glass of warm wine. I hide by the outside of the conservatory and light a cigarette.

I hear the door slide open and Raquel comes to join me.

'Can I have one?'

She points at my cigarette.

'I didn't know you smoked any more,' I say.

'I don't,' she says.

I hand her the packet along with the lighter.

'Where's Fleur?' I ask.

'Running around like a mad thing with your cousin's kids. I guess they're too young to know they're meant to be sad.'

'Lucky them,' I say.

'I know what you mean,' Raquel says. She peers back to the door before saying, 'Look, is it OK if I talk to you now? I know it's a funeral. I wouldn't say anything if it wasn't important.'

'What's wrong?'

I can't think what's got Raquel so rattled. She pauses to light the cigarette and takes a deep breath before blowing out a long stream of smoke.

'There was a guy at the graveside; I've seen him before. It's been a long time but I'm sure it's the one I told you about. He used to wait outside if we went to McDonalds or something. It was weird. He followed her everywhere, spied on her, hung around outside her school, wouldn't leave her alone. He followed her home once.'

My mouth goes dry. Raquel is waiting for me to say something. I feel sick.

'Do you know him, Tess?' she asks. 'Your cousin called him Max.'

Chapter 34

Edie: November 1997

Edie was standing with Aveline and Char in the school corridor, when Michaela came up and said 'hi'. Tess stood a little apart from the group, as she often did, always hovering, never joining in.

'Hi,' Edie said.

Aveline looked at her, perplexed.

'Thanks for the CD. Got any more?'

Michaela had asked Edie about Northern soul and Edie had got Uncle Ray to burn a 'Best of' CD. They'd chatted about music and Michaela had introduced her to Isaac Hayes. It wasn't as different from Uncle Ray's Northern soul as she thought, but she didn't like it as much. What she did like was knowing Michaela. She'd always felt a little on the outside at Joseph Amberley. Edie knew she and Tess were different. Most JAGS thought everyone who came from the Limewoods Estate were benefit scroungers and criminals. Edie never mentioned living there. She spoke in the right way and wore the right clothes, but she still didn't fully fit in. Hanging out with Michaela meant she was a proper JAG.

'There's loads more. I'll make a new CD at the weekend,' Edie said.

'Yeah? Good. Here, listen to this.' Michaela passed her a disc. 'Just a few good ones. See if you like it.'

'Thanks.'

'We're going to lunch. Coming?'

'Yeah. This is my sister, Tess.'

Michaela flashed her a smile. Edie tugged Tess's arm and didn't say anything to Aveline and Char as she followed. They would be jealous and want to know how she knew Michaela. It would teach them a lesson. Maybe they'd think twice before they organised something without her, or try to set her up with some stupid little boy at a party, to make her look like an idiot.

*

The cafeteria was filling up. Michaela took them to an empty table at the end. Edie followed her. Tess followed Edie.

Even though Edie was starving, she copied Michaela and chose a tiny portion of rice salad. Michaela killed her appetite with cigarettes. Edie would have to raid the vending machine later. Tess had a bag of crisps and an apple. No wonder she hardly grew.

'My boyfriend's going away this weekend,' Michaela said. 'He's in London with the band.'

'Are they getting signed?'

'Not yet; soon, I think.'

'Yeah right,' Tess said.

Edie tensed. Michaela looked at Tess.

'What year's your sister in?' she asked Edie as if the thought Tess could answer for herself was ridiculous.

'The same one as Edie,' Tess replied.

Michaela looked puzzled.

'But you're...'

'We're twins.'

'You can't be.'

'We are,' Tess said.

Michaela looked to Edie again for an explanation.

'Non-identical,' Edie said.

Tess opened her bag of crisps and began shoving handfuls in her mouth like a toddler, with broken pieces falling down her chin. Edie wanted to grab the bag off her. Why was she doing this? Michaela gave Tess a sideways glance then turned back to Edie.

'Anyway, with Bob away, I thought we could have a girls' night out at The Hub.'

'I'd never get in,' Edie said.

'Sure you will. I'll do your make-up and Vonnie knows the doorman.'

'On Friday?'

'Saturday,' Michaela said.

'Great.'

'Not you, Tess.' Michaela was smiling. 'I'm sorry, I can only do so much with make-up and the doorman, I mean he can't let anyone in who's too obviously underage.'

'Sounds crap anyway,' Tess said through a mouthful of crisps.

'Your sister's so funny, Edie,' Michaela said. 'Why does she speak with that townie accent?'

'I can answer for myself,' Tess said.

'What did she say?' Michaela asked.

Tess was staring at Edie, daring her to speak. Another group of Michaela's friends arrived at the table and began discussing The Hub, saving Edie the trouble.

*

'You're not going are you?' Tess said on their way home.

'Of course I am.'

'Dad won't let you.'

'I won't tell him,' Edie said. She stopped walking. 'And neither will you.'

They both knew Tess wouldn't break that sibling code.

'I don't like her,' Tess said. 'She spoke about me like I wasn't there.'

'She was trying to be nice.'

'And said I couldn't go to that club.'

'You said you didn't want to go.'

'What am I supposed to do on Saturday?'

'It's one night, Tess.'

God! It was so exhausting being a twin.

Chapter 35

Tess: July 2018

Raquel's face is a mixture of excitement and fear, which changes to confusion when I don't react.

'Tess?' she says.

'I know Max, Raquel, and I know he knew Edie.'

'I don't understand, how do you know him? Why is he here?'

'Max and I were together until a couple of months ago.'

Raquel's mouth falls open.

'How could you, after what he did to Edie?'

'He didn't do anything to her.'

'He terrified her,' she says.

'He hardly knew her.'

'He was obsessed with her and now I find out he's with you. He frightens me, Tess. You need to be careful. He shouldn't be here.'

I think of my chance meeting with Max in a North London bar, miles from home, and hear Vilas's words, 'I don't believe in coincidences.' He was right. For Max, Edie being my sister was not an additional link to bind our relationship but its foundation.

My head feels heavy and my legs weaken. I have to lean back against the wall and put my hands on my knees. Raquel steps forwards and touches my arm.

'You didn't know?' she says.

'No,' I whisper.

How could I not know? At some level I think I did. Smaller, plainer, less academic and four minutes younger, I was always second to Edie. A poor replica, but good enough for Max when the real thing was unavailable.

'You need to tell the police. It's creepy, weird. You don't think he...?'

'Think he what?'

Raquel spins round. Max is standing behind her.

He's glaring and walking towards us. Raquel draws herself into the wall, to create as much distance between them as possible. Max stands a few inches from me then turns to Raquel. I try to stand upright.

'Think he what?' He spits out each word. 'I remember you. It's Raquel, isn't it? Is that what you told Edie about me? That I was creepy and weird. Is that why she wouldn't see me?'

'No,' Raquel says.

'Why then?'

Raquel is no longer the bold girl, swaggering up to lads and demanding cigarettes. She shrinks into the wall.

'Max, stop it,' I say.

'It's people like her...'

He's still glaring at her.

'Max.'

I move to stand between him and Raquel.

'You should go now, Raquel,' I say.

Raquel slides from behind me and goes towards the door into the conservatory.

'Yeah, go, and keep going,' Max says.

I keep my eyes fixed on Max's face.

'I'll call you,' Raquel says.

The door bangs shut. Max and I are alone.

'It was you, the boy who followed her home, wasn't it?'

'And that makes me a murderer? It's not surprising Raquel believes it, when even my own girlfriend—'

'I'm not your girlfriend,' I say.

'No. No, you're not.'

He shakes his head.

'What am I supposed to think?' I say. 'You pretend you only knew Edie in passing and now I find out you were stalking her.'

'Stalking?' he says. 'It's stalking now? I was a teenage boy with a crush. That's all. Nothing weird, nothing creepy. Just a normal, loved-up teenager.'

'Following her around, spying on her movements. Are you the reason she started leaving school by the back?'

'No, of course not.'

'Do you know who her boyfriend was?'

'No.'

'But she had one?'

He hesitates.

'I don't know.'

'You're lying.'

He turns from me slightly and takes a breath.

'Tess, I would never have done anything to harm her, do you understand? I really liked her, cared about her. You don't know how it was for me when she disappeared. I couldn't eat, I couldn't sleep and I couldn't tell anyone. Not my friends, not my dad, definitely not my mum. I know it's nothing to what you went through, but at least you could acknowledge it. You had a right to suffer. You weren't alone.'

His brows contract, the pain spread across his face. I want to feel sorry for him, but I can't. His betrayal runs too deep.

'It wasn't a chance meeting between us in that bar, was it?'

He gives the tiniest shake of the head.

'Was it so bad, wanting to see you?'

'It wasn't me you wanted to see, was it? It was Edie.'

He looks up to the sky. There's nothing left to say. He looks back down and we stand staring at each other, saying nothing until Cassie opens the door.

'Is everything alright?' She looks at both of us. It's very obvious everything is not alright. 'You should come inside, Tess, you're being missed.'

I don't look at Max as I move away.

Dad told me I could be in danger. If someone had a reason to hurt Edie, they knew her, which meant they also knew me.

'What do you think the killer would do if he knows you're after him?'

Do I need to be scared of Max?

Chapter 36

Edie: February 1998

'Most people know the Soft Cell version, not the Gloria Jones original. I managed to find this on a market for fifty pence. The stallholder had no idea what he'd got.'

Uncle Ray's diamond patterned steps fell into easy time with the music. The heavy bassline kicked in. Edie barely danced, just shifting lightly from one foot to the other. Recently, she'd become aware how her body moved differently and that her shape had changed from just a few months ago. She felt self-conscious of her dancing, even in front of Uncle Ray. Especially in front of Uncle Ray, if she thought about it.

He stopped mid flow.

'What's up, Edie, you don't feel like dancing today?'

Edie shook her head and turned away from him slightly.

'You look just like Gina from this angle,' he said and stepped closer.

The door banged behind him. Auntie Becca came in. Uncle Ray took a step back.

'I was just saying how Edie looks like Gina,' Uncle Ray said.

'It's only the height,' Auntie Becca said. 'You're more like Vince in the face.'

'Yes, you're right,' Uncle Ray said. 'She's more like Vince. It's just when she turned her head like that.'

No one spoke for a moment. Edie looked at Uncle Ray and Auntie Becca. Their expressions were unreadable.

Edie hated people talking about Mum. She tried to squeeze down on those memories to make them disappear. Sometimes she recalled birthdays and Christmases, when Mum must have been there, but the presents were wrapped by Auntie Becca, the turkey brought in by Dad. Mum was missing.

'So, did you make the CD?' Edie asked.

'Sure, it's here,' Uncle Ray said and reached for the sideboard. 'I've made some notes.'

'Thanks,' Edie said.

She would copy them later into her own handwriting.

'Is that for a boy, Edie?' Auntie Becca asked.

'No, a friend at school.'

'So you're not courting?'

'I'm not what?'

'You're not seeing anyone, a boy?'

'No,' Edie said.

The idea seemed ridiculous, though lots of girls her age did have boyfriends.

'There must be someone,' Uncle Ray said. 'A pretty girl like you. You must have admirers.'

'There's this one lad,' Edie said.

'Yes?' Uncle Ray said.

'Oh, it's nothing. I met him at Aveline's party. He's at the boys' school. He just follows me around.'

'What do you mean, follows you around? He's not bothering you, is he?'

'No, nothing like that, he's harmless.'

'Because if he is, I'll have a word. I know Vince...' he paused. 'Vince and I would talk to him.'

'Really, Uncle Ray, he's harmless. He's shorter than me; he just turns up wherever I am. He never says anything or does anything. I've told him to get lost, so he keeps his distance. I feel sorry for him.'

Uncle Ray laughed.

'Never feel sorry for boys, Edie, we rarely deserve it,' he said and winked at Auntie Becca.

'That's true enough,' Auntie Becca said. 'I'll drop you home if you like, Edie. I'm going over that way.'

'Thanks, Auntie Becca. And thanks for the CD, Uncle Ray.'

'Anytime,' he said.

Edie thought back to when she'd seen him with Valentina in the park. She'd never asked him about it. After Mum was killed, everything else seemed unimportant. Now, she wondered if he was still seeing Valentina. She was old enough to realise her fatness hadn't been due to eating her own cakes.

As they left, the strains of 'Tainted Love' faded and the record player reset itself.

*

'Where've you been?'

Tess was coming out of her room as Edie came up the stairs. Where've you been? Where are you going? Tess never stopped.

'Were you with Michaela?'

'No.'

'Where then?'

'At Uncle Ray's,' Edie said.

'You didn't ask me.'

'I only went to pick up a CD.'

'For her?'

'Who?'

'Michaela.'

'What if it is?'

'You do everything with her now. You said it was just that once. Now it's all the time. She's so fake. I don't know how you can't see it,' Tess said.

'You say that about everyone at school.'

'They are.'

'If you tried to make friends—'

'I don't want to. They're so stupid. All they talk about is boys and rubbish bands.'

'Michaela doesn't,' Edie said.

Not exactly true. She spent a lot of time talking about Bob, whose band was probably worse than the ones Tess was thinking about. According to Michaela, Bob's band was amazing and about to get signed by a big London label. From the tape Edie had heard, she doubted this; though it would explain why Michaela liked him when he didn't seem her type.

She'd met Michaela's parents at her enormous house out near Bromsgrove and was pretty sure they'd agree. But Michaela liked the music Edie gave her and Uncle Ray was always pleased to burn a new CD and make notes on the artists. This was the basis of their friendship. No one else understood why Michaela liked a girl from the year below, but she was too popular for anyone to question it. Anyone except Tess.

'She's so up herself,' Tess said. 'And she's just using you so she can look like she knows about music. She thinks she's cool but she probably listens to the Spice Girls when no one's about.'

The same thought had crossed Edie's mind.

'Don't talk rubbish, Tess.'

'And you're the same. That stuff she gave you on her CD was crap. You only say you like it cos she does.'

'That's not true.'

'You never mentioned any of her stuff to Uncle Ray.'

Actually, Edie had mentioned it to him. He had laughed and said it was for losers who couldn't dance.

'I'm allowed friends, Tess. Why has it just got to be the two of us all the time? You didn't mind Raquel.'

'She was different.'

'What do you want, Tess? Go back to hanging around garages and traipsing up the high street for something exciting to do. Don't you want to go out, have some fun, meet boys?'

'I've tried. It's boring. They're boring. Why do you pretend? You don't like those girls any more than I do. And the Joseph Amberley boys are all idiots.'

'There are other boys.'

She thought of Michaela's boyfriend, Bob. After every night out with him, and a few ones in, Edie and the other girls would huddle around Michaela as she told them of the previous evening's exploits.

The only person waiting for Edie was that stupid boy from the party. Sometimes he'd wave to her or cross the road as if to come and chat, and she'd go back into the school to avoid him. She'd started leaving by the hole in the back hedge to swerve him altogether. This stopped her from seeing Bob coming to pick up Michaela. It came as a shock that it both-ered her so much.

Once, after a couple of bottles of Smirnoff Ice, she'd allowed herself to be groped by one of the boys from Bridges, who wore too much Lynx and was covered in acne. It had been a one-off. In general, she had no time for boys and held in slight contempt the girls who put on make-up after school and hung around the Joseph Amberley boys from opposite.

But Bob wasn't like those boys. He had a car and a job. He smoked cigarettes that weren't stolen and played the guitar. She didn't understand why she felt the need to see him. She didn't like him. He was a bit of a show-off and his band was unlistenable. It had been kind of him to stop those lads teasing her in the café, but it was to show them who was boss rather than a compliment to her. It rankled that her fears about Bob telling Michaela were groundless. He wouldn't recognise her. However much he occupied her thoughts, she was of no importance to him.

'I'm not interested in boys. I'd rather watch TV,' Tess said.

'Well do it on your own. I can't be bothered arguing. Just don't keep asking where I'm going and why I don't take you with me.'

Edie pushed past Tess and went to her room.

It had been much simpler before. Edie hadn't realised they fitted in, until they didn't. There had been no need to be grateful for friends at St Luke's Primary, no need to pretend about anything. She could always be herself with Raquel. She'd promised to go back and see her but never had. A little guilt tinged her memory of the fun they'd had together over the years. It was odd Tess never mentioned her.

Had Tess been as jealous of Raquel as she was of Edie's

new friends at Joseph Amberley, and Edie just hadn't noticed? She put her Discman on its highest volume, but today it wasn't loud enough to shut everything out. Her old life, Raquel, her mum, she missed them all.

Chapter 37

Tess: July 2018

The morning after the funeral I come downstairs to find Dad's slept in the armchair again, cigarette burnt down to the filter, dead between his fingers. I tiptoe in, slide the butt from his hand and decide to leave the TV on.

My head's aching and I'm feeling a little overheated. I wonder if I'm coming down with a virus. I don't suppose the wine and vodka helped. I go to the kitchen, knock back two Nurofen and bring a cup of tea into the lounge. I check in on Facebook. Laura Andrews has been blocked from the JAGuars' group and on Twitter, people have moved on from #EdiePiper.

The doorbell rings. Dad stirs but doesn't wake. I get up, shutting the lounge door softly, and pad down the hall.

'Can we come in?' DI Vilas asks.

DS Patterson is with him.

'Dad's asleep,' I say. 'I don't want to disturb him.'

'You said you wanted to speak to us.'

I narrow my eyes. I have a vague memory of slurring words into a phone at two in the morning. When Vilas said to call him anytime if anything new occurred to me, I'm sure he didn't mean any time. After the wine I moved onto vodka. I can't even remember what I said to him. I pull the door open and lead them to the dining room. It's the best-maintained room in the house, owing to the fact we have always eaten on our laps or in the kitchen. The room faces the front, so I tilt the venetian blinds to let light in but shield us from view. The ticking of the carriage clock on the dresser echoes round against the near empty walls.

Vilas looks mystified at my choice of room. I cut short his chance to question it by sitting down. He hesitates then follows, as does Patterson.

'It must have been a difficult day for you yesterday,' Vilas says, his head cocked to one side. 'Though sometimes the funeral can bring closure.'

The mild thrum across my forehead is strengthening. I press my eyes shut for a moment.

'I'm glad that part's over,' I say.

'Quite a turnout considering the time that's passed.'

I didn't see Vilas there. He must have been watching from a distance. My head hurts and I'm angry that he's effectively been spying on us, and at the idea that placing Edie's bones in the earth will somehow bring us comfort, as if she were an elderly aunt who'd died after a long illness.

Vilas clears his throat.

'I picked up your voicemail this morning,' he says. 'I couldn't make all of it out.' From the corner of my eye I catch Patterson trying to suppress a grin. 'But I understand you have something to tell us about Max Arnold.'

Max, of course, I told him about Max. And now it comes to it, it feels like disloyalty. Max has been good to me, helped me through some bad times, and now I'm denouncing him to the police.

242

'It might be nothing,' I say.

'We've scant information as it is, if you can tell us anything about Mr Arnold, that's of use to the case, you're actually legally bound to do so.'

I should never have called him whilst drunk and I can't back out of it now, so I recount what Raquel told me, that Max was obsessed with Edie. That he followed her, spied on her, made her anxious.

'And she confirmed what I said about a boy following Edie home. I mean, he denies it, but he would, wouldn't he?'

Vilas nods.

'And you never had any idea about any of this?'

'How could I?'

'I did suggest to you before... but that's irrelevant now,' he says. 'Has Max ever been violent towards you?'

I nearly laugh. Max moans and sulks, occasionally shouts, but he's never physically aggressive.

'No.'

'Towards anyone else, you've never seen him lash out?'

'No.'

Vilas leans forwards.

'Do you believe him capable of harming Edie?'

'No.' The word comes easily. 'But I think he's not telling the whole truth. I don't know why.'

'The thing is, Edie was found thirty miles away from where we know she was attacked. Looking back at the original case notes, I can see he was exceptionally small for his age. It seems unlikely he could move a body thirty miles.'

'Unless he had help,' Patterson says.

'Max lived with his father at the time. His mother had left the family home, is that correct?' Vilas asks.

243

'Yes,' I say.

'And he's close to his father?'

'Not really.'

'Hmm. I'll make more enquiries. But Max doesn't fit the description of the boy Edie was seen arguing with. Our witness was adamant the young man wore jeans and a white T-shirt. Max was a Joseph Amberley boy, wasn't he? And he'd still have been in his school uniform at that time of the afternoon.'

'No,' I say. 'He wouldn't. His dad pulled him out of school after the Mr Kent thing, the teacher his mum ran off with. I don't think he started his new school until the next term.'

'So he wasn't in uniform?' Vilas stops, narrows his eyes and looks at Patterson. 'But he still doesn't fit our description.'

'It was twenty years ago,' Patterson says. 'And travelling at speed in a car, the light, the angle, all that could affect what our witness saw.'

Vilas nods.

'Look, Tess, thanks for getting in touch. We'll follow up on this and probably need to speak to this Raquel. I don't know why she wasn't questioned before,' Vilas says.

'No one knew they were still in touch,' I say.

'Really?' he says.

'I told you before, Edie liked keeping secrets.'

'I see. Well, we'll find out what she's got to say. And obviously be speaking to Mr Arnold again. You're staying here, with your father, for the foreseeable?'

'Yes.'

'Good. I would advise you not to return to the flat you share with Mr Arnold at present.'

I've betrayed Max. They'll go back and grill him, bring up

244

all that stuff about Mr Kent, which he hates talking about more than anything. And he'll know it's me who's told the police, after all Max has done for me and when I know he would never hurt Edie. If he hadn't lied, I wouldn't have had to do it. But then why did he lie? Ever since Raquel told me, I've been telling myself it's because he's embarrassed, shy. But how many reasons are there to lie about the disappearance of a girl you know, a girl you follow? The slow, endless drips of suspicion are eroding my certainty.

*

In the lounge, Dad is awake and on his first cigarette of the day.

'Who was that I heard leave?' he asks.

'The police, they had a few more questions.'

'More questions but no more answers,' Dad says.

I try to ask one more time about Max.

'They asked about a boy who used to follow Edie around. He came to the house here once, do you remember?'

'No, Tess, I've told you before, you're misremembering.'

'But Raquel said Edie told her.'

'I don't know then, but there was no boy,' he says. 'Is that what the police were asking about? They could have come to me.'

'You were asleep.'

I can't tell him that his surviving daughter has been shacked up with the main suspect for nearly the last decade.

I leave Dad to his cigarette and go upstairs, when my phone beeps. It's a text from Mr Vickers:

I've just learnt about this dreadful business with your sister and I've decided that, if you still want to talk to me, I'm ready to answer your questions. You know my number.

I can't quite believe it. Even Mr Vickers can't ignore the glamour and intrigue associated with the death of a young girl.

Vilas focusing on Max reminds me of my childhood game of detectives and I know that fixing your mind on one outcome blinds you to other possibilities. I think back to that time, plodding around the estate in my disguise, notebook in hand. It's ironic my investigations led me right back to that first one, 'The Case of the Missing Cakemaker', and Mr Vickers.

Chapter 38

Edie: February 1998

It was the kind of street and the type of people Edie was wary of. Strange to think she'd once lived here on the Limewoods Estate and been one of them. It wasn't as she'd recalled. Even the layout seemed to have shifted. She wouldn't have known Raquel's house, if the pottery lion wasn't still sat on their doorstep.

Her old house was next door; she remembered it nearer to the top of the road. The door had been painted red and the number was missing. The pots and plants Dad put there were long gone, replaced by weeds, a couple of children's bikes and some empty beer cans. By now, she was sure the back garden would be overgrown or concreted over. Had the green man Mum had attached to the fence survived, protected by layers of ivy?

The day she brought it home from a junk shop Edie hadn't liked it. It was ugly and strange. Later, its strangeness created an odd attraction and she grew to love it as much as Mum, even if she did tell Tess it came alive at night and ended up scaring herself. They had left it behind in the scramble to leave. It seemed to Edie they'd been told of the move only

moments before the removal men came and half their possessions were lost. That same day she'd been replanted in a place
as alien to her then as this street was to her now.

They'd been happy here. She hadn't known they were poor,
or that she should be ashamed of her accent and address.
And Mum, who must have known all these things, had also
been happy. Happier than Auntie Becca in her executive new
builds with en suite bathrooms, instead of a single-glazed one,
tacked onto the back of the kitchen, where you could see your
breath in the winter.

Edie stood staring at the door, as if opening it would lead
her back to early childhood and Mum. The daydream was
broken by a ratty-haired woman opening the door and two
young children bounding their way out and grabbing the
bikes.

'What are you staring at?'

The woman stood with her hands on her hips. Instead of
answering, Edie turned and walked towards Raquel's.

'Oi, I asked you a question.'

The woman came to the gate. Edie thought she was going
to follow her. She swung quickly into Raquel's and knocked
on the door.

The woman was still standing at the gate, glaring at Edie,
when she heard the slap of slippers on carpet, signalling Mrs
McCann's approach. Raquel's mum looked exactly as Edie
remembered, with thick tan tights and her hair curled up into
an improbable cloud, perched on her head, and Edie had
never seen her indoors without her floral housecoat and sheep-
skin slippers. If Mrs McCann hadn't changed, Edie must have,
because she stared at her without recognition.

'Can I help you?'

Out of the corner of her eye, Edie saw the woman from her old house still watching her.

'It's Edie. Gina's daughter. I used to live next door.'

Mrs McCann continued to stare.

'We used to...' Edie began before Raquel pushed past her mother, threw her arms round Edie and pulled her inside the house.

Always a chubby child, she was now lathe thin and the pudding-bowl haircut had been changed to long layers. But she was still unmistakably Raquel, with a small mouth and deep-set eyes.

'Don't mind Mum,' she said. 'All that daytime TV's turned her brain to mush. She wouldn't recognise me if she didn't see me every day.'

'Raquel, that's just not true,' Mrs McCann said. 'I'm sorry, Edie, it's been a long time. I was confused for a moment, you're nearly a woman.'

'It's been a while, Mrs McCann.'

The McCanns' house had an identical layout to Edie's old one, with the front door opening directly into the living room, which was separated from the kitchen by a steep flight of stairs. Narrower than Edie remembered, the lounge was made even smaller by the brown-and-orange wallpaper and matching carpet, which must have looked dated by the time Edie left the street.

'Make us a tea, will you, Mum?' Raquel asked.

'How do you take it, Edie?'

'Milk, one sugar, please,' Edie said.

Mrs McCann shuffled off to the kitchen whilst Raquel sat on the sofa. It faced a TV, where a bouffant-haired quiz show host had been put on mute. Edie took the armchair by the gas fire. She had time to study Raquel. She looked older than Edie, despite being a little shorter. It was those deep-set eyes and the faint imprint of lines across her forehead.

'It's been forever,' Raquel said.

'Feels like it.'

'It was never the same after you left. We've had about ten families in and out of your place and most of them are vile. That one at the moment is a total cow. Her two little 'uns rode their bikes into Mum, knocked her over, she didn't tell them off or even say sorry. I would have strangled her if those kids hadn't been there. I gave her a piece of my mind, I can tell you.'

Edie smiled. Raquel always spoke in a slightly old-fashioned way, maybe because her mum was so much older. It wasn't what you expected from a girl like Raquel, who dressed in tracksuits, hung out at Roswell Park and lived on the Limewoods Estate.

'I was looking at our house as I came by,' Edie said. 'She came out and started shouting at me.'

'That sounds like her.'

'Do you take sugar, Edie?' Mrs McCann called from the kitchen.

'One, thanks, Mrs McCann.'

Raquel rolled her eyes.

'She's getting batty,' Raquel said. 'Forgetful. Is that why you never came to see me? Did you forget? You said you would, that nothing would change just cos you moved. Don't you remember, that's the last thing you said, right before you left?'

'Leaving was a bit of a blur,' Edie said.

She was aware of Raquel watching her face.

'My mum had just died.'

'At least you had a time with both your parents.'

'You've still got both of yours. I mean, I know your dad's not around much...'

Raquel snorted.

'You could say that.'

'Do you ever see him?' Edie asked.

'No. He's got two other kids now. A boy and a girl. I'm not allowed to visit. It might upset them.' She pulled a face.

'You're better off here with your mum.'

'That's not the point. And it's not the point that your mum died. You should've come to see me. I was really lonely. You and Tess were my only friends around here.'

'What about that lot from Roswell Park?'

Raquel shook her head.

'That didn't last long. They were all taking drugs and getting into trouble.'

'Like what?'

'You don't wanna know.'

'I'm sorry. I think I wanted to forget what happened.'

'I thought you wanted to forget that you're from Limewoods and used to speak like me. Bet no one at your fancy school knows where you're really from.'

Once, Edie had spotted Raquel in the town centre when she was with Aveline and Char. She had ducked into a shop doorway to avoid her. Her JAG friends would want to know who Raquel was and how she knew her. She could imagine their whispering and giggles as they relayed the details to the rest of the school. Edie fudged where they'd lived before, just as she gave only a half-truth about what Dad did for a living. She was ashamed. And she was ashamed of being ashamed. Raquel was right to be angry.

'It's not like you think, Raquel.'

'No?'

Mrs McCann came in carrying a tray with mugs of tea and a packet of biscuits.

'It's lovely to see you, Edie,' she said and looked her in the face and smiled. 'It's such a pity you moved; we still miss you. But I understand that you wouldn't want to stay, after what happened to Gina. Best to make a new start, eh?'

'Yes,' Edie said.

Mrs McCann handed her a mug.

'Poor Gina,' she said. 'Who knew she was so unhappy?'

Raquel glanced at Edie.

'She wasn't unhappy,' Edie said.

Raquel was staring hard at her mother.

'She must have been.'

'Mum,' Raquel said.

Mrs McCann looked up.

'No, of course not,' she said. 'Why would she be unhappy? Have a biscuit, Edie. Only Rich Tea, I'm afraid.'

Edie reached for a biscuit because she couldn't think of anything to say.

'And how's Tess?' Raquel asked.

'Same as ever,' Edie said.

'Why didn't she come today?' Mrs McCann asked.

'I was just passing. It was unplanned or I'd have brought her.'

'Tell her to come next time,' Mrs McCann said. 'I remember you two, joined at the hip, always up to mischief with our Raquel. But not like this new lot. You were always polite and listened to grown-ups. And look how well you've turned out.

Just like Gina, so tall and you speak lovely. I suppose they teach you that at Joseph Amberley. I'd loved to have sent Raquel there. They had scholarships, but Raquel didn't want to take the test.'

Raquel pursed her lips. By the time she was diagnosed with dyslexia, she'd fallen behind, and playing truant hadn't helped. She'd never have won a scholarship. None of the girls from St Luke's had, much to Edie's relief.

'So what brought you over this way?' Raquel asked.

'I was coming along the canal and took a detour. Decided to see the old place.'

Mrs McCann didn't appear to be listening.

'You know, Gina was a wonderful neighbour,' she said. 'Always helping out. When I had to go to work and leave Raquel, she'd step in. Helped everyone when she could and I know it wasn't easy, what with Vincent not working. She even had time for Martin Vickers, which was more than the rest of us. My god that man! So above everything and everyone, but not above gambling.

'If I'd been born with that sort of privilege, I'd have made something of it, not throw it all away on horses or whatever it was. But he looked down his nose at us like you would not believe. You know, he should have gone to prison. He had a job at a top accountancy firm before he stole their money to gamble. They wanted to keep it all hush-hush, doesn't look good for their clients. So they just sacked him. He was doing the books for some haulage firm when he lived here, the only people who'd have him.

'His wife wasn't like that. Valentina, beautiful name, posher than him, not a snooty bone in her body. I can't blame her that she upped and left. This isn't what she was used to.' Mrs McCann waved an arm at the window. 'That and being married to that miserable man.' Mrs McCann shook her head.

'Well, Mum—'

'I remember when I went into hospital, you know, with my woman's problems. My sister, Agnes, was going to have Raquel, but she couldn't find the space. Then her dad said he'd have her, but his new wife wasn't having it. That didn't last. Not saying Harry was a saint, still he didn't deserve that.'

Edie didn't know what that was and from Raquel's darkening look, she thought she'd better not ask.

'And Gina turned up at the hospital with flowers from the garden. Bluey-purpley ones, I've forgotten the name. Anyway, she took Raquel to stay with you until I was out.'

'Yes. We made a tent in our room out of sheets and pretended we were camping,' Edie said. 'Do you remember, Raq?'

Raquel smiled.

'Yes, I remember.'

'Well, it was such a relief,' Mrs McCann said. 'Because I was more worried about Raquel than the operation. Thought she'd have to go into care. And when I came home Gina would come over and cook a few meals for us and leave them in the fridge. I always paid for the food, mind. I always pay my way. Wouldn't want you to think I was a scrounger, Gina.'

'Edie,' Raquel said.

'Yes. Edie, of course. I wouldn't want you to think I was a scrounger.'

'No one thinks that,' Edie said.

'My point is, she did so much for other people and now I feel no one did anything for her. We didn't know she was unhappy. I suppose that's how the driver managed to get off so lightly.'

'Mum,' Raquel said.

'What, dear?'

'Come out the back, Edie,' Raquel said. 'I want to show you the garden. I've been planting.'

'Edie hasn't finished her tea,' Mrs McCann said.

In fact, she hadn't started it. She reached unconsciously for the mug.

'Bring it with you,' Raquel said.

'Oh Edie, I hope—' Mrs McCann began.

'It's fine,' Edie said, not sure what Mrs McCann was about to apologise for.

'Come on, Edie,' Raquel said.

Edie followed Raquel, leaving Mrs McCann on the sofa.

'Don't mind Mum. I told you, she gets confused.'

Mrs McCann started singing 'It's Too Darn Hot' as they left for the back door.

'What she said about Mum, is any of it...?'

'Ignore her. She makes half of it up. All that stuff about Mr Vickers' gambling. She doesn't know why they ended up here. Maybe it was gambling. Who knows? Anyway, look at the garden.'

Edie stood in the garden Dad had created for Mum. It was like stepping back four years. An overgrown, reckless blur of greens, blues and purples. Mum never allowed Dad to plant anything yellow or red. Terracotta pots spewed indigo blooms and a green man hung on the fence.

'How did you...?' Edie began.

'I know you thought I only came to yours to get fed. But I always loved the garden. The family who came after you

255

weren't like this lot. They were friendly, let me go over and take cuttings.'

'Did you do all this yourself?'

'Yes.'

'Is that our green man?'

'No. I got that at a charity shop. I get everything from them. No one wants most of this stuff. None of the pots cost more than fifty pence.'

'It's unbelievable, Raq. I should bring Tess.'

'It would be great to see her again,' Raquel said. 'I'm not just recreating your garden; I've got my own ideas. I want to go to horticultural college, that's why I actually go to school these days.'

'I thought it would take a gun to your head.'

'I still don't like it. But I need five GCSEs. I know you must think I'm thick.'

'I've never thought that.'

'Well, I'm not smart. But I should get five. I suppose you'll go to university or something?'

'Dunno.'

'You were always top at everything.'

'I'm not now.'

'What happened?'

'It's not primary school any more. You have to work.'

'I know, it's a bugger, isn't it?'

Raquel started laughing then stopped.

'So why did you really come back here?'

'Really? Because I wanted to see the place.'

Edie looked across the garden.

'What your mum said...'

'Forget that, she rambles on.'

'But what she said about Mum being unhappy.'

Raquel shook her head.

'Mum gets mixed up. Your mum was always fun.'

'I suppose so.'

'And about that man getting off lightly.'

'At least he went to jail.'

Raquel looked puzzled.

'I thought...'

'What? He went to jail right, two years?'

'If you say so.'

Raquel seemed embarrassed.

Nathan Bexley. His name was one of the memories she'd not managed to crush. That and Auntie Becca telling her that 'he'll be in prison for a long time'.

'You're saying he didn't go to jail, Raquel?'

'Maybe I got it wrong.'

She handed her mug of tea to Raquel.

'I've got to go, Raq.'

'Off already?' Mrs McCann said as they came back through the lounge.

'Have to go, Mrs McCann. Dad's expecting me.'

'Of course.' She paused to look Edie up and down. 'You know, Gina would have been so proud of you. You're quite the young lady and you speak in that lovely way, not too posh, just nice.'

Mrs McCann was still talking as Edie pushed through the front door. Raquel followed her outside.

'I'm so sorry, Edie. You shouldn't have found out like this.'

'I'll see you, Raq.'

Edie was glad to be back out on the street. The two children from earlier were pelting along the pavement on their bikes.

She couldn't see the woman from her old house but the front door was open. The front room had the same wallpaper as when they had left, but now it was peeling off. Free newspapers and takeaway leaflets littered the carpet. How could she have thought of it as their house? Their house didn't exist any more.

Chapter 39

Tess: July 2018

Mr Vickers is unrecognisable, close to bald with a body that has thinned from lean to gaunt. I guess when we knew him he was in his early thirties, which seemed ancient back then. However, now he really does look old, bordering on elderly, worse than Dad. I think he must be ill. An impression added to by his limp handshake, though he's lively enough and makes no reference to his health.

He's moved to Kidderminster, into a low-rise council block, brick with PVC windows. It's obvious he's just tidied for my visit. The hall cupboard has a coat arm trapped in the door and after I sit down in the lounge, I find a jumper stuffed under one of the cushions. It's a large room with one enormous sofa, a wooden chair and a TV. Its emptiness gives the feeling of cold despite the day being warm. Mr Vickers pulls the chair up next to me on the sofa.

'Thanks for talking to me, Mr Vickers,' I say.

'Call me Martin. When I heard they'd found Edie, well, I knew I needed to talk to you. So sorry, by the way.'

'I'm surprised you remembered us.'

'Of course I remember all about you,' he says. 'You and

your sister, little imps. Tell me, who was it used to lead who astray? I could never work it out. Valentina always said Edie, she was the cheekiest, but then, it's always the quiet ones, you know.'

He says it with warmth as if reliving cherished moments. Though, the only memory I have of being discussed by Mr and Mrs Vickers is when, through the thin walls, we heard him ranting about us always being at his house when he wanted his wife to himself, accusations that misplaced items had been snaffled by 'those two strays from next door' and a conviction that most of his salary went on feeding us. He didn't realise those were our best days. I had the excuse of being a child. Maybe Mr Vickers had managed to reach his thirties with no experience to lessen his belief that having two noisy and nosey kids next door was the worst life could throw at you.

'It was almost like having our own children. I think Valentina would have adopted you if she could have.' He pauses and brushes his forehead as if to erase an unpleasant thought. 'So, what have you been up to? It's been a long time. I won't say how you've grown, but I'd still recognise you if you hadn't said you were coming. Same hair, same solemn face.'

'Was I solemn?' I ask.

'Oh yes, you always looked like you had the weight of the world on your shoulders.'

I've always thought being solemn was a result of losing my mother and twin. When I think of Gladstone Road I remember Mum singing and Edie and I getting up to mischief. I don't remember being solemn. Perhaps my memory is as flawed as Mr Vickers'.

'So, Tess, how exactly can I help you? If you've come to raid my fridge, I'm afraid there's only half a pack of sausages and they're out of date.'

I try to laugh at his little joke.

'It's a bit awkward, Martin.'

I stumble over his first name.

'Is it about Valentina?'

'How do you know that?'

'Why else would you be here?'

Edie is with me now. I hear her nervous giggle and nearly laugh myself. How silly it was to break in next door when we could have just asked him. It's taken us twenty years to find the courage. Us, the word just comes to me.

'You'll think it's odd but I wondered if you know where Valentina's living now?'

Whatever response I expected, it isn't this. Mr Vickers chuckles and shakes his head.

'You come here and ask me that. I thought you could tell me.'

'Me? No.'

He looks puzzled.

'You really don't know?'

'How could I?'

He laughs again.

'He's sly. I'll give him that.'

'Who?'

'Ray, your uncle.'

I must be slow today.

'She left me for him. Valentina left me for Ray.'

What he's saying makes no sense.

'Ray's still with Becca. They've been married over thirty years.'

'Then she must be a very understanding woman, your aunt.'

He laughs then looks at me and stops.

'I'm sorry, I shouldn't have blurted it out. Only I was sure you knew.'

'How can he be with her when he's with Becca?'

'I don't know the arrangement, Tess.'

Is he lying? He has no reason to. How does it work? Does Ray divide his time between two houses? I think of Becca's nervousness when Ray arrives late. Is she worried Ray won't turn up? Is that why they move so frequently, so the neighbours don't ask too many questions?

'Ray can't still be with Mrs Vickers or... I'm not sure what to call her.'

'She's still Mrs Vickers. We never got around to divorcing.' I look down and notice the wedding ring still on his finger. 'I've not met anyone else and I think your aunt would draw the line at bigamy, even if Ray wouldn't.'

'So you still speak to her, Mrs Vickers?'

'Occasionally, over the phone, for legal reasons. We were left some money a while back, had to sort all that out.'

'I can't believe they're still together.'

'There's something else you should know, Tess, perhaps why they've lasted so long. There's a child. Apparently, Ray adores him.' Mr Vickers glances at me. 'You're upset. Of course you must be. Valentina said you and Edie were close to Ray and his wife, they were your second parents.'

'Yes,' I say.

'I really thought you knew. That's why I laughed. I thought you were up to something.'

'Why were you so sure I knew?'

'Something Valentina said once.'

'What?'

'I got the impression Edie knew, so I assumed you did, too.'

'Did Mum know?'

'Yes. She was very kind, often came to see me after Valentina left. She seemed as upset as me.'

'It was around the same time,' I say.

'Val and your mum were good friends, but Gina had no idea about this Ray business until Val left. Thank God she never lived to hear about the baby. Gina and I talked a lot. She helped with sorting out bills and working the washing machine. Valentina used to do all of that. All I did was go to work and come home. I didn't realise. Too late now.'

He speaks the words as if he doesn't believe them. The wedding ring is still on his finger and the sofa is far too large for a man on his own, has he been waiting twenty years for her to come back? My childhood dread of Mr Vickers made me cautious about coming; I didn't expect to end up feeling sorry for him. And Becca, all those years of lies and the permanent strain on her face. 'Sour-faced', Raquel called her once. She must love him more than she ever shows.

'Do you remember when the police came to your house that time, after Valentina left? They handcuffed you.'

'Not my finest hour,' he says.

'What happened?'

'I went to Ray's work and punched him. One of his workers recognised me. Of course Ray wanted it all brushed under the carpet and the police were happy to let me off with a caution. What made you remember that?'

263

I decide it's not the best time to tell him that Edie and I thought he'd murdered Valentina and stashed her body in the freezer.

'Nothing,' I say. 'Would you be able to give me Mrs Vickers' address?'

'I don't have it.'

'You said you spoke to her.'

'Over the phone and no, I'm not going to give you her number. Let sleeping dogs lie. If your aunt accepts it and I've accepted it, there's no point stirring things up.'

'I don't want to stir anything up. I just want to ask her something about Mum.'

Mr Vickers takes on the stern expression I remember from childhood.

'The past is best left alone, Tess, trust me.'

'Will people stop saying that? I'm sick of it.'

'Who else said it?'

'It doesn't matter.'

'Ray, your Dad?'

I don't reply.

'When you're my age, the past is hard to ignore. There's more behind you than in front. You're young. Move on.'

'I can't. I need to know. After all I've been through with Mum and now Edie...'

Her name acts as a code word. Mr Vickers sighs.

'Very well then. I'll tell you where she works. Just turn up; if you ring she'll try to avoid you. And don't tell her it was me who told you where she is.'

Chapter 40

Edie: March 1998

The blurred image on the microfiche held in the library looked nothing like Mum. She doubted Nathan Bexley's resemblance was any more accurate. Edie moved to the next sheet.

She had imagined Mum's death had made the national news. But it barely made the local papers. The front pages on the week it happened were dominated by a controversy about city councillors granting planning permission to a new shopping complex, in which they had a financial interest. On the week of the trial, a charity match at the local football club gained extensive coverage. Mum's death was tucked away, several pages in, next to a dog returning to its owners after being lost on holiday hundreds of miles away, and another about confusion over school uniform policy.

Where Mum's death was reported, the journalists noted that she had excess alcohol in her system. All hinted at suicide. A passing motorist had seen her running from the waste ground behind the road. Nathan Bexley claimed a man was running after her. Gina Piper had not run straight into the road. She had stopped, looked behind her, then walked calmly into the path of the lorry. At the last second, she looked back, to face where she'd run from.

Nathan Bexley admitted to being drunk in charge of a motor vehicle, he denied causing death by dangerous driving. The jury disagreed, his argument that Gina had run into the road was dismissed. The speed and amount of alcohol were the overriding factors. Sober and within the speed limit, he would have been able to brake in time.

The judge had taken into account Gina's presence on the dual carriageway as a mitigating factor. Bexley was not wholly responsible. The sentence was two years' imprisonment, suspended for twelve months. Gina Piper was not a regular drinker, had no history of depression, no recent trauma and had written no note, but no one had come forward to explain why she was wandering along the dual carriageway on a Wednesday the week before Christmas.

Who knew she was so unhappy? Mrs McCann had asked. Well, someone must have known.

It had never occurred to Edie that Mum wasn't happy. She was too young. What child thinks about its mother's happiness? Mothers are there to feed, clothe and amuse you. Mum did all these things and more. She laughed, sang, danced and played with them. She organised barbecues and made them a tepee in the back garden out of an old blanket, painted with birds, animals and flowers. Mum was fun. That's what everyone said when they mentioned her, wasn't Gina fun?

If you're fun, no one suspects you of being desperate and depressed, which she must have been. But looking back, Edie couldn't point to anything. Mum cried when Grandpa Len died. The only other time she could remember her being sad was when Valentina Vickers left. She'd been quiet then, no fun. That silly story she and Tess made up about Valentina being murdered explained it at the time. Mum was sad because her friend had gone. Edie had found her. She should have been happy.

The papers didn't know her. She would never have left Tess and her. Mrs McCann just loved a gossip. Hints in the newspapers became facts, repeated and embroidered. Mum wouldn't kill herself. It was an accident. That it happened soon after Valentina left, a coincidence.

She printed out a copy of the Stourbridge News report on the inquest and put it in her bag.

*

At home, Edie lay on her bed and opened the scrapbook, 'The Case of the Missing Cakemaker', and read through the notes. The date Valentina left. The date Edie lost her nerve, trying to talk to Mr Vickers. The date they raided his house. Conclusions drawn: Valentina is dead, the body hidden. Childish games. But in amongst the wild superstitions and warped logic there was a death, their mother's. Edie took the short, photocopied newspaper report on the inquest that showed Mum's picture, wrote suicide? in the border in blue ink, folded it up and slipped it under the cover they'd made from a wallpaper scrap.

'What are you looking at?'

She hadn't heard Tess come in. How did she manage to do that?

'Nothing,' Edie said.

'That's our old scrapbook, the one we had for Valentina.'

'So?'

'What do you want it for?'

'I just needed some spare paper.'

'Well don't use that.'

Tess walked over to the bed where Edie was sitting.

'We don't need it any more,' Edie said.

'We still don't know what happened to her.'

'Nothing happened to her. It was just a silly kids' game.'

'It's not silly; she went missing. I suppose you want to get rid of it because Michaela wouldn't think it's cool.'

'Don't go on, Tess.'

Tess snatched the book and hugged it to her chest.

'I'm sick of Michaela. This book is ours and if you don't want it, I do.'

She marched off and slammed the door behind her, taking Edie's precious photocopy with her.

Chapter 41

Tess: July 2018

I'm reminded of my first investigation as I wait, half hidden in the bushes, outside the insurance firm, where Valentina is an office administrator. That silly story of her murder, 'The Case of the Missing Cakemaker', filled the gap in our lives when she left. Edie and I were hurt that she never came back to see us. A substitute parent while Mum worked and Dad watched TV, she'd fuss over us and stuff cake down our throats. She and Mum were nearly the same age and both were different from the other women in the street, more chic and glamorous; though I wouldn't have used those words at the time. If I'd have been asked, I'd have said they were nicer.

How exciting it used to be, sneaking around and making notes. I don't think we really believed she was murdered, or it wouldn't have been such fun.

I'm not excited now, though my hands are shaking and sweat trickles down my back. It's hot, no cooler at five o'clock than midday.

Workers start to spill out from the office. Men in short-sleeved shirts and women in cotton print dresses. Some of them stop in the shade of the building and light cigarettes;

they form a small group near the door. No one notices when I go over to join them and light up. I watch for Valentina to leave.

I needn't have worried about recognising her. She sweeps out of the front entrance at ten past five, still slim, with her hair swept back into a neat chignon, large eyes, barely any make-up. She's more formally dressed than her colleagues, in a beige suit and white blouse. Some of the male smokers look up as she passes; she doesn't return their glances.

She walks straight past me then turns back on herself down a path at the side of the building. I drop my cigarette and follow her. When I reach the path, Valentina turns around.

'People saw you outside the building, they'll have seen you follow me here,' she says.

'Valentina it's me. Tess. Tess Piper.'

'I know who you are.'

I don't understand her reaction. I expected a smile, a hug, talk of the old days, not this nervous hostility.

'I just want to talk,' I say.

She looks over her shoulder. No one's there.

'We'll sit on the wall at the front.'

'OK,' I say.

'You first.'

I walk in front of her, go back the way I came and sit on the wall facing the building, so all the smokers can see us. Valentina sits down, an arm's length from me.

'I don't suppose this is a chance meeting?' she says.

'No.'

'A social call?'

This is the woman who spent hours making me drop scones and Welsh cakes, who asked about my day at school and sewed on the odd button. Something's wrong, more than a passing bad mood. Does she think I'm here to confront her about her affair with Ray?

'In a way, it is a social call,' I say.

'In what way?'

She crosses her arms.

'I wanted to ask about Mum.'

She makes no response.

'I was so young when it happened. None of it makes sense.'

Valentina's arms stay folded.

'What are you trying to make sense of?'

Her voice is flat and hard.

'I was told she killed herself.'

She shows no reaction. Another one who knew.

'I'm not sure what I can tell you.'

'You were friends,' I say.

'Neighbours. It's not like we confided in each other.'

She sounds like Becca.

'You'd spend hours talking together.'

'You were a child. It may have seemed that way to you. We didn't speak that much.'

'Mr Vickers said you did. He said you were close. It's not just my memory.'

'What does he know? Pathetic little man.' She spits the words out. 'He was jealous of me talking to anyone, even you two. He told you where to find me, didn't he?'

'No.'

'Don't lie.' She looks at the passing traffic. When she turns back to me she's angry. 'I really can't help you and I have to go.'

'I know about you and my uncle, I'm not here about that. It's none of my business.'

She tilts her head to one side.

'You've only just found out?'

'Yes.'

She shakes her head.

'Do you think I'm stupid?'

'I don't know what you mean?'

'What exactly did Martin tell you?'

'That you'd left him for Ray.'

'That's all?'

'And that you have a child.'

She's on her feet.

'So that's why you're really here.'

'No.'

'You're not going anywhere near Thomas.'

'I didn't even know his name.'

'And the home has strict security.'

'What home?'

'You stay away from me and you stay away from Thomas or there'll be consequences. I'm going to my car now. I don't want to see you again.'

'Valentina,' I call to her.

She doesn't turn back. I feel like I've been punched in the stomach. I stay seated on the wall. I don't even want a cigarette. What did I say to frighten her so much?

Chapter 42

Edie: March 1998

E die had to get out of the house. It didn't matter that the day
was wet and windy. She'd go to Irregular Records and do
some browsing, anything to get away from Tess and her moods.

The two-mile walk into town let her save on bus fares and
meant more money for buying vinyl. Wet squalls battered her
and by the time she reached the coach station, her thin coat
was wet through and her hair had blown and stuck across
her face. The coach station wasn't somewhere she'd come at
night, but it was too cold and early on a Saturday morning
for the drunks, druggies and prostitutes the area was famed
for. An empty bus trundled past, spraying her with muddy
droplets. Edie didn't care. It was better than being at home,
at least here she could breathe. Even if that breath was filled
with mud, stale urine and diesel.

A man carrying a guitar case came out of a side street
ahead. He walked with long, quick strides, not the slow trudge
of a drunk. Edie looked ahead to her destination. The high
towers of the town centre rose in front, a futuristic safe haven
from the dirty streets surrounding her. She didn't notice that
the man ahead had stopped.

'Alright?' he said.

She looked up at him through wet strands of hair. It was Bob, Michaela's boyfriend. On Friday lunchtime Michaela had been boasting about their weekend away together. They were going to London and seeing some bands. Had Michaela been lying?

Bob was standing in front of a hairdressers. The Upper Cut's windows were covered in faded photographs of women with haircuts she'd only seen in 1970s' TV series. It looked out of place amongst the bars, bookies and boarded-up shops.

'Don't I know you?' he asked.

'No,' Edie said and hoped he didn't link her to Michaela.

'Weren't you at The Green Leaf?'

'The what?'

'The café on the ring road.'

'Oh, yeah.'

She guessed he expected her to thank him for getting rid of those boys. She didn't say anything.

'What were you doing there?' he asked.

'I was going to Irregular Records.'

She waited for him to mention that his girlfriend went there.

'I go there myself sometimes. What do you buy?'

Edie thought she should say Stax, that's what Michaela liked, but she still didn't know enough about it.

'Northern soul.'

He raised his eyebrow and nodded.

'More into the classic Motown and Stax myself.'

All the stuff Uncle Ray looked down on.

'Sounds good,' she said.

'Do you ever go to Reckless?'

Edie shook her head.

'Where do you go?'

'Nowhere really.'

Edie started walking. She shouldn't be standing in this area, talking to a strange man. If she hadn't recognised him she would have crossed the street. He started walking, too. His easy lope kept alongside her, despite the fast pace she'd set.

'So you weren't out last night?' he asked.

'No.'

The rapid clack of her shoes on the pavement filled the silence. She felt too young and awkward. She didn't want to look him in the face, sure that he was sneering.

'Were you out last night?' she said at last.

'Yeah, just playing with some mates.' He lifted the guitar an inch. 'Had a few drinks, nothing special.'

He spoke in a strong local accent. It suited him. Rough but friendly. It reminded her of being on Limewoods, where no one cared how you spoke or what your dad did for a job, or even if your dad had a job. Tess often pointed out how much she'd changed to fit in at JAGS. How much effort she put into her vowels, how she skimmed over what Dad did for a living. Edie knew just from his voice that none of this would matter to Bob.

'Are you in a band?' she asked.

'Yeah, I play bass.'

Edie didn't know how that was different from a guitar and couldn't think of anything else to say. Did he recognise her from the school gates? She doubted it; she was just another girl in uniform.

'Are you going to work? Is that why you're up early?'

'No, not today,' Edie said.

'What do you do?'

She thought of the faded 1970s' beauties in the window of Upper Cut.

'I'm a hairdresser.'

'And what do you think of my cut?'

'Very nice,' she said without looking at him.

He laughed and stopped walking. Without thinking, Edie stopped, too.

'I can't work out if you're shy or just stuck up.'

Edie's face felt hot.

'Neither.'

'Prove it.'

'Prove what?'

'That you're not stuck up.'

'I haven't got anything to prove,' she said and started walking again.

'Come to Reckless with me next Saturday then.'

Edie carried on walking. Did she really like him or was she only interested because Michaela talked about him so much? Next Saturday and another endless evening with Dad and Tess would stretch before her, or she'd be with Aveline and Char comparing Joseph Amberley boys to the St Philip's ones.

'Alright,' Edie heard herself say.

She turned to look back. He hadn't moved from where they'd last stopped. His head was to one side, smiling.

'We'll meet at The Lamb and Flag along the canal side at eight,' he said.

'I don't know.'

'Got plans?'

'No.'

'See you there then.'

Edie nodded and turned to carry on walking into town.

'Hey,' he called. 'What's your name?'

'Edie.'

'Aren't you gonna ask me mine?'

She'd forgotten she shouldn't know it. She turned again.

'What is it?'

'Bob,' he said.

'Bob.' Edie nodded.

He turned down a different street. Edie walked the rest of the way into town without registering where she was going.

Chapter 43

Tess: July 2018

Valentina's upset me. I thought of her as our friend, when she only used us to ingratiate herself with Ray. Now she's frightened of me. I sift through what she's told me to try to understand what's changed so much.

I've missed something. I didn't ask the right questions. Not that Valentina gave me much chance. The moment she saw me she was on edge. Of course I wanted to know about her and Ray. How it had come about, when and why. Were they still lovers, were they still in love? Yet none of this is relevant. Images flit through my mind that I can't form into questions.

I have enough time to walk to the station along the towpath and so cut away from the road. It doesn't bother me that it was on a path like this that Edie was killed. In fact, it makes me feel closer to her. Green slime floats on the water and the odour of decaying vegetation hangs in the air. I imagine her walking along the path, lost in thought. Happy. I like to think of her as happy before she died.

The other pedestrians are travelling in the opposite direction to me, away from the town centre. A pub garden backs onto the canal. It's filling up as workers flee their desks to exploit the heatwave, women in sunglasses and sandals, men looking uncomfortable in shorts that usually only see an outing twice a year. I'm nearly beyond the pub garden when I hear a shout.

'Hey.'

I ignore it.

'Hey, Tess.'

I turn around. A man is at one of the pub tables opposite a woman with her back to me. He's wearing beige shorts and a red baseball cap. I raise my hand to my eyes to block out the sun and see him better. He swings his leg over the bench and jogs towards me. It's Jem. He takes his hat off and scrunches it in his hands. Perhaps he realises it makes him look like a teenager.

'This is a nice surprise,' he says and kisses me on the cheek like a favourite auntie. 'How are you? I saw the funeral on the news. I would have called but you didn't return my texts. Are you upset with me?'

'No, it was just bad timing.'

His companion looks over. She's older than I thought from behind, older than Jem.

'I don't want to interrupt anything,' I say.

'You're not. April's an old friend. We're just catching up.'

I glance at her. She's trying to smile but it's not reaching her eyes. Catching up means more to her than it does to him.

'I was walking to the station. Go back to your friend. See you another time, yeah?'

'No, wait, tell me what's happening.'

'Stay and enjoy your drink,' I say.

He looks over at April.

'We'll go somewhere else. Carry on, I'll catch you up.'

I keep walking and don't look back. I feel vaguely guilty about April. I catch the words 'old friend' being whispered. Jem seems to have a lot of those. I wait for him further along the canal. When he arrives, I'm not sure what to say.

'Michaela never contacted me. I thought she might come to the funeral,' I say eventually.

'You weren't seriously expecting her to turn up, were you?'

'She must have heard about the funeral and they were best friends.'

Jem opens his mouth to speak, then closes it again.

Maybe Edie was best friends with Michaela the same way that Charlotte claimed to be with Edie.

We take a few more steps in silence until Jem says, 'I wouldn't try to see Michaela, if I were you. She isn't the girl you knew from school. She's become bitter and spiteful.' She sounds exactly like the girl I knew from school. 'If she tells you anything it will be a lie, just to hurt you.'

We stop at café-bar Chez Marie. Decked out in primary colours, it resembles a fast-food restaurant more than the Parisian chic its name suggests. Still, they have alcohol and table service, so it's not all bad. We order a bottle of Picpoul and some hummus and pitta chips.

'What were you doing in town today?' Jem says.

'I had to see someone. Nothing interesting, a family matter.'

The wine arrives. Jem's agreed to share a bottle, though I'm sure he'd prefer lager. The waiter offers it to him for tasting.

'Just pour, mate,' he says then smiles at me. 'What can I say, I'm common.'

'Wine's wine,' I say.

'Finally, someone of my opinion.'

'Met anyone who isn't?'

'I had to go to a family thing with Arabella at the Gossingtons'. Lots of Lucinda and Simon clones banging on about the grape and the vintage. I just drank what I was given. Most of them thought the gardener had turned up on the wrong day and was taking advantage.'

I smile. Jem's company is what I need right now. I can't face any more pained expressions and pity. I gulp at the wine and top it up immediately.

'Is it like that in your family?' Jem asks.

'No, I told you, we're fake posh,' I say. 'Besides, there aren't enough of us left to be snobby.'

'What was your thing today? Was it to do with Edie?'

'Yes. No. It's complicated.'

'Have the police got anywhere?'

'No. They won't track down the boyfriend. They're half accusing Max.'

'The boy who used to follow her around?'

'You knew about him?'

'I think Michaela mentioned it once. Do you know him well?'

'Fairly.'

Jem looks surprised but doesn't press me on it. I don't want to tell him Max and I were together and have him thinking what Raquel thinks, that I'm just as much a stalking victim as Edie. I don't want to be a victim. Max may have engineered our meeting but I had a say in it. I chose him. I need to tell myself that.

'There was an article in the newspaper suggesting Jevan Hardcastle was responsible,' Jem says. 'Do you remember him?

He's been in jail for years but he killed three women in the nineties.'

'The police looked into his activities. What happened to Edie doesn't fit. The women he killed were prostitutes. All his crimes were further to the north; he didn't know this area. And he buried all of them within a small area of woodland.'

Jem pours us both more wine.

'I don't think it was a stranger,' I continue. 'That suggests a motive other than some sick fantasy. He knew her.'

'But who would want to hurt her?'

'I've gone over it in my head so many times. And every time it comes back to the boyfriend. Our friend Raquel never met him, but she thought he was older, maybe married. He wouldn't want to come forward, Edie was underage and he'd be worried his wife would find out, or he could have been someone with a reputation to protect, like an MP.'

'An MP?' Jem says, raising his eyebrows.

'I know it sounds unlikely, but everyone really liked Edie. I can't think of anyone else who would want to hurt her.'

'Someone must have disliked her.'

'I did think of Valentina Vickers. She didn't dislike Edie, but she might have wanted to shut her up.'

'Who's Valentina Vickers?'

I've drunk quite a bit now and find it easy to tell him how I was trying to find out why Mum might want to kill herself. About Raquel telling me that Edie came to see her with a newspaper article and my chat with Martin Vickers, which led me to Valentina. I tell him how she made pets of me and Edie and that we investigated her 'murder' after she disappeared. Only to find out, twenty years later, that she'd left him for my uncle Ray and they have a child.

'He's called Thomas.'

'Do you want to see him?' Jem asks.

'I don't know, it frightens me. What sort of home is it? Is he ill? Disturbed? Is it hereditary?'

'Whoa, you're getting a bit paranoid here.'

'She acted like I was insane or dangerous. She was terrified I might try and see Thomas. What does she think I'm going to do?'

'I don't know,' Jem says. 'But you think she could be the killer?'

'Not really, no. However much of a two-faced cow she's been and however much it would be convenient for her to have Edie out of the way, I can't see her killing anyone. She might break a nail.'

Jem laughs and shakes his head.

'You're mental,' he says. 'Do you think it's your uncle she's really scared of? He can't have wanted your aunt to find out.'

'That makes sense but you don't know Ray, no, he's a softy, he worshipped Edie and Martin Vickers thought Becca already knew.'

'But they're still both married to other people. Sounds weird to me.'

'I did say it was complicated.'

'You're not wrong.'

Jem refills our glasses.

'I'm missing something,' I say. 'You know, like when you're talking about a film to someone but you can't remember the actor's name. And just as you're falling asleep, you sit up and go John Hurt.'

For some reason Jem finds this amusing. He's getting through his wine as quickly as me.

283

'I'm thinking all this stuff with your uncle and this Valentina woman, this was all going on around the same time your mum died?'

'Pretty much.'

'So they could be connected.'

'How?'

'I don't know. Were they close, your mum and Ray?'

'He was her brother-in-law. We all spent loads of time together. What are you saying?'

Jem leans back in his chair.

'Nothing, I was just asking. You did say she was really upset when this Valentina left her husband for Ray.'

'She didn't know that at the time.'

'Stuff like that gets around fast. Everyone loves a scandal. It's hard to believe rumours never got back to her.'

'Mr Vickers assumed I knew and said that Edie did. We had a whole scrapbook dedicated to finding Valentina and that's where Edie chose to put the newspaper article. To hide the newspaper article. It wasn't a mistake; she hid it in that scrapbook deliberately.'

'If you replace the rumours about this Vickers bloke for your uncle...' Jem says.

'No,' I say. 'That's not possible.'

'Why?'

'It just isn't.'

'OK,' he says.

He picks up the wine and drains the remnants into our glasses.

'Is there anyone else you can ask?' he says. 'What about Rachel or whatever her name was?'

'Raquel?'

'Yeah.'

'I'm pretty sure she told me everything she knows. Her mum might know more, but she's got dementia.'

'My nana had that. Didn't know what happened in the last five minutes but could go on forever about something that happened fifty years ago. You should go and ask her.'

'Yeah. Maybe. I'll think about it.'

I finish my glass in a couple of gulps. The bar's filling up with suits.

'It's rubbish here,' Jem says. 'I know a place ten minutes that way. They play live music later on.'

'I've got to get back,' I say.

I stand up. My head is spinning. I put my hand on the table to steady myself.

Jem comes round to my side of the table.

'You don't have to go home,' he says.

Jem pays the waiter and asks him to call a cab. He puts his arms around me and kisses me. And for a second the pain's gone, there's only the evening air and his lips on mine.

I've been the grieving twin for twenty years. Don't I deserve some escape, deserve to live, be something more than poor little Tess? I can be like Ray, taking what he wants from life and not caring about the consequences. Could Jem be right about Mum, was she just collateral damage in Ray's appetite for life?

Chapter 44

Edie: March 1998

It was unusual for Auntie Becca and Uncle Ray to come to their house. Normally, they all piled round to whichever place Auntie Becca had just decorated, where she would make trayfuls of food for everyone and only nibble from a small plate herself. Here, she observed her usual habit of not eating in their house, despite the lasagne, salad and cream gateau she had brought with her. Instead, she told them about her plans for their new kitchen.

'We're going to knock through to the dining room then open it up onto the garden at the back with sliding doors. Though I'm not sure about the man opposite. He's got too many cars on that drive and they're always changing, always coming and going. I was woken up by an engine revving at four o'clock this morning.'

Dad wasn't eating either; he preferred to smoke and was standing at the kitchen door, his cigarette held behind him.

Edie looked at her full plate of food. She wasn't hungry. She watched Tess munch through the salad and Uncle Ray piling lasagne into his mouth, slopping cheese sauce and tomato down his chin. At that moment she hated all of them.

'What happened to him?' she asked.

Auntie Becca stopped talking and looked over to Edie.

'You mean Mr Ahmed?'

'Who's that?' Edie asked.

'The man I was just talking about, who lives opposite.'

'Why would I ask about him?'

'Who are you talking about then, Edie?'

'Nathan Bexley.'

'Who's Nathan Bexley?' Tess asked.

Dad carried on smoking, his eyes fixed on the floor. Auntie Becca's were turned to Uncle Ray, who had a pile of lasagne dangling halfway between his plate and his mouth. He glanced towards Dad, then put his fork down.

'Who's Nathan Bexley?' Tess asked again.

'Come into the dining room, Edie. I got a couple of new singles at that record fair last week.'

'Can I come and listen?' Tess asked.

'I've got you a CD,' Uncle Ray said. 'We'll put it on later in the lounge where we can all listen.'

'Don't you want some gateau first?' Auntie Becca asked.

Tess hovered between the two before opting for the gateau. Edie followed Uncle Ray to the dining room.

'Why were you asking about that man?' Uncle Ray asked.

'What happened to him?'

'Don't go upsetting yourself, Edie.'

'What happened?'

Uncle Ray rubbed the stubble on the side of his face.

'You know what happened, Edie, he went to jail.'

'Did he?'

Uncle Ray looked at her.

'Yes.'

287

'You're a liar, Uncle Ray.' She said it softly.

He appeared to jump.

'What's come over you, Edie?'

'You've always been a liar,' she said.

'Edie, come on.'

'Are you still seeing Valentina? I know about her. I saw you together once.'

Uncle Ray stared at her then went to shut the door.

'Keep your voice down, will you?' Ray said.

'You lied about her.'

'I didn't actually lie.'

'And about Mum and Nathan Bexley.'

He leaned towards her and took her arms.

'Edie, we all thought he'd go to prison and get a long sentence. We'd told you and Tess that's what was going to happen. We couldn't face telling you when he got off virtually scot-free. You were much younger then, you'd been through enough.'

'Why did he get off?'

'It's ridiculous. Gina had had a bit to drink.'

'Mum hardly ever drank.'

'And another motorist said she looked as if she...'

'Yes?'

'As if it were deliberate. It wasn't, of course, she was just careless. If that man hadn't been drunk and speeding, he could have stopped in time.'

'So they think she killed herself?'

'No one thinks that. It was a legal trick, to get Bexley off.'

'And he never went to jail?'

Uncle Ray shook his head.

'Where's Nathan Bexley now?' Edie asked.

'I don't know,' Ray said. 'I don't trust myself with knowing.'

'You're telling me the truth this time?'

'Yes, Edie. And that business with Valentina was a mistake. Your aunt knows and she's forgiven me. You're not a child any more, you must know these things happen.'

Edie thought of Raquel's father. She knew these things happened.

'And what about the baby?'

'What baby?'

'Valentina was pregnant when I saw her.'

He pauses.

'Did you tell Gina about this?'

'Yes, why?'

He leant back and didn't say anything.

'What did happen to the baby, Uncle Ray?'

He didn't answer for a moment, seemingly lost in thought, his lips moving, talking silently to himself.

Eventually, he said, 'He died, Edie, and I haven't seen Valentina for years.'

'Uncle Ray,' Tess was calling. 'Where's my CD?'

'I'll get it for you in a minute.' Uncle Ray lowered his voice. 'Have you said anything to Tess?'

'No.'

'Well let's keep it that way. Come back to the kitchen,' he said.

Edie waited a moment before following. Uncle Ray must be used to telling lies. Why should she believe him now? She didn't care about Valentina but she did want to know the truth about Mum. She was going to find out exactly what happened. She was going to find Nathan Bexley.

Chapter 45

Tess: July 2018

It's half ten. I'm alone in Jem's flat. He didn't bother to wake me before he left. I check my phone then slump back onto the bed. Clouds of dust puff up from the sheets and catch in my throat, making me cough. I'm desperate for some water.

I've not seen Jem's flat in daylight before. It's a studio and, even by my standards, a total mess. The kitchen area is a few feet away and I have to clamber over piles of clothes and magazines to reach it, then hunt for a clean glass. I can't find one and the sink's too grimy to wash one up. The effort of moving has made my temples throb, so I go to the bed and collapse on the rough sheets.

Why am I here? Who is Jem other than Michaela's ex? Hardly a recommendation. He's left me here alone in his grubby flat. I presume he's gone to work. But I don't know that or what he does for a living. I don't even know his last name. Going without saying goodbye doesn't bother me but he could have left me a clean glass, my throat's so dry it's about to crack.

A beer can's standing on the floor next to the bed. I pick it up and shake it. A small amount of liquid swills back and forth. Anything to relieve my throat, I lift it to my lips. A stale yeastiness wafts up my nostrils. I have to put it down or I'll throw up. Jem's such an arse leaving me here in this dump and it irritates me that he's so sure I'm a nice girl and won't go rifling through his stuff and take something.

I should teach him a lesson. And if I take something I can't come back, so it's a good idea. I rouse myself to leave the bed and search through his drawers to find something. He's got some unopened letters addressed to Jeremy Robertson. I thought he might be a Jeremiah or something interesting. I consider opening them but they look like bills. A disused mobile lies next to some loose change and a near empty bag of weed. It's of even less interest than value.

I don't need to take something to make sure I don't come back. I'm not interested any more. Maybe it was just the lure of Michaela's ex, a revenge she'll never know about, twenty years too late.

My throat's getting worse. After a quick spray with his deodorant, at least he's got some, I leave.

At the corner shop I grab a can of Tango. It's sickly sweet, but I need the sugar and the fizziness wakes me up enough to try to find my bearings. I take my phone out of my pocket. It shows two missed calls. The transport app tells me I'm the wrong side of town and I need to get a bus to the centre and another one out to get home. Post-rush hour, the top deck of the bus is empty, apart from a couple of schoolboys playing hooky and rolling a joint. I ignore their protests when I open the window and it flutters their Rizla paper away.

'No smoking,' I say and point to the sign.

'Bitch.'

The missed calls are from Max. I decide to ignore them.

291

By the time Dad gets home I'll feel more awake. Maybe I'll make dinner, pasta with tuna, even I can make that, and we'll chat like father and daughter instead of strangers.

*

'Tess.'

Dad calls to me as soon as I step inside the hall.

I stop.

'Tess, is that you?'

He comes out of the lounge. He's supposed to be back at work.

'Where have you been?' he asks.

'Out, with a friend.'

'I need to talk to you,' he says.

He walks back into the lounge and lights a cigarette.

Need to talk. I'm sure most daughters have heard their fathers speak these words, in anger or concern, at some point in their life, but Dad has never said them to me before. His voice sounds strained and flat.

The ashtray is full. It's emptied every night. Perhaps Dad didn't go to bed again. The light from the French windows emphasises how grey he's become. Not just his hair but his skin, as if a fine film of dust has settled across it.

We need to talk. We never talk.

'I waited up for you last night. Where were you?'

'I told you, I was with a friend. I didn't call because I thought I'd wake you. You could have called me.'

'I suppose so.'

He pulls on the cigarette. Half of it disappears in one drag.

'There're things I have to say to you, Tess.' He shuffles over

292

to his chair by the TV. It's on mute, showing a football match. 'Sit down.'

I take the sofa. Dad stays standing but he's looking at the floor. If there's something difficult to say, Dad won't say it. Edie's death and Mum's have always been non-subjects. What's so important that he's prepared to put himself through this?

'I loved your mother.' He pauses. Am I supposed to speak? He sits on the arm of the chair, eyes still glued to the floor. 'I wanted the best for all of you. Wanted to keep you safe. I failed.'

'You can't think it's your fault,' I say. 'What...'

Dad raises his hand. I fall silent.

'It is. I sat back, when I should have done something.'

'What could you have done?'

'You're all I've got left, Tess.'

'Well I'm not going to die. Not soon, anyhow. Dad, you know I'm always here. London's less than two hours away.'

He shakes his head.

'The way you carry on, Tess. Again, I never stopped you. Probably should have. I thought Max would calm you down.'

'I'm not that bad.'

'Edie was a teenager when she died. She was wild and I didn't know how to control her. I thought she'd grow out of it. She never got the chance.'

'Why are you telling me this?'

'You want to be her so much.'

'That's not true.'

'I can see it. Trying to live the life she would have had. But that wouldn't have been her life, she would have grown up, got a job, found a fella and had kids. Not out all hours with God knows who.'

'I just stayed out with a friend, Dad, it's not a big deal.'

'I watch the TV every night, waiting for a knock from the police about you, like I did for Gina and Edie. And then you start this.'

'Start what?'

'Ray rang me. You've been to see Valentina. You've got to stop this, Tess.'

The cow said she wouldn't say anything.

'I have the right to know,' I say.

'We're trying to protect you.'

'From what?'

For a moment Dad looks up and catches my eye. I think about what he said before, that I must know the killer. I hadn't believed him, but the expression on his face makes me start to. He looks down again.

'I'm sick of people trying to protect me. You say I need to grow up but you treat me like a child, not even a teenager. We can't tell Tess this, we mustn't mention that. I need to know the truth. Edie had to go to the newspaper archives to find out that Mum killed herself.'

Dad takes a sharp intake of breath.

'And I had to find out from a note Edie wrote. You never told me anything. A man got a criminal conviction for something that wasn't his fault.'

'It was his fault he was drunk. There's no proof Gina killed herself.'

'We both know she did. And you still can't say it to me.'

He doesn't reply.

'What aren't you telling me about Edie?'

Dad shakes his head.

'You don't understand, Tess.'

'What don't I understand? Do you know who it was? Was it Ray? Edie knew stuff about him.'

'It wasn't Ray,' he whispers.

'Valentina looked terrified when I went to speak to her. Who else would she be scared of?'

'Tess, please.'

The cigarette is down to the butt. It stays wedged between his fingers as he puts his head in his hands and starts to cry.

'Please, please stop, Tess. You're all I've got.'

'But Ray?'

His shoulders are shaking.

'Honestly, Tess, it wasn't Ray. I don't know who it was. But you're putting yourself in danger.'

'How?'

'You just are. I can feel it.'

He's still crying and even though I'm angry with him and don't believe he knows as little as he pretends, I say, 'OK, Dad.'

Not because I'm going to stop, but because I can't bear to see him like this. And I am a little scared. What if I am in danger, from something, or someone?

Chapter 46

Edie: March 1998

The Lamb and Flag was as dirty and neglected as the old men sitting at the end of its bar, smoking roll-ups. They were clustered round a small television set, watching a boxing match. The pub was sectioned into alcoves made of dark wood and mottled glass. A musty sweetness rose from the carpets and mixed with the stench of tobacco. Was it the smell or her nerves that made her nauseous? Why had Bob chosen this place? She was sure he'd never bring Michaela here. And it was obvious that she was far too young. At any moment the barman would turn from changing the optics and tell her to leave. And Bob would be standing behind her laughing. But no one looked up and before the barman turned, Bob was at her side.

'I didn't think you'd come,' he said.

'Why not?' Edie asked.

'You didn't seem the sort somehow.'

She had the same feeling she'd had last Sunday when she'd bumped into him, that she was the butt of some private joke.

'What sort?' she asked.

'Dunno,' he said. 'Let's find somewhere quiet.'

He linked his arm with hers. His elbow brushed against her breast. She suppressed her impulse to pull away as he led her to an alcove. She sat down and shuffled along the seat.

'What do you want to drink?'

'Bacardi and coke,' Edie said.

She thought it sounded sophisticated.

'My nana drinks that,' Bob said. 'Are you sure?'

'Well, I...'

'How about a Smirnoff Ice?'

'Is that...'

'Is that what?' asked Bob.

She was about to ask him if that's what he bought for Michaela.

'That's fine,' she said.

While he was at the bar, Edie looked at herself in the mirror on the wall opposite. The pub's darkness, her eyeliner and blusher couldn't hide how young she looked. Vonnie's friendship with the doorman had got her in to The Hub, not Michaela's make-up. She was still worried that the barman would say something, but perhaps the pub was desperate for any trade. It was fairly empty for a Saturday night.

Bob returned with her drink. She sipped on its sharp, sherbet fizziness.

'Is it OK?' Bob asked.

'Yes,' Edie said.

Bob drummed his fingers against his glass.

'I've been thinking,' he said. 'We've met before, haven't we? Before the record shop. But I can't place it.'

Edie felt sick again. The schoolgirl polyester skirt and blouse were pushing through the black top and make-up.

297

'I'm not sure,' Edie said.

'It'll come to me,' he said.

And if it did? She tried to change the subject.

'Is this pub your local?'

'Nah,' he said. 'But we'd never get a minute to ourselves at The Railway.'

Edie supposed that was where he took Michaela and she mustn't be seen there.

'And it's nearer the club,' Bob added.

'Club?'

'You didn't think we were staying here all night, did you? We're going to Reckless, remember?'

She worried that the doormen at Reckless might be sharper-eyed than the barman at The Lamb and Flag. Reckless would be only the second club she'd ever been to. She longed to tell Char and Aveline and of course couldn't. The one person she should be able to tell was Tess, but she seemed to disapprove of everything Edie did these days, and even worse, she might tell Uncle Ray or Auntie Becca.

Seeing Bob behind Michaela's back didn't bother her. She knew Michaela had been out with other girls' boyfriends. Natalie had never forgiven her for stealing away a St Philip's boy called Zac. To Michaela it was a challenge, one she always won. Bob might not last long, anyway. She'd been telling Edie all about a rugby player from Birmingham University who she might meet for a drink.

'Where's Reckless?'

'Downstairs at Finley's.'

'Right,' Edie said, none the wiser.

'We won't stay here long. It's not up to much.'

Edie looked at the soggy carpet and the old men with their pints of bitter.

'No,' she said.

'Just a couple more,' he said. 'Drink up.'

*

'Any ID, love?'

The doorman was about seven-foot tall. His love wasn't friendly. Edie opened her mouth to speak. Bob jumped in.

'She's with me,' he said.

'She still needs ID.'

'Sure,' Bob said. 'It's here.'

Bob passed him a ten-pound note. The doorman glanced behind him before slipping it in his pocket and stepping back.

'Enjoy your evening.'

Bob took her hand and led her down the steep, narrow stairs, which vibrated beneath her feet to the opening bars of Jackie Wilson's 'Whispers getting Louder'. Edie's neck tingled.

The Reckless club was as dirty as The Lamb and Flag, but that was all they had in common. Not much larger than Auntie Becca's living room, the floors and walls were in stripped wood and it was lit by low-glow red lights. Edie stopped at the bottom of the stairs to look round. Bob pulled her towards the bar. A crowd of mixed age and styles leant over it, screaming their orders above the music.

'Same again?' Bob shouted into her ear.

Edie nodded. He dived into the crush. She edged towards the dance floor. People not much older than her were dancing with others nearer to Dad's age. She spotted the owner of

Irregular Records crafting some complicated steps, making light of his large belly. It was the sort of place Uncle Ray would come, if he ever went clubbing these days.

Bob returned and pushed a bottle into her hand. She slurped at it. She'd already had three in The Lamb and Flag and was enjoying the warm alcohol running through her.

'Can we dance?' she asked.

'Huh?'

'Can we dance?'

She had to shout in his ear.

'Finish this first.'

He raised his bottle. Edie took no time at all finishing hers just as the thumping bass of 'The Night' came on.

'We have to dance to this,' she said and dived onto the dance floor without waiting for an answer.

The music merged with the alcohol, spinning her round, the dance floor a blur. She forgot the time, and that she was only fourteen and shouldn't be here with her friend's boyfriend. All she felt was the movement of her body combining with the beat. Everyone was too involved in their own dancing to notice her, except the guy from Irregular Records, who nodded. She smiled back.

Edie danced every song. Before she knew it they were playing 'I'm on My Way'. Uncle Ray had told her this was always the last track of the evening. She looked at her watch, it was just before two, not like the all-nighters she'd heard about. The club was still full, the dancers savouring every last note.

Bob put his arm around her.

'Better go,' he said.

The cold night air was a shock after the heat of the dance floor. She shivered and Bob pulled her close. She bent her head a little, he reached down and kissed her. The same tingle she'd had on the stairs coming into the club ran down her neck.

'You can come back to mine if you like,' Bob whispered in her ear.

It would have been easy to go with him, to carry on her adventure.

'No, I can't,' she said. 'Not tonight.'

He smiled, he'd not expected her to say yes.

'Let's get you on the bus.'

He put his denim jacket around her shoulders when it arrived.

'Give it back next time you see me,' he said and kissed her again.

She hugged the jacket to her and ignored the drunken shouts and songs of the other passengers. She'd found something away from her little world, something she loved.

*

Edie shut the front door as quietly as she could and tried to listen for movement in the house above the ringing the music had left in her ears. She took her shoes off and padded along the hall. Light was flickering along its floor from a black and white film, playing on mute in the lounge. Dad was snoring softly in his armchair.

She climbed the stairs. Tess's light was off. Edie went to

her own room, slipped Bob's jacket under her pillow and switched the dressing table lamp on. In the mirror she could see her eyeliner had smudged beneath her eyes. The effect pleased her. In one night she looked five years older.

Then she heard footsteps and her door swung open.

'It's nearly three, Edie,' Tess said.

'So?'

'Where have you been?'

'Nowhere you'd like.'

'You stink of smoke.' Tess came into the room and sniffed. 'And alcohol.'

'Go back to your own room, if you don't like it,' Edie said.

She was light-headed from the drink, music and Bob. He had kissed her, she could have been with him now. Instead, she'd come home to Tess. She envied the girls at school, who only had their parents to deal with.

'Were you out with Michaela?' Tess asked.

'What do you care?'

'I was really bored here on my own.'

'That's cos you are boring. Anyone would be bored stuck here with you for company.'

'Just cos I don't want to hang out with boys and smoke and get drunk like you. You can hardly talk.'

'Go to bed, Tess,' Edie said. 'I need to sleep.'

She dragged a cotton wool pad across her eye to remove the make-up. In the mirror she could see Tess behind her, standing by the door. Edie carried on taking her make-up off. Tess slipped away. She pulled the cotton wool across the other eye. It was covered with a pleasing amount of mascara. She should have face cream and a negligee, something sophisticated, not her pink pyjamas.

One day she would escape. She could have done it tonight, not come back at all, gone with Bob. The thought excited her and scared her at the same time. She put Bob's jacket on over her pyjamas, lay on the bed and dug her nose into its collar where it had rubbed against his neck. It smelt of him, the club, excitement and escape. She closed her eyes. Soon, she thought, soon.

Chapter 47

Tess: July 2018

Mrs McCann stares wide-eyed out of the window from the front seat of the car. Her expression of wonder makes me think she only leaves the care home when Raquel takes her. Or it's possible she went on a trip yesterday and doesn't remember.

'Are you alright, Mum?' Raquel asks. 'Do you want the window down?'

'That would be nice.'

Raquel presses the driver-side button for the passenger window and a blast of air cools the car. Mrs McCann raises her chin and the wind brings colour to her cheeks. She could be young again.

'I'm not sure how much she can tell you. I doubt it's anything the police will be interested in. Have they made any progress? They came to see me about Max.'

Her pitch strays higher as she stares at the road straight ahead.

'You don't think...'

She glances over.

'No,' I say. 'Max. He's not capable of violence.'

Raquel looks unconvinced. Her father was good with his fists. She thinks all men are capable of violence. It makes me worry about her husband. Then I think how she smiles when she talks about him, which reassures me.

'I used to come here as a girl,' Mrs McCann says when we reach Coughton Park. 'It was different then, they had a witch's hat and swings over there. I don't recognise these new things they've got.' She points to the climbing frames in the shape of a train. 'Do they still have swans on the bottom lake?'

'Yes, Mum,' Raquel says. 'We were here last Wednesday. Don't you remember?'

She turns to me and shrugs.

'She doesn't ask about Fleur when I don't bring her,' Raquel says. 'It makes me want to cry. She always wanted a grandchild, now she's got one, she doesn't remember. She talks about your mum sometimes, and Edie. How can she remember all those years back and not what happened last week?'

I can sympathise. I often find memories from twenty years ago are clearer than the previous night's.

'It's common with dementia, isn't it?' I say.

'People tell me that. It doesn't make it any less frustrating.'

'She recognised me.'

'Not really. She thinks you're Gina.'

Not as pretty, Raquel is too polite to add.

Mrs McCann pulls out the bread Raquel has brought and walks along to where the swans have gathered in a shaded spot below overhanging willows.

I wait till she's out of earshot before asking Raquel, 'Do you think it will be alright to talk about Mum or will it upset her?'

'No,' Raquel says. 'She likes to talk. And she seems quite good today. Buy her an ice cream, she'll love that.'

After she's fed the swans, I fetch ice creams, a 99 with strawberry sauce for Mrs McCann and mint Cornettos for Raquel and me. We sit at the edge of the lake, on a bench carved out of a tree trunk, to eat them.

'Oh Gina,' Mrs McCann says. 'It's like the old days.'

'This is Tess, Gina's daughter, remember?' Raquel says.

Mrs McCann stares at me.

'Tess?' Her brow creases. 'I do get confused. Time seems to fold, like curtains.' She pats me on the hand. 'Tess. All grown up. Without Edie. Never thought I'd see you alone, could never separate you. Where's she gone?'

'Mum,' Raquel says.

'Has it really been so long since I last saw you, Tess?' Mrs McCann asks.

'Nearly twenty-five years. We moved away from the street after Mum died.'

She nods.

'Poor Gina. When they told me I thought, she's finally done it. But they said it was an accident.'

The ice cream's sugar cold bubbles in my stomach.

'And Mr Vickers took it bad. I didn't think he would. But he was never the same. Neither was the street. It lost its heart after Gina. Just families coming and going. A man was killed a few years later, an accident at work. I only found out because it was on the news.'

I take a deep breath to quell my nausea.

'Do you know what happened?'

She looks at me.

'A wall collapsed. He was crushed.'

'I mean to Mum, to Gina.'

She licks her ice cream and I'm not sure she's heard, until

she says, 'I wasn't sure it was an accident. No one was. Poor Gina.'

She starts humming 'It's Too Darn Hot' and laughs and carries on licking her ice cream.

'It's a good one, plenty of strawberry sauce.'

I glance at Raquel. She shuffles in her seat.

'Why do you think it wasn't an accident? Was it something to do with my uncle Ray?'

'Ray, oh Ray, yes, so handsome. Too handsome. If he'd married Gina, none of this would have happened.' She puts her head to one side. 'Poor Vince. Poor Gina. It's no wonder that the whole Valentina thing pushed her over the edge. It's always the same, she thought she was the only one he loved. They all thought that. He was a charmer, like my Harry.'

Mum and Ray. Jem was right and I should have known. You're so like Gina, Ray had sighed. His devastation at her death had been more than the familial love of a brother-in-law. I remember how he used to dance with mum, how they spun round laughing, as Dad watched on from the edge of the room. When had it started, how long did it last?

'And I did always wonder about those two girls,' Mrs McCann says.

'What? What did you wonder?'

My voice is fast and urgent, which seems to have scared her.

'What did you wonder, Mrs McCann?'

She doesn't respond. Her eyes retreat under the folds of skin. I look at Raquel; she shakes her head.

'Come on, Mum, you're tired.'

'But if I could just ask her,' I say.

'No,' Raquel says. 'Not when she's like this.'

307

I no longer feel sorry for an old woman who had once been kind to me. I want to shake her, shake her until she remembers something, anything. I stand up and walk away to hide my frustration.

'Tess,' Raquel calls.

I turn around and she flicks her head in the direction of the car park. I follow them. Mrs McCann is no longer so sprightly; her walk is slow, as an old woman's should be.

On the way back she doesn't look out of the window and stares at her hands instead.

'I'm sorry I got angry with you,' Raquel says after we've dropped her mum off.

'It's alright.'

'I think I'm overprotective because I get so annoyed with her myself.'

I nod.

'I've never heard that before,' Raquel asks. 'About Ray and your mum. I knew they were together before your Dad but not that they kept seeing each other. What made you suspect?'

'Something someone said. What did she mean, "I wonder about those two girls?"'

'I don't know, Tess,' she says.

But she does know what she meant. As do I. Is Ray more than just my uncle?

308

Chapter 48

Edie: April 1998

She had to concentrate, check the street names and find the right stop, but when the bus reached Marlborough Drive, she hesitated. The address had been easy to find, there was only one N. Bexley in the phone book. She'd scribbled it down along with the phone number on the school exercise book she was carrying with her. Now she'd arrived, her courage evaporated. Only the bus driver staring at her impatiently, as she hovered at the opened door, made her jump off. She landed on the pavement with a jolt, looked up and down the street and realised she had no idea why she'd come.

What would a man, who downed alcohol before ploughing two tons of metal over a woman without looking back, care about anything she said to him? He would make her feel stupid and hysterical. Still, she found herself turning off the main road and heading up Marlborough Drive.

Her step slowed as she neared number fifty-seven, a semi-detached bungalow. Next door had a neat hedge and a caravan in the drive. Fifty-seven's drive was empty. An attempt at a shrubbery, with only three plants, lay under a window, framed with flaking paint.

Edie loitered at the end of the drive. Two cars passed. She must look odd just standing there, shifting from one foot to the other. Two more cars passed. She didn't have to stay, she could just go home, forget about it. A lorry rumbled by and the ground trembled. She closed her eyes, heard the screech of brakes, the screams of passers-by and her vision flooded with red.

She walked up the drive and rang the bell. No one answered. A vacuum cleaner was humming away inside. Edie banged on the door. The humming stopped and the door opened.

Edie looked down to see terry towelling slippers on top of a deep-pile carpet, both in dusky pink. Above the slippers hung thick tights running up to a grey skirt and a lilac jumper. The woman was shorter than Edie, shorter even than Tess. Her grey hair was cut close to her head and finished just below the ears.

'I don't want anything.'

She barely looked at Edie as she spoke.

'I'm not selling anything.'

'And I'm Church of England and already give to charity.'

Edie stayed and said nothing. The woman looked at her properly for the first time.

'What are you after then?' she asked.

'I'm looking for Nathan Bexley, does he still live here?'

Edie spoke slowly and clearly to counteract her urge to gabble.

'Who are you? What do you want with him?'

Again, Edie didn't reply. The woman glanced over to her neighbour's.

'You'd better come in,' she said.

Edie hesitated. She didn't want to go inside. She'd imagined confronting Bexley on the doorstep. But something told her he wasn't in, the vacuuming, the empty drive.

The bungalow's interior matched its exterior, tidy but unloved. Coming from the lounge, Edie could hear a radio, tuned to a local station.

Edie turned to go into the room. The woman reached in front of her and shut the door.

'This way,' she said.

She led Edie to the kitchen at the back. It was cold and smelt of bleach.

From her hair and clothes, Edie had thought she was Mrs McCann's age. When she turned to face her, she could see the woman wasn't much older than Dad. She frightened Edie. She might be small but the close-cut hair gave the impression of a helmet and her eyes were fixed and intense.

'So, what do you want with Nathan?' she asked.

Edie tried to think of something to say.

'Well?' the woman said.

Edie hadn't practised this scene. However awkward or painful her conversation, she had always imagined it would be with him, Nathan Bexley, not this woman. Who was she? His wife?

'You're not the first,' the woman said.

Her voice wavered and Edie realised she was more upset than angry.

'The first what?' Edie asked.

'The first girl to come and find him.'

'No?'

Had Tess come to find Nathan Bexley and not told her? Would Tess really do that? Maybe Edie wasn't the only one with secrets.

'The other one was older. Of course I knew,' she said. 'He was always away on the road, always staying a night longer here and there. Never thought it would come back to haunt me.' She raised the corner of her mouth in a sneer and looked at Edie again. 'How old are you?'

'Fourteen.'

'Fourteen?' She stared out to the cracked patio behind. 'So what did your mother tell you about him?'

'I'm not sure...'

'Or did she not know him so well?'

This woman thought Edie was someone else.

'Did she think she was the only one, your mother? Cos she wasn't.' The woman's voice was louder now. 'There were loads of them, a string of floozies up and down the M6, probably in France too, for all I know. They were just an amusement on the road, like listening to the radio, or a glass of beer in the evening. Did your mother tell you that?'

Her eyes ran over Edie's face.

'After the accident he gave all that up. I bet she wondered why he never came back.'

'Accident?'

'So he didn't even tell her about that. I thought not. Some stupid bitch ran out in front of him. She'd had more to drink than he had, ran into the road, deliberate. He had no time to stop. I did wonder if she was another one, did it to spite him, but I couldn't find any link and she was too close to home. He preferred them at a distance. Where are you from?'

'London,' Edie said.

'If she'd wanted to kill herself, why didn't she throw herself into the canal instead of ruining someone else's life? Selfish bitch. Stupid, selfish bitch.' The woman was too involved with her story to see Edie flinch. 'Lost his job. Lost his licence. They would have put him in jail if that other driver hadn't come forward. The other witness disappeared. It destroyed Nathan. He was never the same.'

'Where is he now?' Edie asked.

'Gone.' She looked at Edie and smiled. 'Heart attack. Two years ago. That woman may as well have killed him at the same time as herself. So if you're after money you're too late.' She looked at Edie. 'That other girl cried when I told her her daddy's dead. Are you going to cry?'

'No,' Edie said.

'Good. I hate scenes. What are you going to tell your mother?'

'My mother's dead.'

The woman changed her stance and looked hard into Edie's face.

'Who are you?'

'Thanks for your help,' Edie said.

'Tell me your name. You're not from London, I can tell from your accent.'

Edie was already at the front door.

'Tell me your name.'

Edie opened the door. The woman reached from behind and tried to push it shut. Edie used both hands to pull it open enough for her to jump outside.

'I know who you are,' the woman said.

Edie's legs felt weak. She had to force them to move and take her away from the house.

'I know who you are,' the woman shouted. 'You look like her.'

The woman followed her down the drive.

'What did you come here for? She got what she deserved.'

Edie kept going until she reached the main road. She turned to see if the woman was still following her. She wasn't there and the drive wasn't visible from where she stood. Her legs were shaking and barely held her upright. She grabbed onto a lamp post for support. Sickness overwhelmed her. She tipped forwards and threw up. A woman walking a toddler yanked the child away.

'Bloody disgusting this time of day,' she said.

Edie squatted down. She thought she was going to faint. She had to consciously push air in and out of her lungs until the nausea lessened, then used the lamp post to pull herself back to her feet.

The woman wasn't lying. It all fitted too neatly to be a lie. Her anger was real and raw and Edie's matched it. Mum had left them. Deliberately. Left them with Dad and a house filled with cigarette butts and ready meals. She thought of the woman's words.

'Stupid bitch. Stupid, selfish bitch.'

Chapter 49

Tess: July 2018

I don't go straight home after Raquel drops me off; instead, I head to the local park and walk the long route around it. When I reach the other side, I turn back and make another circuit. The heat has started to drain from the day, though dusk's a long way off. Between hot and cool, between day and dusk, I hate it. It makes me restless.

The insurance company Valentina works for has its number on the website. She must know about Mum and Ray. Given her hostility when I went to see her, I don't hold out much hope but give it a go anyway.

'Who's calling for her, please?'

'Tess Piper. It's important.'

There's a pause, fast whispering in the background.

'Please don't call this number again and if you're found on the premises, we'll call security.'

The line goes dead.

That bloody bitch. What is wrong with her? Threatening to set security on me, as if I were some escapee from Broadmoor.

I make two more circuits of the park. By now, the light's

fading and I'm bored. It's a short walk up from the main road to the mini-roundabout next to Dad's street. A car slows behind me and beeps. I think it might be Jem. I turn and see Ray's Mercedes. The window opens. I lean down and get a blast from the air conditioning inside. Despite the cold air, Ray's shirt is half unbuttoned and his hairline moist with sweat.

'Get in,' he says.

Ray's my uncle and I've known him my whole life but I feel like a small child being lured into a stranger's car. I hesitate.

'Tess, I'm holding up the traffic.'

I climb in. Ray pulls away without indicating and gets honked. I expect him to turn right towards home. Instead, he turns left and pulls over.

His face is hot and he grips the steering wheel with both hands.

'What the hell are you playing at, Tess?'

'What do you mean?'

'Don't play stupid. Tell me what's going on.'

Ray's never spoken to me harshly before. It intensifies the feeling that he's a stranger. But then Edie was always his favourite. I've only ever been a poor substitute. A role I've been happy with until now.

'I've got a question for you, Ray.'

'What?' he says.

'Are you my father?'

Ray hits the steering wheel with the palm of his hand. A deep line runs from his forehead to his nose.

'Is that what... of course I'm not your bloody father.'

'How can you be sure?'

He raises his eyebrows.

'I know the facts of life.'

'I don't doubt that,' I say.

I press the down button on the window. I hate this air-conditioned cold. Ray takes a deep breath.

'I'm sure, I'm not your father. It's not possible,' he says.

I don't respond. He's a good liar. If I hadn't known he'd had years of practice, I might believe him.

'You're not to contact Valentina again. Do you understand me?' he says.

'Why are you so bothered? What do you think she's going to tell me?'

'You're harassing her.'

'Did she know about you and Mum?'

Ray hesitates.

'I don't know what you mean.'

'Come on, Ray.'

I stare at him, he can't hold my gaze.

'It was a long time ago, all over before I got with Valentina.'

'Did Mum know it was all over?'

'It's not how you think, Tess.'

'Then why won't you answer my questions?'

'I've never lied to you.'

'What about Edie, did you lie to her?'

He doesn't answer at first then says, 'She was too young to understand.'

'To understand what?'

He sighs.

'About Gina and me.'

'I'm not a child, Ray.'

'I don't know what you want me to say. I loved her. She loved me.'

317

'And?'

He shakes his head and releases the steering wheel.

'You know, me and your dad, you wouldn't believe our childhoods. We grew up in a slum. Limewoods would have been luxury. All those old houses have been knocked down long ago: outside taps, sharing a toilet with eight other families, rats running everywhere, going hungry cos your grandfather drank all his wages.'

'What's this got to do with anything?'

'What I'm trying to tell you is when you're offered wealth on a plate, wealth you could never earn for yourself, even if you worked for a hundred years and all you have to do is...'

'Marry the boss's daughter.' I shake my head, 'I never took you for such a cliché, Ray.'

'Becca's dad, Roger, suggested it. He knew he was dying. He was worried about Becca. She'd never worked, had no idea how the business was run. He didn't let her have boyfriends and she couldn't look after herself.'

'Daddy's little girl,' I say.

'Things aren't always as they seem.'

'This is exactly as it seems.'

'Becca always liked me. I was just a labourer on the sites at first, then I became foreman, thanks to Becca, I think. I was too young to be a foreman. She used to come out to the sites just to talk to me. She was so young, she hadn't finished school. I never thought anything of it, until Roger said about his illness and the company. It was too easy and I was stupid. I thought Gina would understand. I thought I could have them both.'

'You're right, you were stupid.'

'Gina wouldn't speak to me. Next thing I knew she was engaged to Vince. What could I say?'

'Did Dad know about you two?'

'Of course.'

'Then why?'

'She was different, your mum. I remember the first time I saw her, I asked her if she was from Brazil; it was the most beautiful and exotic place I could think of. Vince was too shy to talk to her, but I know he felt the same. She had so much life about her.'

'Until she killed herself.'

'That nearly killed me too, Tess. It was a bad time. I came close to losing my mind. Becca pulled me through. She's strong, your aunt. People think she's all about frills and china cups. There's more to her than that.'

'Did you keep seeing Mum after she married?'

'No.'

He's lying.

'And the other women?'

Ray pauses.

'I know what you think of me, Tess, but things are complicated. Becca had, I don't know how to say it... she had problems. She took Valium for years. Thank God she's off that. But it meant we were never close, physically I mean. And Valentina was, well, she was just there.'

'How many other women were just there?'

He spreads his palms.

'None of them meant anything. Gina should have known that. It's only because Valentina fell pregnant that things got out of hand. She turned up at the office with a suitcase. What could I do? I found her somewhere to live and looked after the boy.'

'Your son.'

'Yes, my son.'

His face is set hard.

'What's happened to him? Valentina said he's in a home.'

Ray nods.

'He has a degenerative condition. Had it since birth. He won't live much longer.'

'Do you love him?'

'I care for him as best I can. There's not a lot anyone can do.'

There's a hardness to Ray no one knows, because he's fun and friendly. He doesn't love his wife or son and still everyone thinks he's wonderful.

'Is it hereditary, whatever he's got?'

'You're not worried, are you, Tess?'

'Should I be?'

'I don't know. Maybe if you have children.'

'Not exactly on the cards.'

He looks across the car bonnet, his eyes unfocused.

'I always loved you and Edie, more than Thomas. And no, not because I thought you were mine.'

'You loved Edie,' I said.

'And you, Tess.'

'Not like you loved her.'

'You sound like Becca; she always thought we were too close. She was nearly as jealous as you.'

'I wasn't jealous.'

Ray raises his eyebrows but doesn't contradict me. I don't remember being jealous of Ray. Michaela yes, but not Ray.

'How long have you known?' Ray asks.

'I only just pieced it together. I was never as smart as Edie.'

'And now you hate me?'

The strange thing is, I don't.

'I think Edie must have found out about the baby somehow and told Mum.'

'She saw Valentina in the park with me.'

Ray brings his hands to his face.

'I thought Gina would grow to love Vince.'

'She did,' I say.

'He never made her happy.'

'And you did?'

'No. Neither of us did and she punished me. I saw the whole thing.'

'You were the other witness, the man who was running after her and disappeared?'

'She confronted me about Valentina. We were just talking and she ran off into the road. Gina looked at me. She ran out in front of the truck and turned back to look at me. To make me suffer. And I have, believe me, I've suffered.'

'You put those lilies on her grave,' I say.

He nods. For a moment I feel sorry for him, this man who drove my mother to her death.

'Was it guilt that made you give Dad a job and pay for us to go to JAGS?'

'No. I always wanted to do that. Gina wouldn't let me. Vince was easier to persuade.'

'Dad's always been easy to persuade.'

We sit in silence. It's dark enough now for cars to have their lights on. The beams swirl around us. Ray turns to me.

'You won't say anything to Vince, will you?'

I think of the pain on Dad's face when he talks about Mum and Edie.

'No,' I say.

'Good, I'll drop you home.'

'I can walk.'

I open the door and get out.

'Bye, Ray.'

'Bye. And if you've got any more questions come to me, not Valentina.'

I turn and lean on the door frame.

'I do have something to ask.'

'What?'

'Why was Valentina so scared of me?'

Ray draws breath.

'I don't know. Maybe it was just surprise.'

'That's not the reason, Ray.'

I push myself upright and shut the door. Ray presses a button and the window slides up. I walk back to Dad's. If that's who he is, my dad.

Chapter 50

Edie: April 1998

'Are you still seeing what's-his-name?' Edie asked.

'Paul? No. Got someone else, Nev,' Raquel said.

'And?'

'He's alright, I suppose.'

They were seated in McDonald's in the town centre, drinking diet coke through a straw. She always met Raquel away from the estate now. She didn't want to go back to Limewoods.

Today they'd been shopping together. She'd told Tess she was meeting Michaela. That stopped her wanting to come.

Raquel had her first boyfriend three years ago. At fourteen she must be an expert and Edie wanted to know about them. She felt lost with Bob. She didn't understand him. Raquel was bound to have some idea.

'I'm kind of seeing someone,' Edie said.

'That skinny boy who follows you around?'

Raquel had spotted Max the last time they met.

'Of course not,' Edie said. 'This is someone different. Bob.'

'Bob? No one's called Bob any more. Is he fifty?'

Edie laughed.

'No. I think it's a nickname.'

'For what?'

'Not sure.'

She waited for Raquel to ask her something else about him, but she was more interested in swirling the remains of her diet coke and ice round the bottom of her cup. The problem was that Raquel assumed Edie had had loads of boyfriends. Apparently, everyone knew JAGS were boy-mad and the second you arrived they lined up to take you out. If only. Edie had never told Raquel this wasn't true because she didn't want to admit she knew nothing about boys.

'He's a bit older,' Edie said.

'You need to watch out then.'

Watch out for what? Why couldn't Raquel tell her plainly?

'I'm seeing him tonight.'

'Yeah?' Raquel slurped on her diet coke. 'You gonna get that top then?'

Edie let it drop. Raquel wasn't interested.

'I'll go back and get it,' Edie said. 'By the way, you were right, Raq.'

'About what?'

'My mum.'

'What do you mean?'

'About suicide.'

'I never said that,' Raquel said.

'Your mum said she was unhappy.'

'What does your dad say?'

'Nothing. Uncle Ray said it was Nathan Bexley's fault.'

'That's probably how he sees it.'

'I guess so.'

Edie sucked hard on the straw. There was something else

she needed to ask Raquel, something that had been swirling at the back of her mind and recently surfaced.

'Do you remember once, you asked me if I knew why my mum and dad got married?'

'No,' Raquel said.

She didn't look at Edie and she was sure it was a lie.

'You did.'

'Can't remember,' Raquel said.

'Why would you say something like that?'

'Dunno. I told you, I can't remember.'

'I could ask your mum.'

'Don't,' Raquel said. She put her coke down and stared at Edie. 'You can't. She's ill.'

'What's wrong with her?' Edie asked.

She liked Mrs McCann, despite her gossiping.

'Not sure, she's going in for tests. You can't talk to her.'

'Then tell me why you said it.'

Raquel fiddled with her straw.

'It's just more stuff Mum comes out with. I don't know if it's true. It's something she told me once. I think she'd had a couple of sherries, because when I asked her again she wouldn't repeat it.'

'Repeat what?'

'Are you sure you wanna know?'

Edie wasn't sure. Wouldn't it have been better if she'd never known the truth about Nathan Bexley? She should get up, leave and forget she'd ever asked. But she knew she wasn't going to do any of those things.

'Tell me.'

'She said your mum and uncle Ray used to go out together.'

Edie waited. Raquel fiddled with her straw some more.

'And Ray married Becca because her father gave him the business.'

'That doesn't explain why Mum married Dad.'

'Mum said it was the next best thing.'

Raquel wasn't lying now. She looked nervous, as if Edie was going to get angry with her.

'That doesn't make sense. You don't marry someone's brother because he's gone off with someone else. And Mum could have had anyone she wanted.'

'Yeah, you're right.'

Raquel didn't sound convinced.

'I think your mum got it wrong,' Edie said.

'Probably. You know, that top really suited you. We should go back before it's gone.'

Raquel slurped down the last of her drink and tossed it into the bin on the way out. Edie followed her.

Mum and Uncle Ray together. It wasn't possible. Raquel's mum was a gossip. A lovely lady but a gossip. The guy at Irregular Records said that Uncle Ray went to dances with a girl called Gina. It must be a coincidence, Gina's a common enough name. She didn't believe it. She'd not think about it again.

The memory of Mum and Uncle Ray dancing together in the front room of the old house came to her. They were sharing jokes and laughing. No, Edie thought, it's not possible. I won't believe it. She wandered out of McDonalds in a daze and was only brought to her senses by Raquel's elbow digging her in the ribs.

'Hey, look. It's that boy again.'

Edie looked in the direction Raquel was pointing, just in time to see Max's green parka disappear into a doorway.

Chapter 51

Tess: July 2018

Dad's not home when I get in. I wonder if he's out looking for me, Ray probably called him. The lounge curtains are drawn. I pull them back and open the patio doors to lift the smell of stale smoke, a little pointless as it's interwoven with the furniture and carpets.

I always imagined Dad sitting here every day, his brain as silent and passive as him, when it must have been whirring. His wife wasn't really his wife, his children may not be his children, and all the time he loved us, even if he was unable to protect us. How easy it was to ignore Vince, the unemployed loser to Ray's fun, successful businessman. Other people had paid a high price for Ray's fun and success. Dad was one, Becca another, and neither of them seemed to realise.

I've realised and Mum did. What about Edie? Had she found out, confronted him, angered him, stripped away the veneer of the indulgent uncle? It's no use, however angry I am with Ray I can't see him as a murderer, especially not of Edie. They had a special bond; they were alike in so many ways. People were drawn to them and they didn't have to try. If they wore strange clothes or listened to unfashionable music it was because they were cool and didn't follow the crowd, not because they were out of date and odd.

No one minded their selfishness, their casual cruelty, they were just happy to be with them. It's not like that for most people, for Dad, for me. OK, it's like that for me, but only with Max, and now I'm starting to guess why. And now I can finally answer Cassie's question of why I stayed with him, he makes me feel how the Edies and Rays of the world must feel all the time, more wanted than wanting, more needed than needing.

It's a pity Dad never found someone who made him feel like that. I sit in his chair and take out a cigarette. Mum was the very worst person he could have fallen in love with. She only emphasised how much he wasn't Ray. How did that make Dad feel, how long did he put up with it? Did he snap one day? Did he find out Edie and I weren't his daughters? Was it revenge on Ray and Mum, taking their favourite child? It makes no sense. Mum was dead by then. Besides, Dad couldn't hurt anyone; he could never even get angry with us, let alone violent.

I stub my cigarette out. I can't face Dad today. I need to get away and think. I'm no closer to finding Edie's boyfriend and I can't find a link between Mum's alleged suicide and Edie's death. This house, this town is sucking me in. If I don't go soon, I'll never leave. I could go back to London now, take the next train. The police investigation is going nowhere.

My throat's becoming scratchy, so I fetch some cold water to soothe it then check my phone for the train times. There's one in an hour, I could catch it if I leave now. I'm about to go upstairs to get my case, when the phone rings.

'Hi,' I say.

'Hello.'

A moment's silence.

'Who's this?'

'Hello, Tess. It's Simon here. Simon Gossington.'

It takes a couple of seconds to remember him. Michaela's father.

'I wasn't sure if I should phone you. It was difficult to say anything at the time, what with Lucinda and Arabella being there. My wife doesn't know I still go to see Michaela and Arabella gets upset if she's mentioned.'

'I see.'

'Lucinda thinks it's best to leave her to it. Tough love.'

The line goes quiet again before he continues.

'I saw her yesterday and said you'd been looking for her. She wants to see you.'

'Really?'

'She remembers you well. I think it's a good sign, wanting to be in touch with her old friends. Don't you?'

'Yes,' I say without thinking.

Michaela took no notice of me at school except to sneer. Why would she want to see me now? Perhaps she's another drama-chaser and has heard about Edie. It fits in with what I remember of her, holding court, always the centre of attention.

'I tried to persuade a couple of the others to go but they're fair-weather friends. Do you remember Vonnie?'

'Not really.'

'They were so close at school. But she doesn't want to know. Might as well ask her to go to Kabul as the Glades.' He pauses. 'Maybe I'm being unfair, I don't know what happened between them. Michaela can certainly be strong-willed.'

'Yes,' I say.

'So I really appreciate your going.'

'No problem.'

He reads out the address and I write it down.

'Go in the morning when he's out.'

'Her boyfriend?'

'Yes. Best avoided. If he turns up, leave.'

'OK. And thanks for your help,' I say.

'To be honest, Tess, it's a relief. You'll go and see her soon, won't you?'

'Of course,' I say.

'And if you could just talk about the old times, say that you've been to see us, that we'd be happy to have her home...' He stops. 'I know it's unlikely she'll come back.'

'I'll talk to her,' I say.

I look at the address I've written down. I still can't believe Michaela lives on the Glades.

Chapter 52

Edie: April 1998

Just like the first time she was in The Green Leaf Café, it was raining. And just like the first time, she felt awkward. She and Bob had been to Irregular Records, where she'd bought a couple of forty-fives she couldn't really afford. He must know, as she did, that Michaela was bridesmaid at a cousin's wedding that weekend and there was no chance of running into her.

All the things she would normally talk about would let him know she'd lied. She couldn't tell Bob about Max; he would guess her age straight away. Sometimes she thought she'd seen him when they were out together, but she was never sure. Today, she thought she'd seen Tess. As they'd left the record shop, a small figure had leapt into a doorway at the other end of the parade. But she couldn't tell Bob about her twin. No one believed Tess was fourteen, let alone seventeen years old, the age Edie claimed to be. School was off limits, because she was supposed to be a hairdresser, and she obviously couldn't talk to him about her friends and Michaela.

Instead, she told Bob about Mum, Nathan Bexley and what Raquel had told her about Uncle Ray. Bob stirred three spoonfuls of sugar into his coffee, smoked a cigarette and listened to Edie without interruption.

When she finished, he asked, 'So when did your parents get married?'

'Not sure. Why? Does it matter?'

'Well if it wasn't too long before you were born...'

Edie traced the dirt running through the cracks on the table with the tip of her finger. She thought of all the trips with Uncle Ray, the presents and now he was paying their school fees.

'You think Uncle Ray's my dad?'

'It's possible. I mean, he's sounds like he gets around a bit. He had a child with this Valentina woman too, right?'

'It died.'

'How long did their affair go on for?'

Edie remembered a hot summer day. Her birthday. She came out of the house. Uncle Ray and Valentina were standing close to one another. When they saw Edie, Valentina stepped back.

'Uncle Ray's not like that,' Edie said. 'And he's been so kind since Mum died. Like...'

'Like a father?'

Edie's arm tensed and her fingertips tingled. Bob must have sensed her anger.

'Look, I'm sorry,' he said. 'I didn't mean to upset you. But it makes sense of what you've told me, doesn't it?'

Edie didn't answer.

'Hey, finish up your drink and we can go to my mate Jim's. He's got a record player. We can put on some vinyl there.'

'Won't he mind me coming over?'

'He's not in. I've got the key.'

'OK.'

Her mind was elsewhere. Uncle Ray in Stevenson Park all those years ago. Mum asking about Valentina's weight. It had seemed a long time between finding Valentina and Mum's death. Looking back, it was only a few days. Bob kept talking, something about music. She finished her tea, scalding hot and tasting of nothing.

'Do you think he was seeing Mum and Valentina at the same time?' Edie asked.

'If he's that type of guy, he's not going to stick to one woman.'

Bob squashed his cigarette butt into the ashtray. Edie looked up into his face. He should know about not sticking to one woman.

'Have you got a girlfriend?' Edie asked.

She wanted him to come clean, to tell her he was trying to escape from another relationship. If she only waited it would be just the two of them.

But he said, 'Of course I've got a girlfriend.' He leaned over and kissed her. 'You. Come on, let's go; it's stopped raining.'

Edie stood up.

Two days between telling Mum about Valentina and her death on the dual carriageway. Had telling Mum pushed her to despair? She would have guessed Valentina's fatness was pregnancy and would have known the peacoat belonged to Uncle Ray. Was she responsible for her mother's wish to die?

'Don't forget your records,' Bob said.

Edie realised she'd left them on the seat next to her. Nearly twenty pounds' worth.

She picked up the plastic bag.

'Are you OK? Don't get so upset about your uncle. He's probably not your dad,' Bob said.

'And Valentina?'

'It's all in the past, isn't it?'

'Yeah,' Edie said.

The bag felt heavy in her hand. Outside, the traffic was too loud and the air too thick. Bob took the bag off her.

'You can have a lie-down at Jim's,' he said.

Edie leant against him and didn't reply.

If he's that type of guy...

*

Bob pushed the door open against the weight of leaflets and free newspapers. Dust floated up, swirling in the shafts of light and making Edie cough. It was hotter than outside, far too hot. She had the urge to run, but Bob had stepped in behind her and closed the door.

She brushed against the radiator and pulled back. Someone had left the central heating on.

'Why's the radiator on?'

'Dunno,' he said. 'It's upstairs.'

She wanted to stay where she was and talk about the radiator but couldn't think of anything else to say, so climbed the stairs. The carpet was dark green and fraying. It led to a room with leaf-patterned wallpaper, a floral settee, turned grey by dust, and a kitchenette at the back.

'Do you live here?' she asked.

'No,' he said. 'My mate owns the shop below. He lets me use it sometimes.'

The heat pressed upon her and she couldn't breathe. She fell back onto the settee.

'Why's it so hot?' she said.

'I'll open the window.'

He struggled with the sash before it finally lifted. The heat didn't get any better and the noise from the road was worse.

Her limbs hung heavy and her brain slowed. She didn't want to be with this boy in this flat, with its threadbare carpet and once floral settee. She couldn't remember what she'd liked about him. He seemed so ordinary. The sort of boy she'd normally avoid. She wanted to be alone, walking by the canal, reading, anywhere but here.

Bob picked up her bag and took out 'Glory to Love'.

'Shall we play this?'

She looked at the record player; it was dusty and unused. The needle probably hadn't been changed in twenty years.

'Not now,' she said.

'I'll play one of mine then.'

A loud thump came from the speakers when he switched them on. He took a forty-five and flipped it in his hand before placing it carefully on the turntable.

She knew this song. Not one Uncle Ray played; it must be off the radio.

'What's this? I know this.'

'"In the Midnight Hour", Wilson Pickett. Do you like it?'

'Is this Motown or Stax?' she asked.

'Huh?'

He sat next to her, reached over and pushed the hair from her face.

'Because most of the best Northern soul tracks are actually unknown Motown.'

He leaned in and placed his hand on her knee. She didn't stand up. It seemed easier to get it over with. It was, after all, where this had been leading and what she thought she wanted.

The scent of his aftershave mixed with the dust, traffic fumes and cigarettes on his breath.

'U-huh,' he said.

She closed her eyes and the rumble of traffic drummed through her head. And she thought of Mum's death on the road not three miles from here. His breath against her cheek was hotter than the air in the flat.

Wilson Pickett's voice filled her head. She wondered if Wilson took the girl he was singing about to a grubby flat above a launderette.

She turned her face away and watched the dust rise in the shards of light from the window. Soon it would be over and she could leave, go to the canal, find some cool air, be alone.

Chapter 53

Tess: July 2018

I'd pictured Michaela as a skeleton with greasy hair, cold sores round her mouth and track marks up her arms, living in a squat with stained mattresses strewn across the floor. When she answers the door she is very thin but looks well enough apart from the smudges under her eyes. She's barefooted and wears just a plain grey T-shirt dress. The flat's messy but not some junky hellhole. She shows me into the lounge, which has a mismatching armchair and sofa and a pine coffee table.

'I didn't think you'd come so soon,' she says.

Her voice is unchanged. It holds a commanding quality that still makes me feel inferior. And though she's not quite as tall as I remember, she towers over me.

'I've got to get back to London,' I say.

'Oh, you live in London.' She looks me up and down, a sneer twitching at her lips. 'Why did you want to see me?'

I decide it's best to be straightforward.

'I wanted to ask you about Edie.'

She doesn't offer condolences and her face remains neutral. Perhaps she doesn't know.

'They found her body three weeks ago. The funeral was last week.'

'Yeah, I saw the news.'

'I thought you might come.'

'Me? Why would I come?'

'You were best friends.'

She snorts.

'Who told you that?'

'Well, one of her best friends. I just wanted to ask you about the time, just before Edie when missing. It might offer some clues as to what happened.'

'Like I told the police, it was a long time ago. I can't remember.' Vilas's uncooperative friend. 'You were her twin. What can I tell you? You must know everything there is to know about her.'

'No. After she started hanging out with you...' after she started hanging out with you she had no time for me any more. She lied and kept secrets. You came between us. You stopped us from being sisters, '...we started doing our own thing more.'

Michaela sits in the armchair and reaches for a packet of cigarettes.

'You don't mind?'

'No.'

I pull out my own, light up and take a seat on the sofa as she doesn't ask me to sit down.

'I didn't know you smoked,' she says.

'I didn't at school.'

This comment makes her smirk. I don't like her any more than I did back then. She's smug and superior, even now, living here with this lifestyle.

'Why did you agree to see me?'

'You asked,' Michaela says.

'Your dad says you've cut yourself off from your old friends.'

'They've cut themselves off from me.'

'Your dad says—'

'Urghh.' She throws her arms down to her side; the ash from her cigarette brushes off on her dress. 'My father says a lot of things. What did he tell you?'

'Not much.'

'You told him we were friends.' She smiles. 'Were we friends, I don't remember?'

I ignore her sarcasm.

'So why did you agree?'

'Curiosity,' she says.

She draws on her cigarette then slumps into the armchair. Her T-shirt pulls across her belly and out of the bones there's a small but discernible bump. She sees me watching.

'Four months.'

'You're keeping it?'

'Course.'

'But Arabella?'

'I never wanted Arabella. Mum and Dad bullied me into it. Well, they can look after her.'

'But...'

'What?' she says.

'Nothing.'

Jem told me her parents wanted her to have an abortion and she'd refused. And after Arabella was taken away, she used to go over there crying, begging to see her. I'm not sure who to believe.

'You think I'm a terrible person leaving my child?'

'No.'

Yes.

'She's better off where she is. Except I wish they hadn't sent her to JAGS and I wish they didn't let her see that bastard.'

'He's her father and...'

He seems to care about her, I want to say. But I don't think letting on about seeing Jem is too smart a move.

'Your dad's nice. He's really worried about you. He'd like you to go back.'

Michaela pulls a face.

'I'm not going back there.'

'What's so bad you prefer it here?'

'It's not so terrible. Don't look horrified, you're from Limewoods.'

'I wouldn't go back.'

'No. You wouldn't, would you? Little Tess, so desperate to fit in, to speak properly and make friends with the right people.' I was never like that. If I had, my life would have been much easier. 'You think nothing could be worse than going back to Limewoods? Well, how about going back to boredom. To a life you have no say in? To a child you never wanted.'

'OK, but you don't have to live like this.'

'I don't have to, I choose to. You think you're better than me now, don't you? Is that what you always wanted?'

'I didn't come here to argue, Michaela. And I never pretended I was from anywhere but Limewoods. You're confusing me with Edie.'

'You had a mind of your own, did you? No one could tell, you always followed her around, the shadow no one notices.'

She laughs, her baby bump bounces up and down. I want to slap her.

'If I'd always followed her I'd know exactly what happened. Look, Michaela...' I take a deep breath. 'I just thought, as her friend, you might know something.'

'About what?'

'When she disappeared that summer.'

'Disappeared, yeah.'

It's as though she's only just remembered.

'You were hanging out together all the time,' I say. 'Was she in any trouble?'

'There was that boy who followed her round. He was no one, wouldn't hurt a fly, too small, can't remember his name.'

'Max.'

'That's it.'

'We know about him.' I try not to sound angry. 'Anything else? Someone must have wanted to hurt her.'

'I might have wanted to hurt her,' Michaela says and laughs again. 'Oh, don't worry, I never touched her. Didn't find out until much later that she was screwing Bob.'

'So she did have a boyfriend?'

'She had my boyfriend.'

'What? No, she wouldn't do something like that.'

She's still laughing.

'Why is that funny?'

She stops and looks straight at me.

'The dead are always such saints, aren't they? You think she could do no wrong. You think she was a saint?'

'No.'

'Good. Cos she wasn't a saint. She was a little parasite and a slut. Latched onto us, wheedled her way in. And we let her. Pretended we didn't know she was from Limewoods, because she was pretty, smart and funny.' Her eyes fall out of focus.

341

'Then she got her claws into Bob with her doe eyes and look-at-me-I'm-so-innocent act.'

I don't believe Michaela's version and I should defend Edie, only she told me so little I can't.

'Then the silly bitch gets herself pregnant. Not so much smarter than me, after all.'

'Pregnant? She wasn't. That's not true. You're lying.'

'That's what Bob told me.'

'I don't believe you.'

She shrugs.

'Believe what you want,' she says.

Could it be true, was Edie pregnant? She wasn't any fatter, but she was having terrible mood swings, but then again, what teenager doesn't? I'd seen her throwing up. At the time I thought it was from going out drinking the night before. It's possible, but Michaela's enjoying my distress and I don't know if she's made this claim to upset me. Jem warned me she would lie. I mustn't get angry. I take a deep breath.

'When did you find this out?'

'Much, much too late.'

'Do you know where he is now, this Bob?'

'Yeah,' she says.

She sounds bored and lights another cigarette, then strokes the bulge in her stomach as if daring me to say anything. I reckon nicotine is the least of that child's problems.

'Have you seen him recently?' I ask.

'No.' She drags on the cigarette and arches her back. 'But you have.'

'Huh?'

'Dad said you were at the house when he dropped Arabella off.'

342

Chapter 54

Edie: May 1998

'I have measured out my life with coffee spoons.' Something Mum recited. The verse could just as easily be changed to Dad's cigarettes, or Tess's questions, or Auntie Becca's complaints about the neighbours. Edie's world was so small. School, home, visits to Uncle Ray's and Auntie Becca's. Holidays would be an escape, something new; even Spain would be an adventure. But Auntie Becca wouldn't travel abroad, said she did enough of that when she was younger. Dad was too lazy to make plans and when Edie offered to make bookings for just the three of them, he looked panicked.

'We don't have to do everything with Uncle Ray and Auntie Becca,' she said.

Only they did. Not just holidays, Sunday lunches, shopping trips, Christmas. They'd had to spend their fourteenth birthday with them at Center Parcs. For the cost of the last holiday, they could have gone somewhere abroad, France or even Thailand. But no, it had to be Center Parcs. She'd rather stay at home. Alone. Tess could go. She'd love it.

Bob was her only escape.

Otherwise it was coffee, school, Dad, Tess, Auntie Becca and Center Parcs.

If Mum were here, it would be different. She always wanted to travel. Edie remembered her sighing over pictures of Rome and Athens, but they hadn't had the money back then. Grandpa Len travelled halfway across the globe to settle in England and that must have been enough for him, because he never travelled anywhere afterwards. Mum said they never went on holiday as children.

Learning the truth about Mum's death made Edie more confused. She wanted to put the knowledge in a box, throw it away and forget it forever, but she couldn't stop thinking about it. She'd sworn never to go to Mum's grave, yet here she was walking to the south side of town to find the cemetery. No one knew she was going. Tess was on a geography field trip and she'd forge her own sick note for school. Tess and Uncle Ray had nagged her to visit the cemetery, it would mean a lot to Dad, but she'd always refused. Now they didn't visit, either. Dad never mentioned Mum and had taken all her pictures down. Edie kept a small one at the bottom of her knicker drawer and one in her purse. She knew Tess had one under her pillow. Mum was probably the last thing they had in common.

It was surprising how many people were visiting the cemetery on a Thursday morning. Regulars, she guessed. They came with flowers and didn't need to look at the plan for the graves, which were laid out in rows and numbered, like a car park. No one else was her age. You could play the 'who have you lost' game. But it was too easy. Older women and a few men, still wearing their wedding rings.

Some of them looked at her, perhaps wondering what she

was doing here at that time and who she had lost: a mother, a father, a sister. The game was harder to play with her.

Mum's grave was G31. Black granite with gold lettering.

Flowers lay on top of the horizontal slab, white lilies. They were wilted and brown at the edges. Someone must have come here in the last few weeks. Someone who missed Mum as much as she did. Was it Uncle Ray? She bent down and touched one of the blooms. The petals fell away leaving the yellow centre, bright against the black granite.

She couldn't remain angry with Mum. She wouldn't have left her and Tess without a reason. Edie wished she'd been older, so she could have understood Mum better. Had she been despairing the whole time and all the sugar and song, the hard work and the care of others just distractions, which in the end weren't strong enough? Dad had his gardening and his sport, Auntie Becca, moving and redecorating. Uncle Ray didn't seem to need this. Perhaps that was why everyone was drawn to him. He was uncomplicated. If you have music and a drink, what's to complain about? Edie wished she were more like him. She couldn't bear more years of the continual dullness at home. She would have to leave, go to London or New York, anywhere that wasn't here.

Aunt Lola had left and despite living in a suburb, thirty minutes from Central London and the local high street having little more to offer than Edie's, it held a faint glamour. Her cousins seemed so much more sophisticated and polished than she and Tess. She'd have to wait until she finished school. She'd feel guilty for leaving Tess. But she couldn't take her. Tess would never change. Edie would have to leave it all behind and never come back.

She wanted to feel something, that this place, this moment

at Mum's grave, was significant but it was just a block of stone spattered with rain and petals on the south side of town. It stood for nothing but the designer's poor taste. When Dad died, which wouldn't be long, given how much he smoked, he would be buried here, too. Edie hoped she'd at least be old enough not to have to live with Uncle Ray and Auntie Becca.

After ten minutes she left. She would have gone sooner, but she was aware of others in the cemetery and it seemed disrespectful to leave so soon. Probably no one would have noticed, all too wrapped up in their own grief. Edie swept up the dying flowers from the grave, scattering them on the surrounding grass.

She took the bus back, got off in the town centre and went to a café she used to go to with Mum for Orangina and Chelsea buns. She ordered both; neither tasted as she remembered, far too sweet.

And it seemed her little world just got smaller because she no longer enjoyed the things she'd once looked forward to. Coffee, tea, cigarettes, questions and complaints were all there was.

Bob had rung her house earlier. Their code three rings then hang up. She could call him from the phone in the café.

She was about to get up, when she saw Max. He was standing outside the café looking in. Had he followed her to the cemetery as well? She'd had enough.

She ran outside, thinking he would run away; instead, he took two steps back before standing his ground.

'What are you doing here? Why are you following me?'

'I'm not,' he said.

'Yes, you are. You should be at school.'

'So should you.'

'Just leave me alone,' Edie said and took a step towards him.

He didn't move.

'I only want to talk to you,' he said.

'I don't want to talk to you. Even if I didn't have a boyfriend, I wouldn't want to talk to you.'

'He's not your boyfriend,' Max muttered.

'What?'

'He's not your boyfriend,' Max said, louder this time. 'He's Michaela's.'

'How do you know that?'

How long had he been following her? Where had he been following her? She thought of the flat above the launderette. Did he know about that? Had he gone there, pressed his ear to the door, tried to gain a glimpse through the upstairs window? She felt sick.

'You're not the only one, you know,' Max said. 'He sees other girls, not just Michaela.'

'You're a bloody liar,' Edie screamed at him. 'You stay away from me.'

People at the nearby bus stop turned and gawped.

'He doesn't care about you,' Max said. 'I care about you. You read Angela Carter and listen to Northern soul. You eat hummus and pitta chips. Your mum's gone, just like mine, we're the same.'

Edie's rage was so strong it blurred her vision. Her throat constricted so that her words came out as a growl.

'How dare you speak about my mum. She's dead. I know about your mother, shacked up with that teacher. She's just a slut. Mr Kent's whore.'

She wanted him to cry and run away, but he stood staring,

as angry as she was. They were standing inches apart. Edie towered over him, though he seemed swelled by rage, taller, frightening.

It came as a shock to Edie that she was frightened by this boy she'd only pitied before. She swivelled on her heels and went back into the café. She sat down and realised she was shaking all over. When she looked up, Max was gone.

Chapter 55

Tess: July 2018

I've slept with my sister's lover. My fourteen-year-old sister. Jeremy Robertson. Bob. A stupid nickname, but not a stupid man. He's sly, manipulative and what else? The charm he used on me, he used on her. The hands he touched me with, he touched her with, a child.

I've talked to him about Mum, Dad, Ray and Edie, and he listened and looked sympathetic, touched my shoulder and said the right things. Part of his charm. His intuition about Ray and Mum should have put me on my guard, it was too precise for people he'd never met and a situation he barely knew. Of course he'd had the same discussion with Edie. I must be like a rerun of an old film, the imperfect copy, a pale shadow.

How could I not have joined the dots? Edie was always smarter. Maybe that's why she's dead.

Michaela said Bob told her Edie was pregnant. It's possible. Her late nights, her moods could point to anything, I knew her so little by the end. She lay in that reservoir for years, only bones when they found her, the flesh long gone. She could have been pregnant. We'll never know.

Did Bob kill Edie? I think his love for Arabella is genuine, but he told me that came later, that he didn't want her at first. Did he use Edie as a warning to Michaela, an example of what happens to young girls who get pregnant? An example or a threat?

It could all be lies. Michaela's a liar and a bitch. She was a bitch at school and she's a bitch now. A lying, junkie bitch. I want to believe this, but her story matches with what I know already. I need to speak to Bob or Jem or whatever his name is. My sister's lover.

Chapter 56

Edie: May 1998

Edie came home at ten thirty after her evening with Bob. They'd been to his friend's flat above the launderette again. They rarely went out any more. When she told him about Max, he went outside to make sure he wasn't about. Afterwards, she had wanted to talk to Bob about going to Mum's grave; he hadn't seemed interested.

She went to the kitchen, poured a glass of water and grabbed some crackers out of the cupboard. Tess came in, wearing her pyjamas.

'Is that boy your boyfriend?'

How could Tess know about Bob?

'Which boy?' she said.

'The one outside.'

Edie walked to the dining room and peered out of the window. The small boy was standing at the end of her road looking up at the house.

'Of course he's not my boyfriend.'

'Who is he then?' Tess asked. 'He came to the end of the road as you were coming up it.'

'Are you spying on me?'

'I was just looking out of the window.'

'Your room's at the back of the house.'

'I'm allowed to look out of the window.'

'What's going on?'

Dad came in, roused by the novelty of the dining room being used.

'What are you looking at?' He followed their gaze. 'Who's that?'

'He's from the boys' school,' Tess said.

'What's he doing at the end of our street?'

Neither of them replied.

'Is he bothering you?'

Tess looked at her.

'Edie?' Dad said.

She didn't answer.

'Edie?' He waited for a response then said, 'Right,' and was out of the door.

'No,' Edie said.

She ran to the door and watched Dad charge down the street towards Max.

'You! Oi, you,' Dad shouted.

Max took a moment to realise what was happening then took off, with more speed than his spindly legs looked capable of. Dad's tar-clogged lungs couldn't keep up. At the end of the street he stopped and bent over, his arms resting on his knees, his back rising and falling as he gasped for breath.

He returned to the house still panting.

'Give me his name. I'm calling the police.'

'He's Edie's boyfriend,' Tess said.

'No, he's not. I haven't got a boyfriend,' Edie said.

'Tell me the truth now, Edie.'

If Max were questioned about following her, he might tell them about Bob.

'I've no idea who he is. It might not be me he was watching and he's not there any more.'

'I'm worried for you, Edie. You think boys like that are harmless. I know what boys can be.'

'It's nothing, Dad.'

The energy suddenly drained from him. The mental, as much as the physical, exertion taking its toll.

'OK, Edie, but you have to let me know if he gives you any more trouble. I'll go around with Ray, sort this out.'

'I've no idea who he is. I don't think he was here for me.'

'Are you sure?'

'Yes, honestly.'

Dad looked back towards the door and hesitated before saying, 'You go to bed now, girls, it's late.'

'This is your fault,' Tess said as they went upstairs.

Edie didn't know what was her fault and was too tired to ask. She went to her room and put her Discman on, listening to 'Run for Cover' on repeat.

At first, Max had just been irritating. Then he served as a useful excuse for leaving the school through the back hedge and avoid running into Bob. The problem was that Max had quickly realised what she was doing and started waiting at the back of the school. And now he'd followed her to the cemetery and turned up at her house.

She dismissed what Max had said about Bob, that was jealousy, trying to turn her against him. What she couldn't dismiss was his anger when she'd called his mum a whore. It was a terrible thing to say and she felt bad. She'd hoped it would make him stay away; instead, it had made him more determined. He must have wanted her to see him standing outside. He'd made no effort to conceal himself. Why was he following her? Why wouldn't he leave her alone?

Chapter 57

Tess: July 2018

I ring the bell.

'Who's that?' a voice calls from above.

I step back from the door and look up. Jem is leaning out of the window. He's bare-chested and his shoulders are large compared to his thin torso and concave stomach.

'Wait a sec,' he says.

He disappears for a moment then comes back and throws me a set of keys.

'The lower lock's broken. Just use the silver key on the end.'

I should have called Vilas, but I'm too angry to be wise. The stairs are dusty and piled with unclaimed mail and take-away menus. I think of Dad's words, You could know them, you could be in danger. I should be scared. I'm not. I'm angry.

Jem opens the door in just his jeans.

'Come in.'

It's as messy as before, with clothes, beer cans and magazines strewn across the floor. Deodorant has been used as an air freshener just before I came in. The spicy scent fails to hide the smell of stale sweat and un-emptied ashtrays.

'Didn't expect to see you.'

He's relaxed and smiling. He's no idea why I'm here. Was Michaela lying?

'Everything alright? You look serious.'

'I'm fine.'

'It's a bit early, but there's half a bottle of wine going if you want it.'

The bottle's on the floor next to a glass with lipstick on the rim. Jem realises this at the same time I do and picks it up. I wave my hand.

'I don't want any. I've not come for that.'

'What then?'

He passes the glass to his other hand.

'I saw Michaela this morning.'

His body stiffens.

'What did you do that for? I told you not to see her.'

'And now I know why.' I can't read his expression. 'Was it you? The boy Edie was seeing.'

'Michaela hates me. She's a nutter.'

'Because of you.'

'I never started her on drugs, not the hard stuff, and I stuck with her longer than anyone else would. Longer than her parents.'

'Is it true?'

He takes a deep breath.

'I was seeing Edie for a bit, yeah.'

His casualness maddens me.

'She was a child.'

'Oh, come on, you're not that naive. What do you want me to say?'

'You should have told me.'

'I didn't know how to tell you.'

'No kidding.'

He passes the glass back to the other hand.

'Look, I didn't know I was going to end up seeing you.'

I can see why Michaela hates him. It's all no big deal, why are you making a fuss? Because he's not the one who has to deal with the problems he's created. Michaela's the one who ended up living on the Glades and his child is being paid for and raised by someone else.

'Of all these women,' I gesture to the lipstick-stained wine glass, 'wasn't there one you could leave alone?'

'Look, about the glass.'

I wave my hand at it. My fingers catch the rim. It flies from his hand and smashes against the edge of the kitchen cupboard.

'I don't care what woman you were screwing last night. I care that you were screwing my sister. My fourteen-year-old sister.'

'I didn't. I mean, we never actually did it.'

'Bullshit. You told Michaela Edie was pregnant.'

'It wasn't mine.'

'Immaculate conception?'

'She was seeing other guys. Your aunt believed me.'

'Becca? What's she got to do with it?'

'She came to see me.'

I don't believe Becca went to see him. She would have told me about it and Ray would have been sent round for any confrontation. But why would Jem lie?

'How did she know where you were?'

'I thought Edie told her, or maybe you?'

'Me?'

'Edie said you used to follow her sometimes.'

357

'It wasn't like that,' I say.

'I don't know then. But your aunt came to see me after we'd already split up, said Edie was pregnant. I told her it couldn't be mine.'

'When was that?'

He sighs and looks down at the shards of glass at his feet.

'The afternoon she disappeared.'

'If you thought she was pregnant, what would you have done to stop her having it? It was you that woman saw arguing with her that afternoon, wasn't it?'

'For Christ's sake. Is that what you think?'

Jem's face hardens. There's a menace, an ugliness in him I've not seen before.

'If you really think I killed her you're taking a risk coming here, aren't you?'

'I've told Dad where I am.'

Jem's lip curls.

'What do you think I'm going to do to you?'

He moves closer. He's standing between me and the door. I'm aware of how much taller and broader he is than I am.

'You think I killed her?'

He holds my arm, his thumb and middle finger barely touching. I'd be less scared if he grabbed and shook me. This slow, deliberate anger is more frightening.

'Do you?' he says.

If I move, I know the grip will tighten.

'The police were looking for her boyfriend. You never came forward.'

His face is an inch from mine.

'So you think I'm a killer. I seduce schoolgirls then kill them.'

I hold his gaze. I wish I had told Dad where I was going. I've been stupid to let rage rule my actions.

He presses his fingers a little tighter into my arm.

'Do you think I killed her?' he says.

'Why didn't you speak to the police?'

His grip slackens.

'I was young, I didn't have a clean record and I was seeing an underage girl. No, I didn't come forward. Neither would you.'

He lets go and steps back.

I can't look him in the face. I clench my fist to stop my hands shaking and move around him slowly, towards the door. At any moment I expect him to push past me and slam it. He doesn't. But just before I leave, he starts talking again. He's turned away from me and his voice is quiet and soft.

'That last time I saw her I wanted to call her back or walk with her. If I had, none of this would have happened. I was angry when she finished with me and when I thought she was pregnant. If I'd walked with her, she'd have been OK. Maybe things would have worked out. You're right to blame me. But I didn't kill her.'

I watch him. He still doesn't turn. I click the door shut and make my way back down the stairs. Out on the street, my mouth is so dry I can barely swallow. I go to the same newsagents I went to before and buy another can of Tango to unstick my tongue from the roof of my mouth.

I probably asked him the wrong questions. It doesn't matter. The one I need to ask, he can't answer. Why did Becca never tell the police about him?

Chapter 58

Edie: June 1998

'Who's this man, Edie?'

Tess looked up from her homework. Auntie Becca rarely raised her voice. So this was the real reason Auntie Becca had insisted they come to hers for dinner, not because Dad had gone to the cricket with Uncle Ray. Edie had said it was stupid; they were old enough to look after themselves. But no, they had to eat yet another pasta bake in Auntie Becca's dining room and wait for the table to be cleared before she got to the point.

'Which man?' Edie asked.

She glared at Tess. She must have said something about Max, who hardly counted as a man.

Auntie Becca placed both hands on the table opposite Edie and leant forwards. She was silhouetted by the bright light from the window behind and her face lay in darkness.

'Don't bother lying to me,' she said.

Edie glanced at Tess, whose eyes were darting between Becca and Edie, her mouth slightly open.

'Auntie Becca, I don't know who's said something.'

'You know exactly who's said something and what he said. Going out with this man, drinking and going to clubs.'

Edie looked at Tess. Auntie Becca lowered her voice.

'Do you even know what you're doing?' she asked.

Edie tried to push the images from her mind: the floral sofa, the dust rising in swirls above her head, Bob's hot breath against her cheek.

'He's a man. Far too old for you, Edie. You should be concentrating on your schoolwork and if you are interested in that sort of thing, you should find a boy your own age.'

'He's not that old,' Edie said.

She'd never thought of Bob as a man. Dad and Uncle Ray were men. Bob was still a boy, wasn't he? She'd never asked his age. But he did have a job and drive a car.

'Eighteen,' she said. 'He's eighteen.'

'Still too old, if that is his real age.'

'It's nothing really, Auntie Becca. We're not...' She saw the leaf-patterned wallpaper and smelt his sweat mixed with cigarette smoke. 'I mean, it's really nothing. We're just hanging out together.'

Auntie Becca shook her head.

'You've got to stop this, Edie. You're running around town, playing the slut. If your mother were here—'

'Don't you talk about her!'

Tess slammed her textbook on the table. Edie and Auntie Becca turned. They'd forgotten about her.

'Don't talk about her. You're not Mum. You'll never be her.'

No one spoke for a moment. Auntie Becca drew a sharp breath.

'I know I'm not Gina,' she said. 'But in a situation like this, a serious situation, Tess, I have to do something.'

'You don't have to do anything. You like doing it, sticking your nose in other people's business because you've nothing else to do all day. You're not our mum and you can't speak to Edie like that.'

Auntie Becca stood back from the table.

'Tess, I don't think you realise what sort of trouble Edie could get herself into, hanging about with this man, what's his name?' Edie didn't answer. 'It's my business to—'

'It's not your business,' Tess said. Her voice was becoming squeaky. 'None of it's your business.'

She swept her homework into her bag and stood up, her face wet with tears.

'Come on, Edie, we're leaving.'

Edie picked up her bag and was careful not to catch Auntie Becca's eye.

'I think you should stay, Edie,' Auntie Becca said.

She didn't reply and followed Tess into the hall. Auntie Becca came after them.

'Edie, I'm serious. I don't want to have to speak to Vince.' Tess had opened the front door. 'I suppose you think you're in love. You're not, and I can guarantee he isn't.'

Tess was out and beyond the drive. Edie looked back to the house even though she knew Auntie Becca wouldn't follow. A scene in front of family was distasteful to her and unthinkable in front of the neighbours. Tess had sped off with rapid strides and Edie had to run to catch up.

'Tess,' she gasped. 'Thanks.'

'Don't thank me.'

Tess had stopped crying but her eyes were still red.

'That was brilliant. Telling Auntie Becca where to stick it,' Edie said.

'I didn't do it for you.'

'Come on, Tess.'

362

'Who is he? Why didn't you tell me?'

She was about to cry again. Edie looked away. She didn't want to tell her about Bob. She was sure he was the sort of boy Tess would disapprove of. She disapproved of most boys, even singers and film stars. What would she think of Bob, who drove a red hatchback to their school gates and was going out with Michaela?

'He's just a guy I met. And I didn't tell you because I didn't think you'd understand.'

'What's to understand? You just like keeping things from me, like being different, having different friends, watching different films, pretending you're not my sister.'

'That's not true.'

'Yes, it is. I bet you wish we were at different schools and you could ignore me altogether.'

'Tess, that's not it. How can I tell you stuff when you act like this?'

'Becca's right about you, you are a slut.'

Edie wanted to slap her.

'You're just jealous. Jealous of him, jealous of my friends. I invite you to things and you just sit around and sulk. You could have a boyfriend if you tried.'

'I don't want a boyfriend,' Tess shrieked.

'What do you want?'

No answer came. Tess just stood still and stared at her. The sun was low and caught the glare in her eye. Tess continued to stare before blinking once and walking away. Edie knew not to follow her. At that moment Edie felt she didn't know her sister.

Chapter 59

Tess: July 2018

Becca's out the front cleaning the downstairs windows when I go over to see her. They pay a window cleaner but she always finds fault. She jumps slightly when I call to her.

'Oh, Tess, you should have told me you were coming.'

She's lost more weight, which doesn't suit her; it just makes her look old. She throws the sponge into the bucket and bends to pick it up. Her breathing's heavy.

'I'll do that,' I say.

'Thanks, Tess. Pour it in the gutter. I'll get the kettle on.'

I walk to the end of the drive and sling the water from the bucket. I wobble for a moment and swirl with the water as it runs along the gutter and bubbles down the drain, then walk back up to the house. From the hall, I can hear the kettle starting to boil. I go into the kitchen. Becca's leaning on the countertop next to the teapot. She seems lost in thought.

'Are you alright?' I ask.

'Yes. Fine.' She pushes herself upright. 'Shouldn't watch the kettle, it'll never boil. You look peaky, Tess, are you coming down with something?'

'I'm just feeling a little light-headed,' I say.

'You should see a doctor,' she said. 'The sort of stress you've been under.'

'I'll be fine. It's probably the heat,' I say, though my throat feels like sandpaper.

When the tea's made we sit at the kitchen table. She's less chatty than usual and there are no complaints about the neighbours. I wonder if she knows about my chat with Ray. She always knows all sorts of things without being told. Like how to find Edie's boyfriend. I feel bad asking her anything at the moment, for once she looks vulnerable. I've never thought of her like that before. Maybe it's because of what I know about Ray and what she's had to put up with over the years that I can see a sliver of weakness she'd never willingly reveal.

'Becca. I've got something to say and something to ask and it's best if I just come out with it.'

'What is it?' She sounds bored, as if she knows what the question will be and she's answered it a thousand times before.

'I went to see one of Edie's old friends yesterday.'

'Oh?'

'She told me the name of Edie's boyfriend and where to find him.' There's no point in going into my history with Jem. 'His name's Jeremy Robertson. I spoke to him. He said you went to see him twenty years ago.'

Becca's face doesn't move.

'You never told the police about him,' I say.

'No.'

'Why?'

'There was no point. He had nothing to do with Edie's death.'

This is the old Becca speaking, firm and assured in everything.

'How can you know?'

'I just do.'

'You could only be sure if you do know who did it.'

She sighs.

'Becca, if you don't tell me what you know, I'll go to the police. It's new evidence.'

She gives a slow shake of the head.

'Don't go to the police, Tess.'

'Was it Ray?'

She looks bemused.

'Of course it wasn't Ray. How can you say such a thing?'

'Who then? You have to tell me. You can't sit there, cold-blooded, not caring.' I stand up. My tea spills across the tabletop. 'Why? Why did you never tell the police if you know? It must be Ray. Who else would you protect?'

Becca doesn't move. Not even to mop up the spilt tea, dripping onto the floor.

'Sit down, Tess. I have something to give you,' she says.

She leaves the room and I hear her climb the stairs with a slow tread. She returns with something in her hand. Her expression remains blank. She places a plastic wallet in front of me.

'Speak to your father,' she says.

'You're telling me it was Dad?'

'Open it. I'm telling you, you need to speak to Vince.'

I peel open the wallet. Inside is the missing photograph, the one Edie used to keep in her purse, with the two of us and Mum and Dad. The photograph I believed proved she must be alive.

'Who took this from Edie's bag? Does Dad know about this?'

She moves her head slightly as if to nod then shakes it instead.

'Do you all know, have you always known?' I say.

She doesn't reply.

'You've said nothing. Done nothing. I don't understand.' My voice is cracking. 'How can you sit there, knowing whoever it is is still out there and you could stop them? She was my sister, your niece.'

'Tess, I know you're upset, angry and confused. But you have to speak to Vince.'

We both jump at a car door slamming outside. For the first time, Becca looks me in the eye.

'That's Ray. You'd better go.'

She puts the photograph in her pocket. I hesitate and look towards the hall.

'Don't ask Ray, Tess. It's Vince you need to talk to.'

A key turns in the front lock.

Becca glances at the side door.

'It's open,' she says.

Ray's in the hall.

'Alright, Becs,' he calls.

'You need to go now, Tess,' Becca says.

I look towards the hall once more before leaving by the side door.

Ray's in the kitchen.

'Everything alright?' he says.

I don't hear Becca's reply. I walk down the edge of the drive, so that I can't be seen from the window.

Becca knows. Ray knows. Dad knows. I'm sure of it. That's why he can't look me in the eye, why he hates me coming up and asking questions. He knows. He's always known. He looks so old because he's carried the guilt with him all these years. Not the guilt of killing her, he could never harm anyone, even if he hated them, and he loved Edie. It's the guilt of doing nothing, of watching me grow up alone, aching for my twin, while her murderer walks around unpunished because of his silence. And again my mind turns to Ray, who else would they both protect? Who else was Edie so close to she could do them harm? And who else would value that photograph? Ray. Only Ray matches the silhouette that flits across the unknown in Edie's life. Ray who's so much fun. Ray who was like a second father. Ray who loved us. Edie especially, maybe too much.

Chapter 60

Edie: June 1998

She took the coward's way out and pushed a note under the door of the flat above the launderette they used to go to. It hadn't been Auntie Becca's warning, or Tess's anger that made her do it. She simply didn't want him any more. Why did Michaela go on about it all the time? It wasn't that great. She'd had a boyfriend now, she knew what it was like and she didn't feel the need to find another one. Bob had been a distraction from her everyday life, a very draining one, not worth the effort.

What had drawn her to him now pushed her away. The sneaking about, the possibility of sex, feeling like an adult. Given that Bob already had a girlfriend, she thought he'd not bother getting in touch. Just two more weeks and the school term would end and it would all be over. No more sneaking about, having to leave school through the gap in the hedge so Bob wouldn't see her as he came to collect Michaela from the front.

The thrill of rebellion she'd felt after the confrontation with Auntie Becca turned to vague panic in case she told Dad. Edie closed the lounge door and phoned her aunt from the hallway.

'I'm surprised to hear from you after yesterday,' Auntie Becca said.

Edie took a deep breath. Auntie Becca's triumph would be unbearable.

'I just wanted you to know, I've finished with him. I listened to what you said and it's over.'

'I'm so glad to hear that,' Auntie Becca said. Edie held the phone a little away from her ear. 'He really is far too old and even if he wasn't, I think you could do better than that. He looks like a tramp.'

'How do you know what he looks like?'

'I saw you together.'

'When?'

'That doesn't matter. What matters is you girls. I'm sorry it upset Tess so much, but I really do think of you as my daughters.'

Edie winced but said nothing. Making it seem as if she'd ended it with Bob on Auntie Becca's advice would soften her and she didn't want her telling Dad.

She was about to hang up, when Auntie Becca said, 'There's nothing else, is there?'

'What do you mean?'

'Things haven't gone too far, have they?'

Edie shut her eyes and could feel Bob's hot breath against her cheek.

'No,' she said.

'Because if they have you'll need to...'

'They haven't.'

'Are you sure?'

'Yes.'

A pause at the other end.

'I've only your best interests at heart, Edie.'

'Yes, you said.'

'Good. You're all coming over next Sunday. I'll see you then.'

It hadn't been as bad as she'd thought, but bad enough. Better than Dad finding out.

Edie looked up the stairs to see Tess shutting her bedroom door. Had she been listening? If she knew it was over with Bob, maybe Tess would start talking to her again. She wasn't sure if that was a good thing.

Chapter 61

Tess: July 2018

I stop in front of the house. It looks dead compared to the rest of the street. The care Dad has taken with the shrubs and flowers can't hide the decay, the cracked driveway and rusted garage door, the smears across the double glazing. I organised a window cleaner for him once; he must have left.

I push the key into the lock, aware of its slow turn and the clunk when it opens. Inside, the smoke is fresh. I follow its trail to the lounge.

Dad's sitting in his favourite chair, smoking, lightly tapping a cigarette and missing the ashtray on the arm to his right. This repeated ritual has left a trail of tiny burns in the material down the side, like a dark waterfall. I always notice this and it doesn't bother me, it's just what Dad does. Today it makes me angry. Angry that he can spend years and years, sitting and tapping and doing nothing. Only today he has done something.

'I just spoke to Becca,' he says.

I wait. He doesn't look up, just taps and misses again.

'I don't want to have to tell you, Tess,' he says.

I sit in the chair opposite him. It's the same as his but

rarely used, so in better condition. He should swap them over. I sink into the cushions. My cigarettes fall from my pocket, but there's no ashtray next to me and I don't want to move.

'Was it Ray?' I ask.

'No.'

Dad's eyelids flutter. He still doesn't look up.

'Go back to London, Tess.'

I don't know how he can sit there so passive, almost lifeless, watching as his family is destroyed by his brother.

'You choose him over me? Isn't it bad enough you let him fuck your wife?'

He flinches and still doesn't speak.

'Becca knows.'

Dad nods.

'How? Why didn't she go to the police? It was Ray, wasn't it?'

'Tess, I'm asking you one last time.'

'I'll go to the police myself if you won't.'

Dad shakes his head.

'You can't.'

'Why not?'

He takes a long drag on his cigarette and places it, still smouldering, in the ashtray.

'Dad?'

He leans forwards so his forearms rest on his thighs, his hands clasped together as if in prayer.

'You break my heart, Tess.'

'Tell me.'

He closes his eyes.

'We all knew it was an accident, a moment of madness, you didn't mean it.'

'Mean what?'

'You went back to Becca's, told her everything.'

'What are you saying?'

'You told Becca you'd just killed Edie.'

The room slips from focus and I see the canal path. I'm running through the bushes, brambles tearing at my skin.

'No,' I scream, at Dad or the images, I'm not sure.

My family's silence, their reluctance to involve the police and it wasn't for Ray. Dad wouldn't do this for Ray.

'I... I can't have.'

The words peter out and I pull my hands to my face.

'Becca told me to come over and we made you shower. She washed your clothes and cleaned your shoes. We told the police you'd come back much earlier. Afterwards, you didn't seem to remember. Blocked it all out somehow. We didn't want to tell you. I don't want to be telling you now.'

'You think... no.'

That day is a blur. I remember leaving school. I saw Edie exiting by the back entrance. Later, I was lying on my bed with damp hair and the smell of strawberry shampoo, Becca sitting next to me. She was crying. It's the only time I remember seeing her cry. I thought her dog, Pepe, must have died.

'I loved Edie. She was my sister, my twin.'

'You didn't mean to do it. Ray and I went to find her. She was half covered in the bushes and we had to...' He starts to cry. 'We had to wrap her in plastic and take her to that place. My baby girl.'

'It wasn't me, Dad. I would never hurt her.'

'I had to take the photograph from her bag; it was the only copy, of us all together and happy. A perfect family. Ray made me give it to him. If I kept it he was worried you or the police would find it.'

That vision I had, of running along the canal-side, it had been so clear, so real. Was it an actual memory?

'I never wanted to believe it,' Dad says. 'But you were so angry with her, Tess.'

'I loved her.' I stand up. I look to the door; it's out of focus. 'It's not true.'

'You were jealous, so jealous. You didn't want her to have friends or boyfriends. You wanted it to be just the two of you all the time.'

Dad gets up from his chair and comes towards me.

'Tess, love, sit down. You're in shock.'

He places his hand on my forearm. I pull away.

'I didn't do it,' I say.

'Tess.'

I push past him and out of the door.

'Tess,' he calls. He comes to the front door. 'Tess,' he shouts again but doesn't follow.

I run from the door to the main road.

I didn't do it. I know I didn't do it. I could never have done it, however jealous and angry. She was everything to me and I would never hurt her.

They all think I did it. It makes sense now. Dad's reluctance to see me, the fear in Valentina's eyes when I spoke to her, Ray's warnings to stay away. Could I have done it?

I stand at the edge of the road, I've no idea where to go. I want to go home. I think of our house on Limewoods. I'll go there. Edie will open the door. Mum will make me hot chocolate, stroke my hair and tell me everything's going to be all right.

I need to go home, but I don't have one.

375

Chapter 62

Edie: July 1998

Sunday came and, as usual, Edie filed over to Uncle Ray's with Dad and Tess. Auntie Becca came to the door. Pepe ran from behind her in a half-hearted attack. He was getting old. He jumped up at Edie and barked three times before returning to his basket.

Auntie Becca kissed Dad on the cheek and gave Tess a quick peck. They didn't speak or make eye contact. Tess wouldn't be forgiven as quickly as herself, Edie thought. It hurts more when a favourite turns on you. As Edie walked past, Auntie Becca tapped her on the shoulder.

'All for the best,' she said and gave a little knowing nod.

Edie ground her teeth.

Uncle Ray was sitting in the lounge with a glass of whisky. He put it down and stood up as they entered.

'Good to see you, Vince,' he said.

They shook hands. He gave Tess a quick hug.

'Hi, Uncle Ray,' Tess said.

Her voice was quiet. Perhaps she was worried Auntie Becca had told him about the argument.

Uncle Ray hugged Edie, a big squeeze that nearly lifted her off the ground.

'How's my favourite girl?'

'OK, Uncle Ray.'

She could smell the whisky on his breath and wondered how many he'd had.

'Can I get you one, Vince?'

Uncle Ray lifted the glass and waved it in his brother's direction.

'Not for me, Ray.'

'And you girls?'

'Really, Ray,' Auntie Becca said as she came in.

'They're not children any more,' Uncle Ray said.

'They're not ready for whisky.'

'Well a little glass of wine with lunch, it can't hurt, can it?'

'I'll have lemonade, if that's alright?' Tess said.

Edie wanted the wine even though she disliked the taste. At the Reckless club she'd seen little smirks when Bob gave her a Smirnoff Ice. Not that he was a factor any more, but she didn't want to be smirked at, in Reckless or anywhere else.

'Edie's been unwell today. Best stick to lemonade,' Dad said.

'Are you sick, Edie?' Auntie Becca asked.

'It's nothing. Prawns last night in the Sainsbury's pasta. I don't think they agree with me,' Edie said.

'That's settled then. Lemonade,' Auntie Becca said. 'I'll get the greens on.'

Dad ambled towards the patio doors, leading from the lounge to the garden.

'The back bed's looking good,' he said. 'Give it a couple more years and it will really come into its own.'

'I'm not sure we'll be here that long,' Uncle Ray said. 'Auntie Becca's keen on a new place she's seen, on a quieter road.'

'Shame,' Dad said. 'Come and look at the roses, Tess.'

Tess followed Dad into the garden. Their shared love of plants kept them close. Sometimes Edie felt like the odd one out. She had nothing to say to Dad and Tess was no longer talking to her.

She looked around the room to the turntable.

'Got anything new?' she asked.

'A few things,' Uncle Ray said.

He wandered over to the stereo, picked up an album, twisted it in his hands then put it back in the stack.

'Actually, Edie, I've been meaning to talk to you.' He sounded serious, which was unlike Uncle Ray. 'I was chatting to Freddie.'

'Who's Freddie?'

'The guy who owns Irregular Records. He's an old friend, we go right back to the Wigan Casino days.'

'Right,' Edie said.

'The thing is...' he picked the same album up and scanned the back cover. He put it down again. 'The thing is, he saw you at Reckless with a guy he knows from the shop.'

Is that how Auntie Becca found out? It didn't explain how she knew what he looked like.

'Freddie asked if you were really my niece and if so to warn you off. Said this guy's bad news, always hanging round with different girls. And Edie, you're only fourteen. I know I joked about you not being children but you're not a woman, either. You don't want to be mixing with men like that. I don't know this Rob guy—'

'Bob,' Edie said.

'Whatever his name is, I know the sort. Becca said you finished with him. Please don't be lying to us. He's not going to make a good boyfriend if he's that type of guy.'

That type of guy. The same words used by Bob. It takes one to know one.

'Edie,' Uncle Ray said. 'Are you listening?'

She didn't reply, she was thinking about what Bob had said about Uncle Ray.

'Edie?'

She looked up.

'Did you love Mum, Uncle Ray?'

'What a question. Of course I did, everyone did.'

'That's not what I mean. You know what I mean.'

'What's got into you, Edie?'

'You said it, we're not kids any more.'

Uncle Ray looked towards the door then went to push it shut.

'I saw you in the park with Valentina. A few weeks later Mum's killed and you all lie to us about what happened.'

Uncle Ray rubbed his forehead.

'We wanted to spare you and Tess the pain of knowing.'

'That you were the reason she killed herself?'

'We don't know it wasn't an accident.'

'You loved her though, didn't you?'

'Once,' he said. 'A long time ago.'

'And she loved you?'

Uncle Ray shrugged.

'Are you our father, Uncle Ray?'

His face fell into a blank stare of shock before he curled his mouth into an anxious smile.

'No, Edie, no I'm not. But I love you both as much as any

father. And Christ, I miss Gina. But that was another lifetime.'

'I miss her, too,' Edie said.

Her eyes felt hot and sore and she realised she was going to cry. She hadn't cried for years. Not since she was a little girl living on the Limewoods Estate. Her breathing faltered and tears began to roll down her face.

Uncle Ray stepped forwards and hugged her. She clasped her hands round his waist and hugged back as hard as she could, her head resting on his chest. He stroked her hair. They stayed in the embrace, Uncle Ray stroking her hair, neither noticed Auntie Becca coming in.

'What's the matter?' she said.

'Nothing.' Uncle Ray loosened his grip. 'Edie's just a bit upset.'

'About that boy? She'll get over it. Will you come and lay the table, Ray?'

'Sure.'

Edie's arms were still wrapped round his waist. She held on tight and didn't want to let go. She felt safe with Uncle Ray, she wished he were their dad, that he and Mum had stayed together.

Uncle Ray prised her hands apart.

'We'll talk later,' he said.

Edie nodded. She turned away from Auntie Becca because she didn't want her to see the tears.

'You're too young to go pining away over someone who's not worth it. And he's so much older,' Auntie Becca said. 'Find some nice lad your own age.'

Edie didn't reply.

Auntie Becca stepped closer.

'Have you been sick before, Edie? Recently, I mean.'

'No, why?'

'Well if it happens again, let me know and we'll go to the doctors.'

'It was just the prawns, Auntie Becca.'

'Good. Call Vince and Tess in from the garden, will you? Dinner's nearly ready.'

No one had much conversation at lunch, except for Uncle Ray, who drank more than he ate, taking his whisky to the table and finishing most of the wine.

Edie had little appetite for the tough beef and soggy greens. She picked at a roast potato.

'Not hungry today, Edie?' Auntie Becca said.

Edie looked down at her plate. It was nearly full. She stabbed at a carrot.

'I'm OK,' she said.

'You're not looking well, Edie.'

'She looks fine, Becs,' Uncle Ray said. 'Looking more like Gina each day.'

Dad flinched at her name but gave no other reaction. He never talked about Mum. Uncle Ray knew that, he should keep his mouth shut.

'In a few years, you'll be the same age as when we first met her,' Uncle Ray continued. 'Do you remember that, Vince, the first time we saw her?'

Dad didn't look up. Tess stopped eating, her eyes flitting between Uncle Ray and Dad.

'Uncle Ray...' Edie said.

He picked up on her warning tone.

'Ah yes,' he said, took a mouthful of beef and swilled it down with more wine.

Tess waited a moment to make sure he had finished before

returning to her food. Edie made a show of piling peas onto her fork. Her neck felt hot, Uncle Ray talking about Mum had disquieted all of them. Edie was aware that whereas Tess was looking at Dad and Uncle Ray, and Dad was staring at his plate, throughout, Auntie Becca had not looked at them once. The whole time her eyes had been fixed on Edie. Her gaze hard, unflinching and unreadable.

Chapter 63

Tess: July 2018

I don't know where I'm going or what I'm doing. I've nothing with me except my purse and phone. But I've no one to call. Who can I ask for help when I deserve none?

I see the mix of disdain and fear in Valentina Vickers' eyes, because she knows, knows I am a killer, that I murdered my own sister.

I keep running. My breath becomes rapid and shallow, my dizziness returns. I slump on a wall by the side of the road. I want to run away but I have nowhere to go.

A minicab pulls into the kerb next to me.

'I'm not supposed to do this without a prior booking, but do you want a lift?' he calls out of the window.

I climb in the back.

'Where to?'

'The train station.'

I need to get as far away as possible, the Continent, America, anywhere. I'll go back to the flat, get my passport then I'll be gone. No one will ever see me again. I'll harvest grapes in the Loire or surf in California as I dreamed Edie did. I'll be the mystery, the missing twin.

I buy a clutch of mini wine bottles at the station off-licence and board my train.

Two hours to London, one to collect my passport and an hour and a half out to Heathrow and it's over. This life, Tess Piper's life, will be over.

On the train, I find a double seat and pull my knees up next to me and rest my chin on them. My breath remains shallow, my forehead hot and clammy. The wine will cool it down. I unscrew the first bottle.

The carriage starts to fill up. People pause at the seat next to me. I glower at them. Sitting here, hunched up, bottle in hand, no one challenges me.

By the time we reach Marylebone, the wine bottles are in a pile beneath my feet, but they haven't cooled me down and my brow is burning. I sway off the train and a man in a checked jacket has to help me put my ticket through the barrier.

At Friday rush hour the station is packed. People pushing to get onto trains, people pushing to leave trains, to cross the station to the underground, to leave the station to find a taxi. I can't move against the pull of the crowd. It feels as if my feet are no longer in contact with the floor and I'm pushed outside and down towards Marylebone Road. Buses, cars and taxis toot as they crawl from traffic light to traffic light. It's cacophonous, disorientating. I need to lie down.

My phone rings.

'Tess, where are you?' Max asks.

I don't reply.

'Your dad called me, said you might be coming back. I'll wait in for you.'

I hang up. I don't want him to wait. I can't face him. I can't face anyone. He sounded worried. Dad can't have told him the truth about me. Unless it's a trap. He's in league with Vilas and Craven. Of course he's waiting. He's waiting with the police.

I cross Marylebone Road and wander down past the library. I need somewhere to go. I could call Cassie. But what if she knows? What if Aunt Lola knows? I turn away from the main road, go into the nearest pub, sit at the bar and order a large glass of wine.

'Are you alright?' the barman asks. 'You don't look well.'

I touch my face. My cheeks are burning, my hairline damp. I nod at him, drink the wine and order another.

The next thing I know, someone's shaking me.

'Sweetheart,' the barman says. 'You can't do that here.'

My head's resting on the countertop. I jerk upright and nearly fall off the stool. The two suits standing next to me laugh. An older man drinking alone shakes his head in disgust.

They know, they all know who I am. They all know what I am.

'Get a cab,' the barman says. 'Go home.'

'I don't have a home.'

I'm not sure if I say it out loud or not.

In the time I've been asleep, the pub has changed from an after-work drinking stop to a destination night out. A DJ's hunched over decks in the corner and customers have moved to the tiny dance floor in front of him. The barman turns away to serve another customer and I dive onto the dance floor and push my way to the centre of the crowd. I'm safe here. I can't be seen.

The music is just a series of annoying beats and beeps and none of my limbs seem to move in the right direction.

I keep knocking into people. No one minds, they're mostly too out of it to notice. A guy in a thin white vest is dancing next to me. He rolls his body in time with the music. He's grinning, wide-eyed and happy. He reminds me of Jem and I move away.

The bodies move faster. As they move their flesh melts and blends into one another until there's a single pulsating mound. The music has got louder, the strobing brighter and the rest of the club darker.

The volume increases until it's not noise any more, just vibrations pulsing through my body. The air's rank with sweat and beer. I can't breathe. I need to get out of here. I try to find the exit and end up in the toilets. Inside, two girls are chatting, one is perched next to the sink, the other facing the mirror, reapplying red lipstick. They stop talking when I come close. They stare at me. I stare back. They're still staring. Do they know? Does everyone know? Dad knows, so does Ray, Becca and Valentina Vickers. I back out of the toilets without taking my eyes off them and hear the tinkle of laughter as the door swings shut.

So as not to miss the exit again, I circle the room, trying not to make eye contact in case anyone else knows the truth about me. Finally, I find the exit, miss the step, trip and land on my knees and gash my forehead on the railing. I get to my feet and stagger forwards. Hordes of people fill the streets, spilling from pubs and bars onto the pavement. Some laugh, some sneer as I stagger. They all know. I'll never get to Heathrow, I'll never leave.

Two young women walk towards me, done up for a night out in strappy dresses and heels. One of them peels away from the other and stops me.

'What's happened to you?' she asks.

I put my hands to my forehead, warm, sticky liquid's running from the cut.

'Blood,' I say. 'It's not Edie's.'

She looks confused.

'I'm calling an ambulance,' she says.

'No need for that,' the other woman says.

'She's hit her head,' the woman says.

She starts dialling 999. I think of the police, of Vilas and Craven.

'No,' I say.

I pull my hand free from the woman and try to walk away. I make it as far as a shop front, then lose energy and lean against it. The woman without the phone follows me and makes me sit down, so that my legs are flat on the floor and my back's against the wall.

'Stay here for now,' she says.

'I think she's worse than drunk,' the other woman says.

I lift my hands and hold them in front of me. They seem a long way away. Not part of my body, these blood-covered hands that killed Edie. The woman watches me with my arms outstretched twisting them in the street light.

'See what I mean?' she says.

A phone rings. It's mine. The woman bends down, reaches into my pocket and takes it.

'Yes, she's here,' she says. 'Yes, I think you should come.'

'I wanted to go to the Loire,' I tell her.

She puts the phone back in my pocket.

'Your friend's coming,' she shouts at me.

'I haven't got any friends.'

She smiles.

'Well, someone's very worried. You need to take care of yourself.'

They stand next to me chatting and I'm drifting off to sleep when a cab pulls up and Max jumps out. He runs over and kneels down.

'What's happened? Are you hurt?'

I shake my head.

'Look, we're going. She needs to be more careful,' the one who answered the phone says. 'Do you know how many young women go missing each year?'

She trots off into the night with her friend.

Max takes hold of me and presses me to his chest. Blood from my cut smears his T-shirt.

'Tess, what's happening?'

'Max, I did it,' I whisper.

He holds me tighter.

'I'm the creepy twin. I killed Edie.'

'You didn't. How could you have?'

He's right. I couldn't have. However much Dad, Ray and Becca believe it, I know I could never hurt her. She was my sister, my twin. From nowhere rage rises within me. How small and stupid, ugly and useless Edie made me feel as she sloped off into the night wearing eyeliner and a tight black top. Her smile as she told me she was going out with Michaela, her love of secrets and blocking me from her life. I did hate her. Sometimes.

But I would never hurt her. And yet she's dead.

Chapter 64

Edie: July 1998

Edie felt the summer heat as a weight on her head, the pressure beating against her temples. Her stomach gurgled with emptiness, though the thought of food repulsed her.

Each school day was a slow torture, but she couldn't stay off sick. She had to sit her end-of-term exams and Tess was watching. She'd think time off school was a chance to sneak away and see a boy. Edie had two more days of this, then she could live in bed all day over the summer holidays and be left alone.

She should be working harder. Even Tess was predicted better grades. At this rate Edie wouldn't even get work in a supermarket and she needed a job that would pay good money, so she could get out of this place. Only she could no longer find the energy.

Natalie pushed past her.

'Come on, you're like an old woman,' she said.

Edie woke from her dreaming.

They were nearly at the school's main gates. She stopped and pushed back. What was she doing? She could have walked right into Bob. Natalie looked at her, puzzled.

'I've forgotten something, Nat,' she said and turned back towards the school. Walking against the flow, she was bumped on either side going into the building. The glass entrance intensified the heat so it became unbearable. Edie teetered and nearly fell but made it the few feet to the narrow corridor, where it was much cooler.

'Are you alright, Edie?'

It was Mrs Stanley. Edie forced herself upright.

'Yes,' she said. 'I forgot something.'

'You're not unwell?'

'No.'

'Are you sure? I could get you some water.'

'No, really, I'm fine. Thank you, miss.'

'OK then.'

Mrs Stanley looked at her. Edie thought she might have stopped, but she had her car keys in her hand, as eager to escape as her pupils.

'Well, see you tomorrow.'

'Bye, miss.'

Edie watched her leave and wondered why she needed a cardigan in this weather. As she turned towards the school's back entrance, she caught sight of someone in the corridor on the opposite side of the atrium, standing still and staring at her.

It was Tess. She didn't speak, didn't approach, just stood and stared.

God, she was so sick of Tess, her moping, her surveillance, her silences and pretend secrets. Edie didn't acknowledge her. She continued to the back of the school, anger giving her the energy she lacked earlier, and stomped out. Nausea was still swilling around her stomach but she felt less faint. In the distance, she could see the thin trickle of pupils still leaving by the front gates. She was tired of this nonsense, lying, sneaking about. Soon, it would all be over. Just two more days.

Halfway across the field, she felt eyes boring into her back. She turned around. Tess was standing at the back entrance staring at her, a cold, blank expression on her face. How long was this going to go on? Edie spun back and marched towards the hedge, her fists clenched. She checked behind once more before stepping through the narrow gap and running straight into Bob.

Chapter 65

Tess: July 2018

'Drink this,' Max says.

I'm in the bed in our shared flat. He's holding a glass to my lips. I haul myself onto my elbows and sip at the weak orange squash. Mum used to give me that when I had flu. I don't have flu now, though I'm frail enough and my head's heavy.

'You've been ill.'

I flop back down.

'How long?'

'Two days.'

I groan and turn my head into the pillow. Neither sickness nor alcohol can explain what's happened to me. I must be losing my mind. For some reason this thought is comforting.

'So you've seen him?' Max says.

'Who?'

'Bob.'

'How do you...?'

'You talked a lot when you were ill.'

I can't remember what I told him. He doesn't seem angry.

'I didn't do it, Max, did I?'

He leans over and tucks the duvet under my chin.

'You do believe me?' I say.

'Yes,' he says.

'Nobody else does.'

'I know. You told me the night I came to pick you up.'

The pub and the fall seems a long time ago and I can't remember talking, only the dreams.

'I don't know what's true any more,' I say. 'I thought it was Ray, then Bob or Jem or whoever he is. Even Dad for a moment. And then there's Michaela and...' I think of Max, that insignificant little boy following her around. 'And maybe others, but they all think it's me. Becca said I went and told her. It must be true, only I know it's not.'

'I'm telling you, it's not possible,' Max says.

'Dad told me—'

'You're not listening, Tess. I know you didn't do it.'

'How can you know that?' I ask.

'Because I was there.'

Chapter 66

Edie: June 1998

Edie pulled her hands across herself as if to hide her school uniform from Bob. For a moment she thought it was a horrible accident, that he was there by chance, until he grabbed her arm.

'What the fuck...' He spat the words at her.

He was a different person now. Not the smiles, jokes and slouchy stance. He seemed taller; his facial muscles were tensed into an ugliness that frightened her. His fingers dug tighter into her arm as she tried to pull free.

'I should have known better than to go with some stupid schoolgirl.'

Edie stopped struggling and looked at him.

'Did you think I didn't know?' he said. 'You must think I'm as dumb as you are.'

Bob grabbed her other arm and pushed her into the hedge. She lost her balance and nearly fell.

'What do you think you're playing at?'

'Just leave me alone,' she said.

'Are you going to leave me alone?'

Edie pulled back and this time he let her go.

'Yes. What did you think, I'd tell Michaela?'

'Michaela. So you're not so innocent.' He stepped back and looked her up and down. He seemed less angry now, though he was still breathing hard. 'What do you want from me?'

'I told you. I don't want to see you any more.'

'Yeah, then you sent your aunt round to find me.'

'What?'

Edie struggled to understand what he was saying.

'Like you don't know. You sent her to see me.'

'I never told her anything about you. I never even said your name.'

'Then how did she know where I live?'

'I don't know how she found out but I never told her.'

Had Freddie known his address?

'I don't believe you,' Bob said.

'I don't care if you believe me.'

'Is she going to come again?'

'How should I know?'

Edie pictured an irate Auntie Becca against Bob's relaxed insolence. But seeing him now, maybe he hadn't reacted like that. She couldn't imagine what Auntie Becca had said, she didn't want to know. Edie went to walk past him. He moved in front of her. She stopped, not wanting him to grab her arm again.

'Don't play games with me,' he said.

'I'm not playing games. Let me past.'

'I told her it wasn't mine.'

'What?' Edie heard herself say as she realised the answer to what Auntie Becca had said.

'The baby.'

'There is no baby.'

He leant in to study her face.

'You're telling me you're not pregnant?'

'Of course I'm not.' She almost laughed.

'Why did your aunt say you were?'

'I don't know. To scare you off, teach you a lesson, I guess.'

'So you're definitely not?'

'No.'

He looked away from her and let his shoulders drop. He was about to say something but Edie took the chance to slide past him.

'No hard feelings, eh?' he called after her.

She didn't reply and didn't look back. She wanted to rub her arm where he had bruised it but wouldn't while he was still watching.

Cars passed by. She looked behind her, scared one might be Bob's. Instead, she saw that stupid boy, Max. He was standing on the opposite side of the road. Why was he still hanging about? She'd told him enough times to get lost. The sun was in her eyes and she couldn't tell if he was looking in her direction or not as he ran across the road.

Chapter 67

Tess: July 2018

'It wasn't you, Tess,' Max says.
He strokes the hair from my forehead.

'Did you hurt her?'

'I tried to protect her. Especially after I saw her with Bob. I knew exactly what he was, and what some of his friends were like. Look how Michaela ended up.' He puts the drink on the side and looks down at his hands. 'Only I couldn't protect her. That's what hurts the most. I should have followed her, even though she told me not to.'

'Was I only ever a substitute?'

'It's not like that. I love you, Tess.'

Maybe he believes this, but it's not true. Someone who loved Edie could never love me for myself. I turn my head back onto the pillow so I'm no longer facing him. For Max, it was always Edie.

'I remember the first time I saw her, at a party,' he says. 'She was different to the other girls. But honestly, Tess, it was so innocent. I never wanted anything from her, not like Bob. I just wanted to be with her, be next to her. She thought I was a silly little boy. I hated that.'

'And it made you angry.'

'No, Tess, it made me sad and that's not what I'm trying to tell you.'

'What are you trying to tell me?'

'I was there that day, the day she disappeared. I was following her. You left by the front of the school. You went a different way. You were nowhere near the canal.'

'And Bob?'

'He argued with her. But got in his car and drove off. I never told the police. I thought if they knew I was following her, they'd end up accusing me.'

'You didn't see anyone?'

'Only a woman.'

'What did she look like?'

'I was too far away to see her face. She drove a green MG and had one of those black and tan terrier-type dogs, the type you see as soft toys that get pushed about on wheels.'

'A Welsh terrier.'

'Might have been.'

'It was,' I say.

The pieces of the jigsaw were sitting in front of me all the time and I ignored their pattern. Now, they slot into place and I can see the whole picture. I know now who did this to us, who killed my sister and drove a wedge between me and Dad. I've been such a fool.

Chapter 68

Edie: June 1998

'Are you hurt?' Max asked as he jogged towards her. 'You shouldn't let him treat you like that.'

'Mind your own business,' Edie said. 'If you follow me again, I'll tell Dad who you are. Do you know what he threatened to do to you?'

Max looked down.

'I only want to make sure you're safe. That Bob—'

'Just leave me alone.'

'Have you finished with him?' Max asked. 'Maybe we could go out sometime.'

'No, we couldn't.'

'I wouldn't ask you to do anything, not like him. Please, Edie, what about the cinema?'

'I'm going home now. And you'd better not follow me.'

She walked past him, looking back several times to check he hadn't moved, before she swung off the main path and onto the winding dirt track, leading to the canal.

Chapter 69

Tess: July 2018

I check my phone's on in my pocket before I knock.
  'I knew you'd come back.' Becca opens the door. 'Come in.'

Her face shows no emotion. A fury overwhelms me. I forget my plan and push her into the house. She stumbles to the floor. I haul her up by the armpits, shove her against the wall and place my hands round her throat. Our faces lie an inch apart. I start to press. She's very thin now and too weak to fight back. I grip her windpipe. Her face is turning purple, her eyes bulge and she's making rasping noises. How long do I have to press?

Becca's fingernails scratch ineffectually at the back of my hands. Her rasping becomes more urgent. She's trying to speak. I want her dead, but if she has something to tell me, something about Edie, I have to hear it, I need to know the truth.

I slacken my grip and Becca starts to slide down the wall.

I grab her arm, drag her into the lounge and throw her into a chair. Her head flies backwards and cracks on its back.

I stand back and check my phone again.

Becca bends forwards, her hands to her throat. She looks up at me with bloodshot eyes.

'You see why Ray and your dad were so easy to convince,' she says. Her voice is hoarse and barely audible. 'You have got it in you, Tess. You could kill.'

'You, yes. Edie, no.'

Her hands rest on her throat.

'It wasn't planned. You have to believe me, it was an accident, a moment of madness.'

'An accident?'

'I saw her with that boy and I just knew I had to do something. I didn't even know what, I think I was only going to talk to her.' Becca stops and blinks. 'She wouldn't listen to me; she was always so stubborn and headstrong. I tried to explain the trouble she could get into, with a boy like that. She didn't want to know. Just tossed her head and sneered. I lost my temper, pushed her harder than I meant to. She tripped, fell head first into the bridge. It split her forehead open. Blood spurted everywhere and I panicked.'

Chapter 70

Edie: June 1998

A dog barked in the distance. Edie shivered, despite the heat. The usual calm she found walking by the canal, replaced with a sense of unease. She stopped and let her eyes adjust to the shade thrown from overhanging trees, and was able to make out the dense criss-crossing of bushes and brambles on the path. As she picked her way through, the scent of decay rose from dank vegetation and mingled with the flowers' fragrance in a heady, sickly-sweet mix. Something snapped in the undergrowth behind her. She picked up her pace and glanced back, half expecting to see Max, but thick bushes obscured her view along the track.

The path turned to run parallel with the canal, its surface covered in a thin film of green. She resisted the urge to look back again. It was afternoon, she had taken this route home from school a hundred times. She wasn't some silly little girl, afraid of her own shadow. There was no one behind her, she was frightening herself. She hurried towards the bridge, its thick iron struts and ornate metalwork a hangover from the city's industrial past. It was barely used these days. This route didn't even save time compared to taking the road. Edie just preferred it.

The bushes swayed. An animal, a fox or a dog flashed through the branches then lay still. Something was rustling behind her. No. It was her imagination. She decided to stop by the bridge and fiddle with her shoe. It would give her the chance to look round without being obvious. Propping her foot onto an iron strut and refastening the buckle, she glanced sideways down the track. It was empty. When she'd finished and stood up, she looked across the bridge. There was no one there. Still she remained uneasy. To double-check the path, she leant over to fiddle with the other shoe. She tugged at its strap and again checked around. Butterflies flitted across the shards of light from gaps in the branches, otherwise nothing moved.

Then came a sharp bark, followed by the crack and swish of something rushing through the bushes towards her.

Chapter 71

Tess: July 2018

'And then blaming me, Becca?' I say. 'Making Dad think I'm his daughter's killer.'

'An accident too, Tess. I might have confessed or not said anything. But you made it so easy. You came to mine after school that day, you were upset about something Edie had said or done. I don't know what.'

That last day, when she refused to acknowledge me in the school atrium. I can feel the heat of my rising anger, even now, twenty years later.

'You were so upset, you could hardly breathe. I thought you were going to pass out. So I gave you a couple of my Valium to calm you down. It sent you to sleep and every time you woke up you refused to talk and became agitated, so I'd give you another tablet.'

It explains why I have barely any recollection of the events surrounding Edie's death.

'I told Ray and Vince you said you'd killed her.'

'And they believed you?'

'You don't realise how easy it was to believe, the way you carried on, you were always so angry.'

'I was a teenager.'

'You resented me, Ray, anyone who spent time with Edie.'

'That's not true. How could they believe any of this?'

Becca grimaces and shifts in her chair.

'Ray believed me and that was enough for Vince. He was always led by Ray, never trusted his own judgement. A bit like you.'

A smile flickers across her lips and I realise she's enjoying this.

Edie's death was no accident.

Chapter 72

Edie: June 1998

The push came from behind and hands drove her forwards, tipping her towards the water. She threw her arms back to regain her balance and hovered on the edge of the canal. Another push, much harder this time. Edie flew forwards. Her head smashed onto the bridge's metal strut. One hand gripped her shoulder, another held the back of her head and thrust it into the canal, forcing it beneath the water.

Cold, algae-rich water engulfed her scream.

The surface lay inches above her. Her head throbbed, her arms wouldn't move. Another scream, another lungful of water.

She tried to twist round. The hands held her fast. She managed to half turn. Through the rippling water, blood and algae, she saw a blurred face. Not so blurred as to be unrecognisable. How could it be? She'd known it all her life. The fight left her.

Edie stopped struggling and let water fill her lungs. Blood and sunlight swirled in ornate patterns around her. She watched them form and reform as she drifted into darkness. The head wound felt far away, the pain unconnected with her. She closed her eyes and let her body merge with the dark and cold.

Chapter 73

Tess: July 2018

'It wasn't an accident. You didn't just lose your temper, did you?' I say.

Becca half closes her eyes.

'She was just leaning against the bridge that day, half over the canal, as if she were waiting for me, almost an invitation, like she wanted to be killed.' The smile's still not disappeared from the corners of her mouth when she opens her eyes again and looks me full in the face. 'Part of you must have wanted to kill Edie, or it wouldn't have taken you so long to come back. You did think you might have done it, didn't you?'

Would I have believed it if Max hadn't told me the truth?

'I could never have harmed her,' I say and I know it's true. 'What possible reason could you have had for wanting her dead?'

'The same one as you,' Becca says. 'I was jealous.'

'Of what?'

She gasps.

'Are you serious, of what... of what?' Then she laughs. 'No, I understand. How could fussy, frumpy Auntie Becca have any feelings worth noting? Do you think I didn't know how you sniggered and sneered at me? Silly old Becca with her home decoration, where's she moving to next? What triviality's going to outrage her about the neighbours this time? Which dowdy clothes will she be wearing? Do you think I actually cared about any of that? Do you think I should just have shrugged my shoulders when my husband's sleeping with every tart in a ten-mile radius?'

'This has nothing to do with Edie.'

'I saw her that day, with her skinny legs and bouncy chest, arguing with that boy, and it was Ray and Gina all over again.'

'I still don't understand.'

'I wanted a baby and then Ray had one with that whore.'

'Valentina?'

She nods.

'I pretended not to know and I didn't mind so much because the little bastard wasn't right, had something wrong with it, died soon after birth. I felt like she got what she deserved.'

Now is not the time to tell her Ray even lied about that.

'And then she was so much like your mother.'

'Valentina?'

'No, Edie. Keep up, Tess, you always were the slow one.' She takes a moment to enjoy her barb. 'But then maybe it's served you well.'

'You killed her because she looked like Mum?'

'Ray and your mother...'

'I know. But you always cared for us.'

'Yes, you were like my own children. Until you weren't children any more.'

'You mean when Edie got a boyfriend? Why did you marry Ray? You must have known.'

'I thought he'd forget her. She was no one. She thought she was special because she was at university studying English and could quote poetry. But she was just the daughter of an immigrant on one side and a family of factory workers on the other. Then she married Vince. It was all her own fault. If she'd married someone else, given Ray up, none of this would have happened. You think she was so perfect? She was a scheming little bitch.'

I ram my hands in my pockets to stop myself striking her.

'She was my mother.'

'And who's your father?'

I examine her face, she gives nothing away.

'You think it's Ray?'

'I don't know. I don't suppose Gina did, either.'

'And you hurt Edie to punish him?'

'No, though it was a good revenge. The truth is I couldn't stand how she and Ray were so close. Then I thought she was pregnant.'

'What are you talking about?'

'I couldn't bear her having a child with Ray.'

'You're insane. It wasn't Ray's. It was Bob's. Ray's our uncle, maybe our father.'

'It happens,' she says.

And I think of what Ray told me about Becca, the princess, daddy's girl, and realise she's talking about her father now. Their trips abroad after her mother died, not being allowed boyfriends. I wonder if this is why she never had children, if she can't have children.

'Why are you with Ray if you believe he's capable of that?'

She doesn't answer.

'Tell me, Becca.'

'You're lucky with Vince. He must have worried you were even his, but even after what he thought you'd done to Edie, he loved you. Couldn't bear the idea of you going to prison; neither could Ray. They moved the body.'

'You made Dad do that?'

'I just wanted things to go back to normal.'

'Normal? You think this is normal?'

'Who's to say what's normal?'

She looks up at me.

'What are you going to do?' she asks.

'I haven't decided,' I say. 'But I have recorded this.'

I hold up my phone. The red button is flashing for record. Becca frowns then bursts out laughing.

'Oh dear, Tess,' she says. 'You're not getting any quicker, are you?'

For a moment I think of what Dad said, that whoever hurt Edie would hurt me. She's going to kill me, this thin old woman slumped in her chair. She has a plan, poison, a gun.

'But have it your way. Call the police if you want,' she says. 'Watch Vince go to prison as an accessory after the fact.'

I put the phone back in my pocket.

'And no one's locking me up. Cancer,' she says. 'I knew straight away. It killed my mother. I didn't go to the doctor until a couple of months back. I deliberately left it until it was too late. It felt like I deserved it. Whatever Edie did, I was wrong.'

'She did nothing.'

'I still hated her. So did you.'

'I'm glad you're dying, Becca.'

She doesn't reply.

'It's not just Edie's life you took away, it's the lies. Years and

410

years of lies. To me, to Dad, to Ray. Have you thought about how it's tortured him over the years, thinking one of his daughters killed the other?'

She still says nothing, just stares into space, then her eyes suddenly close in another grimace. Physical pain from her illness or the pain of memory? When she replies her voice is just a whisper.

'I can't change the past, Tess, and I don't have much of a future.'

'You've had twenty years more life than Edie.'

'Have I?' she says and begins to laugh, before pain erupts across her face and it turns into a sob.

I look around at the house. Their tenth house in fifteen years. All the china figurines and flounces, their wedding photo in a gilt frame, Ray smiling and Becca looking shy. How little any of this means, it's all as artificial as the porcelain flowers.

'So you did all this to keep Ray? What do you think he'll do when he finds out?'

It's the first time she's looked frightened.

'You can't tell him, Tess.'

She sobs again.

'I'm not going to tell him, you are,' I say.

She looks at me and shakes her head.

'No.'

'When I first came in I wanted to kill you. Now I think I'd rather see you live to have Ray hate you as much as I do.'

'Please don't, Tess. They're taking me into a hospice soon. I'll be all alone without Ray.'

'Don't tell me you're expecting sympathy?'

Her sobs overwhelm her.

'I never wanted sympathy,' she says. 'I only wanted Ray.'

I turn and leave the room.

'Tess,' she calls after me. 'Tess.'

I don't look back.

*

Dad paces the lounge as I play the recording. Then stands stock-still.

'All this time she's walking around, fussing about which colour cushions she has, playing the devoted auntie, and my Edie's been lying in that reservoir. And I put her there. I'm going to the police. I'm telling them everything.'

'You can't, you'll go to prison.'

'I don't care, Tess. She can't get away with it.'

'We have to stay together. Prison would kill you and that would kill me.'

He presses his fists to his forehead.

'She can't get away with this.'

He looks at his car keys lying on the coffee table and reaches for them. I dive forwards, snatch them up and stuff them in my pocket.

'No, Dad.'

'So that's it, we all just get on with our lives? We can't do that. You must hate her, too.'

'She's ill. She'll not last long. She'll be dead and you'll be in jail.'

'Dying in a hospital, surrounded by doctors and nurses, like lots of people who've never done any harm.'

He's right. I wish I believed in God as fervently as Grandpa Len. To believe that Becca would be punished in eternity. But

I can only believe in now and there doesn't seem much justice.

'Look at what she's done to us, Tess. What she made me think of you. Aren't you angry with me, for believing Becca?'

'I nearly believed it myself.'

'I never wanted to,' Dad says. 'But you were always so angry with her, Tess. Always.'

'I loved her.'

'You argued all the time. You didn't want her to have friends or boyfriends. You used to follow her and go through her stuff. I was worried. I didn't know what to do. I even spoke to Becca about it.'

'We were just two kids fighting. We were sisters, it was normal.'

'And you've got a temper, Tess, I remember that girl in primary school having stitches after you attacked her. She was twice the size of you.'

'She called me a runt.'

'You don't know the trouble that caused. Her father came round and threatened me with a baseball bat. Ray had to pay him off. No one messes with the Powells.'

I wonder how much more trouble I've caused over the years that Dad's never told me about.

'I couldn't believe it,' he says. 'But Edie was dead. And Becca said you'd admitted to it.'

It's the first time I've had a conversation with Dad when he hasn't been holding a cigarette. He doesn't seem to know what to do with his hands and keeps rubbing his hair.

'You never thought it could be her?'

'She loved you two, like you were her own. That's what she always said. And I wanted you to have a mother of sorts, after Gina died.'

'I'm sick of hearing that from Ray and Becca. I loved you as much as if you were my own. It's a lie that's been repeated so often, everyone believes it. Ray only loves himself and Becca hated Edie, too much like Mum.'

Dad's eyes soften.

'Yes, she was so much like Gina.'

'You knew she hated Mum, didn't you?'

Dad looks down.

'Didn't you care?' I ask. 'Your own brother and your wife?'

'It had stopped,' he says. 'As far as I knew. Sometimes I thought there was something going on, but Ray would never do that to me.'

'Because it was easier to believe. Like me killing Edie? I'm pretty sure Ray did know the truth and kept quiet.'

'No, Tess, Ray has his faults but he's not like that.'

There's no point pursuing it.

'Becca will have told him by now,' I say.

'Yes,' Dad says.

'Why didn't you just go to the police, tell them what I'd done?'

He looks at me as if I'm stupid.

'You were all I had, Tess. All I had left of my girls. I let you down. I should have been there, protected you, not wrapped up in my own problems, but it was hard knowing Gina loved Ray, never me.'

'She did love you, Dad, I know she did.'

'No,' he says. 'I know she tried, but it was always Ray.'

I think of Max. It was always Edie. I tell Dad about it.

'You deserve better, Tess,' he says. 'You're not going back to him, are you?'

I shake my head.

Dad nods.

'I'm going to sell this place. I never liked it. Got it for you and Edie.'

'I never liked it, either.'

'I'll find something smaller, get a gardening job maybe, who knows.'

I go and hug him. It surprises him and he takes a moment before reciprocating.

'I love you, Tess,' he says.

'I know, Dad.'

Chapter 74

Tess: January 2019

Becca died alone on Christmas Eve. Ray got the call at our house on Christmas Day morning. To Dad and me it felt like a release. But Ray wept until the evening. I guess, at some level, he must have loved her. I'll never understand who loves who and why. She confessed to DS Craven a few weeks before and he came to see us with Vilas.

'A trial is out of the question, what with Mrs Piper's illness. We will be closing the case, though. Mrs Piper proved to us she knew enough details for her involvement to be irrefutable.'

Vilas was less satisfied.

'We're still at a loss for a motive and Mrs Piper refused to be drawn,' he said, his face pinched with sourness. 'Have you any idea?'

'No,' Dad and I said simultaneously.

'And then there's the removal of the body. Edie was a full four inches taller than Rebecca Piper and must have been carried at some point. How did she manage that? All in all, there's too much in this case that doesn't add up,' Vilas said.

'So you'll not be closing it? It will remain unsolved?'

'No,' he said quickly. 'We're closing it.'

After they left Ray came to see me and gave me the photograph, the one of the family that Edie kept in her bag.

'I found it, when I was clearing out the house,' he said. 'For once, it's me who wants to move.'

'Was Edie your daughter, Ray? Am I?' I asked.

'The truth is, I don't know.'

Ray's told so many lies over the years, I'm not sure he knows what the truth is, but that day, he had the swagger of a drunk, not a liar.

I've framed the photo, Edie's shot of our family, she and I on our parents' laps, Dad and Mum far younger than I am now. That the span of five years could take both Mum and Edie from us was unthinkable to the smiling faces in the picture. The only one not smiling is me. I like to think it's because I was a wise child and knew what would become of the photo and the people in it. In truth, it's far more probable I spotted something that caught my attention, which took me away from my family in those precious seconds.

I wrap it in tissue and place it next to Edie's old records. We're moving. Dad's selling up and buying a cottage in Malvern, high up on the hill, overlooking the Worcestershire plain. I'm going to help him with the marketing to set up his own gardening business, I'll ask Raquel for advice. I'm hoping he'll find another woman; although he assures me no one could ever replace Mum.

Most thirty-five-year-olds would be horrified at the thought of moving back in with their father, but it's only temporary until I work out what to do with the rest of my life. I'm going to enjoy living with Dad. I'll always call him Dad, whether he is or not, because he's always been a father to me, when he must have questioned if I was his child, when his own mental health was failing and even when he knew his wife loved another man, he stayed.

I look around at the house none of us ever wanted to live in and open a cardboard box and place the photo inside, the first of Edie's possessions I'm going to pack. We will start again, Dad and I, in a new place, with no more secrets and no more lies.

Chapter 75

Edie: June 1998

It was no longer cold. Mum was singing to Edie, her voice swimming through the water and wrapping round her. She didn't want to leave Tess. She wouldn't leave Tess. She'd always be there for her twin.

Barbecue smoke wafted up her nose and the sweetness of the sugar flower lingered on her tongue from their birthday long ago. A perfect day, when she and Tess were ten years old. Double digits. Nearly grown up.

Acknowledgements

I'd like to thank my agent, Kate Burke, for all her hard work and for seeing my potential. Thanks also to my editor, Katie Loughnane, and the whole team at Avon for their enthusiasm and dedication.

Syd Moore and Barbara Zuckriegl deserve a mention for patiently reading through earlier drafts of the novel, and giving me encouragement.

A special thank you to Keith Haworth for reading the manuscript, putting up with endless writer's angst and always believing in me.

And finally I owe my parents a huge debt of gratitude for their many years of support.